D0892108

GALVESTON ROSE

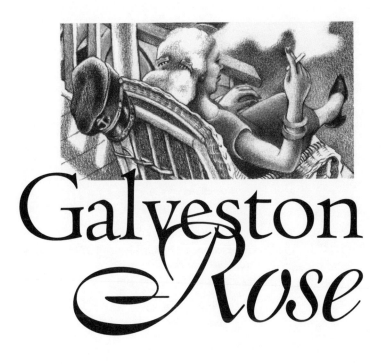

Galveston
Rose

Mary Powell

TCU Press

Fort Worth, Texas

Library of Congress Cataloging-in-Publication Data

Powell, Mary Curtner.
Galveston Rose / by Mary Powell.
p. cm.
ISBN 0-87565-303-0 (alk. paper)
1. Galveston (Tex.)—Fiction. 2. Terminally ill—Fiction. 3. Older
women—Fiction. I. Title.
PS3566.O83266G35 2005
813'.54--dc22
2004013930
Printed in Canada

ACKNOWLEDGMENTS

I am indebted to a number of friends and family members who shared information and gave encouragement during the process of this novel. Thanks to Elaine Seibold, who provided a seed and followed it up with research; to Richard Thompson, lifelong fisherman, boat enthusiast, and devoted resident of west beach; to Tom Eisenhour, an expert on Galveston architecture and history; and to Donna Savell, who celebrated with me the first completed draft and brainstormed relentlessly on a title. Jesse Arbaugh gave an afternoon of his Christmas vacation to help me try to understand the life of a student training in the medical professions, and he allowed me to use his name because it felt right. Middy Larson and Sally Keele let me pick their brains about hospital life from a nurse's perspective. Leandra Contreras contributed a curious tidbit of Mexican folklore and reminded me that Elena is pronounced with two short e's.

Two valuable teachers, also friends, gave of their time and talents to offer insightful, constructive observations. Debra Monroe helped me get my story off the ground, and Miles Wilson was there at the end. Finally, to my sisters, Ann Maness and B. J. Thompson, to my son, Marshall, and my husband, John, all of whom read the manuscript, sometimes more than once, thanks for your suggestions, both general and specific, for listening to my concerns, and for cheering me on.

For Claire

PART I:

The Good Life

Four be the things I'd been better without:
Love, curiosity, freckles, and doubt.
Three be the things I shall never attain:
Envy, content, and sufficient
champagne.

Dorothy Parker
(from *Enough Rope)*

I

"Solitude has its advantages," Rose Parrish liked to say, with a studied tap of cigarette ash, when well-meaning friends suggested she hire live-in help after Nate died. She wasn't inclined to forfeit the freedom of doing as she pleased. Rose especially relished the nights—reading without interruption, watching television at three A.M. if she took a mind to, smoking in bed. It had been more than ten years now and she had never regretted her decision. Until tonight.

For hours, strong winds off the gulf had pushed and howled outside her windows like something alive and malevolent. An old magnolia limb, grown too close to the house, kept scraping the eaves, unpredictable and annoying. Windows rattled. Rain came, then receded. Sleep was impossible. Propped on three pillows, trying to distract herself with a mystery novel, Rose made a mental note to get someone out to trim the old tree. The cement block that seemed to be resting on her chest was a different problem. Her bedside table, crowded with containers of cough medicine, Mentholatum®, tissues, aspirin, water, and cigarettes, had proven an ineffective arsenal. At one A.M., bringing up phlegm disturbingly pink, she phoned the Galveston Yellow Cab Company to take her to John Sealy. It was a respectable hospital, only six blocks from her house. She could walk it, she thought, if it weren't for the damn cough, and the wind, and the rain.

When the taxi rolled to a stop at the emergency entrance, Rose tightened the satin ties of her cashmere robe with shaky hands and leaned forward. An ambulance was unloading up ahead, its red lights dancing crazily off the wet pavement. The possibility of her arrival being delayed hadn't crossed her mind, given the already sufficient difficulties of the evening.

"Sir," she spoke to the driver. Her voice was weak and curdled, unpleasant to the ear, but she maintained. "Tell me how much I owe and then fetch an attendant. I'll need professional help."

The driver hurried off while Rose leaned back to try again for a decent breath. Her heart was working much too hard. She hoped they wouldn't have to use one of those clapper things she'd seen on *E.R.* She wondered how many patients came in by cab. Not as much fanfare as an ambulance, but more tasteful if you could manage it. She had given him, the driver, a bit of a scare—dressed in night clothes and waving with a flashlight from up on her porch. She had sat in the green wicker rocker, her mouth and nose covered with a handkerchief against the wind, hoping he'd come quickly, though she knew that people who drove cabs couldn't always be counted on. Lucky he hadn't had to carry her. He deserved a tip. She moved her wallet over to catch the light and fumbled with the bills. Damn, no tens. A twenty then. And maybe I should get his card in case this comes up again, she thought. Through the front windshield she could see the driver and a couple of white coats approaching.

❖

The next thing Rose knew she was lying flat, in a white cubicle, with two lovely young things working over her. The blond nurse adjusted a tube in her right arm and gave a dimpled smile. The boy, he couldn't have been more than twenty-five, held her left wrist and watched a monitor.

"My vitals?" she asked.

He grinned, eyes still on the monitor. "Some of them. How're you feeling?"

She hesitated to consider. Her breath was coming easier; the marathon her heart had been running was over. "Seems like I've settled down," she said, and after a pause, "I suppose you have papers for me to fill out."

"Someone will be along to help you."

"I'm perfectly capable."

"I'm sure you are, but it's my job to make things easier." His dark hair was cut short and arranged to stand in points. Spiked, she thought they called it. Now why should she remember a thing like that? He actually looked like one of the interns on *General Hospital;* couldn't recall his name at the moment. Not handsome, as she thought of handsome. An oval face, with a vandyke beard setting off his high cheekbones. Interesting, she decided. And, thank goodness, he didn't fumble. He worked, actually, with a high level of certainty. Despite his youth, she decided he had good sense.

"You're a doctor?"

"I'm a third year student. They give me the difficult cases, though." He looked at her then and smiled.

Perfect teeth, she thought. "Your name?"

He hesitated, caught off guard, she supposed, by her forwardness. "Martini," he said.

"And, Mr. Martini, I presume I'm going to live."

"With a little help."

"And that would be?"

"Some medication, some lifestyle changes. You like to jog?"

She shifted her eyes toward an opening in the curtain. "I think I'll wait for the real doctor's advice," she said.

She thought she saw the beautiful nurse frown at the young man as she placed a pillow beneath Rose's head, slipped an oxygen tube around her neck, and adjusted it in her nose. "The doctor will be in soon," the girl whispered. Rose lay back and closed her eyes. She felt no discomfort now. Maybe she was dreaming, or maybe she was dead, which was fine with her, as long as it felt this pleasant.

✣

"Ms. Parrish."

Someone was calling her name. She opened her eyes reluctantly, rising slowly to the surface as if from underwater, fuzzy and irritable. A large black nurse with a take-charge manner was trying to move her.

"Can you help us here, honey? We need to get you off this gurney and into the bed. One, two, three, scoot."

Rose lifted herself as best she could and was dumped into the hospital bed rather like a sack of feed. "Where are the other nurse and that young man?"

"I dunno. They probably worked 'mergency last night. The shifts just now changed, and since you're stabilized, you came to us." As she spoke, the woman moved around the bed, adjusting its position, attaching oxygen, straightening the intravenous tube.

"And the doctor? Did I see a doctor?"

"Did a doctor see you? I s'pose one did, or you wouldn't be here." The nurse poured some water into a plastic cup, inserted a flexible straw and thrust it at her. "You comf'table? I'll be back with your meds."

"What's your name?"

The woman pointed to a rectangular white name tag pinned to her massive chest.

"Victorias?"

"That's right." She winked. "Like the secret. You call me if you need me."

Rose closed her eyes and tried to slip back into the place from which she'd come.

✤

"Ms. Parrish."

It was that voice again, that Victorias person. She stood at the foot of the bed and, as she spoke, gestured back toward the door, which stood slightly ajar. "Someone out there wants to see you. Your housekeeper came earlier and I told her you were restin' easy. She's comin' back. Now this fellow. Nice-looking man. Might be your son. I told him he'd have to wait 'til I see to your needs. I thought you might want to use the bathroom, freshen up."

"That's considerate of you," Rose said, wondering if hospital protocol had changed since she had last visited one, or if this was simply the mark of a unique person. The nurse helped Rose out of bed and into the bathroom, where she took a look in the mirror and gasped.

"I can't see anyone looking like this."

"Now you sit down on the toilet there," Victorias offered. "I'll bring your purse so's you can comb this hair," she ran her hand across Rose's head, "it's mighty thick and nice, and put some color on those lips and cheeks. You'll be freshened up in no time."

Rose sank onto the toilet and waited like a sulking child.

✤

Minutes later, Captain John "J.J." Broussard was allowed to enter the hospital room. Dressed in crisp white slacks, wearing his signature sailor's cap, and armed with a bouquet of fresh mums, he cut a striking figure. Rose, seventy-six, was well of an age to be his mother, but she had never responded to him as one would a son. A few minutes earlier she'd managed to pull her hair back with metal combs and put on the wine-colored dressing gown she'd worn to the hospital. Now she extended a trembling hand and managed a smile.

"You disappeared on me," Broussard said, with a look of honest concern. "When I couldn't get anyone to answer the phone, I finally checked the house."

"Just one of those hellish nights." She waved her hand across her forehead as if to brush away the memory. "Tossed and turned, dozed off, couldn't get my breath. How'd you know I was here?"

"I found your note to Pearl on the refrigerator. 'Gone to John Sealy. Take the day off'," he recounted sarcastically. "Really, Rose." He was frowning now. "You're too proud to call for help?"

"I chose to call a cab."

He stood with arms folded and no hint of a smile.

"I'm going to sell the car," she said, businesslike. "Cabs work just fine." Then her voice, something between a whisper and a croak, betrayed her. It began to fall blank in spaces, like an engine misfiring. "Get rid of other. . .too. Maybe. . .have. . . garage sale. She broke off into a deep, rumbling cough. When the spasm subsided, she lay back, pulled up the oxygen tube, placed it in her nose, and closed her eyes.

Broussard approached the bed. "Call me when you feel better," he said quietly.

She nodded, eyes still closed.

✢

John Broussard, "The Captain," as Rose liked to call him, lived on the far west end of the island, where the Gulf of México meets Galveston Bay. Rose wished he lived closer to town—wished he hadn't chosen to isolate himself out there with those fishermen, most of whom cared more about their boats than their houses. Those people had no sense of history. To them, Galveston was just a strip of sand. Some of them, she was told, were downright strange, not that the west end of the island had a monopoly on eccentricity.

But she couldn't think about that right now. In fact, she found it hard to think about anything, what with the activity that went on in her room. Various people appeared regularly to check on her, others came to check on supplies, to mop the floor, to deliver and pick up food trays, or to simply look in with no word of explanation or apparent need, as if she were a new arrival at the zoo and the keepers were acquainting themselves with her. And for all the faces she saw morning and night, the two young things who attended her arrival never reappeared.

"They were working 'mergency," Victorias told her for the third time, making no effort to mask her impatience.

"Well, surely you can locate them for me."

"Ms. Parrish, I have patients to look after."

Rose pretended to be insulted, but was impressed by the woman's refusal. Most people did her bidding. The next time the nurse appeared Rose asked about the spelling of her name.

"Named after the Queen of England, except my mother, who was a church woman, put an s at the end, as in 'We shall be victorious.' She'd be rollin' in her grave to see it connected with fancy undergarments, but that's the nature of things. Unpredictable. Like that weather out there," she motioned her head toward the curtained window as she put a thermometer in her patient's mouth.

"How long have you been in nursing?" Rose mumbled around the thermometer.

"Thirty-two years."

Rose raised her eyebrows. "Ummm."

"When I first started, people like yourself didn't like the idea of me telling them what to do. I could bathe them and such, but it took some time before they got used to the fact that next to the doctor, I was the boss."

Rose nodded, aware she was being put in her place.

"My momma wanted something better for her daughters than domestic work, so we were told we would be nurses, like it or not."

"And you like it?" Rose asked as the thermometer was removed.

The nurse smiled. "Apparently I do. My sisters, they've stayed with it. too, all but one. They took their business to Houston. More money there. More men to choose from. Me, I like the island. Can't predict the weather here or the people— no more than one can cure the common cold." She removed the blood pressure cuff.

"I've paid my dues. Thirty-two years of puttin' in a good day's work and I get to call the shots on my floor. Long as I do good nursing," she added, almost as an afterthought. She was reading the chart. "Looks like you haven't had a B.M. since you came in."

Rose groaned with displeasure and adjusted her sheet.

"I'm sending you a laxative, and if you don't perform by the morning, we'll have an enema," Victorias spoke over her shoulder as she left the room.

❖

Pearl came to visit, bringing fresh underwear and the mail. Rose almost sent her to the bookstore in search of an Ed Baines mystery she'd been wanting, but then thought better of it. The author's vulgarity would surely embarrass her maid, if she had any notion what she was asking for. But that wasn't likely. Pearl only read the Bible. A simple woman, she had worked for Rose for years and never failed to do as she was asked, though there were times she had to be prodded like a dray horse. If only she had a sense of humor, or some imagination, Rose thought, she could appreciate the woman more. God knows, she was a good person in many ways. She had shown up at the hospital every day, in spite of the incessant rain. . .

Bored and frustrated from feeling bad and looking worse, Rose thought about calling the captain, but discarded the idea. Often she invited him to her house for a drink, or dinner. Regularly, she asked for business advice. Never did she just call to chat. Men hated that. She rang the buzzer instead, tapping her fingers on the bed until an attendant answered.

"Listen, dear," she said, "I need you to get my beauty shop on the phone. The Pink Camellia, on Avenue K."

The young woman did as she was told and handed Rose the phone.

"Lisette? Rose Parrish, here. I'm stranded at John Sealy and need your help in the worst way. Could you come over this afternoon, to do my hair and nails? Fourth floor, nothing contagious." She waved the attendant out of the room and lowered her voice. "And bring me some strong coffee. This decaf is messing up my system, if you know what I mean."

✛

The next morning, when Victorias looked in, Rose was dressed and sitting in the chair, working the newspaper crossword.

"Looks like you're feeling stronger."

"I'm ready to go home. I believe I've met all the requirements."

"So you have. The front desk was abuzz about you all morning—how you called your personal beautician in, and how you got around the enema with caffeine and sugar."

Rose, pleased to have injected a little style into a sterile environment, didn't allow herself to smile. "That always gets me going. You shouldn't deny people things they're used to just because you have them at your mercy."

"Caffeine isn't *recommended* for heart patients."

"I don't *consider* myself a heart patient."

"That's what it says on the chart."

"I read the chart, but I'm not in agreement with it."

Victorias, hands on her hips, shook her head slowly. "You just trying to be difficult?"

"I'm sure I'm not the worst you ever had." Rose went back to her crossword.

"That's true. There was a woman, a long time back, who you bring to mind. Wouldn't listen to anyone. Sharp-tongued.

Impatient. Owned one of those fancy houses used to be on Post Office Street. Thought she owned the town."

Rose's head jerked to attention. "You wouldn't be talking about Big Marie?"

The nurse nodded. "Didn't know who she was 'til someone told me. An awful name, I thought to myself, but it's what they called her. Even called herself that. Told me how the town would turn out for her funeral. 'Ever'one wants to see Big Tit Marie on her back,' she told me."

Rose leaned forward. "Could she really balance a cup and saucer on her chest?"

"Never saw her do it, but she could've if she took a mind to."

"Well, Victorias, this certainly makes my day. I've heard stories about that woman all my life, but I never knew anyone who'd been in the same room with her—or would own up to it. The last of the old time madams. Did she wear fancy nightgowns? Did men come to visit?"

Victorias pulled the bed straight. "She was just another patient for me, one who was dying and not too happy about it."

"But did she manage to go out in style?" Rose persisted.

The nurse cocked her head, as if weighing the question. "I s'pose you could call it that. There were flowers. She put out the word—said she couldn't appreciate them later, so if anyone wanted to send some, do it now. And they came, like four and five deliveries at a time. Her girls came too and kept candles burnin' night and day toward the end and they put perfume on the lamp bulbs. I recall how the room smelled heavy, but not like death, and they kept the blinds closed and played dance music on the radio."

✣

About eight that morning Rose had telephoned the captain and had been surprised when a woman's voice answered.

"Didn't disturb you, I hope," she said when he came on the line.

"Not at all, but I never expected to hear from you this time of day."

"This ungodly place won't let a body sleep. I've been up since six-thirty," she complained. "I've got to get out of here, get some quiet, and a scotch wouldn't hurt. Who answered the phone?"

"The woman who works for me. What's your diagnosis?"

"Severe bronchitis. She certainly comes early."

"She comes when I ask her to. Severe bronchitis. That's all?"

"All I wish to discuss."

"You sound much better."

"I no longer cough like one of those old men you find on city street curbs."

"That's encouraging."

"I'm pumped so full of antibiotics and steroids and vitamins I could run a foot race, but they're reluctant to release me on my own, something about the storm. Seem to have forgotten the fact that I managed to get here by myself. I've lost track of the real world in the past week, Captain, but they tell me this storm has a name now. Wasn't there a movie named *Glenda*? Or was that *Gilda*? Could I impose on you to come and negotiate my release? I'd ask Pearl, but we both know she couldn't talk her way out of a paper bag."

❖

The process of getting Rose out of the hospital took more than two hours, during which time she became increasingly impatient, commenting loudly at one point that she'd passed through customs in Morocco with less difficulty. The doctor was delayed, and when he finally showed up, he insisted on speaking to Captain Broussard, and Rose insisted on sitting in.

"You her son?"

The captain shook his head. "A friend."

"Advisor," Rose said, almost simultaneously.

"Well, it's imperative that Mrs. Parrish quit smoking." The

doctor ignored Rose's presence. He'd had this conversation earlier with her. "I hope you'll do what you can to convince her. In addition to the bronchitis, which we've just about taken care of, she has the beginnings of emphysema and congestive heart failure."

The captain nodded.

"She could also benefit from an exercise regimen."

✢

"My God," Rose said that evening, sitting in her leather chair at home, fitting a cigarette into her holder, "don't they love to scare us! I grant you, I shall die of something or other, but not of boredom. Can you think of anything more tedious than one-two-squat-stretch-bend-pull?"

John Broussard knew better than to argue. "You look a lot better than you did a week ago," he told her.

She smiled. "Thanks to my hairdresser, who was willing to make a hospital call," she told him. "One of the volunteers offered to do me, but I'd probably have ended up with a purple rinse."

"Why don't you see if your doctor makes house calls?"

Rose offered a humpf of disbelief.

"You need regular exams."

"I know." She inspected her polished nails briefly and then rubbed at a discolored spot on her arm where the intravenous tube had been attached. "I don't like to drive anymore," she announced. She tried to sound matter-of-fact, but the truth was, it was maddening, all these little losses. She remembered when driving was one of her favorite things.

"Hire a driver. You can afford it."

She smiled politely, as if she hadn't considered that, then asked him to fix a second scotch, and while he was in the kitchen, she made a quick telephone call.

He brought in the drinks. "Come, sit," she motioned to the wing chair that sat at a ninety degree angle to hers. "I've ordered dinner from Mario's."

"I should get back."

"Pooh. Relax and eat with me. I have some things to discuss. We'll watch the news at ten, and if the storm's kicking up, I want you to stay over. You'll be safer here than way out there, and I'll rest more comfortably all around. These things spawn tornados, and I'm not up to dealing with that thought just now." She said it all rather fast, hoping not to sound needy. The captain had never stayed over, never been invited.

"I've decided to rent the apartment to someone I can count on the next time something like this happens," she rambled on. "And I'm thinking of moving my bedroom downstairs. Pearl's made up the sofa-bed in the library for tonight. We could move out the chairs and the console table, bring in the television and a floor lamp. There are certainly enough book shelves, but I need a work table, maybe something that fits over my recliner, like those tables they roll across the bed at the hospital."

He smiled, as if she'd made a joke. "That won't do much for your decor."

"To hell with decor, Captain. I'm too old for such vanities." She waved her hand as if the comment didn't require a response. "I suppose that sounds funny, coming from someone who refuses to discuss age." She frowned and wrinkled her nose. "Truth is, I've seen the reaper coming, but I've never had to smell his lousy breath before. I'm thinking I can take better care of myself and maybe last five more years. But they don't give you promises on quality. And frankly, I never knew anyone past eighty who was worth a damn anyway." She fit a cigarette into her holder and put it in her mouth without lighting it. "Go up to my office, would you, Captain, and bring down that large, red expanding file that takes up most of the top filing cabinet."

He did as he was asked. When he returned, Rose was stretched back against the chair with her eyes closed. He sat, holding the folder, until she opened them.

"Do you want to do this later?"

"Absolutely not. Here, let me see." While she unwrapped

the ties of the file, he sat back, as if it might contain lingerie. She appreciated his discretion, though they both knew what it held—current records of her financial holdings, along with her will, and the combination to her in-house safe. She had pointed out the location of this file two years earlier at the same time she'd given him a house key, saying she didn't like the thought of strangers ransacking her things.

"I've been thinking about this all week, so don't interrupt me, or give me problems. I've decided to leave you my home and all the furnishings, including the art collection you've so gallantly admired, though I suspect you don't give a damn for those impressionists. But I've seen you eyeing the Wyeths. They're more masculine. Those were Nate's."

"That's. . .too generous," the captain groped for words. Rose had no heirs and had regularly talked about leaving everything in a charitable trust, adamant about not giving more to the government than was absolutely necessary.

"I know what it is you say," she went on, "that you've got plenty of money for your needs and a cabin—a place to live," she corrected herself, "that suits you." She leaned forward, "But, indulge me. I've seen you admire this house, and I want her in the hands of someone who cares."

The captain sat quietly as Rose shuffled through papers and handed him the most recent statement on her Merrill Lynch master account, dated August 30, 1999. "I'm ready to sell out," she told him. "Never intended to stay in so long, but," she looked up and smiled, "it's been quite a ride. Still, things run in cycles, and this should peter out before long. How much money does one person need, anyway? My God, listen to me—a girl who grew up in Amarillo, Texas, during the dust bowl. But the problem is, if I pull out of the market, what the hell do I do with all that cash? I need you to put your mind to that."

There was something else she wanted. "A nice young man was working in the emergency room the night I went in," she told him."His name was Martini. See if you can find him for me, Captain."

As Rose spoke, the hall clock began to chime. It was eight o'clock. Michael, the delivery boy, would be at the door soon in his yellow slicker, sheltering two orders of eggplant parmesan and a side of angel hair pasta from the rain and wind. The island had been battened down for the entire week. Ships were secured in the harbor, but the natives were restless, drinking and eating to stave off boredom, anxious to get back to business. Bookies were taking bets on if and when Glenda would hit, while the fickle girl sat out in the gulf, holding a coastline hostage.

2

Hurricane Glenda didn't change her position the night Rose came home from the hospital, but J.J. Broussard agreed to stay in town all the same. He owed Rose that, especially after that announcement. It had rearranged his priorities like dominos turned face down and shuffled around. What was it she'd said? She knew he didn't need money, or a house. Exactly what he had wanted her to think. Mostly true. But, in the face of $9,000,000, that word, need, loses relevance. Rose's gift, and her request for further advice, had promoted him into the driver's seat of a high stakes game. Should he pass or play? There was pressure to decide quickly, pressure that had his head pounding. He knew Rose would be seriously troubled to discover she didn't know him as well as she thought.

J.J. couldn't sleep. The wind was whistling against the weather-stripping, the chimes downstairs were ringing out at regular intervals, and thoughts were scrambling through his head like mice in a maze. So there he lay, open-eyed, hands behind his neck, and stared into the darkness, where the shadows of the bed canopy looked unpleasantly familiar. His childhood bed had a canopy. His parents had argued about it. His father told his mother a boy shouldn't have such a fancy pants setting. His mother, who had just redecorated his bedroom, told his father she thought it looked very historical, but she wouldn't insist that little John sleep there. He could always choose another room.

He had never thought about money growing up. It was always there, along with other advantages. As the only child of two people who didn't like each other very much, he had been alternately ignored and indulged. He learned to entertain himself, to be non-confrontational, and to be good company when it was called for. Lots of things had come easy for him—like his relationship with Rose.

Boutique investing. That's what it's called inside the business. Find a rich client, hold her hand, answer her questions, send flowers on her birthday. The truth was, he'd never gone looking, never expected something like this. Advising a wealthy widow was far from what J.J. had in mind when he came to Galveston and started a charter boat service. It was Rose who had sought him out, shortly after her husband died, looking to set up what she termed a "risky business" account. She had some good solid securities, but she wanted to play the stock market.

"I don't want to mess with proxies, or annual reports, or any of this other stuff that comes in the mail," she had told him. "Frankly, I think most of it is meaningless. These people want to impress me that they're doing their job, while I'd be much happier if they spent less time writing me and more time seeing how well they could make their widget or drill more wells, or whatever it is they're about."

"All you want is recommendations?" he had clarified, weighing his responsibility.

"That's right. I don't have trouble saying a simple yes or no, when I understand the question, but the financial world seems to have a vocabulary of its own, and much of it escapes me. I'll want you to explain some things and help with the record-keeping as well. I keep orderly records, Captain Broussard, nice, neat lists of when, where, and how much, but uninformed as I am on this subject, I never seem to have the right information handy when tax time comes."

Rose had been testy from the beginning. She had strong opinions on everything from space stations to disposable diapers, but they'd done well together, and he'd never taken advantage. They started with a hunch on Texas Instruments and a long shot on Dell Computers, and they'd made a killing. "Rich as sin," she'd chuckle, after a couple of scotches. She insisted on paying him a monthly retainer, and with that he'd bought the same equities for himself in smaller numbers. With the income, he'd upgrade his truck and boat every couple of years, while his neighbors scratched their chins and wondered how he managed to live so high doing fishing charters now and then.

Meeting Rose had been a stroke of luck twelve years back, but it wasn't the first unusual turn in J.J.'s life, and now he sensed another in the wings. Her announcement spooked him. He'd made it a point not to get too close. Not to Rose. Not to anyone. And then last week, he'd used his key to check on her, and something was set in motion, as if by entering the house he'd stepped over some invisible line. The distance he'd established, his independence, was slip-sliding away—and he didn't want to think about it. *Nine million dollars.* He could think on that. Nine million carried a lot of leverage, if you worked it right. And if not, he thought, there's still this fine old house, antiques, collections, art.

Elena's smile flashed in his mind, and he imagined showing the house to her. That would make those eyes dance! She had an innate good taste that regularly surprised him. There was the almost reverent way she took care of his cabin—polishing a table or a mirror or a tray, and then arranging the blinds so the light could shine on them in the most favorable way. When he teased her about it, she had told him, "Yes, I cleaned them, and they're beautiful now, and they're saying, 'Look at me. *Mires.*' Are you looking?"

He was often looking when Elena was around. She had come into his life after a long time without a woman and was as refreshing as water from a clear spring. She'd probably wear thin at some point. None of the others, four or five he remembered by name, had been important enough, or had stuck around long enough to leave a serious mark. This one was too young. Plus, she had kids. J.J. had escaped parenthood and wasn't about to take on someone else's. It wasn't even a consideration.

But a house. A historic house. That, he could wrap his mind around. He traveled mentally through the lower level, through the massive double doors of the entry into a tall-ceilinged, crystal-chandeliered foyer, which led into the parlor on the right. The paneled library off the parlor was smaller. It had a fireplace and two walls of shelves that stretched from the floor to the ceiling, holding a collection that included an amusing selection of rare books and raunchy ones. Down the hall and back to the right was the staircase, under which was tucked an awkward powder room with a sloping ceiling, that required bending his knees to piss. It could be fixed. Beyond that were a butler's pantry and a huge kitchen, which served the formal dining room, with its table for ten, massive buffets at either end, and elaborate wall sconces that resembled branched candlesticks.

Rose's table was always set. Sometimes it held flower arrangements from the back garden that Pearl tended as if it were her own. Outside the house, a wide, covered porch wrapped around three sides. It had pots of red geraniums, padded wicker rockers, and an ocean breeze. My gin-and-tonic porch, Rose called it. It could have been a movie set, and in her younger days, he was sure she had reigned there, playing Katherine Hepburn.

This night, with Rose resting below, J.J. explored the upstairs on his own. There were four bedrooms, two with private baths, and another separate bath. The bathrooms had been remodeled and were still small by modern standards, but the tile was polished to a shine and the plush towels smelled like lilac. He rummaged in a cabinet for a couple of aspirin and took them with water from a porcelain glass. In a small bedroom at the end of the hall he came face to face with a dressmaker's dummy, standing in the shadows, headless, the actual shape of the Rose he had met some years back. Unnerved, he shut the door. Nine million. A little more than nine, actually. The numbers bobbed in his head like a cork in water.

✥

At home, two nights later, J.J. was still unable to sleep. He lay awake in the dark and listened to the flag mounted on the deck outside his bedroom flapping up an awful ruckus. He kept thinking about Rose. "I need to rewrite my will before this is an accomplished fact," she'd said, "and while I'm at it, I'm thinking of changing the trust. As it stands now, everything goes to the public library, but I'm looking for something a little more imaginative."

J.J. could feel his cabin floor shift and heard it creak. He raised himself on one elbow to check the clock, then shuffled barefoot to the door and stepped out into the warm September wind. Thirty miles an hour, he figured, out of the south, and gusting.

He lifted the flag from its holder and wrestled it back to the bedroom, then went in search of the remote. Light from the television spilled into the room and flickered, greenish, across the bare windows. He reached for his glasses. While a pasty-faced man in front of a map of the U.S. described the frost line just above Cincinnati, J.J. located the culprit himself— the swirling cloud mass in the gulf. Hurricane Glenda, upgraded from a tropical disturbance days ago, had started moving again. When the phone rang, J.J. picked up without a comment, eyes still focused on the weather channel.

"Saw your light on. You still watchin' this thang?" a familiar voice drawled.

"Yep."

"Sure is messin' up the fishin'."

"Your mottled face could use a break from the sun."

Woody, on the other end, chuckled. "This is true. You thinkin' to board up?"

"I'm keeping an eye on her."

"Poker still on?"

"I've never canceled yet."

On the second and fourth Mondays of every month J.J. hosted a neighborhood poker game. He didn't welcome strangers and kept the stakes low. The island had always attracted gamblers and scoundrels, but he wasn't having anyone questionable at his table.

When he had bought the lot on west beach in '86, there had been only a few houses in the subdivision, a couple of women who lived together near the entrance, and a scattering of cabins along the shell road that led to the bay. He and the women were the only permanent dwellers back then. The rest were weekenders, who didn't show up every weekend. Over time, people had come knocking on his door, looking for a sander, a hand truck, or motor oil.

"Cookin' up the day's catch," the borrower would say. "I'm the gray house on the corner. The one with the wind sock. Stop over about sundown and get some of the real stuff."

He hadn't come to the end of Galveston Island to be sociable, but neither was it in his nature to be rude, so he usually wandered over to sample the redfish or specks or flounder. He'd pick up tips on where the fish were running, and then someone would pull out a deck of cards. Now there were twenty houses. Some were upgrading, spending more time at the coast these days; some felt free to call at four A.M. when they saw his television flickering.

The weatherman was talking about Glenda now. J.J. rummaged in a drawer, pulled out his map, and marked the new coordinates. She had blown across Cuba without doing much damage and then had lost steam. For the past week she'd been stalled ninety miles out. Like a boxer, she feinted this way and that, teased, circled, and gathered momentum. Right now, she was headed for Galveston, a direction that could easily change.

When his charter customers had questions about hurricanes, J.J. told them a good sailor could feel the pressure drop that comes right before one—feel it in his body fluids—and they'd nod, polite but skeptical, maybe a little embarrassed. "Me, I keep an eye on the barometer," he'd add. They'd laugh then, relieved their captain wasn't directed by body fluid intuition. But there were things he didn't tell them—that he kept records and charts from twelve years back, that he could figure odds on where and when the big ones would hit, that the nerves get itchy, waiting.

Out where J.J. lived, the island narrowed to a strip so thin you could walk from the gulf to the bay in five minutes. A man had to know when to clear out. He liked to think about that—watching the water rise on both sides, then taking off at the last minute with the waves licking his hubcaps. In his vision, he'd look back to see the cabin standing there on wooden legs, a matchbox surrounded by water. He didn't plan to wait too long; still, something in him was excited by that idea—driving truck, boat, and trailer through the friggin' Gulf of México.

At five A.M., he put on a pot of coffee and settled in with a novel set in Baton Rouge, his hometown, 250 miles east as the crow flies, and a world away. Mid-morning he climbed into his pickup and headed toward town, with the south wind pushing at the truck like a bully itching for a quarrel. He stopped at a place near Thirty-seventh Street where he could get gasoline and a *Wall Street Journal,* then on to Pier 10. Storm warnings had kept the shrimp boats in again, and the pier was populated with restless seamen.

"Seventh one this season, and a gal's name to boot; she's hopin' to give us fits. Ain't Glenda a witch?"

"Hell, she was a good witch. Heard on the news it looks like she's turnin' to go in between Orange and Lafayette. Anybody willing to wager?"

J.J. bought fresh crabmeat and kept his eyes averted. After twelve years, he still maintained a low profile in public places. Outside the market, he tugged on the bill of his cap, headed his lanky body into the wind, and looked disinterested. On the way home, he stopped at Kelly's Liquors for a case of beer and a quart each of Jim Beam and Chivas, then went next door for a barbecue sandwich.

"Good you caught me early," Mrs. Kelly told him. "I'm going to shut her down about two. Not much business on Mondays anyways, and no tellin' what this thing is going to do. Think I'll just take me a busman's holiday, go home, open a bottle of wine, and watch the soaps. It's no picnic, having a business so near the beach, what with the trash that wanders in and out of here, and spring break, and the hurricane season, not to mention the god-awful insurance I have to pay and the blisterin' heat in the summer and the TABC always checking up on me. I run a clean ship, though." As she talked, she ran her dishtowel in swiping strokes across the counter.

"That you do," J.J. nodded and wiped his mouth, thinking she was more sour than usual.

Mrs. Kelly dabbed at her own chin with the dishtowel. "Got a little spot right there," she directed. "Hard to keep the barbecue sauce off that beard. Always shows up on gray. Don't you shave it, though. It becomes you," she winked.

He nodded and wiped again.

"I left once, after Carla. Now there was a bad one. You thinkin' we'll get any action?"

"If I knew that, Mrs. Kelly, I'd be a rich man."

She laughed, a big, open-mouthed hoot. "And here I always thought you were rich, Captain."

"Think again," he said, reaching into his pocket. He

brought out a packet of bills, neatly clipped with a silver dollar sign. "Now, if you'll give me a sack of ice and tell me what I owe you for today, I'll get out of your hair."

⁘

J.J. regularly cooked a meal for the poker club. Tonight it was gumbo, Cajun style, rich with filé, sausage, and crab. He could fix a hearty lasagna, a white chili, a venison stew, but the gumbo was his trademark. His neighbors appreciated a good meal in the same way they savored fishing in the bay, traipsing the flats at midnight to gig flounder, or shivering in a duck blind on mornings when most anyone would be glad to sleep in. They were a crusty bunch, most of them older than he was, men who had come up in a different time. Their toilets didn't always flush, but their motors were tended. Some of them, when they came to fishing camp, didn't change clothes for days. And they guarded their freedom like it was holy. It comes with a price, J.J. knew, thinking about his own. He felt comfortable with their simple talk.

"Fellow told me th'other day that back in the '30s this place, right where we sit, was Little Italy. Bunch of Eye-talians had a camp here. Probably bootleggers. If you showed up and wasn't invited, you might be picking shot out of your ass."

"Nobody's been shot in my recollection since Eddie forgot to put the safety on his pistol that day we was clearing out snakes. Got hisself in the foot when he was on the crapper."

They laughed, even Eddie, who jumped to change the subject.

"Y'all see we've got another new house goin' up? Bunch of blue tiles stacked by the door."

"You got a problem with blue tiles?"

"Too fancy for my taste. Get a bunch of homeowners in here, and next thing you know they'll be knockin' on my door with a list of regulations and a bill for dues."

"That's what you said when J.J. showed up. You complained

he was building too big a cabin and he kept his boat too clean. 'You think he's queer?' he asked me." The speaker was playing to the crowd now. "Boy, was he relieved to see women comin' in the evenin' and leavin' in the mornin'. Ante up and stop worrying about other people's stuff, Ed. If you don't let it go, you won't be around long enough to see what does happen."

"I've lived through Carla, Alicia, two divorces, and a shark bite," Eddie drawled. "Sure as hell plan to outlive you."

J.J. noticed that even the educated ones slipped into the vernacular at the poker table. He also noticed that their conversation had changed over time. It used to be big on tales of conquest, whether a fish or a woman. Now they commiserated on how hard it was to sleep and argued about whether it was better to treat arthritis with horse liniment or WD-40. They gossiped, too, though they'd deny it all day. A man that moves out here keeps his privacy, they declared, but there was a hunger, too, to learn another man's story.

✧

Late that Monday afternoon, when the gumbo was bubbling, and the beer iced down, J.J. lit his pipe and dialed Rose's number.

"Well, Captain," she cleared her throat. "To what do I owe this pleasant surprise?"

"I wondered if you'd caught the weather report."

"Actually, I've been wrapped up for the last hour with *Oprah* and the story of some young man with a botched circumcision who was raised as a girl, much to his consternation. It's quite fascinating. People will talk about anything these days."

He skipped over her invitation to conversation. "It looks like Glenda's finally on the move and headed our way. We should know by tomorrow evening."

"You know how those things are, weaving and threatening

like a drunken sailor. I try not to give them more attention than they deserve."

Typical Rose, he thought. Two nights ago she had practically insisted he stay over because of the impending storm. Was this her way of advising him she was back to her independent self? He wondered if anything else had changed.

"How are you fixed for supplies?" he asked her.

"I have plenty of scotch if that's what you're asking. However, if we're going to have a real storm, I might want some of that excellent Glenvitis, Glenfiddle, whatever they call it."

"Glenfiddditch?"

"That's it. I finished the bottle you gave me for Christmas and haven't gotten around to replacing it."

"I'll drop some off tomorrow."

"I'd like that, Captain. Anytime after noon."

"How about bottled water, toilet paper, batteries?"

"All taken care of." He could imagine the wave of her hand as she dismissed the ordinary. "No tornado warnings, I assume."

"Not yet. You feeling okay?"

"I'd kill for a cigarette." She gave a throaty laugh and hung up before he could answer.

✛

He had watched her change over the past couple of years. Didn't go out as much as she used to. Had given up her charity luncheons and club memberships. She didn't walk him to the door any more when he left. That rumbling cough they both tried to ignore told the tale. Before she ended up in the hospital he'd noticed how she sat in her chair, with her books and magazines close at hand, and the medicine tucked away out of sight. He'd thought that she was losing weight, too, though she still dressed the same, always pants, bright colored tops, and that big jewelry she liked ordering by mail.

"You think these earrings look gaudy?" she'd ask him, pointing to a picture on a dog-eared page of an art museum catalogue.

He'd study first the picture, then her face. "A good choice," he'd say, or "Eye-catching, not gaudy." She'd shift in her chair, brush an invisible piece of hair off her forehead, then flash an appreciative smile.

3

After prolonged teasing, Hurricane Glenda swirled north to harass the residents of Lafayette, Louisiana. Galveston relaxed its vigil and island life returned to normal. Weekenders and tourists poured across the causeway like ants on the trail of sticky candy. Fishermen filled the bay with skiffs. People on the street were cheering the good weather. But for the doctors-to-be from the University of Texas Medical Branch, gathered at Gunners Bar on Twelfth Street, the talk was the same as always—grades, course work, professors.

"Kerwin's a bastard."

"He's just old and tired. Been around too long."

Jesse Martin stayed quiet and tried not to look irritated at his roommate's show of defending an unpopular teacher.

"You're sure getting generous," someone said.

"Know why The Chip Man is so generous? 'Cause he aced Kerwin's last test."

"No shit?"

"We all studied together. How'd you pull that off?"

"Superior dendrites." Chip's attempt at a swagger looked ridiculous.

"Nothing else? No test copies you didn't share?"

"You think I'd hold out?" He rearranged the designer glasses that looked pretentious on his chipmunk face and continued to protest innocence.

No one answered.

"Isn't Kerwin friends with your dad, Chip?"

"Sure. But that doesn't win me points."

"Says you. It's hell to even get in this place with no doctors in your family."

Jesse nodded agreement. He was trying to count his change without taking it out of his pocket, hoping for enough to order another beer. As he fumbled, the others continued on his roommate's case.

"My name is synonymous with the leading gastroenterology clinic in the state, but I don't get any special points," someone mocked, then turned back to Chip with a grudging smile, "You've got it made."

Jesse, looking away from the conversation, caught sight of a girl standing just inside the door. Susanna, the graduate nurse whose attention he'd been trying to get for months, waved toward their table. He could swear that wave was directed at him.

"Moi?" he mouthed, eyebrows raised, and pointed to himself.

"Looks like it's your day," his lab partner, Gail, nudged him with her bony hip.

When Susanna nodded, yes, Jesse didn't waste any time making his way across the wooden floor toward her. As he reached her, she pushed open the door, and they walked out into the afternoon light.

"Jesse Martin, don't you ever have your fun at my expense again," she spun to face him, obviously irritated.

He shaded his eyes and squinted at her.

"Someone called about that night you came into my emergency area. You weren't scheduled, and now they're asking me about somebody called *Martini,* and what am I supposed to say? 'Oh, that was Med Student Martin, just hanging out, being clever.'"

"What *did* you say?"

"I said I wasn't aware of any *Martini* on duty that night."

"And they accepted that?"

They seemed to, but," she made her point with a single, unwavering finger, "I don't like lying."

"You didn't lie. No Martini was on duty that night. And what's the big deal, anyway? I slipped on a white coat and helped you."

"I didn't need your help."

"You were smiling at the time." He grinned, hoping to defuse the moment.

"Well, I'm not smiling now. You weren't on the schedule, and they think some stranger was walking around dispensing medicine. You're going to get yourself in trouble, Jesse, and I don't want any part of it."

"Gotcha," he said, suddenly serious. "I didn't hurt anyone, you know. It was only that one old woman. Did she complain?"

"I don't know, but if you didn't think you were doing anything wrong, why Martini?"

"It's my stage name."

He finally got a glimpse of that dimple, but it was too late.

Back inside Gunners he told the crowd his version. "She wants to marry me—madly in love, but we have to cool it. She's engaged to a guy who cut off his left hand with a hacksaw the last time she tried to leave him."

"That was a movie, Jesse," his roommate moaned, taking the edge off the joke and, as usual, calling attention to himself.

✢

Jesse knew they liked him in Emergency. They called him to fill in regularly, and sometimes, to get out of the dorm, he'd hang out there. Sure, there were things he wasn't qualified to do, but he was a quick learner—worked with the team and handled the patients well. It looked good on his résumé. The best thing about Emergency—it was real. Much of the doctor game looked like big business—well-dressed people smiling on cue, never getting caught by surprise, or at least not admitting it. As a kid, he'd been blinded by that holy aura; now that he was almost there, he could see that the shine had its rough spots. Managed care, for example. Insurance. The really hot issues like legalizing drugs and abortion were more political than moral. There were rules for medical professionals and big punishments for breaking them. Doctors had to take themselves seriously. Was he ready for all that?

❖

"It's hard work and it has its nasty side," he had told his father a few months earlier.

"It pays well and has a lot of clout. Stick with it, son."

"Not sure I want to do this with my life—be the man with the answers. I like parts of it, but. . ."

"I had a chance at something better and shot it, when I was your age. I'm doing everything I can to give you a better deal."

It was an old conversation. They had it regularly.

"Zey teach us it's psychologically unsound to try and live out ze parental fantasies," Jesse offered, trying for a Freudian accent.

"Do they teach respect for your parents' input?" His father's frown didn't change. Neither did his accent.

"Sure."

"Then stop questioning. You're smart enough to be a doctor. You've wanted this as long as I can remember. Jesse Martin, M.D. Roll that around on your tongue. I do. I was the first one in my line to graduate from high school. You'll be the first doctor. Your brother?" he blew out his breath in frustration.

"I'm having serious second thoughts. How about owing over $50,000 when I get out, assuming I don't go for a specialty?"

"Don't throw this away, Jesse. I'm counting on you."

Jesse would have appreciated a sympathetic ear, but he knew he wasn't about to get one from his dad. He was really fed up with pinching pennies and watching his roommate hit the ATM machine for pocket money. Fed up with his roommate. On opening day they warn you. The competition turns some people into gunners. Those are the ones who go for whatever looks like an advantage—grades, honors, references, connections— and they shoot down anyone in their way. Chip fit the profile. Jesse was tired of the dorm, its lack of privacy and petty jealousies. And he wanted away from Chip.

Once, on a scout outing, Jesse had located a nest of rattlesnakes by recognizing their oily fragrance. This won him the title of "Snake Nose" and provided for campfire games, where he would sit, blindfolded, and identify random items passed across his face by other twelve-year-olds. Recently, during clinical rounds, he'd impressed the supervising doctor by suggesting a diagnosis of internal bleeding based on a strange odor in the room. But more often than not, his ultrasensitive nose was more curse than blessing. He hadn't thought, when choosing to study medicine, about being regularly subjected to the chemicals of body decay, aptly named cadaverine and putrecine. Neither had he considered that location might be a problem. Galveston's warm breezes were overlaid with heavier smells of mildew, decaying timbers, and rotting sea life. Then there was his roommate, whose feet smelled like swamp trash, whose closet reeked of the same sickening odor. That stink was the real deal-breaker.

34

❖

There had been a fantasy about moving in with Nurse Susanna, but when that went down in flames, Jesse started to scope out cheap rooms to rent. One afternoon in mid-October, following four hours in Psychiatry, he wheeled his bike down along the Strand and took a turn chasing the gulls that perched along the posts of the pier outside Willie G's. He couldn't get her out of his mind—a fourteen-year-old he had interviewed that afternoon. She had claimed to smoke six joints a day, financed by selling her body. When he asked her what she was looking forward to, she had told him "Driver's Ed."

He darted in and out of sparse traffic along Mechanic's Row, then turned down Post Office Street, headed for the dorm. He liked the old tree-lined street and its shady reputation. He and every other Texas schoolboy had heard about it— stories from when Galveston was a wide-open town, full of sailors, good old boys, and people looking for a quick buck. They said that whore houses stood side by side here, like porta-potties at a concert, ready to service anyone with a need. His dad had told him, maybe with a hint of pride, about losing his virginity on this street, for seven bucks. A strange confidence, Jesse thought, for someone whose conversation was generally limited to questions and directives.

Midway in the second block stood a once-white house, with circular wooden columns, flaking paint, and a wide upstairs balcony. This one had the look. Jesse could imagine women leaning over the railing, calling out suggestions, quoting prices, doing business. Sex for sale. Jesse wasn't buying. Last year his younger brother had run up a $200 telephone bill with 900 numbers. *Sick,* his dad had called it. Hypocrite, he had thought, about his dad, but hadn't said it, only pointed out that phone sex was safer than the actual thing. His brother thought he was taking up for him.

On down the street he passed a large, well-kept house with an apartment for rent sign. He slowed his bike and sat, flapping worn tennis shoes against the pavement, considering. The place was only five blocks from school, and nothing he had looked at before had a private entrance. It was sure to be too expensive, but maybe someone with a house that nice could rent cheap. Maybe they wanted a reliable med student to house sit or take care of pets when they were gone. Maybe they needed someone to cut the yard or clean out the garage. Maybe he could barter for his rent. He could see it now—Jesse, the jester, at Gunners, entertaining his buds with a story about this old house on Post Office Street. He approached the impressive front door and started to knock, then decided to use the polished brass knocker. It resonated with a couple of solid thumps that pleased his ear.

A woman answered the door, red-faced, graying, all business. He smiled and mentioned seeing the sign, and she disappeared for a minute, then reappeared and led him into a fancy sitting room that faced the street. He stood tall, anxious to see who it was he needed to charm. Women were easier.

An elderly woman—easiest of all—sat forward in her wing chair, extended her hand, and introduced herself as Rose Parrish. She had bright eyes and steel-colored hair that fell past her shoulders and was pulled back with fancy combs. She reminded him of the duchess who hands out trophies at Wimbledon.

"You're asking about the apartment?"

Jesse fidgeted. "I attend UTMB," he gestured toward the school, "and was riding by and saw your sign." He brushed at the legs of his green scrubs and tried to look innocent. "Just got out of lab."

"We put it out today, didn't we, Pearl?" The woman, who had remained standing in the doorway, nodded. "Do I know you from somewhere, young man?"

"I don't believe so."

As she reached for her glasses, Jesse's stomach did a quick flip of recognition.

"Mr. Martini?"

He stood his ground, trying to look blank.

"Come a little closer," she motioned, scrutinizing his face. "I could swear you were the young man I met in the emergency room a couple of weeks ago, but they say there was no one by that name in Emergency that night."

He shrugged and tried to look innocent. "Martin, ma'am. My name's Jesse Martin. Maybe you misunderstood."

She raised an eyebrow. "I've seldom been known to misunderstand Martini." She continued to study him in silence. "So, might it have been you in the emergency room?"

"I work there sometimes."

"Well, Mr. Martin, I forgive you for not recognizing me. I certainly wasn't at my best."

Jesse widened his eyes and nodded again, hoping to look reassuring, hoping they were past the name thing.

"Here, sit down, and Pearl can bring us some tea." She looked over her shoulder at Pearl, who nodded. "And something to eat, Pearl, please. I understand young men are always ravenous. If you're wondering why in the world I was trying to find you, I'm not quite sure myself. I don't meet many young people, Mr. Martin, and you impressed me, even in my witless and disheveled state. Tell me, are you one of the local Martins and how old are you?"

"No, and twenty-seven," he stretched his age a couple of years. "And please call me Jesse."

"And do you like the study of medicine, Jesse?" He wanted to look around, check out the furniture and the pictures on the walls, but she held his eyes.

"Most of the time."

"Aha! I would have mistrusted you if you had told me you liked it unconditionally. Nothing's perfect, is it? What is it that . . . no, I won't ask you that. What do you like about it?"

"I like the idea of helping people."

She nodded, looking unimpressed.

"My favorite thing is probably trying to make a diagnosis. Sometimes it's easy, but sometimes you have to hunt for clues and try to piece them together—like a puzzle."

She smiled and leaned forward. "Have you ever lost a patient?"

"No, ma'am, I don't really have patients. I just assist. I've seen some people die, but then I've been working in emergency rooms since I was a senior in high school. You lose some," he told her, trying to sound experienced. He shifted his position in the chair. "May I ask you a question?"

"Certainly." She sat back in her chair.

"About the apartment?"

"Since I was in the hospital, Jesse, I've decided to make some changes. The apartment, as you can see, is attached to the house, but has its own entrance. It's been vacant for years and isn't in very good condition, but I can have it fixed up. That way, if I need help in the middle of the night, as I did last week, someone will be handy. I put the sign out hoping to catch the eye of one of the domestics who work in the neighborhood. Pearl has a husband and a grown son at home and won't be enticed to live here."

"Would you consider a student?"

"Oh, I don't know. Young people are so flitty and half the time they mumble and have loud music and. . ."

"No, I mean me."

She put her hands to her face in embarrassment. "Oh, my. Of course, you are a student." She then reached out and patted him on the knee. "I had. . . I had forgotten that was why you . . ." She began to cough and reached for a glass of water. When the coughing increased to a level of distress, Jesse moved to the side of her chair, took hold under the armpits, and smoothly lifted her to a standing position. He took the glass from her hand and set it on the table, then raised both her arms over her head.

"This'll open your chest and help you get more air," he told her. "You can do it by yourself, whenever you feel like you're choking."

As the coughing stopped, she sank to a sitting position. Jesse came to the front of her chair then, kneeled down, took a foot in each hand and arranged them, crossed at the ankles.

"Sitting with your legs crossed is hard on your circulation.

It's better if you can sit like this, or, ideally," he walked across the room and brought back a small needlepoint footstool and put her feet on it, "elevated."

"Usually don't use that," Rose's post-spell voice was a whispery gargle. "Made by my husband's great grandmother, circa 1825."

"Shhh," Jesse told her. "Rest for a minute."

She sat back in the chair, her feet resting on the antique footstool, and rang a small bell which advised Pearl they were ready for refreshments.

"Tell me," Rose whispered and waved her hand commandingly, "about your family."

"Well," Jesse sorted through possibilities for the best answer. "My parents were divorced when I was ten. My brother and I have lived with my dad since I was twelve and he was five, and my mom remarried."

"Your father?"

He shook his head. "Didn't remarry."

"And he . . .?"

"Sells insurance."

"Not a doctor?" she shook her head questioningly, eyebrows raised. "Proud of you, I'm sure."

Jesse gave a nod and looked up, relieved to get off the spot, as Pearl entered carrying a tray of small sandwiches with the crusts removed, decorated cookies, and iced tea. They nibbled and sipped in silence.

"Is this the room you sit in most of the time?"

Rose nodded.

"You should have an oxygen tank in here."

"Upstairs in the bedroom," she pointed. "Ugly thing. I prefer to keep it out of sight, though it's a comfort at night."

"You should get another for down here."

"Sounds like you don't think I'm long for this world," she looked at him over her glasses.

"No, ma'am. That's not at all what I was saying. I just think you should make yourself as comfortable as possible during this recovery period."

"Delicately put, Jesse."

This lady was nobody's fool, he thought. She was proud and clear-thinking, but it didn't take much to see she was feeling vulnerable these days. He had paved his path through twenty years of school with a bright smile, an earnest manner, and a sense of what people wanted to hear. His foot was already in Mrs. Parrish's door. She liked him.

"If you're serious, I'll tell you that the apartment rents for $300 a month," she was saying. "I pay the utilities," she waved her hand in dismissal. "I don't have a separate meter, and it's too hard to divide them out."

"I'm serious," he said, almost too fast.

"Call me tomorrow," she said. "It's good to sleep on decisions that require a change."

There were drawbacks to moving out of the dorm. It meant taking himself from the heart of campus—something his advisors would frown on. His dad would be pissed. So would his roommate. But Jesse's main concern was that this lady might change her mind before tomorrow. Coming across her was like finding a bag of cash dropped from a Brinks truck—the kind of stuff you read about in the newspaper that happens to other people. Never to him.

Mrs. Parrish was sure to have some jobs for him. He'd be available. Maybe she had an extra television that wasn't being used. Maybe he'd help her when she had her next emergency, and she'd give him a reward. Maybe she'd be so indebted she'd leave him something in her will. Right. And maybe Susanna would parade down the street naked on a prancing white horse, looking for him.

4

J.J. Broussard had a horseshoe hanging over his cabin door, and, like most gamblers, he had a few rituals he'd just as soon not be called on to explain. Whenever he entered or left his place, he slapped both sides of the pine-stained jamb twice. Simultaneously. Whap, whap. It protected his space. He did it naturally, without half-thinking, so a visitor would scarcely notice, though J.J. didn't have many visitors. There was the poker club, and there was Elena. The poker club came on alternate Mondays. Elena came every Thursday to clean, and she slept over.

He knew Elena had noticed. She couldn't know what the slapping was about and she had never mentioned it, but she had taken to crossing herself when he did it. She was young and not the sort to question. And she had some superstitions of her own, like that thing she did with the condoms. In their arrangement, a lot went unsaid, and he was comfortable with that.

As far as he could tell she wasn't counting on him to make changes in her life. She spent what at his place? A day out of her week. The rest of the time was her own business—working long hours at the boat shop, sharing a trailer with some girl. She was a mystery. Appealing as fool's gold, a butterfly, a neon light. Unexpected—the way she had tapped him, made herself available. And though he kept expecting her to ask for something, she didn't. Most of the women he'd known were playing some kind of angle. But Elena had been around a year and a half now. If she wanted more from him, she had yet to make it clear.

❖

Although J.J. was comfortable enough in his cabin, the idea of a private boat slip was one he'd toyed with a long time. Those advertisements in the Sunday paper that sold "The convenience of launching from your back door" never failed to catch his eye, and ever since Rose's announcement, he'd been looking. He wasn't going to act on anything Rose had said—not until he saw the new will—but she didn't make empty promises. Besides, he had a nest egg, an annuity his father had left, with him as beneficiary. It had been an unexpected, bittersweet gift, considering their history.

Instead of putting his inheritance to work in the market, J.J. had chosen to let it sit and draw interest, like yeast left to bubble. He could sure have a new place if he took a mind to, without any help from Rose. In fact, it might emphasize how little he needed her generosity. He'd simply be someone she named to do her a service—take care of her favorite things—and that should quell any second thoughts she might have about what she'd left him.

J.J. was thinking big, and though it felt strange, it was also familiar, not much different from slipping out of his fisherman's clothes into an expensive new shirt. Why shouldn't he build himself a place with a private dock? It'd give him breathing room from Woody's constant scrutiny. Other ideas kept springing up about a deal for Rose. It wasn't hard to make things happen with sufficient resources backing you up. The law of big money, they used to call it.

Lady Luck was winking at him. If he played his cards right, she might let him win back what he'd forfeited years ago. Respectability? Not a common term on the island, but as good as any. Wouldn't that be a kick? Maybe that guy was right, the one who told him you get a chance at a new life once every ten years. J.J. grabbed his cap and headed out the door. Whap, whap!

❖

He met with a realtor that afternoon, a huge, red-haired, red-faced young man who mopped his face incessantly as he spoke with authority about the local economy.

"Warm for October. Can't complain, though. Always brings in the tourists. Man, it's crowded on the seawall today. That new beach that was supposed to bring half a million new visitors? I think they're all down there today. You watch them build that thing? Pumping sand from the ocean bottom. Men and machines going all which ways. Reminds me of an ant farm I bought for my kid last Christmas. I tell you what—it's good for Galveston. It'll more than pay for itself through sales and hotel taxes."

J.J. had heard this before. It was the latest good news rumbling through town like a freight train. Galveston was going to boom again. The old business district had been revitalized, a new resort area was just completed, with a hotel, an aquarium, and an Imax theatre. Visitors were coming, money was rolling in, and if the beaches began to disappear, they'd make new ones, by God. Invincible, that's the kind of place she was—burned by pirates, battered by hurricanes, decimated by encephalitis, upstaged by Houston, godfathered by the Mafia, controlled by wealthy families, and regularly invaded by dreamers and opportunists.

"You read about that guy going head to head with the Moodys?" the realtor asked. He slapped at a mosquito with his handkerchief and missed. "They say he wants to take us back to the glory days."

J.J. turned the conversation back to bay lots, but that phrase "glory days" rang in his ears. He needed a project for Rose that was glamorous, something she could get excited about, and he could control from behind the scenes. If he could conjure up just the right deal, he could sell it to her. It would be best, he thought, if it tied into philanthropy. J.J. was closing in, and this time he'd play it straight.

✤

They say a hurricane begins somewhere in the planet's ecosystem with a falling leaf or a hatching butterfly, one tiny change begetting another and another until, over time, a swirling mass of natural fury evolves, prances its way across oceans and islands, slams against coastlines, and dances over the map until exhausted. J.J. wondered if his own shift of focus was the result of some similar random motion in the universe. Why now? All through his forties, he'd been content, even determined, to lie low, live the life of an independent fisherman, and keep to himself. But lately, even before Rose's bombshell, he was feeling diff e rent about things. Did it have something to do with a sense of time running down, having passed fifty? Was it—what did she call it—male menopause? Rose had told him about it—another of her *Oprah* stories. He'd listened half-heartedly.

Armed with back copies of the *Galveston Daily News,* he called on Rose. He brought to her attention a series of articles about a developer whose grandfather had been part of the mob-controlled gambling empire that had created and protected Galveston's glamorous reputation in the 1930s and '40s.

"I recognize the name," she told him. "Most of those families moved to greener pastures when the island got closed down."

"Well, this one's back," J.J. told her. The articles outlined how the man was buying up land, refurbishing hotels, building restaurants, and spinning dreams of a return to paradise. He was appealing to those who could remember a time when everyone who came to the island went away bedazzled, and everyone who lived on the island shared in the profits. This guy was challenging city fathers, saying all their "good works" lined their own pockets. And he was gaining support of old-timers who were tired of being tied to the old empire-builders. There were still some who remembered the glory days and were ready to make some money.

"I've been following this," Rose told J.J. "Even started to write my own letter to the newspaper, but thought better of it. Gambling's been voted down a couple of times in the last ten years, and I'm not so sure it's a good thing, though the city did prosper when we had it."

"Are you turning conservative on me?"

She smiled. "Conservative is not a dirty word. I'm older and wiser. When Nate and I were enjoying that particular romance, we were children—well, practically. He was forty something, and I was in my twenties. I remember how we danced all night, countless nights, to Benny Goodman and the like at the Balinese Room, then we walked on the beach in our evening clothes and bare feet. Sometimes we walked, sometimes we drove—back when you could drive on the beach. We came across another couple one night, doing just what we were doing—waiting to see the sun come up—and we built a fire and passed around a flask, to keep the energy going, and swore we'd meet there again the next weekend, or the next night, I can't remember which."

As she talked, her eyes shone soft in recollection. The afternoon light was kind to Rose's still-handsome features, and J.J., able to imagine her at her prime, wished he'd known her then. He appreciated the fact that she wasn't afraid to show her intelligence or her sense of humor, rare qualities for a woman, in his experience. She was generous also, in her way, and she didn't pry. In all the time he'd known her, she'd never asked about his life before Galveston and she'd never shown up on his doorstep, though she actively courted his company. When he turned down her early invitations to dinner, she stopped asking for a long while, but she managed to make meetings in her library feel more intimate than businesslike. Her green eyes were compelling, and she made the most of a shapely, slender figure, but Rose was in her sixties when they first met, impossibly old for J.J., then barely forty. He was fifty-three now and she was seventy-six. Impossibly old. He had managed to treat her with a mix of affection and respect, and their relationship had grown comfortable, often amusing.

Rose had an interesting way of keeping her distance, too. "Life is full of unpleasantness," she had told him. "I don't believe friends should subject friends to tales of woe, past or present." But no other subjects were taboo. She teased him from time to time about his "love life," and he was quick to change the subject. Rose's curiosity was going to have to be her own problem. J.J. wasn't about to try to explain his present relationship to Rose when he wasn't sure what to call it himself. Regular sex? Infatuation? Comfort? Friendship? Exploitation? Hell, it wasn't like Elena didn't have some say in their deal.

"We gambled and drank and ate fine steaks and never thought we were doing anything wrong," Rose continued her recollection. "What could be wrong about having such a good time? Big bands came here from all over back then. I heard Sinatra in '47, when he was just a skinny kid, about as wide as a broomstick, with that gorgeous dark-haired woman in the audience. What was her name? I remember she had on a slinky black gown and a white fur jacket that she intentionally dragged on the ground. My God, we thought that beat all—dragging a white fur on the ground." She paused and sipped on her scotch. "It was good. So why are we talking about this, Captain?"

"I'm wondering if you want to get on the bandwagon."

"And how would you suggest that?"

"Letters to the editor are nice, but a serious investor with a plan could be very welcome."

"I should invest in a developer with Mafia connections?"

"I wouldn't put it that way."

"How *would* you put it?" He could tell she was interested.

"Bricks and mortar, Rose. I'm suggesting you buy and restore Maison Rouge and turn it into a fine restaurant and club."

"Lafitte's old headquarters?" she beamed. "Now, Captain, that's a perfectly glorious idea. We'd have to tear down that warehouse or whatever it is that's over it now, and we'd have to check the archives to see if there's any reference to what it used to look like. If not, an early nineteenth century mansion would do. French architecture, wouldn't you think? Furnished with antiques. I can see it now—a cigar room and a martini bar and Sunday evening jazz and if gambling ever comes back . . ." She trailed off, leaving the thought dangling. Hands together, she leaned forward, one eyebrow raised. "How long do you think it will take, and will I live to see it?"

J.J. outlined his plan to liquidate her market holdings, purchase the land, buy large unit government bonds with the remainder, and use the income to cover the reconstruction of Maison Rouge. They should contact the enterprising developer to let him in on their plans and assure him they were collaborators, not competitors, in giving a facelift to the east end of the island. "You could arrange to leave the whole thing to the historical foundation, Rose, if you wanted to," he added, his final selling point.

Rose motioned toward the marble-topped bar. "Fix us a drink, will you, Captain? This idea is so delicious, I can hardly stand it." She fished in the drawer of a small mahogany table that sat between the two chairs. "What I wouldn't give for a cigarette."

He walked across the carpet and put a scotch and water into her hand. "I'll light you one, if you like, the night Maison Rouge opens for business."

She cocked her head, looked up at him sideways, and smiled.

"You have a penchant for saying the right thing, Captain."

Still a flirt, he thought.

✣

The following morning J.J. lifted the receiver to make a phone call and found the line open. Whenever that happened to him, it brought bad news.

"Got some bad news," a familiar voice said.

It was Woody, who never identified himself. His earthy East Texas twang, as remarkable as mud between bare toes, left no question who was calling.

"What's that?"

"Tyler's dayud." He strung the final word into two syllables.

"I just saw him yesterday, taking his boat out."

"'At's right where they found 'im. Keeled over in his boat, it goin' round in circles out'n the bay, motor still runnin'. Almost hit some kids. Musta been his heart."

J.J., caught off guard, didn't anticipate the next request.

"His brother's comin' down to cremate the body and wants to put his ashes in the water where he loved. Ast me to do it, but that kind o' thing spooks me, J.J., know what I mean? I told 'em you used to do that some and I figured you'd do it for ol' Tyler. That okay?"

"I suppose so."

"So, J.J., they got a new bartender at the Rusty Nail. She came over here from Corpus 'cause she says there's more money in Galveston than Corpus, if you know where to look. And she's lookin'. You interested?"

"Nope."

Woody was a procurer of sorts. Whatever you wanted, he could get for you, or tell you where to get it, or set up a contact. He didn't do it for money; he did it for friends, and it came in handy from time to time. Never hurt to know someone like Woody. But he was rubbing on J.J.'s nerves.

"Haven't seen you 'round much. That girl keepin' you busy?"

"What girl?" he asked, knowing exactly who he meant.

"The one from the boat shop."

"She only comes one day a week. How could that keep me busy?"

"Thought I saw her there on the weekend."

"Nope."

"You got your shots for Hepatitis B? Most of 'em have it, you know."

"Hepatitis B? Anything else?"

"Ever'thin' else. Tuberculosis. Diabetes. The Clap, prob'ly."

"You have your shots, Woody?"

"Nope, but I'm not sleepin' with a wetback."

"Then it's my problem, not yours."

"It'll be a hell of a problem when she shows up at the door with a couple of babies in tow."

J.J. offered no response.

"Jes' thought you ought to think about it before you let this go on too long. She's pretty and all, but she ain't good enough for you. Well, I gave Tyler's folks your number," he rushed to close off a conversation grown sticky. "They'll be callin' you tomorrow, next day, I s'pose."

"I'll be around," J.J. said. He wasn't much on burials at sea. Most weren't as cheerful as his first meeting with Rose had been. Still, Tyler had been one of the poker group, and Woody next door, for all his crudeness and intrusions, was someone you could hardly turn down. Woody was an extra set of eyes, the watchdog of the neighborhood. He reported everything from rowdy kids breaking into a weekender's house to a nest of rattlesnakes down by the pier; he was ready to help work on a motor, repair a roof, or board up for a hurricane. He knew about the tides and the back bayous and how to clean an alligator gar—swore he grew up eating them. For someone who didn't have much use for neighbors, J.J. knew it'd be hard to live on west beach alone.

5

Rose pulled the sheet from her typewriter and began to count.

> *October 2, 1999*
> *Editor,* Galveston County News
> *On a recent visit to John Sealy Hospital, I noted a small band of people huddled beside the front door trying to grab a smoke, despite the wind and rain of Hurricane Glenda. I know from experience that a trip to the hospi - tal is a traumatic time, and the relaxation from smoking a cigarette has helped many through a crisis. Why, then, should a facility used by the public, which receives federal insurance and various forms of taxpayer assistance, force people to smoke on the outside? It's unjustifiable and inconsiderate.*
> *As long as smoking is legal and the personal choice of many individuals, the hospital, which serves the public, should accommodate that portion of the public by estab -*

lishing a comfortable, safe, and ventilated area inside the building where smokers are protected from the elements, as well as from harassment and discrimination.

The fact that she had pared it down to less than 150 words brought a smile of satisfaction. Letters to the editor were her favorite forum for championing unpopular causes. This one was sure to elicit a spate of responses. She signed it with a flourish and set it aside for Pearl to make a copy when she went for groceries. Thank goodness for modern conveniences. She still had a box of carbon paper in her desk drawer, but was happy to forego its messiness.

Since the captain's last visit she was feeling more enthusiastic than she had in years. She had a plan now, and a man to help carry it out. She was proud of herself for choosing the captain and for deciding to stick with him when she'd found out about that mess in Baton Rouge.

Caution had gotten the better of her when they first began to do business together, and she'd asked an old friend from Tulane to find out whatever he could about a J.J. Broussard who went there in the late 1960s. The friend reported back that the only J.J. Broussard from that time period was from Baton Rouge, not New Orleans. She had hired an investigator to find out the rest.

A thief—that's what she'd learned. Well, not what she'd call a common thief, but he had been involved in a robbery ring. They pinpointed houses and only hit when the owners were on cruises or on ski trips or junkets to Las Vegas. Often the victims were off on holiday with the captain and his wife. Sometimes, just out to dinner. The thieves were quick and effective. They disarmed burglar alarms; they didn't ransack; they took only what they came for. The captain had been married back then, but the wife was apparently innocent. Rose thought about the society women she'd known and figured the innocence was a pose. They may appear focused on club work or cruises, she thought, but most of them know what their husbands are up to, and some decide to look the other way.

They called him J.J. in the report. Rose preferred to think of him as "The Captain." It was jewelry and furs and special collections that had been stolen. All trappings of the wealthy. And it was surely covered by insurance. No one was ever hurt, not even scared. But the social circle was furious when they realized it was one of their own, the easy-going, smart, young stockbroker with the pretty wife. One article told how he had been a heavy supporter of local charities and had even challenged his friends to cough up big donations.

The newspaper called it the "Country Club Capers." There were quite a few articles, stretching over a six-month period, all of which Rose had studied scrupulously. She had recognized right away that the man had an uncommon polish, certainly not what you'd expect of the ordinary seaman. Having found him, she didn't want to let him go. But, she was treading on soft turf here, and Nate wasn't around to bail her out of trouble if she made a bad choice.

One newspaper article reported: "Questioned Thursday about the 'double life' he was leading by socializing with wealthy friends while at the same time setting up burglaries of their homes and businesses, former Baton Rouge native Broussard replied, 'It was worse than hell, sir.'"

There was a picture of him, fuller-faced, boyish looking. In the interview he seemed remorseful. Certainly four years of prison should make a young man come to his senses, she thought, though she was aware of the statistics on back-sliding. But she wanted him—had hand-picked him—and he was certainly smart enough to help with investments.

"He was extremely intelligent—brilliant in the stock market," the article went on to quote an ex-friend.

Rose had thought about confronting him. She could tell him she knew his past and she'd know where to look if anything were missing. That's how she'd do it if he were a maid, or butler. But that wasn't how you handle a situation involving someone with whom you share good scotch and books. She was in a quandary. If she cut off the relationship, she'd have to tell him why. If he were a thief sizing her up, he might retaliate. If she continued the relationship without telling him, would she have to be ever-attentive, counting the silver every time he left the house?

She had taken it to the court of last resort—Nate. In the difficult months after his death, she had discovered that a conversation with her dead husband could be very satisfying. He had always been a sounding board, so when she felt touched or confused or at her wit's end trying to pull things together, she'd sit in her blue wing chair and talk to the chair that sat at right angles to her own. Sometimes she shared a poignant passage from a novel she was reading; usually she voiced a concern. And a dialogue ensued. She spoke aloud and heard his answers. They came out as perfectly formed and independent of her thinking as one could imagine. He was still there.

When she aired her dilemma over Captain Broussard, *Les Miserables* popped into her mind. "It's one of your favorite scenes, dear," she could hear Nate saying. "Surely you remember when Valjean stole the bishop's silverware, and the police captured him on the run and returned him to the bishop's house. 'Oh, my friend,' he told Valjean. 'I'm glad you're back. I meant for you to have these candlesticks as well.'"

Rose took that to mean that she should be generous. How much could he hurt me? I have no collections, only a little art and the antique furniture, which would be difficult to cart off without drawing attention. Jewelry? I keep it in the safe upstairs. Credit cards? Only the one, and I keep it with me. She tossed and turned on pebbles such as these for a couple of nights, fashioned some safety nets for her peace of mind, and decided she would continue her association with the captain until it proved untenable.

It hadn't been hard to rationalize her way through it. She had been hungry for male companionship, and this one fit the bill. He was attractive, intelligent, unattached, and unfamiliar to any locals who might see them together. His background lent an air of mystery and a hint of danger. She liked to imagine Nate had sent him to her, to brighten her days.

⁜

Rose, remembering, smiled. The captain had brought great refreshment to her life. It had been nice to have someone to talk to, a man with an opinion and some finesse, but not so sure of himself to be arrogant, or presumptuous. There had been times—times when things might have gone another direction. She was a rich widow, after all, and could have had, she supposed, most anything she was willing to pay for. But he had always been a gentleman, and they had worked well together. If it had turned into something else—their relationship—it would have been short-lived and fraught with doubt. What she liked most was his attention, and he had been smart enough to keep it on just the right level. Anything else would have been distasteful, though flattering.

"Happily ever after," she scoffed one day early in their friendship, "should be happily from time to time. Nothing is ever happily ever after, much as we want to believe it. Have you ever been married, Captain?" she had asked.

"Once," he had said, "a long time ago."

How proud she was to have her hunches validated. What pleasure she had enjoyed in his company over the past years. Had it been ten? More than that, she thought. She could figure it out if she wanted to focus, but just now she had better things to think about. She had a plan, and a man. She liked the economy of that phrase, the simple rhyme. Seemed there was something else that went with it, something that was escaping her for the moment.

Actually, she also had a boy. Jesse had accepted her offer, as expected, and having him in the house was going to be a comfort. She must be careful not to intrude on him. Would he be bringing young women to the apartment, she wondered, and if so, should she make some rule in advance about that? Certainly not, she decided quickly. She recalled a talk show where parents had discussed the relative merits of denying adult children cohabitation with non-spouses under their own roof. In one anecdote, a mother twice divorced and sleeping with the plumber wouldn't allow her twenty-five year old daughter to sleep with her boyfriend when they had traveled a thousand miles for a birthday visit. Principles can be as irritating as poison ivy, Rose thought. And sometimes they need a good weeding.

She wondered about Jesse. She had done it again, plucked some stranger who seemed promising and bright right out of the blue. She didn't do it often. But, it had turned out so well last time. Not that she equated Jesse with the captain. But the boy was competent and charming, not to mention pleasant to look at. The prospect of having him close felt reassuring. She would need his skills at some point, unless she were lucky enough to die in her sleep.

There was another interesting item. She was feeling pretty well. Maybe it was that steroid cocktail they'd given her at the hospital. It had been weeks now, and she was maintaining. Pearl had been tempting her appetite with dishes like last night's filet mignon, with late summer squash and chocolate pudding *à la Gran Marnier*. Pearl didn't cook with alcohol on religious grounds, but softened her position when Rose found a statement in a cookbook that said heat destroys the intoxicating part. Pearl believed what she saw in print. As for Rose's bottle of scotch, she refused to touch it, even to put it away, and wrinkled her nose when she carried away the glasses.

Pearl was a piece of work. Her Czech grandparents had emigrated through the port of Galveston in the early 1900s, when it was a little Ellis Island. Set down roots right where they landed, started a truck farm and raised cattle, never budged from the island, nor did their children or grandchildren. When Nate and Rose had bought the house in 1966, Pearl had been a ruddy-cheeked girl who worked for the previous owners, and she had stayed on. She had been sixteen at the time, a high-school dropout, married to a shrimper, the man she shared quarters with to this day. She needed her job back then and still needed it. Poor woman could never get ahead, what with her husband and that son who never amounted to anything. Thank goodness she only had one child. The husband was a loser, but Pearl was reliable, and Rose didn't dream of interfering in her private life, though she had to bite her tongue, and sometimes she wasn't completely successful.

In the '60s, Rose had been full of feminism, determined to set free every woman who had ever suffered under man's heel. She laughed, remembering her zeal. It turned out to be more complicated. Some women, she had found, choose overbearing men because that's what they want and they feel no need to be rescued. Rose, herself, had chosen an older man, a cross between her father and the boys who courted her. Nate had never tried to dominate her, yet she'd favored him, showered him with attention, been a dutiful wife for her time, and managed her temper tantrums, to a point.

There was the postcard affair. She had found it on the seat of the car when they had stopped at the liquor store on the way to celebrate their engagement.

"Everyone at the office is pleased," he told her. "They say it's time I settled down."

"I agree," she had said with a toss of her hair.

Then he had disappeared into the liquor store, and her hand had come to rest on the card, which displayed the picture of a beautiful woman. Susan Murchison, of the Zeigfield Follies, the card announced. *Nate, Hope you'll stop and visit next time you're in town,* she had written on the back and signed it, *Susie.*

"What, may I ask, is this?" Rose had asked when Nate returned.

"My private mail."

"A little too private for me," she had told him. The next day she put her ring in the mail to him and took off for Kansas City, where she had an aunt. She planned to catch her breath and start again. She hadn't left a forwarding address and didn't want him to follow. The hell with him and his showgirl. Was that what he was doing every time he took a business trip? The hell with him!

She was miserable for almost a week. That's how long it took him to find her. Then she was delighted, enchanted, won over. Surely he would do anything for her. He had left everything to come and find her. She could forgive one indiscretion, if it had been such, but a husband of mine won't dally with showgirls, no matter how pretty they are, she had stipulated. Nate had agreed. They married and lived happily from time to time.

That was long past, the kind of thing that brings a smile in remembering. Rose had come across the postcard a few years back, cleaning out Nate's old desk, surprised he had kept it after all these years. But that was some babe, Rose thought, admiring the dark brown hair, the slender, well-proportioned body, feeling no jealousy, just a longing for lost youth, wishing she had kept pictures of the men who had courted her. Long past. Happily from time to time.

✤

Rose had arranged her day so that she came downstairs in the late morning and went up about midnight. She had difficulty climbing the stairs and often stopped to rest at the landing, where she pretended to be a character in a Victorian novel, pausing for the narrator to insert something philosophical. At such times she'd ponder her own condition. After a full life, here she was—widowed, childless, wealthy, very wealthy, with a few good years left. She had noticed how often people said that—a few good years—because it was simply too depressing to think of death lurking around the next corner. However, Rose did think of it regularly and was determined not to be caught by surprise. She planned to go out gracefully. It was the last arrangement she wanted to make with life. She had watched others go—friends, family, her own dear husband—and knew enough to recognize some of the pitfalls. Keep the mind active. That was her first rule. Have your affairs in order, rule two. Surround yourself with talented, younger people and pay them well, rule three. In case things linger on, find an escape. She was still working on that one.

When she came home from the hospital, she had talked about sleeping downstairs, but had discarded that idea. She wasn't ready to turn her home into an infirmary, complete with rumpled bedsheets and the smell of camphor, or whatever that is that smells old. When Pearl came in each day about ten, she brought a carafe of coffee and the newspaper to Rose's bedside, then left her to wake slowly and dress in peace. She liked a light meal around noon. She took care of paperwork and phone calls after the mail was delivered. Then she read and watched her shows until about five, when she had a scotch and water, followed by a hearty meal. If she had company, which she seldom did, she postponed dinner, had Pearl cover it and put it in the oven. The woman would be irritated when she came in the next day to find the meal still in the oven, but she was getting paid whether Rose ate or not. Occasionally she had her dinner delivered. Overall, it was a simple routine. Pearl worried that she'd slip going upstairs and then be in the house alone all night with a broken something or other, but then Pearl worried about so many things—UFOs and white slavers and witch covens. The poor woman, who seemed to carry the world's woes on her shoulders, was eternally vigilant.

Rose was thinking she needed to contact her lawyer and talk to him about changing her will. She also needed to contact an antique dealer about furnishings for Maison Rouge. What ever happened to that old gentleman she used to do business with in South Houston? Probably long gone by now, but surely she could find someone. She hadn't been out of the house for a coon's age. Maybe when the boy gets moved in, she thought, she'd ask him to drive her into Houston. Would that be too pushy? Well, if he doesn't have the time, he can say so. Even if he looks like a boy, he's well on his way to being a doctor. She must think of him as a man. That's it! The word play that had been teasing her suddenly clicked into place. A man, a plan, a canal. Panama. A *palindrome*—reads the same forward and back. She liked those silly things, and she had known it would come to her. Things always did.

6

Jesse stood, surveying his new apartment and congratulating himself. It smelled of fresh paint and Murphy's soap, like his
mother used to use. He raised the bamboo blinds and discovered he could see the bay from one of his bedroom windows;
the other held an air conditioning unit that was gently humming, not unwelcome, even in November. Turning back the
chenille cover on the bed he found a new mattress still in its
plastic wrapping. He set up his computer in the sitting area, next
to the lamp table and beside the sofa. Over the computer he
installed his bulletin board to which were pinned notices,
receipts, schedules, telephone numbers, a Dave Barry quote
someone had printed out on card stock for him. "Never take a
sleeping pill and a laxative on the same night," it said. His old
roommate had scratched out the word "take" and replaced it
with the word "prescribe."

At six P.M. the following evening, Jesse lifted the brass
knocker at the main door. Rose Parrish answered slowly, frowning, but made an immediate correction when she saw who it
was.

"Well, Jesse, come in," she motioned. "I wasn't expecting you. Almost didn't answer. Thought it was someone collecting for something, and I don't like to encourage them. I give to whom I choose, when I choose, and if everyone did the same maybe we wouldn't have these strangers knocking—little children selling chocolate bars and such. So difficult to turn down. That's why they send them, of course. Marketing. By the way, don't use that knocker thing. I tell my friends when I hear the knocker, I often don't answer. Same concept as an answering machine, though I hate to talk on the darned things, but I screen my calls. Just because it's possible to be reached by everyone doesn't mean we have to. If we were smart, we'd go back to butlers, but I suppose that's not politically correct."

As she spoke she walked, upright, but slowly, toward her chair. "Help yourself to something to drink," she motioned toward the bar, then sat heavily. She exhaled quickly and concentrated on her breathing.

"You okay?" Jesse asked.

She drew her feet up under her, closed her eyes for a moment, then opened them wide, taking another breath. "I'm just fine," she said slowly. "This is nature's way of telling me to let someone else talk."

He told her he was settled in and handed her a slip of paper with his telephone number. When she asked if he could take her into Houston on Saturday, he agreed, though he hadn't expected a request so soon. No problem, he thought, quickly rearranging priorities. He'd combine her errand with a trip home to get some things he needed. He could drop her off, run to the house, and be back to pick her up an hour later.

✥

When Jesse showed up at Rose Parrish's door Saturday morning, a fine car sat in the driveway with the motor running.

"Mr. Green came by to make sure she was roadworthy," she told him. "Checked the battery and oil, filled her with gas. He keeps an eye on her for me."

She was a 1974 Mercedes, 450 SLC two-door, yellow, with a sun roof. It had 70,000 miles on it, not a dent, and only some small cracks in the leather. Jesse, whose auto expertise ran to keeping junkers going, felt a mix of excitement and awe in the presence of the car. Rose's husband had bought it for her fiftieth birthday, she told him. "I never was much for cars, thought it was silly for people to get so worked up over them, but when I saw this, I fell in love. Pretty, isn't she? Like one of my art pieces. Can't bring myself to get rid of her, so I have Mr. Green come by once a month." She handed him the keys. "We named her Colette because she seems to prefer men."

He slid behind the wheel, trying not to feel important. It was just a set of wheels, he told himself, but having worked as a parking attendant on occasions, he had developed an appetite for cars. This felt like a cross between a Jag and a Lexus.

They arrived at the antique store a little after noon, only to find a wreath on the door and a note that included an obituary, a photograph, and an apology to any patrons inconvenienced by the closing.

"Good Lord," she muttered. "It's enough to have to bury someone, without having to apologize for it. But they do seem to have some nice pieces in here," she said, peering through the large, leaded glass doors. "Maybe we can come back another time."

Jesse, trying not to think about the study group he was missing, asked what she'd like to do next. She was already getting tired, she told him, but knew he had planned to stop by his house, so why didn't they just go there and then head home.

When they arrived at the small frame house on the north side of Houston, he immediately regretted his decision. His brother Jerry was sitting in the driveway in a wheelchair, shooting at a rusted hoop that hung over the garage door. When he recognized Jesse behind the wheel, he jumped up, loped toward the car and pressed his face hard against the window in an excruciating grimace.

Jesse turned to his landlady. "This is my brother," he told her. "He's never serious and usually rude."

She rolled down the car window. "You go ahead with your visit. I'm perfectly comfortable here."

Jesse opened his door, while Jerry ran around to Rose's side of the car and leaned down to look at her.

"I'm Jerry," he said.

"And I'm Mrs. Parrish."

"Am I glad you came, brother," he looked across at Jesse through the car window. "Been sitting around beating off all day."

Rose Parrish frowned slightly but ignored the comment. "So you are Jesse's brother," she said.

"And you must be his girlfriend," the boy giggled. "Nice car."

With a wrestling hold around his neck, Jesse teased his brother away from the car and dragged him playfully across the grass toward the open front door. Once inside, he threw his brother toward the wall and kicked the door shut.

"Behave yourself, Jerry."

"Fuck yourself, Jesse."

"I need to pick up some things and then I'm out of here."

"You want me to go entertain your lady friend?" he grabbed the car keys that had landed on the floor in their scuffle and started a slow dance. He was nineteen and still growing.

"You've made a good start on that. C'mon, brother, I need my keys."

"The doctor needs his keys," he chanted, like a child's game. "The doctor needs his keys."

"What's the deal? Last time I talked to Dad he said you hadn't been home for weeks and had no idea where you were."

"Ran out of money, and he won't give me any."

"Jobs are handy."

"He gives money to you, and you don't have a job. But

then, everything's for Jesse. Jesse's going to be a doctor. Jesse's our hope and our salvation."

He studied Jerry's eyes to see if the pupils were dilated. "You okay?"

"I'm cool, dude."

Jesse reached in his pocket and pulled out five dollars. "This is all I have. I need to get back on the road. Take it. Do whatever it is you do."

"Maybe I should come down to Galveston and let the doctor help me."

"Jerry, if you come, I'll make it hard for you. You can't push me like you push Dad."

"Hunh." The sound was something between a sneer and a sniff.

Jesse went to his old room, picked up a gooseneck lamp, some double bed sheets and an alarm clock, and headed out the door where Rose waited.

"Wait," Jerry stumbled out of the house, caught up with Jesse and hung on him. "Want to shoot some hoops?"

"I have to go, Jerry."

He grabbed his crotch and crossed his legs. "Oh, so do I," he said, running back toward the house with a grin.

⁘

"I apologize," Jesse said when they were back on the road. "Jerry had a bad fall on his bike a while back, wasn't wearing a helmet, and, well," he made a motion of helplessness and pulled up something he hoped sounded like professional jargon, "brain-damage manifests in a variety of forms."

"Should he be left alone?"

"My dad has to work. We've tried sitters, but he runs them off."

"And why does he use that wheelchair?"

"It's what he wanted for Christmas last year. We couldn't figure it out, but, well," he shrugged, "that's what he asked for."

The wheelchair had just appeared in their garage, his dad had told him. Possibly stolen. Gruesome thought. Jesse had seen Jerry sitting in it at the mall on New Year's Eve, playing his guitar, with a hat and a couple of dollars on the ground in front of him.

"He seems fond of you."

"I feel bad if I come to town and don't spend a few minutes with him," he lied.

"I have another question, a bit of a clinical issue."

"Sure."

"This 'beating off?' Am I to infer he was talking about self-abuse?"

"Self-abuse?" Jesse did a double take across the steering wheel. "I'm not familiar with that term, but what he was talking about was more like, uh, self-gratification."

"I suspected as much."

Jesse drove in silence. Damn Jerry. Such a jerk. If he truly were brain-damaged, Jesse might summon up some compassion for him. As it was, he was just a huge embarrassment. He couldn't tell if she had believed his story; she was leaning back against the headrest, eyes closed.

"Feeling okay?" Jesse asked.

"A little short of breath."

"I'll have you home in forty-five minutes."

He needed to help her into the house, get her hooked up to the oxygen, and check her pulse. He was scheduled for emergency duty tonight. Needed to get a few hours sleep, too.

⁜

At eight that evening the unfamiliar ring of the telephone jerked Jesse awake. It was Rose.

"I've been thinking. That car doesn't get driven at all these days. You know, cars need to be driven. My husband always said you must take them out now and then and get them up to sixty or so to clean out the engine, or some such male theory. And

I'm sure a young man like you has the need for a car from time to time."

"Yes, ma'am."

"Any time you want, Jesse. I'd like you to use the car. Any time. It's not as easy for me to get in and out of as it used to be. Rides so low, you know. By the way, I'm feeling much better now. That was my first time out of the house for almost six weeks. I just overdid. Did you have some dinner?"

"Not yet. I go to work at eleven. I'll eat before I leave."

"I hope you don't get more old ladies who want to take up your time."

"No problem, Mrs. Parrish."

"Rose."

✤

Susanna was at the hospital when he checked in. He hadn't seen her since the day she called him out of Gunner's to give him hell. He figured she'd told them not to schedule him when she was on duty. So he was surprised to hear her call his name.

"Martin. Can you give me a hand here?"

He walked over to where a patient lay in a half-curtained cubicle.

"It's been a wild night and we're short-handed. Smitty had a wreck on the way to work, messed up his back, and may be out all week. I need you to stay with this patient," she looked down at a small girl who looked terrified, "until her mother gets back, or they come get her for surgery, whichever happens first." She looked down at the child. "You'll be okay, honey. This is Jesse. He'll tell you a story."

By the time the child was taken out, three new patients had arrived and it was almost four A.M. before there was a break.

"I'm going to put on a fresh pot," Susanna called to the team and disappeared around a corner.

"Can I help?" Jesse stuck his head in the door of the tiny kitchen area.

"Yeah," she said, handing him a glass carafe to wash while she measured out coffee into a filter. "Actually you were a lot of help tonight. Thanks, Martin."

"You're welcome, Parker," he mimicked her brisk tone.

She laughed and held her hands up. "Okay. I give. Sorry about the other day, but, at least you know how I feel about the rules."

"No kidding." He filled the reservoir with water and, while the coffee brewed, kept the conversation going by telling her about the coincidence of bumping into Rose, about moving into her apartment, and their trip to Houston that afternoon. "My brother embarrassed the hell out of me, but Rose didn't seem to mind. After we got home, she offered to let me use her car."

"Well, aren't you the smooth operator," she said, looking unimpressed, maybe even disapproving.

"Just trying to catch you up on my life," he shrugged and smiled. Seemed like whatever he tried with this woman, she wanted something else. After a silence he tried again, "So, why don't you tell me about yours?"

He saw the dimple wink, some little trick she did with her mouth, but she didn't really smile. She was busy pouring coffee. "Not enough time, *Martini*. Let's get back."

He followed her through the door, enjoying the smooth way her hips shifted when she walked. Funny, how the anatomy's the same and yet every woman has a distinctive way of moving, he thought. Then they act like you're not supposed to notice.

7

J.J. remembered the day he met Rose. It was fall of 1985, just after he'd settled in Galveston and was getting his charter service started. She'd found his card on a supermarket bulletin board and telephoned one day. Imperious was the word that best described her manner, but he couldn't afford to be choosy back then. She'd said she wanted to go fishing in Hall's Lake and then had shown up late, dressed in white, sporting a cigarette holder and a large Neiman Marcus shopping bag. As he took her hand and guided her onto the boat, his intuition flashed a caution signal, but he figured he could handle whatever she was about.

He'd settled her in the boat, crossed the bay, and was cruising the shoreline, looking for a good place to drop anchor, when suddenly the bark of gulls mixed with troubled shouts demanded his attention. His passenger appeared to be scattering crumbs off the side of the boat while a large congregation of seagulls competed to gobble up the larger pieces that floated on the breeze. J. J cut back the engines and called to her.

"Problem?"

She had put on short white gloves and was holding a lidless, gray box. Her face wore a pained expression. "Can you keep these creatures away? They're ruining everything."

"They won't leave until you stop feeding them."

"I'm *not* feeding them."

"What *are* you doing?"

"I'm spreading my husband's ashes—and," she clutched the box to her body with one hand and batted at a particularly aggressive bird with the other, "they're *eating* them."

J.J. drew the gulls' attention by emptying the bait box at the front of the boat, offering his customer time to gather her belongings and her dignity in the rear. He gave her a few minutes alone, then walked to where she sat, staring out at the water.

"My God, it was a fiasco, wasn't it?" She turned toward him.

He shrugged, helpless.

"I know the point of cremation is to be recycled, but that was more sudden than I was prepared to handle. Like something out of a Hitchcock movie."

He nodded in wordless agreement. She rested her head in her hands and rolled it from side to side in a gesture of helplessness. What at first he took for sobbing, he soon realized was chuckling. She was laughing, head bent, apparently replaying the scene. When she looked up, she pointedly took off her sunglasses.

"My amusement involves no disrespect, Captain. He's been dead six months now. I assure you, I've had time to come to terms with this."

J.J. understood. He liked this woman.

She told him about her husband, Nate, that he had been much older than she, that he had taken care of her in the early years of their marriage, and she had cared for him at the end.

"When he was alive, even sick and feeble, I always felt young," she said in a wistful tone.

And just when the conversation was getting uncomfortable, she asked him to open the bottle of champagne she'd brought for the occasion and share it with her.

"If you'd told me what you wanted to do, we could have made this easier," he said, handing her a glass.

"I suspected rules against such things. People are so touchy about death, you know, so I decided to handle it myself. Usually easier to ask forgiveness than permission, isn't it?" She smiled and sipped on her drink. "Are you a reader, Captain?"

He nodded.

"I suspected as much. What kind of man, I asked myself, names his boat the Odyssey?"

"I was going more for a feeling—you know, a kind of voyage."

"I know exactly. And that's what captured my attention. Your voyage is a kind of journey—a seeking—a story, if you will. And it's through our stories we reveal ourselves."

"I wasn't trying to reveal anything."

"But you did."

He emptied his glass, uncomfortable again.

"You revealed desire, isolation, education."

"It's just the name of a boat."

"Well, you could have called it *Miss Twinkie*."

He had grinned back at her then, thinking she was probably old enough to be his mother. Now it was twelve years later, she was still at it, and he was still there, glad he hadn't taken advantage of her invitation, her generosity, her trust. It had worked out so much better this way.

⁂

Rose's enthusiasm for J.J.'s proposed building project had set him in motion. It had been years since he'd tried to think like a promoter, but he hadn't lost the knack. In fact, it wasn't much different from fishing. After a couple of unsuccessful calls and unreturned messages, he dropped bait.

"This is John Broussard," he told the answering machine. "I represent an investor who's planning a multi-million dollar restoration on the east end of the island and thought a visit would be mutually beneficial."

Someone named Blair Peterson, who identified herself as a public relations person, returned his call and set up a meeting in the lobby of the Tremont House for the following Wednesday evening. Blair advised that her boss was living temporarily at the hotel and his assistant, Mr. Calhoun, would join them.

"We're not ready to release anything yet," J.J. told her, "but we wanted your team to be ahead of the press."

"We appreciate that, Mr. . . ?"

"Broussard."

He hung up the receiver, smiling, and phoned Rose, whose answering machine suggested he leave a message. He looked at his watch. She should be up and about by now. He was counting on her to be in good shape on Wednesday.

She returned his call within minutes. "You won't believe what I was doing earlier that prevented me from answering your call."

"What's that?"

"Walking."

"Walking?"

"That's right. I have a new treadmill—Quasimodo, I've named it—and I'm walking on it. Three minutes is about all I can do now, and it exhausts me, but the plan is to work up to twenty. Twenty minutes a day, Jesse tells me, will invigorate my system. Did you know we're constantly replacing every cell in the body? Even lung cells?"

"Who is Jesse?"

"Well, my goodness. Our last visit was so engrossing I suppose I failed to tell you I've rented the apartment. He's a student over at the medical school. The one we tried to find a while back and couldn't."

"And he has you on a treadmill?"

"What doesn't defeat me makes me stronger. Nietzsche said that."

"I knew I'd heard it somewhere."

"Oh, Captain. Don't pout. I thought you'd be pleased."

"I am. Just surprised. Do I need to meet this Jesse?"

"You must. Oh, and come a little early on Wednesday, will you Captain. We'll take my car to the meeting, but first we need to plan our strategy."

❖

On Wednesday afternoon, J.J. found himself thinking about what to wear and how to present himself. Attention to appearances felt slightly out of character for the man who had lived alone on west beach so long, but things were changing. Something was about to happen; something, hanging in the balance. He hadn't felt that way since the day he and Rose had struck their original deal.

❖

After the memorable spreading of ashes trip, he hadn't expected to see her again. Then he'd run into her at the library. She had told him she was on the board there. Being the wife of a professional has its advantages, she'd said. Her husband had been an architect and a historian, active, until his death, in the island's restoration movement. She had turned her curiosity then to the books he was returning, commenting that he was an eclectic reader, like herself.

"We must talk more sometime, Captain," she had said. She had turned, as if to go and then turned back. "Do you know anything about the stock market, Captain?" she had asked.

A strange question, he had thought, but she was a strange woman. He made an effort to answer casually. "As a matter of fact, I do," he had told her.

After that, she'd sent him customers—an elderly cousin who had come down from Houston for a week and, later, two boys in their late twenties taking a last fling before marriage. Then, she had called one gusty afternoon and invited him to tea. Curious, he had accepted. The house had impressed him before he ever stepped inside.

"It was built in 1905 by George Stowe," she told him, "in the Victorian Colonial Revival mode. Isn't that a mouthful? Architect talk for sturdy and imposing. The original house had seven bedrooms, but when Nate and I bought it in the late '60s and began remodeling, we took advantage of the back stairs to make a separate apartment, with its own entrance, bedroom, sitting area, kitchen, and bath. Nate's mother lived there until she could no longer take care of herself, and we brought her in with us. Used to wheel her out on the porch on good days and let her watch the people passing by, until she started yelling obscenities. Children and blacks seemed to ignite her the most. I have an ungodly fear I'll end up doing something like that and embarrassing whoever has the thankless job of taking care of me. You ever think of such things, Captain? No, of course not. You're young."

She poured tea with exacting grace from a silver service. "Captain, what did you do before coming here?" When he hesitated, she said, "Forgive me. I didn't mean to be intrusive. I know how islanders guard their privacy, but you are unusually well-spoken for a fishing boat captain."

"You've known many?"

"Fishing boat captains?" She laughed and tucked a stray wisp of hair behind her ear. "Of course not. We both know I got your name from the Handy Andy bulletin board. I just didn't expect, well, never mind. Why don't you tell me something about yourself."

"I grew up in New Orleans," he had lied. "Attended Tulane. Worked in a family business for a number of years."

"You see," she laughed, "I knew you were an educated man."

They talked about her antiques, favorite seafood restaurants, and Galveston politics. One minute she was sitting upright making declarations and dispensing advice as if she were his aunt; the next, she was leaning forward, searching his eyes.

"You're a handsome man, Captain, and seem to know your way around."

He lowered his head and smiled, acknowledging the compliment.

"You can drive a ship, open a bottle of champagne, and handle a teacup."

"It's a boat."

"Drive a boat, then. You're educated, suave, unattached—I assume?" He nodded. "And you're not BOI?"

"Born on the island? No. I'm here by choice."

"Much better. BOI holds expectations, history, connections, attracts gossip. My husband, Nate, was BOI, yes I told you that, and it was sometimes ungodly tiresome. He was a wonderful man, but somewhat stiff, and I blame it on this BOI aristocracy. That, and the architecture calling." She caught herself then, aware she had wandered from the subject, and moved back on track. "You're perfect."

He held up a hand and leaned backward slightly. "I've seldom been told that, Mrs. Parrish."

"Rose," she corrected. "Oh, I was planning to do this just right, but my mouth has gotten ahead of me." She leaned forward again, arms resting against her knees, hands clasped. "As you know, Captain, I'm recently widowed. My husband died after a long illness. Most of our friends were his friends and much older. They were an interesting bunch of intellectuals and rebels, many born with silver spoons, right out of Galveston's glory days, but they're dropping off like flies. The only remaining couple is talking about giving each other hearing aids for Christmas this year. Fancy that. Carrying on a sizzling conversation with them is well nigh impossible. I've had time to think about what I want to do with the money Nate left me, Captain, and I have some good ideas, but I need someone to talk things over with, someone to take care of the details. I'm willing to pay for your time."

"You hardly know me."

"I realize that. I've been over in my mind everyone I know, and their children, and no one fits the bill. Oh, yes, there are consultants for hire. Do you remember the "boys" I sent you who wanted a fishing trip for a last fling before getting married? The one who paid the bill was my stockbroker; the other was his brother. No insult intended, Captain, but in a town as—what's that word—as *funky* as Galveston, doesn't that seem like an uninspired choice for a last fling? Yes, there are young men trained in business school who'd be more than happy to help, but I'm prepared not to want them for that very reason. They choose the predictable path. I may not know you, but I have good instincts. Are you a gambler, Captain?"

His palms were suddenly damp. He sat forward this time, looked her head on, and took a moment to choose his words. "I'm appealed to by life's possibilities."

Her eyes twinkled. "I knew it!" She leaned back then, suddenly all business. "My husband left me considerable assets, all quite safe. Suffice it to say, I have more than enough coming in to live on every month. There was also a sizeable life insurance policy—$500,000 to be exact."

She raised an eyebrow and looked past him, as if lost in remembering. "I always thought I'd be a shrewd moneymaker, if given the opportunity, but that was one of the few things my dear husband didn't give me. I have no children, no family, no one who's counting on inheriting my money, and no one I care to leave it to. Some women my age would choose to travel, or make their name as a benefactress, or look for another husband. What I want to do is take that half million and set up an account separate from my other holdings, a risky business account let's call it. The times seem stable, though I don't know what's going to happen with these Democrats in office. But I want to see how much I can make this grow—legally, of course."

"And where do I come in?"

"Basically, advice. I'll pay you a retainer. What's fair? $500 a month?"

"How much time are we talking about?"

"I'd like you to stop by once or twice a week, have tea or a drink, spend a few hours, and we'll talk about investments. Of course I'll expect you to do your homework."

"$500 is too much—especially since you don't know what you're getting."

She leaned forward. "Lawyers charge $100 an hour, and you're never quite sure what you're getting there. So you'll be making less than the lawyer and more than the plumber. Seems fair, considering the subject matter."

❖

That had been twelve years ago. Now, nearing the year 2000, an almost magic number for those who paid attention to such things, the two of them had sparked on something new. She sat tall in the passenger seat as they drove to their meeting, eyeing the festive streets with enthusiasm, still commanding, still enveloped in her familiar fragrance, citrusy and expensive. J.J. found himself thanking his stars that Rose hadn't had to deal with his past, proud he had never given her cause to doubt him. They drove through the old warehouse district, in past years a no-man's land, now the site of a Victorian Christmas that attracted tourists from afar. Garlands, lights, and wreaths dripped from lampposts and swung gracefully overhead. Gaslights spread a rosy glow. In front of the Tremont House J.J. handed off the car keys to a valet and walked around to open

Rose's door. The sky was clear, the breeze luxurious. The island, a place of constant change, was theirs for the moment.

"We've come a long way, Rose," he said, offering her his arm.

"I was thinking the same thing, Captain."

8

"Nate and I attended the grand opening of this building,"
Rose told J.J. She took his arm as they walked slowly through
the authoritative wood and glass entry doors to the Tremont
House. "That was back in the '80s when the Mitchells, George
and Cynthia, I think her name was, were pouring funds into
revitalizing the island and decided we needed a fine downtown
hotel. Actually, the man we're here to meet bought one of his
major beach properties from Mitchell. At least that's what I read
in the paper, if it's to be trusted. Oh, I wish Nate were here to
sit in."

They made their way across a marble-floored reception area,
then stopped to survey the atrium lobby with its white wicker
sofas and chairs, glass-topped tables, and grand piano located
back near the long wooden bar. A middle-aged woman with a
shapely figure and a long skirt, slit on one side, stood up and
moved their way.

"Mr. Broussard?"

"Ms. Peterson?"

He introduced Rose, they shook hands, and walked over to

a sofa, at which point Blair punched a number on her cell phone.

"They'll be right down," she smiled.

Rose ordered a drink and decided to let J.J. handle the conversation. She'd prepared herself to sit back and observe, just as she would have done had Nate been there. Men handled business talk, even when women handled the purse strings. She studied Blair, whom she found to be likeable and quite attractive, even though she seemed to be a glorified secretary for a big shot who couldn't come to his meetings on time.

"Mr. Broussard tells me your husband was an architect," she said to Rose. "Wasn't he involved in restoring some of the houses in the Silk Stocking District?"

"He was," Rose nodded. What followed was ten minutes of polite conversation, with Blair's eyes flicking over to check the elevator each time it stopped. Finally, Rose excused herself, irritated by the waiting game.

On the way to the ladies' room she stopped to browse in the gift shop, where a bright display of Mardi Gras necklaces hung on a display rack amid an assortment of Christmas gewgaws.

"Good stocking stuffers," suggested the elderly male shopkeeper when he saw her admiring them.

"They are quite attractive." Rose fingered the shiny green metallic leaves of the necklace. "A nice change from those ubiquitous beads."

The man grinned an elfish smile. "You don't want to wear one yourself, but if you have any young people in the family, they might get a kick out of them."

"And why's that?"

"Those are cut to resemble marijuana leaves." He chuckled. "I thought, just like you, they were a nice change when I ordered them. First thing I knew, all the busboys and porters were snatching them up. Manager made a rule they couldn't wear them. Young kids, fourteen, fifteen, come in here, buy them, and drive their parents crazy. You going to go to war with your kid over a necklace? I've got these on half-price trying to get rid of them."

"Give me one, will you please." Rose dug in her purse for five dollars and change and considered whether she should wear her purchase or save it for another occasion. She hadn't been outrageous in years and this was as good a time as any. In the ladies room she put on the necklace, which shone nicely against her white silk blouse and picked up the green threads in her jacket.

As she reentered the lobby, a man dressed in a sequined vest began to play the piano, Liberace style. The place was filling up, and her table was now complete. She checked her watch. Twenty minutes after the appointed time.

Everyone stood as she approached, and introductions, but no apologies, were made. Then J.J. started talking.

"We've followed your efforts in developing east beach," he said, "and we think our project can only enhance those efforts."

"What exactly is your project?" The entrepreneur was short and slight. He regularly touched his forefinger to the bridge of his nose and flicked his eyebrows, as if to get his wire-rimmed glasses in a better position. His young assistant, Bobby Calhoun, hugged his side but appeared more interested in the lobby crowd than in following the conversation.

"We're planning the re-creation of a historic site. When we're through, there'll be a restaurant and private club. Approximately 5,000 square feet. We're looking at probably two million in building and decorating costs."

"And you want us as investors?"

"No. We have our financing in place."

"Oh?" He adjusted his glasses.

"Yes. What we do want is to buy the property from you. It's among your holdings, but nothing's happening there at present. Harborside Drive, at the foot of Fifteenth Street."

"A good location, but derelict."

"Our project should make your adjacent property boom."

"What else?"

J.J. looked over at Rose. "We want a fair price. Beyond that, Mrs. Parrish and I prefer to keep our names out of the paper. We're happy for you to announce the project, let it add to the momentum you have going."

"How'd you know I own that property?"

"Public records."

"The Internet?"

"I did it the old-fashioned way. Digging through county records. Took me the better part of a day."

"Quicker on the 'net."

"So I hear."

✤

On the way home, Rose, who felt she had held her tongue admirably during the meeting, found herself babbling, while J.J. seemed preoccupied.

"I was prepared not to like the man, but what he lacked in charm he made up for in decisiveness," she declared of the entrepreneur.

"And seemed willing to sell. As soon as I get a realtor on it and we get some comparables, we should be able to get started."

"What did you think of the other fellow? That Bobby Calhoun? Could he be gay?"

"How would I know?" J.J. said.

"I thought men knew these things."

"It seldom crosses my mind."

"You think he's a bodyguard?"

"Maybe so. He's got the build for it."

"He stared at you incessantly."

"That so?"

"Captain, do you have a computer?"

"No."

"Do you think you need one?"

"I've chosen to get along without. How about you, Rose? You want a computer?"

"Well, I always was a good typist. I've been thinking about upgrading."

It was only nine when she got home, but Rose's mind was so busy replaying the night's action, it was well after midnight before she went to sleep. Everything had gone quite well, she thought, except the captain hadn't seemed to take a shine to that good-looking Blair woman and no one had noticed her necklace.

✣

Rose had done business with the same law firm since she and Nate were married. Jewel, Hokes, and Tewsbury had been in operation for more than half a century, and the elder Sam Jewel had been a friend. The young Sam had written their wills and helped her at the time of Nate's death. She was quite fond of him, though she hadn't seen him in years. When she called for an appointment, a noncommittal female voice informed her that Mr. Jewel had retired from active law practice to take a judge-ship.

You choose a professional for experience and maturity and then they die or retire on you, she thought.

"And who's taking his cases?"

"Any of the junior partners will be happy to help you. I can connect you with Mr. Johnson's office, one moment, please." The girl gave her no chance to respond.

Rose hung up the phone. Telephone manners were abominable these days. She didn't want a junior partner. Wouldn't you think they'd put someone on the front desk with a little more finesse? She turned to the yellow pages.

✣

A few days later, Rose took a taxi to an address near the courthouse. She had found herself a new attorney. However, if his abilities could be measured by his office trappings, Rose thought, this one wouldn't amount to much. Cheap reprints of the Constitution and The Bill of Rights decorated the walls of the waiting room, and some of the magazines were a year old. She supposed that was what she got, choosing a counselor by his name, although it'd been known to work for her with race horses. Will Parker had a ring of integrity she'd been willing to take a chance on.

When he appeared in the doorway, dressed in loafers, slacks, and a sport jacket, she was pleased that he looked young enough to outlive her, but not wet behind the ears. He led her to a comfortable chair.

"How can I help you?" he asked.

She told him she wanted a new will, setting up a tax-free trust for architectural restoration. "I'm counting on you to figure out how to get this done and to put in the proper jargon so the IRS doesn't walk away with 55 percent of what my husband and I have accumulated. I'm happy to give it away, but not to those people."

"Any specific bequests?"

"I want to leave my home, my household furnishings, and personal effects to John J. Broussard, along with sufficient funds to cover the taxes, if that's necessary. My car goes to Mr. Jesse Martin. And to Pearl, my loyal housekeeper, $25,000."

"Her last name?"

"Lowman. Make that $50,000."

He raised his eyebrows.

"You think that's too much?"

"It was quite a jump."

"I want the woman to feel valued, but I'm afraid she'll give it all to the church." Rose thought a moment and sighed, "I suppose that's her business. Leave it at fifty."

There was more to discuss: the naming of an independent executor, someone to oversee the trust, someone to make decisions for her welfare if she became incapacitated.

"Put Mr. Broussard in all three positions."

"He knows the extent of your estate and has access to your records?"

"He has access."

The attorney raised his eyebrows in a silent question, but Rose didn't offer a further explanation. She had some miscellaneous things in the safe, some jewelry, gold coins, savings bonds, deeds to a couple of lots she and Nate had bought when they lived in Houston, another $250,000 or so, but she'd keep that information to herself. Everyone should keep a few secrets tucked away. She'd leave to the present generation the propensity to tell all to strangers.

Will Parker spent more than an hour with her and left her feeling satisfied he could do the job. What's more, he appeared to be a man of character, a quality ascribed to wine more often than to lawyers these days, she told him. The office wasn't actually shabby, she decided on her way out, just understated.

✤

There was yet another project facing her before she could relax and focus on Maison Rouge. That evening she pulled from her files some yellowed papers and proceeded to address the questions therein. "Plans for a Christian Funeral," the title page read, and on the following pages she was to select from six service options, from "Standard Funeral Service" (complete with embalming, lying in state, religious service, and burial after service in a cemetery of choice) to "Bequeathal of Body with a Memorial Service" at a later date. Rose selected "Cremation without Embalming (must be done within twenty-four hours)," with a memorial service at a later date. Should she leave it to the captain to dispose of her ashes? It seemed she had given him sufficient responsibilities; but, he was being recompensed. It shouldn't be too difficult for him to drop them off in Hall's Lake—with Nate's. She couldn't think of a finer setting, with those huge trees dripping moss, the occasional grand home set back from the water, and lovely birds with craned necks punctuating the shoreline.

Planning the service was more difficult. She was to choose a church, a clergyman, hymns and/or scriptures to be used, give a list of people to be notified, and instructions regarding flowers and memorial gifts. No wonder she had avoided doing this before. Church had always served a social purpose for her more than a spiritual one. The coming together of people in a spirit of goodwill couldn't be scoffed at, but the truth was, the older she became, the less she cared for large groups and children running around. So much attention on the young these days—as if people hadn't been having children for years. Most of the sermons were centered on families, with very little food for the soul. Rose had decided she'd just have to enrich herself, which she did. Take, for instance, the poetry of Edna St. Vincent Millay. Now there was food for thought:

When I see my netted veins
Blue and busy, while the grains
In the little glass of ME
Tumble to eternity . . .

Rose decided against a religious service. Who would come anyway? A few doddering friends and some people with whom she did business. Pearl and Willie? Lisette, her hairdresser? Mr. Green from the Exxon Station around the corner? She imagined him scrubbing the grease from under his nails and donning a suit. No, that wasn't what she wanted. Neither did she want an obituary in the newspaper. Under "People to be Notified," she put Will Parker, Attorney. The others who counted would find out soon enough.

She placed the papers in her ready bag and locked the file cabinet, feeling a sense of relief and a driving urge for a cigarette, the perfect finish to a task completed. She cracked her bathroom window, sat on the commode lid, and lit up. Ridiculous, sneaking smokes in her own house. But, she wasn't ready to face Pearl's disapproval, and this did serve to keep her craving in check. Besides, she wasn't hurting anything. She only coughed in the mornings now, after a prolonged period on her back. Seemed as if that damned walking contraption might be helping.

9

Jesse Martin, immersed in six weeks of Obstetrics, was learning to appreciate the complexity of women's bodies in other than obvious ways. When presented with abdominal pain, for example, he was forced to consider not only the appendix and gastrointestinal tracts, but ovaries, fallopian tubes, and urinary tracts. The increased possibilities were clinically exciting, not to mention the challenge of adopting a bedside manner appropriate for a pelvic exam.

With two years of class work behind him, he found this year of clerkships more to his liking. So far he'd done a month in Family Medicine, a month in Pediatrics, and six weeks in Psychiatry. Every day something interesting happened with the medical team or the patients. And though he made his share of mistakes, things were going well. Other students, like his ex-roommate, who had kicked butt on the rote stuff, were losers in the clinic. They might be good book-doctors, but try to get them to make a patient assessment or work out a plan of care and they turned suddenly dense. For them, live people were something to avoid. For Jesse, patients were the meat of it—what he'd been waiting for. Sure, they could be troublesome, and sometimes they got way off base, like the woman with pleurisy who came in complaining of heartworms, or the girl with an easily curable sexually transmitted disease who wanted a hysterectomy to make sure it wouldn't come back.

In the hospital he had to think on his feet and swallow his mistakes. He also had to hold back questions about policy, gripes about paperwork, and complaints about people covering their asses with unnecessary procedures and endless reports. Students were at the bottom of the pecking order, but they were right in the line of fire, expected to be humble with superiors and confident with patients. It seemed to Jesse that the OB-GYNs he found himself with this six weeks were generally nicer than the surgeons he'd run up against. They weren't as gruff as orthopedists, or as nerdy as the ENT men. Wouldn't be a bad specialty, he thought, except for the malpractice claims.

❖

When he stopped in Gunner's before the Christmas break, his ex-roommate was there, sounding off about going skiing in Vail over Christmas.

"Hey, Jesse," Chip called, "Your mail's piling up. Want me to forward it?"

He hadn't given Chip his new address, nor anyone else. He'd been procrastinating, reluctant to face the flack he expected from the school, or his father, or both.

"I'll take care of it when I get back," he told him.

"Whatever you say," Chip said. "You have a good holiday, buddy."

"Yeah," Jesse shot back. "You too." Even when the guy was being nice, he irritated Jesse. He knew part of it was jealousy. He'd much rather be going off to ski than home to sit around the television, eating chili dogs on Christmas Eve with his dad and Jerry.

Gunner's was crowded that night, and the atmosphere was brighter than usual. It was usually a laid-back place where people stopped in to locate someone, set up a study group, or just shoot the breeze with whoever was there. But the night before Christmas break, spirits were high. The bar was draped with tinsel, and icicle lights twinkled across the tops of the windows. Jesse was on his second beer when he saw Susanna come in with a couple of girls. He tried to catch her eye, but she wasn't looking.

"I dare you to go over there," Gail nudged him.

"And say what?"

"Just wish her a happy holiday."

"She'd laugh me out of here."

"What have you got to lose?"

He emptied his glass and walked to the men's room. On the way back, he stopped by the table.

Susanna gave him a relaxed smile, "Hi Martini," then gestured to the two girls with her. "Meet my friends from high school. They've come over from Baytown to shop at Colonel Bubbies."

"And check out the local bars," one of the girls giggled.

"I didn't know you were from Baytown."

"Martini, there's so many things about me you don't know." Her tone was playful.

The girl giggled again.

"Well, listen," he shifted from one foot to the other, "I just wanted to wish you a happy holiday."

"You going home?"

"For Christmas Eve," he said, trying not to project his lack of enthusiasm, "but I'm coming back the next day."

She raised an eyebrow. "Studying?"

"Yeah," he shifted again, feeling awkward. "Well, you take care," he slapped the table, smiled, and started to walk away.

"Listen, Martini, I'm having an Orphan's Christmas, kind of an all day thing on the twenty-fifth, so if you're around . . ."

"Orphans?"

"Not really, just friends who don't have anywhere else to go. Christmas alone is a bummer. Here," she pulled a pen from her purse and jotted an address on a napkin. "Everyone brings a little something for the group meal."

He replayed the conversation as he walked back to the table.

"Gettin' lucky?" Gail asked when he sat down.

"I haven't a clue," he told her.

Chip, who had obviously been watching Jesse, leaned over the table. "Don't get your hopes up, kiddo. She's an ice queen."

"I'll remember that," Jesse mumbled.

✣

He stopped in to see Rose before meeting up with his ride to Houston.

"I don't decorate any more," she said, placing the poinsettia he had brought in a prominent place, "but we used to have one of the brightest houses on the block. I outlined it in red lights, in honor of Post Office Street, and it was written up in the newspaper. People drove by to take pictures."

"I could do it for you next year."

"That's nice of you, Jesse, but I suspect we both have better things to attend to. But I would like you to come to dinner New Year's Day. There's someone I want you to meet."

At the door, he wished her Merry Christmas and, in the spirit of the season, gave her a quick hug. She smiled and gave a few quick pats, not really returning the hug, but he was close enough to detect the smell of tobacco.

"You're working on your treadmill?" he asked.

She smiled and nodded.

"And you've stopped smoking?"

She nodded. "Almost."

"Almost? Rose, it's the absolute worst thing you can do."

She waved him away. "My dear, there are many worse things than an occasional cigarette."

✣

The transition from school to home was often surreal for Jesse. He thought about how soldiers must feel, that movement from a battlefield into an alien place where they're expected to rest and relax. When he got to the house, Jerry was there alone, stretched on the sofa watching television, a huge bowl balanced on his chest. The kid looked up briefly, waved him over, and immediately launched into a recap of the movie he was watching. Jerry was stoned, Jesse would bet, involved in a stupid show, and wanting Jesse to watch with him. He seemed to have forgotten the last time they'd been together, that day he'd been so rude to Rose. Jesse had expected him to still be angry, or jealous, or whatever, but he was only friendly and silly.

"C'mon, look at this," Jerry kept insisting, and Jesse, who had promised himself to concentrate on staying detached and getting along, sank into his dad's chair, grabbed a handful of microwave popcorn and proceeded to watch *Revenge of the Pygmy Dinosaurs.*

While Jerry slept the next morning, Jesse went jogging, cleaned up, and washed two loads of clothes. It was afternoon before they went to the mall. His brother seemed clear-headed enough as they picked out a book and a sweater for their dad.

"Let's find something for you," Jesse told him.

They wandered through Radio Shack, but when everything that caught Jerry's eye was more than Jesse could afford, he drew back from the game.

"Let's go to the music store and find a CD you'd like."

"Or you could give me that," Jerry turned to face him and grabbed his sleeve. He'd been after Jesse's black denim Levi's® jacket for a couple of years.

What the hell, he thought. He took it off and handed it to him. "Merry Christmas, little brother."

Jerry lit up."Cool," he said. He put it on and turned the collar up.

✢

Back at the house, his father was warming lasagna.

"Smells great," Jesse told him. "Can I help?"

"Yeah, but not with dinner." He motioned Jesse aside, then asked when he planned on going back.

"Christmas morning, after breakfast."

"You can't stick around a few days?"

"No, sir."

"Well, could you take him back with you?" He was whispering now, looking toward the living room, where Jerry sat watching a football game.

Shit, Jesse thought. He had let his brother visit a couple of times, but not now. He couldn't take him to Susanna's. There wasn't room for him at the apartment, and no way to entertain him, like there'd been at the dorm. What was he supposed to do with the pygmy dinosaur boy?

"I really can't. I have to study and I'm on call at the emergency room."

"He can hang out with your roommate."

"Yeah, well . . . ." He hesitated, knowing it was time to say there was no more roommate.

"What?" His dad was waiting for him to finish the sentence.

"Nothing." It was the wrong time to open up that subject. "I can't handle Jerry right now," he said, as firmly as he dared.

"We need to keep him out of trouble."

"As long as you give him money, Dad, he'll buy drugs."

"And if I don't, he runs off and does God knows what." His dad gave a deep sigh. "Look, I need to make this trip. I'll be back before New Year's."

"Sorry, Dad. I can't do it."

"Yeah." His father turned away, obviously unhappy with their exchange.

⟐

Jerry approached him later that night. "Dad's got a girlfriend," he grinned and made a crude gesture. "They're going to Austin. I heard him talking about it over the phone. He says it's for business."

"No way," Jesse said, considering the possibility, as it filtered through his brother, wondering if there was anything to it.

"So, can I come with you? It's hell to hang out here alone."

"What about your buddy Jim?"

"He's in some kind of rehab," Jerry shrugged.

"Maybe it'll do him some good," Jesse said.

"Yeah. I know." His brother's face stayed blank for a minute. Then he brightened. "So, can I come with you?"

"I've got a lot of studying, and there's no room."

"You don't have classes, and I can sleep on the sofa like I did before."

He reached out for Jerry's shoulder and tried to look sincere. "Sorry, brother. I'm working Emergency." He tried to make it sound terribly important. "Maybe another time."

"What if I have an emergency here all alone," Jerry said. He was whining, but Jesse recognized the veiled threat.

"Here," he scribbled his phone number on a piece of paper. "Hold onto this. If something happens you can't handle, call me."

Heading back to Galveston on the ten-thirty Greyhound Christmas morning, Jesse wondered what would become of his brother. When he was Jerry's age, he was busting his butt studying for the MCAT. He did well on it too—that's what got him into med school, that and his high school record, volunteer work, and the letters of recommendation he'd courted from the dean of science, his biology professor, and the head of the psychology department. It had seemed so important at the time. And what would he be doing now if he hadn't gotten in? Probably working for a pharmaceutical company, pulling down big bucks, driving a nice car, and dating beautiful women.

✛

On the way home Jesse decided to see if he could borrow Rose's car to go to Susanna's party. When she had made the offer, he hadn't considered taking her up on it, but like she said, it needed to be driven now and then. The other choice was to ride his bike to Susanna's, which wasn't exactly the impression he was going for.

He called Rose when he got to the apartment around noon. She had just gotten up and said she was looking forward to spending the day alone. She seemed surprised at first by his request, but when he explained that he'd been invited to a party and was going to ride his bike, but was supposed to bring food and that was kind of tricky on a bike, she warmed up and told him to stop by in an hour and pick up the keys. And he must allow enough time to have an eggnog with her. She also wanted to know what he was supposed to take to the party. When he told her he was going to stop at whatever market he could find open and pick up something, she wouldn't hear of it.

"Just where did you think you were going to buy decent food on Christmas Day?" she quizzed him when they were face to face.

He shrugged and smiled. "I'd forgotten about the stores being closed."

"Just like a man," Rose shook her head, as if he were hopeless. "There," she pointed to a wicker basket that sat on the hall table next to the car keys. "I've packed you a loaf of Pearl's homemade potato bread and a wedge of Brie I found in the fridge and some gingerbread cookies. And I stuck in a nice cabernet. You can't show up on Christmas Day with crackers from the Stop and Go."

"That's really nice, Rose. Sure you don't mind me borrowing your car?"

"If I seemed vague when you called, it's because I'd forgotten I'd offered it to you. But, then it came back to me. Damned memory, comes and goes. I'm sure you'll take care to park in a place where she won't be subject to someone else's carelessness."

"Definitely."

"And just drop the key through the mail drop when you come in."

"You want me to check on you?"

"I'll leave a message on your machine if I have a problem. Do you have a date for this party, Jesse?" She was sitting, hands folded, eyes dancing, obviously wanting to extend the visit.

He was anxious to get going. "Not exactly."

"No young lady in your life?"

"I'm working on that."

"Working on that today?"

"Sort of."

"Well, I wish you a Merry Christmas, my dear," she raised her glass, "and may your efforts be fruitful."

✥

He didn't know what to expect of an Orphan's Christmas, but he definitely wanted to play it cool with Susanna. Starting out in a Mercedes with a basket of goodies helped his frame of mind. When he arrived, there were six other people, all connected with the hospital. Others came and went during the afternoon. They shared food and small talk and played a game where one person chooses an obscure word from the dictionary and everyone else makes up definitions, which are judged against the real definition. The idea was to be falsely convincing and subtly deceptive. Jesse had never played it before, but picked up on it pretty quick. When the word was "pungar," (actually, a crab) he pulled in three votes for his definition as "the residue from an oil fire." And when it was his time to find a word in the dictionary, he chose grig and slipped it by everyone. Who would have guessed it meant anything particularly small?

"Pretty cool, Martini," Susanna said. "A newcomer seldom does well at that game."

"Beginner's luck," he smiled and set the plate he was drying on the counter.

It was eight, and everyone else had gone. He'd stayed to help with the dishes and found himself in the situation he'd wished for all day. He didn't want to blow it. A silence stretched between them, and it was tempting to fill, but he wanted to let her carry the ball—or at least set the tone. The silence continued. If she'd just say something, he thought.

"Know why I invited you today?"

He shook his head.

"Because you looked so pitiful when you said you were going home."

"I didn't look pitiful."

"Bad choice of words," she said, and rephrased. "You definitely didn't look like you were looking forward to it, and then you told me you were coming back Christmas Day, which was a pretty clear statement. Maybe I'm supersensitive, but it sounded like family problems to me. Want to talk about it?"

"No big deal." This wasn't what he wanted—her acting like a counselor.

"Okay," she emptied the dishwater and dried her hands. "Didn't mean to be nosy. So," she paused, as if weighing alternatives, "you can ask me a question."

He thought a minute. "Want to try a nice cabernet?"

"That's your question?"

He pulled down a couple of wine glasses and got the bottle Rose had provided, along with an opener. "No. But my question may take a while."

"Don't get any ideas, Martini."

"You can call me Jesse."

"Don't get any ideas, Jesse."

"Because. . . ?"

"Because I keep a healthy personal distance between me and doctors, or doctors-to-be, for that matter."

He handed her a glass of wine.

"Because. . . ?"

"This your question?"

"Yep."

She took a deep breath. "I was burned by a med student who I thought I was going to marry. We met here. He went off to Colorado to do a residency while I stayed here, finishing school, planning our lovely future, how I was going to help him set up a practice. Then, when he was through, he called to say he was going to marry someone else, a girl in Colorado whom he'd been screwing for two years, and who he just realized he loved more than me." She blurted it out without a pause. "Bastard!" she added.

"So you've given up on the whole profession?"

"Exactly."

He shook his head. "That's dumb."

She shrugged. "So be it."

"How about us just being friends?" She didn't leave him many choices.

She sipped on her wine and looked at him sideways. "And I get to hear about your family?"

"Sometime." He lifted his glass to touch hers.

She dimpled. "If you make one move to touch me, Martini, you're busted."

He nodded and took a sip. Touching her was exactly what he'd been thinking about most of the day.

✛

Jesse spent much of the next two days studying and daydreaming. If his prospects with Susanna weren't promising, his imaginings were. The second afternoon he went to the gym, hoping to find a pickup game of basketball. When he got back, a message was blinking on his recorder. He played it back, expecting Rose.

"Hey, brother," Jerry sounded pissed. "Dad just left. We had this big fight, and I'm not sticking around here. I'm heading your way, like it or not."

He called home immediately but got no answer. He let it ring a dozen times, considering what he could do. If Jerry went to the dorm room, Chip probably wouldn't be back yet. But someone would tell him Jesse had moved, and no one knew where. He decided to wait for Jerry in the dorm study lounge, but the kid never showed. At eight the next morning, Jesse packed up his book and went back to the apartment to get some decent sleep. There was another message. This time the voice rang with excitement.

"Dude," he said, "I'm hitching, right, and this guy picks me up, and he's really cool and we stop for a beer and I put a dollar in this eight-line machine and won $150!" He could hear music and talk in the background. "So we'll be along after while. Or we won't," he laughed and hung up.

Disgusted, Jesse fell across the bed. He stuck around the apartment the next two days, waiting for the next call, which didn't come until New Year's Eve. Jesse was getting ready to go to work when the phone rang.

"You could have told me you moved." Jerry's voice was confrontational.

"Where are you?"

"Home."

"How'd you know I'd moved?"

"I talked to your funky roommate, helped him unload his car, in fact, and he said you moved out weeks ago and he didn't have any idea where you were living and he was worried about you and I should tell Dad something's going on."

"That jerk."

"That must be the favorite family word. That's what Dad called me when he saw me with your jacket. I told him you gave it to me, and he didn't believe me. Said it was your favorite, and I had to give it back, because even if you had given it to me, I shouldn't have taken it. You were a good brother, he said, and I always found a way to be a jerk. Well, your roommate was nicer to me than you, good brother. He let me spend the night and take a shower and I left your fuckin' jacket with him, since nobody knows where you live."

"You had my number."

"Yeah. But I didn't want to talk to you by then, Jesse. 'Cause you're the biggest jerk of all!" He slammed down the phone.

✢

At six P.M. on New Year's Day, Jesse presented himself at Rose's door, still tired, still replaying the deal with Jerry. He was dressed in his best slacks and a sport shirt. Rose wore a long black dress with a heavy silver necklace. Tall candles burned on the mantel, and Pearl, in a white apron, was passing something he didn't quite recognize. He took a bite. Chicken liver wrapped in bacon. Interesting. He tried not to think about nutritional damage. Captain Broussard had on a sport coat and a turtleneck and was making a production of pouring champagne.

They began by talking about fishing and that led to skin cancer, so then they switched to golf. Before he knew it, he was talking about skin cancer again. The subject turned to biking, which made him think of Lance Armstrong and his testicular cancer, but he didn't mention it. They hit on the big question for the year 1999—who would be the man of the millennium. Jesse liked Nelson Mandela; the captain preferred Winston Churchill. Rose didn't take sides, but told a story about when Churchill was called down in Parliament for being intoxicated.

"Sir, you are drunk," Rose did an imitation of a British noblewoman.

"'And you, Madam, are fat,' Churchill told her. 'What's more,' he drew himself up, 'tomorrow I'll be sober, and you, Madam, will still be fat.'"

They all laughed, Jesse pretending he'd never heard it before.

"I love the way you tell that, Rose," the captain said, and she beamed.

Jesse thought about how his crowd would cut him off at the pass if he started a story they'd heard before.

"How did you two meet?" he asked his dinner mates.

The captain and Rose exchanged amused glances.

"The captain has been a friend and advisor since shortly after my husband died," Rose said.

Jesse nodded. Something about the guy didn't ring true. He wasn't sure if it was the turtleneck or the anchors on his jacket buttons, or the way he offered Rose his arm to go into the dining room. He'd been around all right, but he hadn't spent his life running a fishing charter.

When Rose said she was considering getting a computer, Jesse tried to encourage her. "In a couple of years you won't be able to do anything without them," he told her. "Maybe I should say you'll be able to do almost anything with them. Like order your groceries."

"Pearl does that."

"She could do it on the 'net."

"Pearl?"

"I think you'll be voting on the Internet, if not in the next election, then surely in 2008."

"You think so?" He noticed a look pass between Rose and the captain.

"I try not to look ahead too many years, Jesse." She smiled at him.

The table was set with cloth napkins and crystal glasses and three silver utensils on each side of his plate. Jesse knew to use them from the outside in, but what was he supposed to do with that spoon laid sideways above his plate? He wanted to learn, because he planned on having stuff like this someday. He remembered when he first started thinking about going into medicine, and he had thought how great it would be, not having to worry about paying bills. Then it didn't take long being around doctors, with their new Jaguars and family vacations in the Caymans, before he realized it was more than having good credit. Much more. It was another level of operating. Classy. Buying name brands, never having to jury-rig something to make it work, picking up the ticket, instead of hoping someone else would. Rose lived that way, and he was anxious to learn whatever she could teach him. So what if he had come from low on the social ladder. So what if his father just plodded along and his brother was a loser. So what if he let them down now and then. They were heavy sometimes, and he had big plans.

Pearl served avocado soup, followed by baked ham, black-eyed peas, and wild rice with apricot dressing. Rose, presiding over the table, insisted on hearing about his New Year's adventures in the emergency room.

"It was fairly quiet. A couple of stabbings; a teenager with alcohol poisoning; a middle-aged woman, depressed; a baby with the croup—when they start sounding like a seal, the mothers get scared; some old guy, mid-fifties, came in with chest pains, and we sent him on for a bunch of tests. What did you do for New Year's, Captain Broussard?" he said, trying to pass the baton smoothly.

"Nothing to match that."

After dinner they moved to the sitting room.

"That was delicious," Jesse told Rose.

"Did you think so? I was afraid it was a little plebian," she said. "I used to cook myself. Sometimes five entrees, sometimes simply soup and a choice of desserts. My guests never knew what to expect, but they never went away hungry." She sighed. "Pearl, however, is a stickler for a balanced meal. She's loved it since I'm out of her kitchen. Captain, would you fix us a scotch? Jesse?"

"I'll take a bourbon and Coke," he said, feeling stuffed,

wanting nothing, wishing he understood the mysteries of scotch, wishing he hadn't said that thing at the table about an old guy in his mid-fifties.

Rose proposed a toast, "To those who can laugh at themselves, for they shall never cease to be amused."

They all laughed then and touched glasses. Ice cube tumbled against ice cube; crystal rang against crystal. They sipped. The fire crackled in the fireplace, the candles flickered and reflected off Rose's polished necklace. The captain sat erect, smoking his pipe, a special blend she had ordered for him. It was January 1, 2000, and Jesse felt like he'd been sucked into a vintage movie. He bowed out early, went up to his apartment and called home. Apparently Jerry hadn't blown the whistle on him. News of his move came as a surprise, but his father seemed surprisingly calm and willing to give Jesse credit for knowing what he needed.

103

✢

It wasn't until the middle of January that the shit hit the fan. Jesse was summoned to the office of Dr. Jefferson, Professor in Medical Jurisprudence and Dean of Student Affairs. He wasn't named Jefferson for nothing, was the joke. Because Jesse had done well in class, he thought—hoped—he was being singled out for something special.

"Something has come to my attention," the professor began in a friendly tone, "and I'm going to present it to you straight out. Do you have a drug problem, young man?"

"No, sir." Jesse felt like he'd been sideswiped.

Jefferson reached under his desk and pulled up a black Levi's® jean jacket. "I understand this is yours."

Jesse fingered it, saw the Martin written in black ink on the label, and nodded. The teacher fished in his drawer and laid a plastic baggie on the dark, polished wood of the desk; it sat there, looking slick and ominous, holding two tiny slivers of white paper, with burned ends. Roaches.

"These were in the pocket," Jefferson said. "Unquestionably cannabis."

"This is my jacket," Jesse told him, struggling to stay calm, "but those aren't mine."

"Your ex-roommate's concerned about you," Jefferson said, studying Jesse's eyes. "He tells me you moved out on him unexpectedly, that your family isn't aware where you're living, that you've separated yourself from your classmates, missed regular study groups."

"All explainable, sir." He struggled to control his anger. He could imagine his face red and his blood pressure off the chart. He felt like he could explode—but he wouldn't give old Chip the satisfaction. Fat jackass jerk.

"When I got this information, I turned it over to the Disciplinary Committee, hoping you could exonerate yourself. They set a hearing date, and you didn't show. Can you explain that?"

"I didn't get the message. I haven't," he struggled for a better explanation, but knew better than to say anything but the truth, "changed my address, or picked up my mail."

Dr. Jefferson pushed the jacket toward him and dropped the baggie back into his desk. "Unfortunately you've breached procedure and the rules are clear. I refer you to page 126 in the *General Information Bulletin*. It's an automatic suspension."

"But. . .."

"There's nothing I can do, Mr. Martin, except offer some advice. If you ever intend to be a doctor, you need to pay attention to business and keep your nose clean."

✢

Jesse called home again.

"Jerry's here," his dad said. "But he doesn't want to talk to you."

"Tell him I have to talk to him."

"He won't come to the phone."

"Tell him he owes me."

Jerry came to the phone, his voice blank.

"I'm in big trouble. You happy?"

"What?"

"You left roaches in my coat."

"Damn! I was looking for those." He sounded surprised, and Jesse believed him. It cleared the question of whether Chip had planted them. But, it didn't really matter. Whether accidental or on purpose, he was suspended. And he needed a new game plan.

10

When Rose asked J.J. what he thought of Jesse Martin, he made polite sounds about being glad she had located him. What he actually thought was that this doctor-in-training she'd found was a little short on finesse and maybe a smart-ass to boot. Jesse's comment at dinner about "some old guy, in his mid-fifties," hadn't set well with J.J. It struck him as sloppy talk from someone doling out help in an emergency room. If Jesse had the least idea what fifty was all about, he would have given his patient more respect. Besides, what kind of person chooses to s u round themselves with disease and degeneration? You couldn't pay J.J. enough to do that. All that medical talk didn't impress J.J.; in fact, it could be a smoke screen. What else was going on in the boy's head? Rose seemed to dote on him, which was her business, but just because he was studying to be a doctor didn't mean his motives were above suspicion. J.J. knew one thing—con-men are everywhere.

✢

Prison leaves its mark, and J.J. was no exception. He still got a jolt in the pit of his stomach when he heard the ring of steel

doors clanging shut. But, he'd been lucky. His had been a federal offense, which qualified him for a federal lockup that had a
good-sized library, a gym, a golf course, tennis courts, and
white-collar type inmates who were, for the most part, benign.
J.J. swore off trying to manipulate people and events and tended his own business. He read a lot and played golf every day the
weather and the rules allowed. He picked up the name "Skins"
playing a complicated money game on the course, a game he seldom lost. By the end of his four years, he knew he could make
a living hanging around country clubs, playing for money, but
his counselor advised against it.

J.J. had a passion for gambling. The counselor had called it
that and backed it up with pointed questions. Does it make your
heart race? Give you a rush you can't find anywhere else? Do
you prefer it to sex? Can you stop when your good sense tells
you to?

J.J. came to realize that his gambling had never been about
money. It was about pitting himself against another, or a lot of
others, or sometimes just blind chance. And it often got out of
hand, like the day he bet his new car on the draw of a card. Two
people lived in J.J.'s head—the gambler and the guy who
thought about consequences. Sure, he won more often than
not, because he was smart, but the gambler in him took risks
that could have landed him in serious trouble half a dozen
times.

"You don't appear to have a split personality," the counselor
told him, "or any unmanageable psychological problem."

"That'd make it easier."

"Yeah, everybody likes to think their problems are beyond
their control. Tell you what, 'Skins,'" he used his nickname to
make his point, "you need to give it up."

J.J. was irritated. "You make me sound like one of those
poor bastards who can't walk by a crap table without losing his
shirt."

"No. Your problem is more complicated, but if you don't come to terms with this propensity for risk, it'll get you just the same."

✤

J.J. had other reservations about young Jesse Martin. He didn't like to fish? And didn't read anything but textbooks?

In prison, J.J. had read Hemingway and found escape in elaborate daydreams that sometimes carried into the night—scaling mountains, hunting elephants, fishing off the coast of Cuba. Three weeks he spent with *The Old Man and the Sea*—reading and rereading, slipping back to summer days spent with his mother's father, a gruff old Cajun who ran a grocery at the edge of the backwoods, who knew about life on the bayou and never strayed from his comfort zone.

When J.J. got big enough to sit still, his grandfather began to pass on what you couldn't learn in the city. They spent slow, salty days together, days his mother would have frowned at if she'd stayed around, but she never did. She dropped him off for a week or so during the summers, sandwiching his visits between riding lessons and swim club competitions. It was his grandfather who taught him to read messages in the taste of the wind and the changing colors of the water. He learned which fish took which bait, and how to cast, and when to move on. He grew to like the silence, to anticipate the catch, to let the motion of the boat calm whatever churned inside his adolescent head, and he developed a lifetime affection for the day's catch, rolled in cornmeal and spices and fried in a cast iron skillet. And then the old man had died, and J.J. had gone on to college to discover women, alcohol, cards, and other games of chance.

✤

After New Year's dinner with Rose, J.J. filed some papers she had sent home with him and then straightened his desk. He was orderly by nature, a trait that sometimes drew sarcastic comments when a poker buddy, looking for cayenne, discovered his spice rack arranged alphabetically. He also kept a journal, another remnant from prison, where he recorded the weather and fragments of his days. The millennium demanded some comment, but J.J.'s entry was characteristically spare:

01/01/2000 A blustery day. Rose more demanding; her health improves, thanks in part to Martin. Tech stocks falling. Good time to liquidate.

He put down his pen, switched off the lamp, and noticed the answering machine flashing.

"Bobby Calhoun here. Why don't you meet me for lunch at Clary's tomorrow at one," a brusque voice snapped, more an order than an invitation. Calhoun hadn't given away much of himself at their first meeting, but was clearly someone who knew his way around. J.J. sat at the desk and scratched his beard. He hung up his clothes then, brushed his teeth, and checked the thermometer. Fifty degrees outside and the cabin wasn't airtight, not in this wind; still he felt a flush, almost a sweat. Damn, he thought. What does this guy want?

When he tried to return the call the next morning, he found there was no Bobby Calhoun listed, and the Tremont House declared he wasn't on their guest list. J.J.'s options were limited—he could show up or not.

✣

"'Skins' Broussard," Calhoun said, when they'd been seated and the waiter had taken a drink order. J.J. said nothing.

"I gave you that name—'Skins.' You prob'ly don't remember me, though. I wasn't much of a player back then—just a kid hungry for action—and you were the action." He smiled. The wide gap between his front teeth seemed familiar.

"Back when?" J.J. didn't blink.

"Back when I did time for mail fraud. Learned the skins game in the lockup, following you around the course. It's my *job* these days to watch people, but I was always good with faces. I'd know you anywhere."

The waiter brought their drinks and recommended baked oysters.

J.J. picked up a fork and ran it across the white cloth. He sat, silent, and studied the tine patterns.

"You've done well for yourself," Calhoun said.

"I've been lucky," J.J. said.

"Always were. You got another Robin Hood deal going? Stealing from the rich, giving to the poor?" Calhoun grinned.

In prison, everyone had a story, and there were those who made it their business to learn them all. J.J. only remembered a couple of guys from back then, certainly not this one. He'd kept to himself inside the walls, just as he had after he got out. Hell, he'd hung himself on the end of an island, hoping never to have to deal with that part of his life again, and after twelve years, the first time he makes a trip downtown, this gap-toothed joker shows up.

J.J. shook his head and offered nothing.

"Whatever," Calhoun shrugged. "How's your golf game?"

They talked for a while about golf. Calhoun said he had been a punk kid when he went in and had gotten into body building in prison.

"After I got out I started looking for something to do and got a job at Gold's Gym that didn't pay for shit, but that's where I met the boss. He had me tending bar at parties on weekends, and if someone got out of line I was supposed to usher them out. A year or so later, he took me to Vegas with him for a week." Calhoun spread his huge hands, palms out. "Tell you the truth, I don't know what the hell all his business is and don't want to. I've been on the full-time payroll for eight years. Sometimes I run errands; sometimes I just stand around and look pretty," he grinned again and rotated a toothpick in his mouth. "It's good money, and I usually don't carry a gun. So, that's my story, 'Skins.' What's yours? You're not in Galveston for your health."

J.J. reached into his wallet and pulled out his business card for fishing charters on *The Odyssey*. Calhoun studied it a minute, then looked up with a question on his face.

"That's what I've been doing since I got here."

"I noticed the old lady called you captain. So, you're her right-hand man?"

"Yes and no. She's a friend. I advise her on investments, and she trusts me."

Calhoun continued to pick his teeth, now using the card J.J. had handed him. "She know about your doin' time?"

"Not yet."

He shook his head. "I'm not here to give you trouble. However," he paused, "the boss knows a lot of people. You hang with him, and someone will come out of the woodwork to blow the whistle on you—if that's what's worrying you. Me, I think it's better to tell 'em right off. Gives you the upper hand, and you don't spend your life looking over your shoulder."

J.J. was relieved, temporarily, to hear that all Calhoun wanted was to renew a contact, maybe play some golf. He didn't have much life of his own, Calhoun had told J.J., and Galveston was tame compared to Houston. Figured J.J. could point him to a high stakes card game. Maybe the two of them could partner in a local tournament, have a little fun, win a few bucks. And what did he think about the Blair woman? She wouldn't give him the time of day. Could J.J. put in a good word for him?

✦

"I have to quit the project," J.J. told Rose.

"What in the world?" Always up for a dramatic moment, she pinned blazing eyes on him.

He hesitated. "You don't want to hear this."

She leaned forward. "Try me."

He had decided on a calculated confession. Didn't want to

take a chance she'd learn the truth from someone else. So, he told about the jail time and how it had happened when he was young and living a different life, and that he had come to Galveston to escape his past. Told how Calhoun had caught him by surprise and how he figured the guy would need to pass it on to his boss to show he's on top of things. Sooner or later, the story would surface to jinx the project and embarrass her.

As he spoke, he studied her reaction. She looked intent, but not overwhelmed. He knew he was important to her; what he couldn't predict was how she'd respond to having been deceived. There was a chance she'd close the books, change her mind about the house, cut him off. So, in the telling he did his best to separate the captain from the felon. Maybe she'd decide to drop the project. Better yet, she'd hire a front man and let him continue to pull the strings. He wanted this deal.

"Quite a story, Captain," she said, when he was finished. She took her time fitting a cigarette into her holder and put it in her mouth, unlit. "Now I have one for you." She told him about hiring an investigator who had discovered his colorful past back in 1987, before they started working together. Told him about talking it over with Nate. About feeling validated at how well it had turned out. "I don't know what happened to you in prison, but I'm certain there was an epiphany of some sort. Like Saul on the road to Damascus, you changed your life completely."

J.J. sat, speechless, and tried to hide his discomfort. He felt like a visitor at a nudist colony, stripped bare, and here she was, acting like it wasn't worth a raised eyebrow. Rose wore a smug smile and looked anything but disturbed. He lifted his glass in a small salute. Epiphany, he thought, wryly.

She tilted her glass back at him. "Let me tell you, I'm comfortable with this. So what if you have a record? You've paid your debt and been straight with me. I wish I had another good day on earth for every man or woman on this island with a less than pure background. People live here because they like to think they're invincible; and those types crash hard. You, my dear, will be a small flash in the pan, if you flash at all."

J.J. was having trouble processing the fact that she'd known for years. Had she questioned at every turn, or just jumped in, trusting? Rose, trusting?

"I had reservations," she admitted. "But you kept your distance, never asked for more than I offered, resisted my advances," she smiled. "I made a commitment to give you the benefit of the doubt, and you proved yourself."

"But . . ."

"*Caveat emptor,* Captain. It's still a good rule, even if the courts have taken the fist out of it." She shifted positions in her chair and fiddled with her cigarette. "How much do you know about Jean Lafitte?"

"That he was a pirate who operated out of Galveston in the 1800s." J.J.'s answer was brusque. He preferred to stay on the subject right now, not travel one of her side paths.

"He was a pirate—in the days when piracy and smuggling were not only common, but sanctioned by some governments as a way to deplete their enemies. They say Lafitte was fluent in French, English, and Spanish, and was the darling of New Orleans society. He showed up with men and ships to help Andrew Jackson at the Battle of New Orleans. Then he moved his headquarters here and set up a fortress town with its own government, on the east end of the island, at the very spot we have in mind."

J.J. sipped on his drink and tried to smile. "Interesting."

"I think you miss my point. Lafitte came here from Louisiana—handsome, educated, an outlaw in his way, but with ideas and a code. You, Captain, are a modern day Lafitte—and I think you should come out of the closet. This island appreciates a touch of wickedness. Your background has the potential to work in our favor, make the restoration of Maison Rouge more intriguing, and get you off that desolate beach and back in town where you belong."

At home, J.J. thought over Rose's presentation, wondering how long she'd been formulating a marketing strategy with him at the center. The woman's mind was seldom still. Out of the closet, for God's sake. He'd be surprised if that phrase just popped into her mind. She had caught him off guard, but the reluctance he felt now had nothing to do with her. He wasn't ready to have his life laid open; he had spent too many years sewing it up, putting the outlaw in him to rest. Lafitte never came to terms with that, never considered himself a pirate, called himself a privateer. He even tried to be a patriot, until his reputation got in the way. J.J. recognized danger in that kind of complexity. He had the education and the brains to move in other circles, court new adventures, but why tempt fate? He'd be wiser to work behind the scenes, with room to retreat to his fishing boat and Elena in his bed.

✢

When J.J.'s troubles had first erupted, his father, Dr. John Broussard, had been a respected professional in Baton Rouge. He had unraveled quickly. Humiliated, he didn't know how to face his patients, his colleagues, or friends at the country club when his son turned out to be a thief. He fumbled apologies, ran his hands through his hair when he talked, and had a hard time staying on track. He had visited J.J. in prison, making an issue of standing by him, in spite of the mess he'd made. "Your mother has a harebrained idea about selling the house," he told J.J., "and I'm indulging her. I've put it on the market for much more than it's worth. She'll get over the idea before we ever get an offer. Poor woman's having a hard time losing her social status. When I married her, she was a real beauty—intelligent and strong-willed—but she never rose to her potential."

J.J.'s mother had escaped from the backwoods as soon as she turned eighteen. Even though she sent him to visit his grandparents in the summer, J.J. was in college before it dawned on him how high she'd married up the ladder. He'd never known what spark had brought his parents together, because it was long gone before J.J. was old enough to recognize it.

From his earliest recollections, his mother had her own bedroom, slept late in the mornings, and spent the afternoons shopping. J.J. had been cared for by a succession of housekeepers, whose responsibility it was to deliver him to private school in the morning and see that he was picked up in the afternoons. There was another woman who came daily to clean house and cook. At night, dinner was served in the dining room, with silver and china, and J.J., from age ten on, was expected to put on a tie and make conversation. His father told about his day, asked J.J. about school, and his mother reported on her remodeling projects, her women's club work, and her growing collection of antique clocks. When his father wasn't present, she referred to him as "the good doctor," as if he were a character in a book.

✢

His mother came to visit him in prison, wearing pants and a vest and a long gold chain in graduated loops around her neck. She looked thinner and younger, with her hair grown out to her shoulders and colored darker than before.

"You didn't need to come," he said. "I know this is hard for you."

She fumbled with her chains. "I came because I have something important to tell you." She leaned toward him, and he noticed how bright her eyes were. "I'm leaving your father."

"Is it because of this?" his gesture took in the prison.

"Yes. And no," she said, obviously agitated. "Your problem just woke me up. This isn't the 1950s any more. I've spent the last thirty years letting your father tell me what to do, keeping me dopey with those pills because he said I was depressed." She was whispering now, "I think he wanted to keep me a zombie. Don't you?"

"How should I know, Mother? That's between you and him."

"Well, we've put the house up for sale, and he doesn't know this, but with the proceeds, I'm buying a bed and breakfast. In Canada. With a friend. So when you get out, if you have no place to go, you come and stay with me until you get on your feet."

"What about Dad?"

She reached out and patted him on the knee. "You're not the person I thought I knew, but neither am I. Neither is your father. With luck, we'll all find ourselves."

She had left then, walking briskly, turning to smile and wave as she left the visiting area. J.J. waved back, befuddled. Strange to see her so suddenly changed. His mother. Coming to tell him her plans. With a friend? Who would that be? She had offered him a refuge. Not that he planned to take her up on it.

His father eventually sold his practice and moved to San Miguel, a village in México favored by successful Americans and Europeans. It was a move J.J. suspected hadn't turned out all bad. He'd gotten postcards—a bowl of limes, big as apples, and a note in his father's medical scrawl: *Rx: take 1 three times a day* con tequila y sal. An open doorway, dripping bougainvillea, leading into a dirt courtyard where two dogs lazed in the sunshine. The message: "Living a dog's life." He'd never known his father to have a sense of humor.

❖

J.J. had made no friends in Galveston other than his poker-playing buddies and Rose. And, of course, Elena. He belonged to no church, no clubs, no seaman's association. They knew him at the golf course and the bait store and Kelly's Liquors, but most people just called him Captain, and, if pressed, wouldn't be able to pull up his name. If he followed Rose's suggestion, things would change. He'd become visible. People might look for him; they'd ask questions. He didn't want reporters knocking on his door, looking for a follow-up. He didn't want anyone from the past finding him, though it was becoming more likely every day. He refused to be Rose's modern day Lafitte, even though the comparison amused him.

Rose climbed onto the treadmill, gingerly snapped the ON button, then carefully put her feet on the black runner. Getting on was tricky. It was an ugly thing, its hulking design distinctly out of place among her batik prints and beveled glass. Still, she kept at it, probably because Jesse had her recording her walking times in a small book, and she considered herself too old and proud to lie. It worked best if she watched television, but the treadmill's noise was distracting, and if she turned up the television so she could hear it, Pearl appeared at the doorway with a tormented expression, hands over her ears. Jesse had a solution for that as well. He had brought her a video tape of the English countryside flitting by at the speed of a slow-moving car, complete with background music, which gave her the sensation of a vigorous walk.

When Jesse had asked if he could work for her because he was going to drop out for a semester, she'd been reluctant.

"Why in the world would you want to do that?" she had asked.

"Pressure," he had told her. "I need a break. This way I could have more time for my most important patient."

Rose knew a snow job when she heard one. "Sit down, Jesse," she motioned to the chair beside her and when he had settled himself she leaned forward. "You'll excuse me for being nosy, but this decision seems awfully sudden. Has something happened?"

He had studied his hands for a while before answering. "I've been going to school since I was five years old," he said finally. "And I've been at it without a semester off since I was a junior in college."

He did look tired, she thought.

"Burnout," she said. "I saw a show about this."

He nodded.

"But won't this put you off schedule with your schooling?"

"It's not that unusual. It can be worked out."

"And there's nothing special troubling you?"

He had hesitated. "Well, there's some personal business I need to take care of, and this would give me time to, you know, get it done."

She rubbed a swollen knuckle, thinking. "I can give you enough work to cover rent and, let's say, another $100 a month. Will that suffice?"

"That'll be great," he flashed her an appreciative smile. "And I promise not to get in Pearl's way. I don't think she approves of me."

Rose raised an eyebrow as if to say that was up to him. She didn't think he should devote too much time to winning Pearl's approval, which was iffy on the one hand, and without rhyme or reason on the other. Her plans were to use Jesse to research Maison Rouge. She wanted him to take her to the Rosenberg Library in search of information about the old building in the days of Lafitte. If nothing turned up, they'd contact the Galveston Historical Foundation or the Architectural Society or the French Legation in Houston. She needed information on the architecture of that period. Possibly, they'd have to recreate the place from an enlightened imagination. Of course, there'd be a professional to do that, but she wanted some clear ideas before she turned things over to an architect.

She thought she was up to traveling around, although today she had a nagging pain on her right side. Tomorrow it will be on the left side, she thought, or in the middle of my back. These things travel around like nomads, camping first one spot, then another. Actually, she hoped that tomorrow there would be no pains. Tomorrow was Fat Tuesday, and Pearl, who overlooked the fact that it was a Catholic celebration, was preparing a festive meal, much of which she'd take home to her family and neighbors. It was a Mardi Gras ritual established early in their relationship. Pearl agreed to work on this holiday only if allowed to spend her time cooking. Though the day was repeatedly colored by this grudging concession, there was a distinct energy to it. Pearl would be seriously out of sorts if Rose's appetite wasn't up to appreciating her succulent creations. There would be wild duck, shot last fall and stored in the freezer for this occasion. It was to be stuffed with olives and pearl onions. There was an oyster dressing—Rose's mother's recipe—orange-candied yams and pecan pralines the circumference of a silver dollar and mounded half as high.

Tuesday afternoon, when she had dressed and made her way down to the parlor, Rose was surprised to hear voices in the kitchen. She listened more carefully—perhaps it was the radio. Pearl often played religious music, or hummed to herself. Rose had forbidden preaching broadcasts. However, this was more like—indeed it was—laughter, and a male voice as well. She arranged herself in her chair and rang.

Pearl greeted her with an uncharacteristic smile. "Would you like French toast?"

"You never fix French toast."

"Jesse stopped in, and I fixed him some."

"Jesse?"

"Your renter."

"I know who Jesse is. I'm just surprised by your sudden change of heart. I thought you were suspicious of him."

Pearl said nothing.

"Well, all right then, bring me French toast and orange juice, and," she hesitated for effect, "ask Mr. Martin to join me when he's finished in there."

Jesse appeared with brunch on a tray, along with a bud vase that held a silk rose and a sprig of fresh-cut rosemary.

"What's this?"

"Fat Tuesday celebration."

"You and Pearl?"

He set down her tray with a proud smile.

The boy's youth and energy were infectious, she decided. Not that she was foolish enough to believe she could catch it, but with him around she felt better. Apparently, she wasn't the only one. Almost motherless, the boy would have them both looking out for him now. Well, Pearl could do the cooking part, though she mustn't overdo it.

Rose had her own ideas. Timing was everything; she had always believed that. Jesse hadn't come into her life at this juncture for her to let him slip away. No, he needed to stick around. Of course, she didn't understand how he could be in such good humor when he'd just dropped out of school. Staying with things seemed to have more importance when she was young. When she asked if he was worried, he shrugged and said life was too short. She chewed on that without a comment.

When she mentioned she had a research project, Jesse popped to attention. "The best way to do research is over the Internet. Why don't you get yourself a computer, and I'll teach you."

One of Rose's pet peeves, of which there were a number, was to approach someone with a request, only to be diverted, like a stream running in an inconvenient location. She had envisioned Jesse driving her around, like Miss Daisy, except she'd of course sit in the front seat. She looked forward to having him accompany her into the Historical Library or the Architectural Society Archives as her special consultant. On the other hand, working from the comfort of her front room had its appeal. Getting dressed to go out had become a chore.

✛

"You pick it out," she had told him. "Not too many bells and whistles, mind you."

Prepared to begin immediately, she was disappointed to see him remove the thing in parts. He sat on the floor, reading manuals, locating ports, attaching cords, loading programs.

"Is it always this complicated?" she asked.

"This is a simple one," he said.

Finally, they began. "This is your mouse," Jesse told her. "It will take a little getting used to." An understatement, if she ever heard one. The damn thing jumped around on her and wouldn't go where it was bid. And the keyboard repeated letters whenever she rested her hands to think. Getting in and out was a mystery. She had a list of directions he had written out for her, nothing as simple as hitting a switch. Then there was that silly sign he had taped prominently on the monitor that proclaimed "Jesus Saves," to remind her to use the save command so as not to "lose" anything. All she was doing was composing letters, which she could do just as easily on a yellow pad. There was nothing yet to save. And she still hadn't reached the information highway. Her teacher was saving that until she had conquered the basics. It would be Easter at the rate she was going.

Rose read her manuals carefully and, as a word person, was intrigued with the cryptic language that accompanied her computer: ROM, RAM, bits, bytes, giga-, mega-, virtual memory, hyperlink. She appreciated the principle of keeping things in files, and these became increasingly clear as she fiddled with them. The icons were clever, often intuitive, especially that trash can.

Jesse checked on her computer progress daily, in addition to monitoring her exercise. He now had her strapping on one-pound weights to strengthen her legs and arms. He took her blood pressure and insisted she buy nicotine patches—and wear them. She complained, but followed instructions. When he turned that smile on her, she felt flutterings of some instinct or other. It was a motherly thing—a grandmotherly thing—a woman thing. He treated her like a recovering patient, which she was, and seemed to take his work seriously.

By the middle of February Rose had raised the boy's monthly compensation to $250. One hundred dollars, for goodness sakes. What had she been thinking? She discovered, through repeated questioning, that he was out of school because of some trouble, which he was trying to sort out by himself. He was worrying. She knew he was. Every thinking person worries. Meanwhile, he claimed to be enjoying himself, and she thought he had put on a little weight, due most likely to the friendship with Pearl.

123

❖

The idea came to her late one night watching an old Joan Crawford movie, and she acted on it the next day by calling the medical school and setting up an appointment to talk about planned giving. She was warmly received by the Vice President for University Advancement.

"How can I help you, Mrs. Parrish," the vice president asked. He seemed young for such a title.

"Actually, I'm here to see if I can help you," she said, removing her leather gloves. "My husband, Nathaniel Parrish, was a Galveston architect until his death in 1986, and I'm in the process of setting up a foundation in his name."

The man leaned forward attentively. "Did your husband have connections with the medical school?"

"Not *per se;* however, he was involved in restoration of some of the buildings the school has acquired as it has expanded."

"You'll be offering grants?"

"Up to $500,000, for architectural restoration."

The man nodded. "That's most interesting. We have a project on the drawing board we're seeking funds for. Would you like to see it?"

"I'll get you some guidelines, and you can make us a proposal."

The vice president smiled and relaxed in his chair, delighted, she suspected, to have something like this dropped in his lap. "May I get you some coffee, Mrs. Parrish?"

"No, thank you. But, you could do me a small favor."

"Of course."

"I need to talk with someone on a student-related matter."

Fifteen minutes later she was ushered into the office of Dr. William Jefferson, Dean of Student Affairs. By the warmth of the man's greeting, she suspected news of her offer had been passed on.

"I wanted to talk with you about a student by the name of Jesse Martin."

He folded his hands and nodded. Rose recognized the classic look of a man in power behind a desk. "I know Jesse," he said, in a voice without expression.

"I understand he's in some sort of trouble. Can you tell me what that is?"

"I'm not free to discuss a student's business without his or her consent."

"Well, what I'm here for is to set that business right, if possible." She leaned forward and spoke softly, "I hope this doesn't sound crass, Dr. Jefferson, but I have funds available to be tapped by the university, and I'd appreciate in return that the school look favorably on Mr. Martin."

William Jefferson sat tall behind his polished desk, framed by shelves of textbooks and pictures of himself and family on the ski slopes, on a sailboat, with children, with dogs. He studied his manicured hands for a moment, then looked back at her.

"I like him as well, Mrs. Parrish, and acknowledge your concern, but the school couldn't possibly enter into an agreement like that."

Rose was surprised and embarrassed. Had she gone about it wrong? If so, what was the right way? "I mean no disrespect, Dr. Jefferson, but it is common knowledge that alumnae and major donors to any institution have certain *privileges*. I simply want Mr. Martin to receive any courtesies that might be extended a donor. Imagine that this support comes in his name."

Dr. Jefferson shook his head. "I hope Jesse will return after this issue is cleared. He's a promising young doctor," the man looked up and appeared to soften. "But he's going to have to stand on his own feet."

Rose gathered her gloves and her purse. "He's unaware that I've come to see you. I assume your code of privacy works in both directions, Dr. Jefferson. Shall we forget this conversation?"

✛

Going home in the taxi, Rose felt mortified. She should have known better than try to throw her weight around like that. Nate would have been furious with her—as she was with herself. She should have asked the captain what he thought, but he hadn't seemed impressed by Jesse. He certainly wouldn't have advised her going off to negotiate clemency for him— whatever the boy's problem is. *Must be getting senile, letting this child push my buttons or pull my strings, or whatever.* There was that pain in her stomach again. She rubbed her right side below the rib cage. Stress. It wasn't Jesse's fault. She took full responsibility for being a fool. Not the first time, and probably not the last. I shall grow fat eating crow, she thought. Her mother-in-law used to say that, before she lost her mind.

At home she consulted her AMA book of medical symptoms: recurrent abdominal pain, mainly below the waist, intermittent bouts of diarrhea. "Consult your physician," the book recommended. Well, it would have to get a lot worse. She'd eat a bland diet for a while and take some Pepto-Bismol, and maybe the symptoms would go away. None of the diagnostic procedures were acceptable: sigmoidoscopy, barium x-ray, analysis of stool samples. Humiliating.

She should have been prepared for this wearing out of the body, having gone through it with Nate. Still, she'd never given it much thought. Always healthy as a horse. Cigarettes? Of course she'd known they weren't good for her. They called them "coffin nails" back in the '40s, but back then young people weren't interested in health. They were trying to get through a war. She didn't regret a one she had smoked and was of a mind to tear off the damned patch. She was also of a mind to stop the daily treading and give the computer to her young friend. The thought of opening Maison Rouge was worth some effort, but how sweet would that be if they rolled her in wearing diapers? The next thing would probably be a stroke, cancer, Alzheimer's, diabetes. It was true, what that advertisement she had gotten in the mail yesterday said, "You are slowly dying. Being *Murdered* From Within. . . *One Cell at a Time.*" Of course, they had a remedy, a line of products at $70 for a one-month supply. Only $235 for a six-month supply. She had considered it briefly, with its pictures of smiling grey-haired couples jogging and necking on the beach, then thrown the damned thing away. How could she get through all this gracefully?

Nate didn't wait to be consulted. "Feeling a little sorry for yourself, are you, dear?"

She answered out loud, irritated. "As a matter of fact I am."

"You always get depressed when you do something to embarrass yourself."

"Well, I certainly pulled a doozie today at the medical school. I think I offered them more than the foundation will generate."

"Cheer up. They're not likely to apply."

She sat down, put her feet up and clicked on *Oprah*. "Today's show is about the quarter-life crisis—twenty-somethings facing the meaninglessness of their lives," the announcer said as the camera panned a line of beautiful, bright-eyed young women who apparently had grand disappointments of their own.

12

A windstorm had brought down the last leaves of fall, and the bare branches of trees along Post Office Street were now decorated with strings of beads flung by some of the thousands of Mardi Gras revelers who had invaded the island. Rose looked out one morning and declared her yard a "disaster." When she discovered the gardener wasn't available until the first of March, she took the issue up with Pearl, who wouldn't budge from her position. Pearl only tended flower beds; she didn't rake or pick up trash. Rose had refrained from asking Jesse, but he had heard her complaints and seen her frowns when she looked at her lawn, usually so carefully tended, now decorated with clumps of brown matter, strewn with leaves, and punctuated with printed circulars and miscellaneous debris. It offered him a window of opportunity.

On Fat Tuesday morning, he'd gotten up early and had three bags of leaves and assorted trash piled up when Pearl came around the corner. He nodded good morning, and she, unsmiling, had acknowledged him as she entered the house; a half hour later, when he'd moved to the back yard, she opened the kitchen door and asked if he wanted coffee. It was a beginning. If he was going to work for Rose, he wanted Pearl on his side.

"Good coffee," he told her.

"Ms. Parrish only buys the best."

He sniffed at his cup. "But this has a special touch."

"A pinch of cinnamon," she said. "I do it now and then. She don't always favor it."

"She's rough on you sometimes," he said.

Pearl was beating eggs. "Her bark is worse than her bite," she told him. "Been worse since Mr. Nate died." She tightened her lips and breathed in. "Such a gentleman. Wore white suits—all the time—and a white hat, and sometimes carried a cane, when he didn't even need it, but then he did need it after the first stroke." She stopped, studying her mixture. "I'm going to have extra here. You like French toast?"

Jesse nodded heartily, then asked how many strokes there had been.

Pearl stooped to pull the griddle from a lower shelf. "Three, or maybe it was four. She took care of him all through, and it got plenty bad. If it was me, and I had their money, I'd of had someone in, at least some of the time, and I told her so. I took care of his mother when they first moved here, but I told Ms. Parrish I didn't want to do that—wasn't up to any more nursings. At the end, she bathed him every day, took him for walks, kept him by her side. She planned his meals, watched his medicine, even read to him, though I thought he'd just as soon watch the television, and she never once complained. At least, not that I ever heard."

"You admire her."

Pearl looked up as if he'd suddenly opened a new subject. She tilted her head toward the parlor and lowered her voice. "It's hard to admire someone who won't save her own soul by accepting Jesus Christ."

"Still," he was reaching for the right words, "I can tell you're loyal."

"I'm loyal because she's my employer," Pearl cut a slice of bread and dipped it in egg, "and because whenever I've needed help, she and Mr. Parrish, may he rest in peace, they've come up with it."

Jesse didn't want to argue any of that, and he quickly changed the subject to the day's menu before Pearl started asking about the state of his soul. If it ever came up, he'd tell her about joining the church and being baptized when he was eleven and hope that would satisfy her.

⁜

So much time on his hands made Jesse itchy. With the little he was required to do, his mind played constantly with what he could do and from those possibilities emerged feelings ranging from anger to anarchy, from self-pity to submission. He concocted elaborate scenarios of ways to get revenge on his roommate, punish the school for injustice, and teach his brother a lesson. He imagined walking away and never looking back, turning his energies to something more glamorous and less demanding than medicine. Then, again, he envisioned himself trudging back and paying his dues, a tiny cog in the institutional infrastructure.

He took to running twice a day—in the mornings along Water Street, where piers stretched out for miles to accommodate shrimp boats at one end and cruise ships at the other. He liked watching the island come alive with its hustle of goods and people coming and going. In the afternoons he ran along the seawall, or down on the beach, where the scenery captured him—the water, never the same color for long, the surf, sometimes crashing, sometimes quiet, boats and swimmers of all shapes and sizes, solitary fishermen in hip-high waders, deposits of seaweed, packed with particles of ocean life. Driftwood. An occasional rainbow.

Late one afternoon, when he came across a group of pony-tailed girls in warmups listening attentively to a guy talking about stranded mammals, he'd signed up for the Dolphin Rescue Team. The instructor was a graduate student in marine biology who found out Jesse had medical training and quickly started treating him like second in command. One night after class, the two of them went to watch an autopsy being done on a beached dolphin that had died. They went for a beer after, and the guy told him he was organizing a beach cleanup for the fol-lowing Sunday. Jesse, burdened with the mess of being sus-pended, wondered if he dared invite Susanna.

He wasn't sure how suspension would affect his place at the hospital, and he needed the money, so he'd kept quiet about his situation. His story, if pressed, was that he had decided to lay out a semester to cure mental breakdown or poverty, whichever occurred first, and he'd be back next semester. As for Susanna, he wanted to tell her before she heard it somewhere else, even though it was likely to wipe out any progress he'd made with her.

❖

"Is this a couples deal?" Susanna had asked, when he called to invite her.

"It's a work deal. We're going as a team."

"I guess I can handle that, Martini," she said, teasing.

He knew she called him that to remind him she'd seen him in action—charming old ladies and shading the truth. And he wasn't going to deny it or apologize. He'd been taking stock ever since the suspension and had decided that one of his strong points was convincing people to take a chance on him.

The Sunday they set out to clean the beach was an overcast day in the low sixties. Susanna was dressed in jeans, a wind-breaker, and a red baseball cap. She brought gloves and plastic bags for both of them and was enthusiastic despite the day's

131

chill. She told him walking the beach was her favorite thing, that she wasn't much for swimming or sunning. He liked to surf, he told her, but had never gotten good at it.

When they arrived, eleven people, a variety of ages, were gathered at the end of the seawall, and his instructor buddy was saying that no, they wouldn't need to list their trash, like they did on the Adopt-A-Beach days in April. That was official, he told them, but this was just a thing he put together from time to time. He directed teams into the back of a pickup to be dropped off at mile intervals. "We'll pick you up in an hour and a half," he told them, "and there's a prize for the most interesting piece of trash."

On the beach, Jesse and Susanna quickly decided to do a quick jog of the mile, stopping for large items, then a slower walk, looking for the small stuff. He adjusted his pace to meet hers, which was respectable, and they stopped to pick up a beach chair, drink containers, and a weathered straw hat. On the way back, they slowed to a walk as she put on her gloves, rubbed them together, and said,

"I like this part."

"What?" Jesse asked.

"Research, Martini. The life of the beach. Whenever I do this, I feel like a scientist studying the artifacts of a culture. It's a careless and messy culture, I admit. But we share something in common. We're all caught in the power of that." She motioned to the water. "Feel the pull? I feel it all the time. I stick around here because I don't like the thought of being separated from it. Probably good I didn't end up the wife of some big city doctor. This is my place, and," she looked up and smiled, "I'm pretty passionate about it."

"Passionate is good." He'd never seen her so animated.

"Give me a break," she looked down, embarrassed, he thought, at exposing that side of herself.

They chose to walk the middle of the sandy expanse and to circle out in either direction, with the effect of covering the beach in an hourglass design. Each had a plastic bag into which they deposited cigarette butts, coins, plastic containers, pieces of rope, beach toys.

When they had finished the walking mile and were waiting for the pickup to come by, Susanna dug in her bag, came up with a striped bikini bottom, and held it out with a grin.

"So what's the most interesting thing you found?"

"This," Jesse pulled a corked bottle from his pocket.

"Cool. Does it have a message?"

"It appears to," he held it to the light, where a slip of dry paper could be seen. "I wish it had a genie."

"Wait," she took the bottle. "This is a gift. You shouldn't take it lightly."

"I'm not taking it lightly."

"Well, you're wishing for more. You got a message, now you want a genie."

"I always wish for more," he admitted. "You read it. I bet there's a name, a date, and an address, and it's somebody's science project."

"And you promise to follow up on it?" she smiled, eyes bright.

"If you promise to help me."

She shook the bottle, trying to release the paper stuck just below the throat. She blew into the bottle repeatedly, then walked over to pluck a firm stem of dune grass, which entered the bottle easily and brought the paper forward. She pulled it out and read in a solemn voice:

> YOU WILL BE CALLED TO A POST OF HIGH
> RESPONSIBILITY AND GREAT FINANCIAL
> REWARD.

Jesse reached for the rectangular piece of paper, which looked like it could have come from a large fortune cookie. The words were printed in a single line, all caps.

"See, Martini, it's your fortune. You don't need my help."

"I need something more than words on paper," he said, tucking the paper into the bottle.

Susanna rolled her eyes to the sky. "The man gets affirmation from the universe and he still isn't satisfied. What's your problem, Martini?"

"I've been suspended."

"Oh, Jesse. I'm sorry." She reached across and lightly touched his arm.

✛

She got the story out of him, the one she had wanted before. She got it while they were waiting for the pickup truck, and later, at the picnic, where everyone roasted wieners and marshmallows, and still later, at her condo. She was a good listener and seemed genuinely interested. He told her about his father and his brother, about the plans he had for something better, and how his brother had compromised him with his drug habit. He told her how he felt somehow guilty in the whole thing, and mad too, and not sure whether he wanted to go on with doctoring or not.

She told him she knew it was hard to take, but getting somewhere in medicine demanded a lot of a person, and there were almost always hitches along the way. She said he'd better take time to listen to himself, because if this wasn't something he really wanted, it wouldn't be worth the effort. She also said she knew of people who'd been suspended and reinstated who'd done worse things than not keep their address current, or miss a hearing, so she thought his chances were pretty good.

And she shared some stuff about herself, too—about growing up in Baytown, about when her father left, and her mother turned up with breast cancer. She told about driving her mother into Houston for treatment, through downtown traffic, when she just had a learner's permit. She told him the beginning of her connection with nursing was taking her mother home after chemo and watching her retch for hours.

"I learned to do a lot to help her, and she finally got better," she told him. "In my junior year, she went to a high school reunion and met an old flame and they got married. My senior year I lived with my grandparents and started going out with a wild crowd. I'd always been serious and shy and had hardly dated. Took up with a bull rider and his friends, and we hit the rodeos on weekends." Susanna shook her head and stopped talking.

"Don't stop now," he said.

She got up from the sofa and refilled his cup. "What are you going to do about school?"

"Talk with the Disciplinary Board. Apply for reinstatement. Get it straightened out if I can. And if not . . . "

"Maybe you could be a nurse," she smiled and turned back to the kitchen.

He threw a pillow at her. "So what happened with the rodeo guy?"

"He got me pregnant."

He tried not to register surprise. "And?"

"I got an abortion."

"Sorry."

"It was a huge relief."

"Did you drop out of school?"

"No. It was just a blip. I was two months along. I told my grandmother, and she said I was too young to have a baby and she was too old to raise one and she didn't think we ought to put it on my mother right then. So, she took me to this nice doctor on a Friday afternoon, and he was very clean and proper, and I was back in school on Monday. My gram didn't lecture me, she just told me, 'Some guy's always going to be after your cookie. You mind who you share it with.' She also said if I slipped up again, I'd break her heart."

"And you didn't."

"Nope. I turned myself into a good nurse, and that kept me going when Mr. Wonderful let me down. What if I'd been counting on him to take me away? You could consider it good luck that life is forcing you to work on yourself."

"Okay. Okay." She was sounding like a counselor again.

"How old are you, Martini?"

"Twenty-five."

"I thought so."

"What?"

"I've got four years on you. Not to change the subject, but I had a nice time today. I think your fortune was appropriate, and so was your prize."

He smiled and shook his head. "A kite. God, I wish I was as laid back as that guy is. He just organizes beach cleanups for something to do in his spare time."

She wrinkled her nose.

"You don't like him?"

"He's a sweetheart," she said with a shrug. "Maybe I just like bad boys."

At home later that evening, Jesse couldn't stop thinking about Susanna—her enthusiasm, her encouragement, her ponytail sticking out of that red cap, her dimple, her cookie. Never heard that term before, but it caught his imagination. She'd obviously shared with the med student who let her down. He wondered what it'd take for her to share with him.

❖

Rose didn't appear to have a clear idea what she wanted Jesse to do to earn his keep, but she asked that he meet with her on weekday afternoons. Some days she had small chores or errands; some days she wanted to talk. She wanted to know about his life in the present, and she seemed to enjoy telling him about hers in the past.

"When I left home, typing was my only marketable skill," she told him. "I lived in a boarding house and worked for a law firm in Houston for two years before I married. I wanted to be either a telephone operator or a Martha Stewart—no, that's not her name—a Martha Graham dancer. Now she was something. Anyway, I almost signed up for the WACs in '42 because I was feeling patriotic and their uniforms were very snappy, but my parents objected, and back then young people had to listen to their parents."

"They still do, Rose."

"What does your father think about your being out of school?"

"I haven't told him yet."

"Well, don't you think it's time?"

✛

At Rose's insistence, he took her car to Houston. On the way, he considered how best to deliver his news. He had studied communication skills. With patients, the rules were clear: Don't tell them more than they can handle; don't offer conjecture; expect anger, denial, non-compliance, and even lawsuits. Jesse had found it hard to adopt an all-knowing tone with patients, considering there was so much he didn't know. So he had talked sports, complimented the ladies, pasted stickers on kids. None of this was going to help with his father.

It was hard to think of his father these days without feeling irritated, but Jesse could remember other times and other feelings. He remembered watching his father fix things around the house, following him around, wanting to help, thinking his dad was really smart. But when he started making his mother cry, Jesse got mad at his dad and didn't want to see him.

And then there was the night of beer and tears. He was ten, and his parents had separated, and he and his brother had gone to his dad's apartment to spend the night. It was like living in a closet, the smallest place he'd ever seen—one bedroom, with the bed so close to the walls you had to get in it from the end. There was a bathroom that let you sit on the toilet and wash your hands at the same time. The big room had a kitchen sink, a half-size refrigerator, a sofa, and a television. The refrigerator had a six-pack of beer and some little plastic containers of mustard and mayo. They went out for pizza and came back and watched some scary show. Then his dad put the boys down in the bedroom and took a pillow and a blanket out to the sofa.

Jesse woke to the sound of thumps and grunts and wandered into the other room, where his father was stretched out with a bunch of pillows at his back. He was naked, drinking a beer and watching wrestling. Jesse, embarrassed, turned to go back into the bedroom, but his father sat up and patted the sofa beside him in invitation.

"Want a beer?" his father asked.

"Unh uh," Jesse shook his head.

"Not embarrassed to see me like this, are you?"

"Unh uh," Jesse shook his head again, focusing on the wrestling.

"We're just men here. Like in the locker room. We can do anything we want. Don't have to go by anybody else's rules." He said the word with a kind of sneer that made Jesse know he was talking about his mother now. Jesse said nothing, and after a while his father started up again. "All I want you to do, Jesse, is the right thing. Every chance you have, just ask yourself what's the right thing and then do it." His voice broke then, and Jesse peeked up to see a tear running down his cheek. One fat, round drop, and then another, and another. His father batted at them, but they kept coming. Then he put his head in Jesse's lap and hugged him around the legs. "Stick with me, boy. I really fucked up."

He'd never heard him use that word. He didn't even think his dad knew that word. Jesse patted him on the head and later, when he thought he was asleep, turned off the television and went back into the bedroom. But he had a hard time going to sleep. He felt like a top running out of spin. Off balance. Sad, too. He worried for himself and for Jerry, who was too young to talk to about this kind of stuff. The next Monday at school, he told his best friend about the crying and the beer—not the naked part.

"Oh, yeah," his friend said. "Dads act really weird when they're getting a divorce. Mine quit his job and slept in a hammock in the back yard and showered under the garden hose until my mother got a training order."

"What does a training order do?" Jesse asked, hoping he'd stumbled on a solution.

"It says they have to stay away."

✣

Those first two years after the divorce, he and Jerry had lived with their mom. She was interested in everything he did and usually came in to talk to him last thing at night. It was pretty nice, really, even if she did have a lot of rules because she was a single mom and she kept reminding him of that. And he had to help her with Jerry, because he was the oldest, and she knew she could count on him. Then his mom had met this friend of a friend who lived in Colorado, and this guy started coming down to visit her, and the next thing he knew, she was going to get married. He was almost twelve then, and he and Jerry decided they didn't want a new dad and didn't want to move away, so his mother and dad talked and his dad said they could come live with him—but they'd have to be responsible. Jesse had experience in that. "What else is new," he remembered thinking.

After that, he watched out for Jerry and his dad, too. His dad was always stressed about money, half-mad all the time. It was like he spent all his niceness on his customers. Jesse heard how he talked to them on the phone—real anxious to please— and he felt jealous. Why couldn't he talk to him and Jerry like that? 'Cause they were kids and pretty much trouble, he answered his own question. Jesse wanted to please his dad and so he tried harder. For a long time, he had asked himself what was the right thing to do, but the older he got, the stickier that got. Right now, he had to tell the old man about school, and it wasn't going to set well.

✛

"Now do you see what I'm up against with Jerry?" he asked, with eyebrows raised, and waited until Jesse nodded. "As for yourself," he went on, "I hope you've got a job because I can't be sending money if you're not going to class."

"I can take care of it," Jesse told him.

His father nodded. "So what's with the fancy car? Not shacked up with some woman are you?"

Jesse laughed at the suggestion. "No."

"Looks like a woman's car."

✛

When he got back to Galveston, Rose was pleased to report that she'd been investigating the Internet. "I located a site," she announced with an air of importance. "It had a drawing of Lafitte's house in New Orleans and a description." She reached for a yellow pad of notes: "Two-story brick, facing the sea, with a wide-arched door. It said the house was filled with the scent of chamomile, and the man could often be found resting in a hammock made of red cloth."

"Did you print the picture?"

"Couldn't figure out how to print."

"But you bookmarked the site?"

"Oh, Lord, no," she sighed.

He could see her satisfaction turning to frustration. "We'll find it again."

"Or we won't. If there's a picture, it can be found in a library, too. Maybe we should go hunt it up on Monday," she told him.

"I'm at your disposal," he grinned.

"Dear Jesse, did anyone ever tell you, you have perfect teeth?"

"I worked after school for a dentist," he told her, "in

exchange for braces and pocket money."

"Have you always been so responsible?" she asked, lingering over the word as if it were slightly distasteful.

"Until recently," he grinned again and was gone

✤

March in Galveston was windy, and the beaches were mostly deserted by tourists and locals alike, but there were occasional fine days, and Jesse's new-found freedom allowed him to grab them. One day, with the temperature in the low seventies, he took his bike out along the seawall. The water was green and white-capped, the sky blue with a scattering of clouds, none threatening. He stopped in one of the shops for ice cream, then paused to read a monument. The wall was twenty feet wide at its base, it said, five feet across at the top, seventeen feet high, built after the 1900 hurricane destroyed most of the city. It was the city's answer to the worst natural disaster the world had known at that time. The wall. Man's attempt to conquer nature. And it had worked. Galveston had never suffered again what it went through back then, what would have driven less gutsy places off the map, and they credited the seawall. You couldn't live here long without catching some of that sense of island pride and stubbornness. They still obsessed over storms— Audrey in '57, Carla in '61, Alicia in '83, the last really bad one, and the only one in Jesse's lifetime. Watching the weather was, for islanders, like a doctor taking vital signs, he thought, a constant gathering of data and a requirement of survival.

At the end of Seawall Boulevard, near 7-Mile Road, Jesse stopped and looked into an expanse of unwalled beach that extended as far as he could see. To his right, some high-rise condos had water lapping at their back doors, where the beach had eroded hundreds of feet since the wall was built. It was convincing proof that what he had read was true—that the west end of the island was washing away. According to the experts, it was being deposited on the east end.

Galveston Island was a strip of constantly shifting sand. An exercise in denial, Jesse thought. The people who live here count on their wall, even though they know everything has limits. Much like medicine—trying to outsmart nature, holding onto territory, determined to win a contest against the inevitable.

Had he chosen the wrong profession? The thought of going back to school summoned up a knot in his gut, but the thought of leaving it for something else loomed like a storm cloud on the horizon. He rode west down the San Luis Highway, stopped at a deserted stretch of beach, and took his new kite out of the bike basket. It was a dragon, black, with red fire in its mouth, and yellow stripes on its tail. Jesse walked his bike down the beach until he found a perfect spot. Then he set himself against the wind, took a few running steps, and began to let out the string.

13

When Dr. John Broussard learned his firstborn was a son, he named him John Jones, after himself first, and secondly, to incorporate two famous names in golf—that of Bobby Jones, the player, and Robert Trent Jones, the course designer. Dr. Broussard considered golf a gentleman's game, preferable, in his mind, to tennis, and he set out to make his boy a golfer, as he wished his own father had done. Starting at age nine, J.J. had been given weekly lessons and had been taken regularly to the driving range to practice. He wasn't allowed to play a round until the year he turned twelve, at which time he celebrated his birthday playing at the club with his father.

As J.J. looked back, it wasn't a bad plan. The waiting created in him a kid's thirst for action. When the appointed day came, he'd been waiting and practicing for a quarter of his life. He shot a ninety-six that day and Dr. John got it written up in the club newsletter. Every birthday after that, until prison interrupted their lives, the two marked the day with a game of golf. It was the closest thing to a ritual they shared.

Over the years, the character of their game shifted. First, J.J. was a kid trying to please his father, and the doctor, a stiff man, trying to be fatherly. At about fifteen, J.J. began to think about beating his father. "The Good Doctor" wasn't that good, he realized. At eighteen, he began to beat him regularly, but winning didn't change things much. J.J. might be on top when they came off the course, but in the clubhouse, it was, "How're you doin' today, Dr. Broussard? You need anything, just let me know. This your boy?" And his father would take the reins again.

Of the things that had shaped J.J.'s character, golf was on the list as a more consistent teacher than his father. Golf taught him patience and focus, which came pretty easy. Harder, was the lesson on attitude. He had to take what he was trying to do seriously and stay cool when things went wrong. He'd seen guys break clubs against trees, and throw bags, clubs and all, in the water, but J.J. learned to control impulses like that because he could see they didn't work. He wasn't fond of over-thinking things, preferred to act on instinct, and, over time, learned to bury issues he didn't want to deal with.

❖

J.J. and Bobby Calhoun had made a date to play at a small course across the causeway, where, though they had his name somewhere on the books, they knew him as "Captain." It was a Tuesday afternoon in mid-March.

"How often you play these days?" Bobby asked as they waited to get off the first tee, swinging clubs to loosen up, neither looking at the other.

"Once or twice a week."

"Handicap?"

"Five," J.J. told him. "You?"

"Ten," Calhoun said. "So, what's the bet?"

"I never play for more than a dollar a hole these days," J.J. said.

"You have gone straight. How about five?"

"A dollar and drinks," J.J. said.

J.J. won eight holes; Calhoun won five, and they tied five. He was the kind of golfer J.J. liked to play with, someone with a good pace who didn't talk too much. In the clubhouse, over a beer, Calhoun told him how he'd been working on his game for the past fourteen years.

"I was psyched up to beat you, Skins. Thought I had you, too, given the age difference," Calhoun said.

Thought he could beat this old guy in his fifties, J.J. thought.

"And you don't bet any more?" Calhoun still looked doubtful.

"I follow sports," J.J. told him, "but it's all small potatoes."

Calhoun suggested they team up and play some local tournaments. They'd win some, J.J. figured. Their pictures could get into a local paper, which would mean more shots at being recognized. But why not? If Rose didn't care, he was willing to let the chips fall.

✢

J.J. had cashed Rose out of the stock market and invested in long and short-term government securities and tax-free municipal bonds. It was a good time to get out, with technology stocks going sour. There had been times he'd have laughed at making 5 percent on an investment, but with the market this shaky, it sounded okay. Besides, it was Rose's call, as had been her idea to buy the lots surrounding Maison Rouge. They'd acquired a full block of land facing the water, with room for a large building and parking. A back alley divided the block neatly, lengthwise, and gave additional access to the property. After the land purchase was closed, they made an appointment to talk with an architect named Ellsworth King.

"Architects are strange birds," Rose had told him. "Exceedingly proud of their knowledge. But this one has cause. He's a recognized expert in historic restoration."

King showed interest in their proposal. "We're not talking a real restoration," he told them. "Even if we find sketches or a design layout, there's no hard evidence of what the original house looked like."

"I found a reference on the Internet," Rose said, pulling out some sketches of her own. "A two-story house of heavy masonry, painted red. It had a tower and cannon ports mounted across the side that faced the bay. Beautifully decorated rooms for fine living and entertaining. Barracks, outside, in the back." She read from notes until her voice was coming in breathy jerks. J.J. watched her laboring, unwilling to stop talking.

"The site has seen a multitude of changes over the last 200 years, including other buildings," King told her, "but the structural remains of the original wine cellar give us a starting point." As he talked, he doodled—a fortress, cannons, waves, seagulls, a tall-masted sailing ship. He suggested Rose continue her search, and he would search as well. He'd prepare a preliminary design in about a month, based on the information they could gather.

"Have you thought about the overall image you want to convey?" he asked.

"Opulence," Rose said without hesitation.

"Escape from the ordinary," J.J. added.

"Just make us a pleasure palace," Rose chuckled.

King nodded, jotting notes.

✣

J.J. hadn't consulted an architect about his own new house. He'd found his plan in a book at the grocery store, and it was taking shape, with a wall of windows facing the bay and storm shutters to protect them. There'd be no more boarding up. In the kitchen, cook tops were going to replace the old four-burner gas flame. The upper deck would be covered, and, down at dock level, there'd be an electric boat lift and a lighted spot for night-fishing. Each time the builder offered choices, J.J. went for the best. His friends, watching the house take shape, uncomfortable with change within their group, were giving him hell. Woody was stuck on the idea that he was trying to impress Elena. "You can do better than that señorita, J.J.," he told him.

J.J. wondered how his friends would react to the rest of his story. A phony—that's how they'd see him—hiding out all this time, keeping secrets from people he'd known for ten years. If it came out—when it came out—it'd probably mean the end of the poker, the fishing, the easy camaraderie, but he couldn't help that. He was being pushed toward something new, and he'd ride the wave. The world was tilting for J.J., centering around the axis of Rose and the pull of her money. Nothing to complain about there, but experience had taught him that when a major change comes, there'll be good and bad to follow, and it's almost impossible on the front end to recognize one from the other.

⊹

Rose called and left a message on his recorder. "I've ordered some books so you can familiarize yourself with the architecture of the city. Then I realized," she said, "if you don't know anything about architecture, you need a general book, too. So, read the general first and then the specific. As if I had to tell you that. Sorry, Captain, we get bossy as we get older." She took a quick breath. "You have that to look forward to." She paused, then, as if wondering whether her next item was appropriate to discuss over a recording machine. "I also want to talk with you about a successor trustee. This is for after I'm gone and you decide you don't want to be trustee any longer. You're in the same position as I—no one to leave the family jewels to." Breath. "Goodnight, Captain. I'll hope to talk with you tomorrow or the next day. Jesse and I are going to the library tomorrow and then he wants me to go fly a kite."

⊹

J.J. had avoided thinking during his twenties, which wasn't too unusual for someone coming of age in the '70s. But in prison, forced to confront not only his addictions but his actions by a counselor with the unlikely name of Simon Wise, he came up with the following scenarios: (1) Everything had always been easy for him and he never dreamed he'd get caught; (2) He was rebelling from a father who had dictated his life, from Boy Scouts to Tulane to marriage; (3) He was regularly indulging in recreational drugs which clouded his judgment; (4) He was a gambler by nature, destined to push things to the limit; and (5) He was a self-centered, conscienceless smartass looking for a quick way out of a money crunch.

"Take your pick," Simon said.

Simon Wise had a master's degree in Psychology and a philosophy that drew from his Native American background. He volunteered at the prison because he was testing a new theory. Some of the inmates he considered bad subjects. J.J. he liked.

"Whatever the reason, I messed up," J.J. told Simon. "My father told me I fouled my nest. Really pissed me off when he said that, but when I think about it, it's a good enough description of stealing from your friends. Shitting where you sleep. It was a lousy thing to do, and I figure I'll be paying for it forever."

"Is that good, or bad?"

"It's not my first choice." He had been irritated the first time Simon asked what seemed like such a stupid question, but it turned out to be the essence of the counselor's cognitive theory.

Simon told the story of a young Indian boy, crippled when a horse trampled him, crushing one arm and one leg. His injuries prevented him from proving himself as a hunter or warrior, so he was left behind with the old men to guard the women and children. He longed to be like the others and cursed his fate. And then he found that when the others were on extended trips the young maidens brought themselves to his tent, sometimes two and three a night. What he lacked in other manly skills, he made up for in sexual prowess, and time spent in the company of women had increased his sensitivity and gentled his approach. He was a lover in great demand, and for this gift he offered thanks to his totem. And then the tribe began to notice—the squaws began to talk, the warriors grew suspicious, a rash of infants with his distinctive birthmark began to appear. The men tied him to a stake in the ground and forbade the women to approach him except to bring food and water. He was in despair. One morning by the first light of dawn, the village was overrun by an enemy tribe who killed the warriors and took the women. But they spared the staked creature. Because of his deformities they thought him holy and took him with them to bring good fortune.

"What do you think happened then?" Simon asked.

J.J. shrugged. "Hard to tell."

"My point, exactly," Simon said. "Whatever happens, happens—and it carries seeds both good and bad. Nothing is written in stone—not your life, not mine."

With guidance, J.J. had gotten a handle on his gambling and drugs and learned to think his way through things. His story had made its way into Simon's book under the bogus name of John Jay Phoenix. But if prison had evoked an epiphany, it wasn't so much about seeing the light, as seeing the handwriting on the wall. If he'd continued in the same path, he'd be back in trouble in a New York minute. The old calls were still there, but J.J. learned to work with them. The sea is a gamble, he knew that much. Stocks are a gamble. Creating a new identity is a gambler's game.

❖

On a poker Monday in early April, J.J. decided to serve crawfish. He bought ten pounds at the pier and brought them home in a cooler full of water. The condemned creatures sat, scrabbling in his kitchen, awaiting their fate, while J.J. washed greens for a salad and considered telling his story at the table. That's how Charlie had dropped it on them that he had colon cancer. That's how Jumbo did it when he gave his place to his kids and moved back to town. You drop it late in the evening, so nobody gets too uncomfortable, and there's always the next hand to get to. There were other ways that information got spread. You could always tell Woody, who got the word out in his own style.

Woody showed up about the time the sun went down, carrying an extra boiling pot. "Specs are runnin'," he told J.J. "We was baggin' 'em this mornin'. Want to go out tomorrow?"

J.J. shook his head. "I've got business in town."

"There was a kid askin' for you yesterday. Ridin' a bike. Skinny legs, no socks, hat on backwards, that type. 'Bout twenty-five, I'd guess. Wanted to know where your house was. I pointed him in that di-rection, but tole' him if your truck was gone, you was gone. He rode down here, roun' the block, and headed back toward town."

Woody had a way of making things sound ordinary and mysterious at the same time. He delivered his information in short bursts and punctuated it with raised eyebrows and a cocked head that seemed to say whatever he was telling you was a curiosity worth relating. He seldom ventured a judgment in the telling, which left things up to the listener's imagination or willingness to question. J.J. wondered why the hell Jesse Martin was way out here looking for him. It was probably ten miles into town—no small trip on a bicycle.

J.J. finished chopping onion and threw it in the salad. He buttered two loaves of French bread and sprinkled on garlic salt. Then he lit the fires under two huge pots.

"Woody," J.J. said, adding pinches of salt to the water, "I was in federal prison from 1981 to '85. Burglary and theft. It's well behind me. I don't want to talk about it—just thought it was time for you to know."

"That so," Woody said, studying the pots. "This kid have anything to do with that?"

"Not a thing."

"What made you come out with it?"

"Other people may come around."

"To do you harm?"

"No good reason to."

"Anyone else roun' here know?"

"You're the first."

"Well, I'll be damned," he rubbed the stubble of his beard and grinned.

"What about the wetback?"

"She's not a wetback, Woody."

"She don't have papers."

"How do you know that?"

"Donnie at the Boat Rack told me. He pays her out of pocket 'cause he can't put her on the payroll. Says she's a natural. Whoever heard of a Mescan woman mechanic? You're both thinkin' with your dicks. She's not workin' on my boat."

Woody had only part of the story and, as usual, was willing to believe the worst about an outsider, especially Elena. What J.J. knew was that she was in the states on a visitor's pass, under the guise of helping an aging family member. She'd shown up at Donnie's place looking for work. Said she'd learned to clean and detail sailboats for rich people in Guadalajara. He'd let her do a couple and realized he could charge $300 for it, pay her $150, and turn a good profit. Then he found out she could work on a motor too, and he paid her peanuts compared to a real mechanic.

She had twin boys, seven years old, and sent money back to her parents in Monterey, who were keeping the children. She was determined to give her boys a good education and better opportunities than the ordinary kid in Monterey. When J.J. had asked how she planned to do that, she'd told him God would provide. He didn't expect her to say, "Marry an American," but that had to be part of her thinking.

"She'll get you in trouble," Woody said.

"We have an agreement," J.J. told him.

He'd hired her over a year before, on Donnie's recommendation, to come to his place and help refurbish his boat. At the end of the job, she said she had Thursdays off. Did he want her to come on that day and clean the cabin?

"I don't need much help," he'd fumbled for an answer.

"Once a month?" she'd asked, her head tilted in invitation. "Thirty dollars?"

When they started sleeping together, she was very clear. "I like you. You're the only one. Only you. Only on Thursday. After the work is done."

And he had buried his face in her hair, breathed in the clean scent of her, and said, "I like you, too."

He liked her independence and the serious way she absorbed things. Liked her dark, brooding eyes. And then the sudden smile, like a flash of lightning. He liked that she didn't talk about her children, or show pictures. He didn't worry about her bringing him trouble, but he knew she'd be taking off one of these days. He wasn't her answer.

Elena needed someone like the Martin boy, he thought. They could probably match each other for ambition. And she could teach him a thing or two, though he probably wasn't smart enough to learn from anyone who didn't carry the proper credentials. When you're Jesse Martin's age, J.J. thought, you're big on judging. You see other people's lives and are certain yours will never get fucked up. That kid thinks he's here to change the world. J.J. felt a rising irritation. Taking Rose out to fly a kite. She's likely to have a stroke.

14

Rose balanced herself on Jesse's arm. They'd walked from the car, down a few steps to where the beach began, where she stopped to take off her canvas shoes. Jesse stood in his flip-flops and waited for her to make the adjustment. He had already set up a folding chair and a small beach umbrella and had come back for her and the ice chest filled with Cokes and pimento cheese sandwiches.

"It's been years since I've been to the beach," she told him.

"That's what I thought when I saw all this stuff in the garage. It's right out of *Ozzie and Harriet*."

"It's still perfectly good," she pretended indignation.

Rose was of the opinion that things were good until they wore out. Jesse was of the throwaway generation, she said. In reply, he would point to his worn tennis shoes and swear he hadn't thrown anything away for three years, at which she'd scoff, saying three years was a flea on an elephant's behind.

He settled her in the chair, watched insistently while she put on sun block, then headed down the beach to the kite shop. Rose adjusted her straw hat and used the opera glasses she'd hung around her neck to watch the surfers. She had previously witnessed this activity on television or from the distance of a car. Up closer, she could see it was quite a feat. She quickly located the most adept young man and became engrossed in his efforts. Behind him, sailboats dotted the gulf. The water near the shore was a murky gray, foamy from whitecaps that spewed high and wild, but farther out, where sunlight hit on still water, the surface shone emerald green. Such a dear, familiar sight, this beach, right at her front door, and she hadn't looked in years. She blinked away sudden tears.

Young women in skimpy bathing suits walked at the water's edge, playing tag with the incoming tide. Rose, dressed in long pants and a long-sleeved shirt shook her head, amused at their need to rush the season. Let a sunny day present itself, and the girls poured out to the park across from her house to watch the boys play ball. They dressed in halters and tiny shorts, which sometimes revealed parts best kept covered. She understood it was part of the mating drive, but wished they'd be a little more circumspect. Hadn't their mothers told them that covering the body is often more interesting than exposing it?

A couple jogged by, talking. A man and dog ran by, the man, well-toned for middle age, the animal's golden coat wet and shining. The two stopped in front of her, as if seeking an audience, while the man threw a disc and the dog bounded to catch it in the air. She waved approval. Two older women strolled by, hand in hand. One had short gray hair, cut like a man's.

On the horizon she could make out the shadowy outlines of two huge oil tankers and a vertical line of gray rising to a darker cloud. She raised the binoculars again. Could be a waterspout, but no, it was only smoke from the tankers. She leaned back, relieved. That fear of whirling winds had been with her since childhood, ever since her parents had taken her to see *The Wizard of Oz* in the silent version. It had terrified her. The barren landscape of that early movie was much like the Texas pan-handle where she grew up. The storm cellar, the wide sky, the black funnel advancing in an ever-widening circle, things being sucked up and tossed to kingdom come. It was a foolish fear, born of some movie-maker's vivid imagination. More people are struck by lightning than flung about by tornadoes, she was certain. Nevertheless, the anxiety stuck around and had to be dealt with. She rode out storm warnings with a stiff drink of scotch.

"Anything exciting happen?" Jesse threw himself on the sand and began taking things out of his sack.

"Do none of these people work?" Rose asked.

"They probably work shifts. Like hospital personnel," he said. "Or maybe they're on vacation, or maybe they're slackers like us." He chuckled.

She lowered her sunglasses and sent a frown in his direction.

"I'm not sure what you mean by 'slackers' but I'll tell you this. My husband didn't want his wife to work. It wasn't the norm in certain circles, back then. So I kept myself busy other ways."

"Like what?" Jesse had opened a Coke and sat on the sand, concentrating on assembling a kite.

"In the '50s I took courses in landscape architecture. Thought I might work my way into my husband's office as a professional, but I had to think again. Architects don't have much use for landscape architects, nor did men have much use for wives in their offices back then."

Jesse nodded and continued working. Rose knew he wasn't paying attention, but she slipped off her shoes, ran the warm sand between her toes, and kept on.

"In the '60s I went into the Fifth Ward in Houston to register blacks to vote. Republican women, that's who we were, dressed in our Sunday best. We drove into an area the police were reluctant to enter. People warned us we'd be robbed, or worse, but we had an invitation and support from the churches and the Negroes lined up to be put on the rolls. These were people who had never voted before and never would have, except that the time was right, and we were sitting there, almost begging them." She smiled to herself in memory. Jesse didn't look up.

"In the '70s I got into a local fight to keep the shrimp boats down at Pier 19. The Mosquito Fleet, they call them. Business powers thought the smell and the sight of simple fishermen would run tourists off. That's what the tourists love to see, we said, the real thing, not just T-shirts with pictures of fishing boats. In the '80s we started Keep Galveston Beautiful, an environmental movement that attacked, among other things, dumping sewage. . ."

"What do you think?" Jesse interrupted, holding up the finished kite, a large fish with multi-colored scales that flapped freely.

"Lovely," she said, willing to forgive his lack of interest. She did run on at times.

He ran then, along the beach, heading the kite to catch the wind. Before she knew it, the paper fish was up, up, sailing in its own blue ocean, scales glimmering like a sequined blouse. Rose clapped her hands. He brought her the string, and she stood to hold it, letting it out a little more, walking first this way, then another, toward the water's edge, bare feet in foamy froth, toes in wet sand, her heart, light as a feather.

Jesse stood back, smiling, proud of himself. "Great, isn't it?" he shouted over the wind.

✤

"I would have been a terrible mother," Rose had been heard to say more than once. "Is it possible to read and have children, too? Don't they keep interrupting you with questions and having to go potty? I told the doctor I'd only have a child if he could wrap it safely in a cocoon until it was twenty or so, and then we'd bring it out when it was old enough to mix drinks and tell us jokes."

After a first miscarriage, Rose and Nate Parrish had made a conscious decision. He was forty-five by that time, just getting reestablished after the war, and no longer considered young. If he started a family at that age, would he live to see them graduate from high school? Worse still, could he provide life insurance to take care of the family if he died at fifty-five? That was the life expectancy for a male born in 1900, though Nate had already beaten the odds by surviving childhood, not to mention the war. Then there was the Rh factor. Rose had Rh negative blood, already sensitized by the miscarriage. "The body remembers," was what her doctor had told her, "and creates antigens that can kill the infant and the mother." The doctor painted a gloomy picture, and Rose and Nate, happy with each other's company and having many interests to pursue, decided to forego parenthood. They didn't just forego it, they laughed at it sometimes. As it turned out, Nate lived to be eighty-six, and modern medicine learned how to help Rh negative women safely through pregnancy, but with the irrevocable decision made, the childless couple never experienced walking the floor with a crying baby or waiting up for a delinquent teenager. She was well aware of the demands of parenting, and took comfort in the fact that she had redirected that energy toward worthwhile causes.

157

✥

Exhilarated but tired from her kite-flying adventure, Rose was at her typewriter at midnight, determined to address something that had irritated her from the paper that day.

March 16, 2000
Dear Sir,
    An article in your paper this date accuses "elderly" homeowners of defeating the Galveston Independent School District bond issue on the grounds that they didn't under - stand their property taxes were frozen when they reached age sixty-five. This assumption stigmatizes the "elderly" as

a monolithic group intent on preserving the status quo at the expense of the young and ignores the fact that through - out their lifetime these people have paid taxes that make public education possible. The idea that a significant num - ber do not know their taxes are frozen at sixty-five is non - sense. It's a rite of passage.

I suggest that those concerned spend their time educat - ing the public and getting out the vote (a very low percent - age of eligible voters showed up at the polls for this issue), rather than using the mature citizens of this community as a scapegoat.

⁜

At two A.M. Rose was still awake, mentally editing her letter, replaying her day at the beach, feeling vaguely uneasy. Tossing. An occasional cough. Fitful dreams, though she could swear she wasn't sleeping. A scratchy throat. At three A.M. she awakened, nauseated. She struggled up and sat on the side of the bed. There was a sharp pain in her back, between the shoulder blades. She reached to rub it, but it was too much of a stretch. She took a sip of water. It tasted metallic. Was she going to be sick? Needed some time to make it to the bathroom. Such a chore. But a cold cloth would feel good. She forced herself up and crept to the bathroom sink, where she wet a washcloth and leaned against the counter, holding the cool to her head, then her throat. A little better, she thought. Aspirin? The thought of swallowing anything was uninviting. Cloth in hand, she dragged herself back to bed, but no sooner had she put her head on the pillow than she was coughing. Her throat felt raw now and her chest was tight. Damn, she thought. My pleasure has its price.

When Pearl arrived the next morning, Rose was resting, motionless. Pearl set the carafe of coffee on the bedside table and turned to go. Rose opened her eyes and held up a finger. Pearl, a woman of few words, stood, awaiting instructions. Rose motioned for her to come closer.

"I'll stay upstairs today," she whispered in a raspy voice. "Bring the paper and the mail when it comes."

"Hungry?" Pearl asked.

Rose made a grimace and turned her head. The nausea was gone, but the thought of food had no appeal.

"Cream of Wheat?" Pearl's answer to whatever ailed one.

Rose closed her eyes and waved the woman away, then had to call her back to get her pills and pour some coffee, though she wasn't sure she could get either down. The simplest task seemed a mountain climb.

She dozed off and on. She dreamed of fish and brown pelicans and herself, swimming underwater, looking up at a surface dappled with sunlight. When she was awake, she lay and stared. A book was too heavy to hold; the crossword took too much thought. The mail was confusing. She retreated, face to the wall—aspirin for the fever, fluids, sleep. Her throat began to feel better, her chest, worse. Coughs were painful. Fortunately, they were controllable. Pearl came and went. She mumbled things and seemed to be moving the furniture about. Why was she so tired? So tired.

"Rose?"

She opened her eyes to see Jesse standing at her door. She grabbed at the covers and tried to sit up. Damn Pearl.

He came closer. She reached up and tried to smooth her hair. He took her hand.

"You're parched. Got a thermometer?"

She nodded toward the bed table. He shook it and put it in her mouth. Then he took her hand again and checked her pulse against the second hand of her alarm clock.

"I want to listen to your chest," he said, all business. "Can you lean forward?"

She shook her head.

"Of course you can. Here." When he had her situated, he put his ear to her back. "Take a deep breath."

She tried.

"Deep breath, Rose."

She tried again, ending in a cough. She hugged her arms to her chest to brace against the pain.

"I can't hear anything," he said, "but I don't have a stethoscope. Let's call an ambulance and get you over to the hospital."

She shook her head.

"Pearl tells me you've been getting worse all weekend. She came in on Saturday and Sunday to check on you, but you kept waving her out. One of you should have called."

Rose shook her head.

"So I was working. You leave a message. Wasn't that our agreement?"

"No ambulance," Rose whispered.

"I'll take you," he said.

Pearl came in then and helped her put on a dressing gown. She packed a small bag for her, never saying a word. The two women shared the room in silence.

"Look in on the cat," Rose said finally.

Pearl nodded.

⊹

"Ms. Parrish."

Rose wished they'd let her rest in peace. She had coasters at home with her initials RIP—Rose Inez Parrish. It had been such a joke, back then, serving drinks on cork circlets that suggested dying when they were all so alive. She opened her eyes to see that nothing had changed. The hospital room was beige and spare, and a large, familiar-looking nurse was standing over her. "Time for your meds," she said.

"Do you usually wake people to give them their pills?"

"If they need it," she answered, attaching something to Rose's finger and then taking hold of the opposite wrist. "How you doin' honey?"

Rose closed her eyes and ignored the question and the intimacy. It was the same nurse she had last time. Strange name.

"You ready for a bath?"

Rose shook her head.

"You plan to let Jesse and Pearl see you looking like this?"

"How do you know Jesse and Pearl?"

"Honey, Victorias knows ever'thing." As she talked, she filled a small basin with water and brought it to the bed table, along with soap, a washcloth, a comb, and a toothbrush. "Now you get yourself together, and I'll be back shortly."

Rose did what she could. She thought she'd been here a while, but this was the first time she'd looked around, or washed up. Must be getting better, she figured, though what she felt could hardly be described as better. The nurse returned and stopped in the doorway, hands on hips.

"You miss your ring? He brought you in here with it on an' 161 I sent it back. You're mighty lucky, that's all I have to say."

"This is luck?"

"Well, it never hurts to have a warrior on your side."

"A what?"

"You heard me. Your woman, Pearl, she goes to my church. She's a prayer warrior."

"Never heard of such a thing," Rose dismissed the conversation. "What's wrong with me?"

"Pneumonia." She chuckled. "That's what it says on the chart. You're stubborn and contrary as a cat, but we don't put that on the charts."

"Are you sure you're a registered nurse?"

"Trained right here," she said with obvious pride.

"Where's your cap?"

"We don't wear them any more. You hungry?"

"I might be."

"Ice cream? Soup? Peaches?"

"When can I get out of here?"

"When you're strong enough to walk out on your own steam."

"Bring me some of everything."

15

When the University of Texas decided to set up a medical school in 1890, Galveston was only one of the locations under consideration. It was a major Texas city then and one of the richest cities, for its size, in the country. Galveston wanted that medical school. According to local lore, the city fathers used the fact of killer storms and yellow fever epidemics as a sales pitch. The island, they said, could offer students good practical experience.

When Jesse heard that story at orientation, he wondered if it was intended to warn students or impress them. The general attitude on the island was pride. You have to be tough to withstand the salt, the sand, the heat, the humidity, and the biting insects.

There were still killer storms, but yellow fever, thankfully, was gone. In the mid-1800s, it wiped out 10 percent of the population. Rose told him that identifying those born on the island started in the Civil War to indicate which soldiers could be quartered in Galveston. This was because BOIs, most of them, carried a tolerance to yellow fever. Lucky if they did. The symptoms had imprinted themselves in Jesse's medical memory: Chills and fever, then the eyes turn yellow, and in the final stages, black vomit. Every time he slapped a mosquito he thought about that.

Houston was the only city Jesse had ever known, and it was too big to fully comprehend. Galveston, however, was accessible and begged to be explored. He spent his now abundant free time getting acquainted with the island's streets, its beaches, and some of its inside pockets. After listening to Rose's stories of how it used to be, he paid more attention to old buildings and monuments, but he especially liked the crusty characters in the bars, bait shops, and souvenir stores. Talk was their daily fare. They had stories about all sorts of Galveston people—society types, fishermen, tourists, gamblers, gays, and sailors. Jesse imagined them talking to other people about him. "Waited on a kid yesterday, used to be a med student. Says the competition's cutthroat. Things are tough all over, I told him."

West-enders, they said, were a special breed. Didn't belong to the historical society, didn't attend Dickens on the Strand at Christmas, and some didn't evacuate when a storm beat down on the island. Dutch Voight ran a smuggling operation from that end of the island back during prohibition, and Lafitte was said to have buried treasure there a hundred years before that. Living on west beach was a statement—a taste for life in the raw—and those who chose it were self-sufficient, sometimes reckless, and often private people. Jesse couldn't help wondering about Rose's friend, Captain Broussard. He seemed to fit the description. And why would he choose to celebrate the millennium with a woman old enough to be his mother, laughing at stale jokes? Jesse saw how he flattered her. He had to be after her money.

✛

Jesse had shared more with Susanna the night of the beach cleanup than with anyone in years. Usually, he liked to keep people laughing and at arm's length. He wasn't keen to expose his private world, the conflicts with his father, the guilt about succeeding where his brother hadn't, and the anger about money. He'd learned to pretend he wasn't interested in expensive clothes, or a decent car, wasn't interested in dating girls who expected to be taken to nice places. This had eaten at him through high school and college, and it still stung.

Working for Rose had helped him keep his sanity after the suspension, but the brief relief he'd felt from being out of school had turned into a damn clock ticking in his head. Despite the fact that he was getting plenty of sleep and exercise, exploring the beach, cruising the city, and trying to get something going with Susanna, it was impossible for Jesse to relax and enjoy the present because he was so busy wrestling with the future. He had programmed himself to achieve. If he couldn't do it in medicine, he'd have to find an alternative. He also had developed a 165 sore knot just below his rib cage on the right hand side—probably the beginning of an ulcer. He rubbed at it, concentrated on deep-breathing, and hoped it would go away if he got a positive response to his petition for reinstatement.

✤

Jesse almost ran into his ex-roommate outside the hospital when he was there checking on Rose. The first instinct was to duck, but it wasn't necessary. The big guy was with his clinical supervisor, hanging on his every word, and wouldn't have noticed if the place had been invaded by killer bees. And why should he hide from Chip anyway? Shouldn't it be the other way around? The guy hadn't lied outright; but he had been a weasel, and Jesse ached to get back at him. "Revenge is a dish best served cold," he could hear Rose saying. His employer thought in quotes and passed them his way daily.

At Gunners, later that afternoon, Jesse made an appearance.

"We heard you were in detox."

"Nope."

"Well, you disappeared, dude, dropped off the face of the clock. They said you had a drug problem. I said no way, but shit happens. You know?"

"I got swallowed by the great white whale," Jesse said.

"Chip?"

"Who else?"

"Speak of the devil," someone muttered in a low voice, and Jesse looked up. Chip was moving toward the table, hand outstretched. "Jesse! Good to see you man. Where've you been?"

Jesse kept his arms folded. "I thought you knew."

Chip looked around to find all eyes on him. "Well, uh, I heard something about, uh, rehab."

Jesse stared him down. "Where'd you hear that?"

Chip looked around again, like he was taking roll, then came up with a name of someone not present. "Franco."

"That's funny. Because Franco said he heard it from you."

Chip shook his head in a show of innocence. "No. I think I heard it from him."

Jesse unfolded his arms, erased the anger from his voice, and sat down. "Truth is, I probably have you to thank." He hooked his foot around a chair and pulled it toward Chip in an invitation to sit.

Chip remained standing. "How's that?"

"If you hadn't done what you did, I'd never have come to terms with my shit. You did me a big favor, man. Let me buy you a beer."

Chip looked nervous. Suspicious, Jesse thought, but he could be diverted.

Jesse turned to the table at large and changed the subject. "Try this one. A thirty-year-old comes into the clinic. He's trembling all over. Has no fever; appears to be well-rested. What's the diagnosis?"

"Parkinson's?"

"But you notice that the trembling continues whether he's moving or at rest."

"Alcohol withdrawal?"

"He says he doesn't drink."

"Does he have thyroid symptoms? Bulging eyes? Sweating?"

"Nope."

"Is he a coffee drinker?"

"He's had about six cups in the last eight hours."

"Caffeine poisoning," Chip barked the pronouncement, anxious to beat someone else to the answer.

The game continued, with the one who answered correctly throwing out the next challenge. No one came to Gunner's without first arming themselves with a set of symptoms. It was mainly practice—a replay of the humbling dialogues the students were subjected to in teaching clinic. Chip, now in the spotlight, sat down, and Jesse ordered him a beer.

In some ways it didn't take long for the surroundings to feel normal again, but Jesse couldn't help noticing how pasty these people looked, like they hadn't seen the sun in weeks. Most had circles under their eyes, and he'd be willing to bet no one knew it was the first day of spring. They only knew it was Saturday and tomorrow was Sunday and the next day was Monday. They were bright young zombies, marching toward a carrot with an M.D. carved on it. They also had a stick beating at their backsides. Clinic doctors weren't teachers. They showed you once, then stood by to clean up after stupid mistakes. Did he really want to get back to this, Jesse wondered?

The talk continued. They called for another round, and a third. Jesse reached in his pocket for the pain killers he'd lifted from Rose's medicine cabinet. He slipped them in Chip's beer while the big mouth argued the relative weight of various body organs. Chip picked up his beer and guzzled, drinking like he ate, like it was going to disappear if he left it untended for any length of time. Jesse sat back. He figured it'd take about fifteen minutes.

⁂

"So, Jesse, what are you up to these days?"

He told them about driving *Miss Rose,* about the Mercedes, and dolphin rescue training, and flying kites. His audience groaned with envy.

"You coming back next semester?"

"Not sure."

Chip, who had gotten quiet, looked up. "Think they'll let you back in?"

"Why not?"

"You know. The drug problem."

"Who said I had a drug problem?"

"You said you were in rehab." He was beginning to slur.

"No, I just didn't deny it. In fact, everyone here heard it from you." Jesse draped his arm over Chip's shoulder. "This man, my friends, reported me to Jefferson as a potential drug addict."

"There were roaches in your jacket. I was worried," Chip's eyes looked heavy as he searched the faces for a friendly affirmation.

"Shit, Chip. You took it to Jefferson without going to Jesse?" Disapproval rose from the table like steam.

Chip reached in his pocket. He fumbled with a handful of bills, straightened them, counted and recounted. Finally he laid some on the table. "I'm out of here." He stood up and wavered, out of balance, surprised.

Jesse stood too, catching him by the shoulder. "I'm worried about you, Chip. Looks like you've had too much to drink. Shouldn't be driving, should you? A DUI wouldn't set well with the school."

Chip pushed him away, then sank into a chair. Someone slid

him a glass of water. A few minutes later he laid his head on the table. One of the girls leaned over to check him.

"He's gone," she said and shook her head.

Jesse took off shortly after that. Someone would see that Chip got home. There was always someone around to do the right thing. This time, it wasn't going to be Jesse.

He left Gunner's and jogged home, sucking in cool, salty air, working on the answer to his own question. Why would anyone want to be a doctor? *It's a high calling.* That's what he'd written on his required statement of intent. He remembered sweating over one paragraph for weeks and running it by people who were good with words. "Say what's in your heart," an English teacher told him. "Insincerity rings particularly false on a white page." And so he wrote what he believed, or wanted to believe back then—that medicine forces you to sharpen and use every skill you own and some you don't, and that it gives you a chance to make a difference every day.

He slowed down to walk the last block home, then stopped to push against an iron fence, stretching out his calf and back muscles. He breathed deeply and looked up. Clouds scudded across an almost full moon; the stars were mostly obscured. The anger that had been gnawing at him had dissipated. Seeing the old gang had been good. His knock on Chip had felt good. The time off had been good. Not everyone can do it—be a doctor, Jesse thought. That was a big reason he wanted it. He wanted people to pay attention when he talked.

When a letter from the school arrived a week later, Jesse opened it with trepidation. As he read, his right hand worked at the knot in his side. It was from Dr. Jefferson's office, saying the board had reviewed his petition favorably. He could apply for the Summer Research Clinic, but would be under probation for the period of a year and subject to certain restrictions. It was businesslike, but friendly, and probably the most welcome news he'd ever received.

He visited Rose in the hospital with the letter in hand. "I've decided to start back in the summer," he said, expecting to please her.

"I need you this summer." She handed the letter back to him. Her voice was weak, but her eyes were demanding.

Uncomfortable, trying to avoid her look, he searched for something to say. "I thought you wanted me to be a doctor, Rose."

"Changed my mind." She turned her head. Now she wouldn't look at him.

"You have something else you want me to be?"

She turned back to face him and managed a smile. "A soap star."

Jesse agreed to help Rose through the summer. Now that he was back on track, he found that her talk about the captain and their project got on his nerves, as did the way she had of petting his arm. She seemed more demanding than before, but the worst part was being locked in her pace. Everything she wanted to do—find a television program, make a grocery list, look up something in the dictionary—took incredibly long. But she had increased his stipend to $500 a month, plus free rent. He'd be in good shape to start back in the fall. Move over, Chip, he thought, mentally elbowing his obnoxious ex-roommate off a bench.

16

The year he was twenty-seven J.J. Broussard had shown up on the eligible bachelor's list in the society section of the *Baton Rouge News Journal*. He'd been out of school three years, had a degree in finance, a broker's license, a nice apartment, and money to burn. That was the summer he met Brenda, the girl from Biloxi who'd signed up to crew a sailboat. He couldn't remember now exactly how she looked, only long blonde hair that flew across her face and a lean body, smooth, and tanned. He remembered cut-off jeans, no makeup, wide eyes, a sense of wonder, and a reckless edge. She liked to say and do whatever came into her mind. His father called her a hippie.

J.J. and Brenda sailed and biked and camped on the beach with bonfires. She made up rituals for them to perform by the light of the moon. J.J.'s father got her fired. "You've had your fun," he told his son. "She's not the kind of girl you can take out in public."

Six months later, J.J. and Saralee got engaged. She had just graduated from LSU in Home Economics and invited him to escort her to the debutante ball. People said it was a great match. She was pretty, and he was smart. And they were from good families. She liked to dress up and give dinner parties. She was a good cook and taught him to like working in the kitchen, the only plus he could now recall from their marriage. She wanted children, but he convinced her to wait because they were only young once, as if that were an original idea.

Six years later, J.J., then thirty-three, was in financial distress—drowning in losses at the track, credit cards maxed out, a call on his margin account. Between Saralee's shopping and his gambling, they tossed cash around like confetti. J.J. had to scramble to find a way out.

He knew the houses of wealthy clients, knew about their alarm systems, their Toby Mug collections, their Royal Doulton and Lalique, not to mention coins, stamps, guns. He arranged for the houses to be visited when the owners were away. It was so easy, and everything was covered by insurance. A damn good plan, he thought. A jeweler contact disposed of the merchandise across the state line, and most of the profits were used to cover J.J.'s losses. Some went up his nose. Some, he gave to local charities and challenged his friends to come up with matching gifts, a little piece of one-upsmanship to make himself look good and solvent.

❖

When Saralee was a freshman in college she'd done a bit part in a movie, and in the credits she'd been billed as "Cute Girl in Car." After J.J. had heard the story of her movie career enough times to be tired of it, the realization set in that he'd probably be listening to it for the rest of his life. It had been one mistake to marry her, and another to use her innocence as a cover. She never suspected, even when someone suggested the robberies looked like the work of an insider. "That could have been our house that was robbed," she said on more than one occasion, remarking on the awful coincidence that so many of their friends had been hit. She was never charged with the crime, and he'd been quick to state her lack of complicity.

He didn't spend much time thinking about Saralee. She had divorced him the second year of prison and gone to work selling real estate to their wealthy friends and friends' friends, who were convinced that no one had been more taken in by J.J. than Saralee. In their minds, for her to succeed without him would add to his comeuppance.

⁜

On April 1, at the Bay Area Golf Championship, J.J. and Bobby Calhoun walked away with team honors. In the celebration and banquet that followed, photos were snapped, and one of them made the newspaper. Within a couple of days, someone called looking for a John Broussard who used to live in Baton Rouge. The caller left messages, which J.J. didn't return. He called again, and then again. J.J. let the answering machine do its job, even when he was there. At night, in bed, he tried to fit a face with the voice he heard on the machine.

Meanwhile, Woody, who'd been overly attentive since J.J. had chosen to reveal his past, stopped in almost every evening on one pretense or another.

"Saw that same kid again t'other day, jes' ridin' up 'n down the streets, with a kind of ignamatic look on his face."

"Stupid or just blank?" J.J. asked, trying to decipher Woody's vocabulary stretch.

"Can't tell. Doffed his cap at me. First I thought he was makin' fun."

"Doffed his cap?"

"You know," Woody lifted the cap off his own head and tipped it toward J.J.

"I know doffed. I'm just wondering."

"Frien'ly sort. Said his name was Dooley."

"You had a conversation?"

"Not much a one. He's still lookin' to ketch up with you."

J.J. looked out at the bay, wondering. If it wasn't Jesse, who the hell was it?

⁜

Rose's week in the hospital had set things back. Ellsworth King was ready with preliminary drawings for Maison Rouge, and J.J. had lined up a couple of contractors willing to give him a bid. Things were waiting on Rose.

"I'm half goofy from these medications," she told J.J. on the phone. "The old catch-22. The meds make me heal faster, so they say, but when I take them, I'm not worth talking to. Can't remember whether I'm washing or hanging out. Go ahead without me."

J.J. remembered when Saralee used to ask about fabrics and colors, and whether he liked one furniture style more than another. It was a woman thing. He'd never cared about the shape of a lamp, or whether a doorway was arched, or if there was molding at the top of the ceiling. But suddenly he was thrown into a situation where huge amounts of money were being committed to architectural and design details, and he had to pay attention.

King had sketched an exterior of brick and arches that included a lookout tower topped by a flag. He had an attached portico marking the entrance and a balcony with iron grillwork bordering the back to offer a view of downtown. There was a large entry, an inviting gathering place, with overstuffed chairs and sofas in small groupings, and a huge, narrative mural. There was a wood-paneled dining room, with indirect lighting, exotic plants, and a dance floor. The cigar room was wood paneled too, with floor to ceiling bookcases, leather chairs, Tiffany lamps, and a copper fireplace. Another room had a bandstand, intimate tables and booths, walls crowded with pictures and island memorabilia, and a huge oak bar backed by mirrors. A broad, curved staircase led to large, fanciful restrooms, a billiards room, and a long balcony, where drinks or exotic snacks would be available.

"I've gone for a mix of French and Spanish colonial," King explained. "Lafitte came here from New Orleans, but it's easy to recreate New Orleans. Most of us have seen more of it than is probably good for us. You know where it's hard to go?" King raised his eyebrows in an exaggeration. His pupils were surrounded by white. "Know what we haven't seen?"

He insisted on holding J.J.'s eyes, making him squirm a bit before he delivered his own answer. "Cuba."

J.J. nodded.

"Pre-Castro Cuba was a playground for rich Americans. It was lush and sensual—just what you're looking for. A tropical pleasure garden. If you want to recreate that atmosphere, we need Spanish touches, bright colors, baroque lines."

J.J. knew he was out of his element. He nodded again. "I like what I see here. Let me take it to Rose."

"You'll explain the style mixtures?"

"Sure."

✣

"He's mixed styles," Rose said, studying the drawings. She was home after five days at the hospital, weak and short-tempered.

"He's going for something he calls Cuban baroque," J.J. told her. "Says it's reminiscent of opulence."

"That so? Is he aware Lafitte hated the Spanish? That theirs were the only ships his men were allowed to take?"

"It was the Spanish government he hated. Not the culture." J.J. leaned over and pointed to the sketches, trying to mimic King's air. "Look at the common elements in the styles—these arches and columns. I think it works."

She cocked her head and looked up at him. "Look who's turning into an authority."

He dumped a dozen copies of *Architectural Digest* on the end of her bed and made signs of leaving. "While you're recovering, you need to think about colors and lighting and windows."

"Where are you off to?"

"I'm going to start getting bids—unless you want King to rethink his plans."

"Go on," she waved him out. "It'll grow on me."

When he looked back, she was thumbing through one of the magazines with a no-nonsense look on her face.

❖

J.J. sat on his deck watching the sun slowly melt into the bay. It was poker night, and things would be starting up soon. At the horizon, a puddle of rosy gold spread across the water and held on long enough to capture his attention, before it slipped away. He sipped on a beer and looked in the direction of his new house that was taking shape two blocks to the north. He'd put his father's money to good use. Elena was especially pleased. She showed up earlier than usual on Thursdays now and demanded a tour before she started work. Last week she'd wanted to watch the tile man set the counters. This week she wanted to try to put in the bathroom floor by herself. She had even winked at him when she said she wouldn't charge for her labor if he'd let her do it. *Por nada.* Raised her hand and swore she'd do a good job. *Juro.* He had told her to give it her best shot.

"What does that mean?" she asked.

"Go for it. Do it the very best you can, understanding that you'll make some mistakes and it's not going to be perfect."

The builder had given him a move-in date of June 1. Ground should be broken on Maison Rouge by then too. Things were moving along. Blair had called to see when the press release should go out and wanted to know if he and Rose still wanted to keep their names out of it.

❖

"Hel—lo?"

He heard the voice first. When he looked around there was a lanky figure in a baseball cap coming up the steps, two at a time. At the top, he straightened up and took off his cap. Sandy hair. Skinny. A friendly smile.

The boy came toward J.J., hand outstretched. "Finally caught you at home. My name's Dooley."

"J.J. Broussard."

"Yes, sir. I know." His eyes were as soft as his voice. "Sorry to intrude on you like this, but I've been trying to catch you for some time."

"You left the messages on my answering machine?"

"Sure did."

"And you've ridden your bike out here how many times now?"

"This makes four."

"It's a long way."

He shrugged and fiddled with his cap. "I'm off for ten days and don't have much else to do. Met the lady who works for you the other morning. She was nice. Pretty protective of you, in case you'd like to know. She talked to me in Spanish. I'm not as good as I'd like, but it's important to keep in practice. I use it in my work sometimes. I'm a marine biologist at the A&M Oceanography School. We're charting crustacean life up and down the bay."

"What can I do for you, Mr. Dooley?" J.J. cut off whatever else the boy was planning to say.

"No, sir. Dooley's my first name. I think you knew my mother, a long time ago. In Baton Rouge. Her name's Brenda."

Something knocked at J.J.'s chest, a sudden thump, before his mind clicked in. "Brenda Thomas?"

"Yes, sir."

He was conscious of a long pause before he said, "How is Brenda?"

Dooley shrugged. "She's doing good. Mom's always doing good."

J.J. nodded.

"Last time I talked to her she was in Key West. Always manages to be around the water. She was living with a friend, doing aromatherapy. She sells herbal medicines, too, but she can practically do that out of her car, you know, wherever she goes."

J.J. took out his pipe and lit it. He sat down and motioned for Dooley to sit. "Did Brenda send you to find me?"

"No, sir. This is my doing. She didn't even want to tell me your name. Said she'd tell me when I turned twenty-three, which was how old she was when she had me. I started looking for you in Baton Rouge. The people there remembered you all right, but nobody knew where you settled after. . ."

"Hold on!" J.J. jumped up. "I'm not sure what you're getting at."

"Well, sir. I believe you're my father." The boy was undaunted. "I saw your name and that picture in the paper, congratulations by the way, and I called the golf course for your number and then got into a directory that matched it with this address and, well, here I am."

J.J. willed himself to stay cool. "You want a beer, Dooley?"

"Yes, sir."

"Why don't you call me Captain," J.J. said. "Everyone else does." He walked over to the bucket where beers were iced down and brought up two at the same time that Woody came up the stairs.

"Hey, Dooley," Woody said.

"Hey, Woody." The boy smiled and extended his hand.

"You playin' with the big boys tonight?" Woody asked.

Dooley looked at J.J.

"You play poker, Dooley?" J.J. asked.

"A little."

✢

J.J. could tell a lot about a person by the quality of his poker game. Dooley made no apologies, no bluffs, no distracting conversation. He started slow and dropped back when he had a questionable hand. As the night progressed, he got a little braver. J.J. noticed the way he watched the cards and used his head. He was a sharp kid and mild mannered.. But he's not mine, J.J. thought. This is a scam.

When the game was over, J.J. insisted on taking him back to town in the pickup. It was too late for a bike ride, and a good chance to put this visitation to rest.

"I don't know what you want, Dooley, but I'm not your man."

"I figured you might think that, so I've got something I'd like to leave with you. You take a look at it, and you can call me or not. If you don't call, I'll let it be." He fumbled in his jacket pocket and came up with an envelope on which he wrote his telephone number before handing it to J.J.

Back at the cabin, J.J. opened the envelope.

Dear J.J.

If you get this, I'm sorry. I never intended you to know about Dooley, but when you have a kid, you don't realize they're going to grow up some day and want some - thing you didn't want for them. This boy wants to know his father. In case you're in doubt, here's a copy of his birth certificate. Now you count back and you think back and you'll remember I wasn't sleeping with anyone else that summer. We had a good time, didn't we? There's a pic - ture of us I gave him, so he'd have something to go by, but I'm hoping he won't find you because, after all this time, it's going to be some kind of shock. He's a good boy. My parents helped raise him and are sending him to college so this isn't about money. He's never given us trouble and he's brought joy into our lives. Maybe he'll do the same for you, wherever you might find yourself.

Brenda

P. S. Remember how we liked that song, "Tom Dooley?" If he was a girl, I was going to name her "Delta Dawn."

17

Rose remembered writing a report on the Plains Indians when she was growing up in north Texas, sixty-something years ago. They were nomads, those Indians, and moved their camps with the seasons. When the old ones could no longer manage to walk long distances, they lay on a travois and were pulled along by a horse. At some point in the journey, the old ones often elected to roll quietly to the side of the trail. It was an accepted way of death. As a child, she hadn't much liked the idea. As a grown woman, she didn't think about it. Approaching her own end, she found it simple and appealing.

She had been sick before, but it had never taken so long to recover. This was normal, the doctors said. Pneumonia at her age, given the condition of her lungs, was no small thing. She should count her blessings she was still alive, they said. *Oprah* had a show on giving thanks. Every day one was supposed to wake up and find at least three things to be thankful for. Jesse, J.J., and Maison Rouge were what Rose came up with. That was it—same three things almost every day. Sometimes she included her money, or her house, or the fact that she wasn't bald. Not yet at least.

She had shamed Jesse into working for her this summer, when he was ready to be back at school. But she wanted him around and didn't care if she stole three months of his life. That's how it gets when you're old and sick. She'd seen it before. Many times. The world gets smaller and smaller, so that all that remains at the end is a tiny circle with you in the center. She frowned and consulted Nate.

"If you're taking three months of his life, you owe him something," Nate told her.

"I'm paying him."

"I'm not talking money. I'm talking recovery. Get well, Rose, if you can."

She groaned. His advice was always sensible, and demanding.

✥

"I'm putting myself in your hands," she told Jesse. "I want you to get with my doctor, work out a program of care, and let's get on with it." 181

"Whoa," he staggered backward, making a show of being thrown off balance. "I thought you wanted errands—a driver and a go-fer."

"Those will be secondary. Getting me stronger is your first priority. Think you're up to that?"

His usually playful face got serious. "You're not discouraged?"

"Of course. Aren't you? All that time you invested, just to see me fall out like a ninny. But you're determined to be a doctor and, believe it or not, I still have some things I want to do."

"How much are you willing to change?" he asked.

"What else do I have to change?"

"Your outlook."

Rose raised her eyebrows and said nothing.

"There's anecdotal evidence that people with optimistic outlooks recover better than those without."

"And you don't think I'm optimistic?"

"I think you take pride in saying the worst before someone else does."

She sat quietly. "This is true, although no one but my husband and my mother ever dared tell me so. Are you going to preach sunshine and roses every day?"

"I hadn't planned to."

"Good. Because that's not what I want. I want a regimen, and a kick in the rear if I'm lagging. And a little encouragement on the side."

"You want a personal trainer."

She brightened. "That's more like it. Oprah has one. Why not me? Now go work up a plan for me before I change my mind."

Who am I kidding? she wondered. She got tired walking from the bed to the chair. Getting a bath exhausted her. What did she think Jesse could accomplish in three months? And wasn't she going to regret giving him this responsibility? He'd take it too damned seriously, and she'd spend her last days trying to live up to his expectations. She picked up her crossword puzzle in an effort to distract herself. *Miracle worker* was the clue. Seven letters. Sullivan, she tried, for the teacher. Too many letters. Bancroft, the actress. Still too many letters. Doctor. Not enough letters. Healer. Still not enough. Trainer, she thought, still pondering the morning's conversation. She filled in the spaces, checking connecting vertical words. Was this supposed to be a sign? She sighed, wishing she could renege.

Jesse insisted on taking her to the specialist's office in a wheelchair. It was mortifying, but like using a bedpan or being examined in private places, the mortification didn't last long. There are lots of wheelchairs out and about these days, she discovered, especially in medical offices. Still, she had him wrap her foot so it appeared she had a temporary injury. Together they had a conference with the doctor, who was businesslike.

"You're getting along in years, Mrs. Parrish. Given your history of smoking, I'd say you were pretty lucky. Your heart's reasonably healthy. Blood pressure's a little high, but I don't detect significant blockage in the arteries."

Jesse asked about her medications and was given a brusque answer that he thought was intended to establish who was in charge.

"I'll schedule a follow-up chest X-ray in six weeks," the doctor said. "She should be clear by then. You need me to look at that foot?" he turned to Rose, who shook her head quickly.

"Lucky," she grumbled, when he had left the room. "I'm more interesting to them when I'm at death's door."

Ready to get back home after the doctor's office, Rose was irritated when Jesse stopped at Moody Gardens, helped her into the wheelchair again, and proceeded to walk her through marine and flower exhibits. After she stopped protesting, she found it delightful. She hadn't been out and around like that in years. Jesse maneuvered her through the walkways, reaching down to make comments in her ear from behind, like an individual tour guide. People stepped aside and held doors and smiled at the two of them.

When they got home, Pearl had set up a temporary bed, with oxygen, downstairs.

"Whose idea was this?" Rose snapped.

"Your trainer's," Jesse said.

"You're taking this too seriously."

"It's the only way to take it," he said, looking authoritative. "Get comfortable now," he told her, "I've got something I want to show you." He disappeared for a few minutes and came back with some pictures and a plastic model. "These are lungs."

She shuddered and turned her face aside.

"I want you to get acquainted with them. Picture your own— which are pretty much like this, except less pink, less elastic."

"Seen better days," Rose grumbled.

"True. But, they're going to improve with everything we do. I want you to focus on that."

Rose frowned and nodded while Jesse outlined a plan of exercise, diet, and visualization that he promised would take her back to better than she'd been the day they flew the kite. He'd take her vitals every morning and they could chart them together. He planned to press the doctor about a new medication for improving lung function and wanted to talk with him about changing her blood pressure medicine. If he'll give a lowly student the time of day. There were breathing exercises she had to do on a silly little machine with a ball at the bottom. She wasn't going to be allowed to sit around, he declared. He wanted to go out in the afternoons to places she used to go, so she could show him Galveston.

"I need to be home for *Oprah*," she told him.

⁙

Three weeks later she was measurably better. But Rose, who had never exerted herself, except in the pursuit of pleasure, was tired of what she called "the grind." Jesse made her watch films about superhuman athletic feats. He brought her stories of people over eighty who were still conducting symphonies, creating art, teaching, changing the world. She accused him of trying to make her feel guilty. He insisted he was trying to inspire her. They argued and kept on.

"I'll be glad when you go back to school and leave me alone," she told him.

"Me too," he answered. "And I'm not planning to specialize in Geriatrics."

⁙

J.J. stopped by, bringing flowers and scotch.

"Fix yourself a drink, Captain," she said. "I'm on the wagon."

He raised his eyebrows in question.

"It doesn't taste worth a damn since I've been sick. As Jesse would say, 'Isn't that the pits?'" She patted the sofa. "Come tell me how things are going."

184

He told her they'd broken ground on Maison Rouge, that the press release would come out in Sunday's paper, and asked what she thought about Labor Day the following year for an opening date. "It might be ready sooner," he said, "but we'd be pushing our luck to set it too early. A lot can go wrong."

Rose pouted for a moment. She'd hoped for Memorial Day, or surely the Fourth of July. Then she asked if he'd decided about a successor trustee, and he fidgeted.

"What's the matter, Captain?"

"Nothing." He fingered his beard.

Rose leaned forward. "We haven't talked for a while. Is something wrong?"

He let out his breath. "Not really."

She motioned toward the bar and he fixed himself another drink.

"How's Jesse doing?" he asked.

"I guess I told you he's going back to med school. Which is a blessing because he's driving me crazy."

He laughed politely and waited.

She smiled. "When you get my age you get to thinking the upcoming generation isn't worth a damn, and then someone comes along and puts the shine back on things." She leaned forward and touched J.J. on the arm. "This boy feels like kin. I plan to make provisions for him, but it's my opinion you can spoil someone, giving them too much, too soon, Captain. Do you think providing for Jesse will take away his incentive?"

"I don't know, Rose."

She sat up. "Well, that's a first. You always have an answer."

He took another deep breath and let it out noisily. "I'm short on answers these days."

He got up to leave and, uncharacteristically, leaned down to kiss her cheek. "Check with you on Sunday."

As he walked out, she called to him. "When you're ready to talk . . ."

He nodded and waved a thank you. She'd never seen the captain so out of sorts. Maybe he was sick, she thought. Or could it be a woman?

⁂

She had a list of things to talk with Jesse about the next morning. After the exercises, and the blood pressure check, and the chart, she had him sit down.

"Now be still a minute, because I have some things to cover and I don't want to have to repeat myself. First, I want you to figure out how much money you need to finish school and get established, and I'm going to take care of it."

He shook his head in disbelief. "You can't do that."

"Let's get down to it, Jesse dear. I can do just about anything I want. You have problems with money? Tell me what you need."

He sank down to sit beside her. "This is . . ."

"What do you owe to date?"

"About $50,000."

"And how many years for a specialty?"

"Two, four, eight. It depends."

"We can handle it," she beamed. "You know, I used to say I wanted to go to my grave proud, witty, and brave. But I've changed my tune. What I'm going for now is the grandmotherly approach. I've already stuck my nose in your business unbeknownst to you." She told him about her visit to the school and her embarrassment when turned down. "But they didn't forget me. They're wondering if I'd like to set up an educational trust." She fumbled in her drawer and pulled out a glossy photo. "This is the award they want to give me. It looks like a cross between a Rodin and an Oscar." She dropped the papers on the table in exaggerated disgust. "My name would, of course, be inscribed."

She leaned forward and patted him on the knee. "I don't

need to go through the school. You're the only one there I give a damn about."

He sat, speechless.

Rose consulted her list. "If you're feeling in any way beholden, don't. There are a couple of things I need you to do for me. First, I want a pill. I want something I can take when it's time, so I can go quietly and not wake up." She held up her hands. "Don't shake your head. This is perfectly sane. By the time people are voting for president on the Internet, they'll be able to control their own deaths. At least I hope that's the direction we're going. There's entirely too much prolonged care going on, keeping people alive instead of letting nature take its course."

"The Hippocratic oath is a promise to support life, Rose."

"It's also a promise to live with purity and holiness. How many doctors take that one seriously? I'm not asking you to give me a fatal injection. I simply want something like a cyanide pill at my disposal, like spies get when they're going behind enemy lines."

Jesse closed his eyes and shook his head.

"We'll talk more about this later. I have another request."

"Which is?" he asked. He didn't really want to know.

"Captain Broussard. He was here to visit me yesterday and something's bothering him. I want you to find out what it is."

"Rose, I hardly know the man, and he doesn't like me. He avoids me, in fact."

She waved her hand. "I don't care how you do it, just see what you can find out. Now, help me onto this treadmill and I'll try for three minutes."

18

In pychology's hierarchy of stressful life events, a sudden financial gain is rated equivalent to sudden financial loss. Jesse had always read that as a Puritan exaggeration—until it happened to him. He slept fitfully now and jerked awake every few hours, like he used to on nights before a test. He wanted to feel good about Rose's offer. He did feel good about Rose's offer, but she had attached some big strings, expecting him to be a cross between Jack Kevorkian and *Magnum P.I.*

He took off for the beach on his bike. The late summer day was overcast; the sky, pewter. All week thunderstorms had circled the area. They gathered mid-morning and played out through the afternoon, moving east. Sometimes it cleared, and the sun broke through for a few hours, then the next cell would develop, and the process repeated itself. The water was choppy and uninviting, but the air was cool when he decided to venture out to west beach.

An hour later, when the sun came out, Jesse found himself pedaling in an outdoor sauna. Dripping with perspiration, worn from fighting the wind, he stopped at Kelly's Barbecue. The place was dark and the counter deserted. Ceiling fans stirred the air, and open windows provided a warm cross breeze.

"Hot enough for you?" an oversized woman with curly red hair greeted him.

Jesse asked for a glass of water and a large Coke. The water wasn't bottled and tasted salty, but he downed it anyway, then the Coke, while the woman studied his T-shirt.

"Haven't turned on the AC yet. It was pretty cool 'til just a while ago."

Jesse nodded.

"You a med student?"

"Yes'm."

"What do you think about using wild oregano to cure *can - dida?*"

Jesse laughed, "We haven't gotten to that chapter yet, but if I were you, I'd check with a homeopathic doctor."

"A homo what?" She held his eye for a long moment, then laughed. She was missing a tooth toward the back. "Isn't that the damnedest name? Hope that's not what you're studyin'."

"No, ma'am," Jesse said.

"So what brings you out this way?"

"Exercise."

"You want something to eat? I got the best brisket on the island."

Jesse declined. "How far down do the houses go?" he asked.

"You lookin' for someone in particular?"

"Nope."

"Another four or five miles."

Clouds had covered the sun again, and Jesse rode on. The highway stretched out like a slender ribbon with beach and some fine homes to the left, flat land, farms, campgrounds, and subdivisions to the right: Sea Isle, Isla del Sol, Terramar. When the rain came, he turned around and sought refuge once again with Mrs. Kelly. This time, he ordered a hot sandwich.

"Figured you'd stop back by. Most everyone does. A man needs to eat." She threw him a towel from behind the bar, "Bet you're glad the AC isn't on now. Huh?" As Jesse dried off, she kept up a steady stream of talk while she piled a bun high with sliced beef, ladled on barbecue sauce, and slapped onion slices, pickles, and chips on the side.

Jesse ate and nodded while she told him how she'd been there for thirty years, how her husband had been electrocuted in a fishing accident, how she almost left after Alicia. Hell, if west beach had a mayor, she'd run. She knew everyone out here, she told him, 'cept the tourists.

"You know a Captain Broussard?" Jesse asked.

Her eyes danced. "Sure enough. I'd like to know him better, but he's a quiet one. How do you know the captain?"

"Someone told me he ran a fishing charter," Jesse fumbled for an answer.

"I think he's just about put that to rest. Seems he's got business in town, nowadays. I see his truck going in that direction nearly every day, and his neighbor tells me he's building a new house."

"Is he married?"

"The captain? No way. I don't think he has a mind for women."

"You mean. . .?"

Mrs. Kelly laughed. "That he's a homo? Well, I never thought of that. I'd say no, though it's hard to tell these days, but I wouldn't be one to start a rumor. Not that rumor, anyways. They say he's got a little Mescan girlie that cleans for him and provides other favors."

Jesse fit the last bite of sandwich into his mouth.

Mrs. Kelly leaned across the counter and took on a conspiratorial tone. "There was someone else stopped in here a few weeks back lookin' for the captain. 'Bout your age. Sweet-faced boy. Soft voice. Said it was important. Y'all friends?"

"No, ma'am. I was just looking to put together a fishing trip." Jesse wiped his mouth, paid his check, and told his hostess goodbye.

"You come back now," she waved.

Traveling with the wind made the trip home easy. Jesse pedaled and let his mind play with Mrs. Kelly's information. Were there other people who'd be willing to talk about the captain? Could he find out anything on the Internet? Was playing sleuth sleazy? He didn't have any obligation to the captain, and he owed Rose a lot.

He wished there was someone to talk to—someone to bounce things off of. His dolphin rescue buddy would listen, he thought, but they didn't know each other that well yet. "Hey, Dooley, how's this for a Sunday night movie? My roommate turned me in on a false charge to make himself look good, and I got suspended. My brother's headed down the drain, and my father expects me to bail the family out, but I've just about given up on them. I've definitely given up on girls until I get some money, but that shouldn't be too long because I've ingratiated myself to a rich old lady who wants me to get her a final sleeping pill."

He thought about Rose and the quotes she kept feeding him. Shakespeare: *To thine own self be true;* Thoreau: *Whoso would be a man would be a non-conformist;* The Bible: *Don't hide your light under a bushel.* He personally ascribed to the Second Law of Thermodynamics: *All systems tend toward disorder.* He dreamed that night of a naked red-haired girl on a white horse. As he reached up to her, the girl turned wrinkled, the horse dropped a load on his doorstep, and Pearl appeared, shaking her finger.

✛

Early the next morning Pearl let Jesse in the back door. He told her he needed to boot up Rose's computer.

"She's not eating her vegetables," Pearl complained.

"How about the protein?"

"Says she craves dessert."

"No desserts for a while."

Pearl sighed and turned to go. "I baked an apple crisp. If she can't eat it, you'd better have some."

On the 'net he found county public records showing a recent deed recorded in the captain's name for a piece of property on west beach. In the newspaper archives he found a write-up of a golf tournament. It didn't appear the captain had money problems. What else do people his age have problems with? Maybe he was sick. If he was, he wouldn't tell Rose. Jesse thought if he could see him, he might be able to pick up a clue by the look of his eyes, his skin, his odor.

He had talked Rose into putting in a ramp adjacent to the back steps so he could take her out regularly in the wheelchair. In spite of much complaining, she seemed to enjoy the outings. That afternoon he took her for a drive by the Maison Rouge building site she'd been wanting to see. It wasn't far, located in a warehouse district, across the channel from Pelican Island. A couple of bulldozers were working at demolition, and workmen in hard hats were moving rubble. He drove around the perimeter and stopped in front of a sign:

Future home of Maison Rouge
Opening Fall 2001

Rose interlocked her fingers and studied the message like it was profound. "Lovely. Isn't it? I think we should take pictures to get a record of its progress. I showed you the plans, didn't I?"

Jesse nodded. She had shown him the plans. It was a huge project. He couldn't imagine how much it was going to cost and couldn't help wondering if there'd be enough left over for him. Should have given her a number when she asked how much he needed. Something his father used to say about answering the door when opportunity knocks. He needed to call his father, he knew, but Rose was a priority right now. He looked around for the captain's truck.

"I thought Captain Broussard might be here."

"So did I," Rose said. "He'd be pleased to see me up and around. Maybe I'll call and invite him over. See if he's still out of sorts."

"I was thinking, he might be sick."

"I'd thought that myself," she frowned.

"It's the sort of thing he wouldn't want to talk about."

"That makes sense." Jesse couldn't tell what she was thinking, but wondered for the hundredth time exactly what she and the captain had going.

⁘

A few days later, back at the site with a disposable camera, Jesse had his eye to the viewfinder and was intent on getting a shot of the cleared lots and remaining structures when he felt a hand on his back. Jumping around in surprise, he found a short, muscular man in his face.

"You got a reason to be here?"

"I'm taking pictures for the owner," Jesse explained.

"And who would that be?"

"Mrs. Parrish."

The man chewed on a toothpick and stared at him. "Why don't you come with me a minute," he said finally, and led him over to where the captain stood talking with two other men. When he saw them, he broke off his conversation and came over, hand extended.

"Martin," he said.

"He says he's taking pictures for Mrs. Parrish," the tough guy said. "That okay?"

The captain introduced him to Bobby Calhoun and invited Jesse to look around, then excused himself to continue his talk with the engineer and the construction manager.

"Any kin to Nicky Martin?" Calhoun asked. "Used to run numbers in Kemah?"

"No," Jesse said.

"You work for the old lady?"

"I'm in medical school. I'm just helping her out this summer."

"She's a funny one. Ever see that Mary Jane necklace of hers?"

Jesse shook his head. "You must have the wrong person."

"No. I swear to God, when I met her she was wearin' bright green leaves all around her neck."

Jesse, certain he was mistaken, laughed. "So it's okay if I come back from time to time?"

"I'm not here all the time," Calhoun said, "but I'll know you when I see you. If J.J. says you're okay, it's cool with me."

"You work for J.J.?"

"Nope. Spent some time with him back in the late '60s, and then last December he brings this deal to my boss, and my boss says to keep an eye on it. There's people in town don't like this development. Better to be safe than sorry. You take care now, Doc. Hope we don't need you. Lots of accidents on a building site, you know." Calhoun walked away, his huge triceps bulging from a Bowflex T-shirt.

Jesse took a few more pictures and studied the captain from a distance. Wearing a hard hat and sunglasses, motioning across the site, he looked fit and enthusiastic, more authentic than he did in his double-breasted blazer, smoking his pipe.

✛

When Rose sent Jesse on an errand in north Houston on a Friday, he decided it was time to clear things with his dad. They hadn't talked for months, and he knew he was expected to make the first move. He wasn't looking forward to it, didn't relish the questions and doubts he expected to hear, but once he cut himself free financially, life would be easier for everyone. He called before he left Galveston, but the line was busy. He called when he got to his first destination, and it was still busy. His dad was probably working online from home. Jesse headed for the house, found the door unlocked and wandered in.

The living room was surprisingly clean—no papers, clothes, or food containers strewn around. He wandered into the kitchen, where clean dishes were stacked in a drainer. He opened the refrigerator. No furry, indistinguishable dishes; no dried up half sandwiches; no open, dead sodas. The milk hadn't expired. There was a bowl of fruit on the counter. He picked up an apple and wandered down the hall to see what other miracles had evolved. The bathroom smelled fresh; Jerry's bed was made.

"What the hell?" A woman with one towel wrapped around her body and another around her head screamed at him from the end of the hall.

"Excuse me," he said and backed down the hall.

She reached back to pull the bedroom door shut and then came toward him. "I bet you're Jesse. I saw your picture. I'm Serline. Sorry I can't shake hands but . . ."

"Yeah," Jesse said, not knowing where to look.

"Your dad's—uh—in the shower." Her eyes, smudged with black, looked disturbing. "Can you come back in a few minutes?" she said.

He went to the corner store and called.

His dad answered. "You here in town? Good. There's someone I want you to meet."

✢

"This is a surprise," Jesse said, sitting in his dad's chair. His father sat on the sofa, eyes pinned on Serline, one hand on her knee. Streaked blond hair hung down her back in limp strands. She had put on lipstick and cleaned up her eyes, which were sending a silent thank you.

"Yeah. I should have told you, but it happened pretty fast and. . . I would have gotten around to it." His dad fumbled with an excuse.

"The house looks a lot nicer with a woman living here," Jesse offered.

Serline smiled. His dad patted her knee. "She's a great person to have around," he said.

When Jesse told him he'd won a scholarship that would cover the rest of his schooling so he didn't need money anymore, his dad wanted to know if rent and gas were covered, too, and whose car was that anyway and was he sure he'd be okay and wasn't that great. There was no need to answer. Babbling with relief, the man was showing more emotion than Jesse had seen since the naked night of beer and tears.

"How's Jerry with this, Dad?" Jesse asked, motioning generally around the house.

Serline spoke up then. "He's got a job," she said softly.

"Doing what?"

"He's a bank teller."

Jesse was incredulous. "Didn't he have to take a drug test?"

Serline smiled and looked at her hands.

"Serline got him some stuff at the health food store," his dad said. "He drank it all one weekend, and she had him running around the block and drinking gallons of water and. . ."

"Cleansing his system," she finished his sentence.

"Didn't I tell you she was great?" His dad looked adoring.

"So you think he'll stay clean?"

"I talked to him," Serline said. "Told him he couldn't be a bum all his life. I told him twenty years ago I went down that road, did stuff he's doing and more he hasn't even thought about yet, and to take my word for it—it wasn't anywhere he wanted to go. Told him if he'd get a job, we'd help him get a car, and he could even smoke his pot here at the house because it's safer that way."

"Do you think he can swing it, Dad?" He turned to his father.

"We just never gave him a chance. Serline's helped me see that he's smart."

"Smart enough to learn to be a teller. Not so smart he can figure out how to walk out of the bank with some of its money, I hope."

"I'm ashamed of you, Jesse."

"I'm ashamed of myself," he agreed and made some quick excuses. He had to get out of there and think in a different setting. His father's hound-dog adoration and his brother's sudden reformation were too much, not to mention the lady Serline, who was doing some kind of Mary Poppins act in a house he'd given up on.

19

Elena came to work at J.J.'s dressed in jeans or shorts, her hair mostly covered by a cap, with a pony tail pulled through the circular space in back. Not until after she was satisfied with the cabin, inside and out, did she pull a worn leather bag from her truck and disappear into the bathroom. When she exited, she was striking. She usually wore a soft, simple dress and sandals. Sometimes she piled her long hair up, sometimes she braided it, sometimes it hung loose down her back, and smelled like fresh flowers. Her complexion was as flawless as the models on television, and she managed to accent her eyes and cheekbones in a way that didn't look made up. Her mother managed a beauty shop, she told J.J., and there were always products to experiment with. J.J. never failed to appreciate the game of transformation she played for him. But their connection didn't begin, or continue, on anything as simple as looks.

He was very clear on what he didn't like in a woman—helplessness, silliness, demands for reassurance. Elena was serious by nature and self-sufficient. He remembered the first day she came to work for him. He'd gone out fishing and came home late in the afternoon to find her working on the arm of the toilet.

"This thing, she's running," she told him.

"I know."

"That wastes the water."

"I can handle it."

She looked sideways at him, her fingers fiddling with the chain. "Where I come from, *el agua es precioso*."

I don't need instructions from this girl, especially in Spanish, he thought, and headed back outside to clean his catch. A half hour later she came down to tell him she was leaving and the toilet was fixed, but it was going to start running again soon. If he'd give her the money, she'd get the stuff needed to fix it right. He told her he'd pick up a ball kit and fix it himself.

The next time she came, she reset a cabinet hinge that had come loose. The next time, she said she wanted to fix a window that wouldn't stay open. When he told her he'd take care of it, her disappointment was visible.

"I don't expect you to fix things around here," he told her.

"But I'm good at it. I keep that truck going," she motioned to the Chevy pickup outside, "long past its life."

He bought some sash cord at the hardware store and managed to stick around the next time she came.

"Why are you not fishing?" she asked.

"I don't fish every day."

"You always fish when I come," she said, cutting through his evasion.

"Thought we'd try to fix that window."

She beamed as if he'd given her the day off with pay.

A few minutes later, she watched intently as he took the cover panel off the window. Then she moved in beside him, reaching down to retrieve the broken cord. "I can do this," she said.

He stepped back but stuck around to watch her work silently. Unusual, he thought, a woman who doesn't have to talk.

"You like fish, Elena?"

She looked up, surprised. "To catch or to eat?"

"To eat. I'm cooking redfish tonight. Would you like to stay and have dinner?"

She smiled.

"It's a thank you for fixing my house up—for doing more than you need to."

"You could give a present, *un regalo,*" she told him, eyes dancing.

"Or I could fix you redfish veracruzano."

"Okay."

After dinner they had walked along the beach. In the moonlight, a phosphorescent glow rose from the crests of the breakers. J.J. smoked his pipe, and Elena, shoes in hand, tiptoed along the most recent selvage of the water's path. From time to time she looked over at him, smiled, then studied her course, placed one foot gracefully in front of the other, and stretched her arms out for balance, still smiling. He wondered. Back at the cabin she turned on the outside shower to rinse the sand from her feet before going upstairs. Then, with no word or sideways glance, she stepped out of her clothes and into the shower's spray. She closed her eyes, laid her head back, and let it wash over her face. After a minute he handed her a towel from the line, and she wrapped herself in it.

"Would you like that I stay?" she asked.

That had been almost two years ago. Soon she was coming every Thursday, but she continued to work for Donnie at the Boat Rack the other weekdays and half-a-day on Saturday. J.J. took her out on his boat sometimes and cooked for her regularly. At her suggestion, they refinished the cabin furniture, working side by side, communicating in silences, smiles, nods, a finger wagged "no," a hand beckoning, "come see."

She liked old American movies. Romances. Audrey Hepburn. He ordered *Breakfast at Tiffany's, Funny Face, Roman Holiday, Sabrina,* and *My Fair Lady* from a catalogue and surprised her with them one day.

"Now I can really learn," she clapped her hands in surprise.

"Learn what?"

"What to do when I don't know what to say. You see how good she is? Always *graciosa.*"

Elena shared a trailer with a girl who was a waitress, and she watched the girl's child at night. She saved almost everything she made and rode a bus for twelve hours every three months to visit her boys. She told J.J. her husband had been nineteen when they married, good-looking, and believing he was smart enough to get rich quick. They had gone to Guadalajara, against her parents' wishes, and they lived and worked for some rich people, and soon they had a house and a car, and then she found out about the drugs. His job was delivering drugs. She'd gone home when she got pregnant and he'd never seen his sons, never tried, never sent money. Someone had told her he was in Mexico City, maybe jail, she thought.

"I trust you," she told J.J., "because you have kind eyes and you like simple things and because of the fingernails," she said, touching his hand, "always so smooth and clean." She told him she thought the love act was important, because it was known that a woman without a man begins to lose the oil in her skin and dries up before her time. She never asked him to increase her pay, but he did.

❖

J.J. remembered Dooley saying he'd stopped at the house one day and talked to Elena. He said they'd spoken in English and in Spanish. She couldn't have forgotten. When J.J. asked why she hadn't mentioned it, she'd shrugged. She knew he didn't like people in his business.

"Did he tell you why he wanted to find me?"

"Yes." She rubbed her finger against a spot on the table. "He says you may be family. That is true?"

J.J. nodded. "Apparently so."

"So why is it necessary he comes looking for you?"

Her frown spoke disapproval, but J.J. wasn't going to try to vindicate himself. He needed to talk to Dooley and see where they were going with this thing. He'd ask him to keep a lid on it, too. The boy was guileless. No telling who he'd told about searching for a long lost father.

❖

J.J. had tried to call Dooley after he read Brenda's letter, but there was no answer and no machine. He called every day for a week before he went back to the house. No one answered the door, but beside the mailbox he found a well-crafted wooden box. On the box was painted a large arrow, pointing down. J.J. looked around to see if anyone was watching before lifting the lid to find a spiral notebook and a handful of pencils. So it wasn't a joke, after all. The book was full of dated messages. He flipped to the end, where the first clean page was dated July 5 and said:

> *I'm working in the field until August 18. Leave a message and I'll get back.*

J.J. read the messages.

> *Your apartment was serviced 7/10. Acme Pest Control.*
> *Hi Dooley, The PTA cookbook you ordered is in. We'll bring it over when you get back. Sara and Susan*
> *Dooley, End of semester party at Zapatas Thursday 17th. If you get back early, be there. Cathy*
> *Surf's up. Call me when you get back. Doc*
> *DT, Mammal rescue classes rescheduled for the last weekend in August. We need you. TNT*

J.J. added his own message: *Dooley, I'd like to talk. Call me. J.J. Broussard*

On a Tuesday afternoon in early August, J.J. called Rose and arranged to stop by for a visit. He found that she had rediscovered her taste for scotch.

"That's a good sign," he told her.

"I've been diligent these past months, Captain," she told him. "Don't believe I've ever worked so hard at anything as I have at recovering from that last setback."

"Have you decided what you're going to do for Martin?" he asked.

"It involves you."

"I'd just as soon stay out of it."

"I don't know what you have against the boy, Captain, but I ask you to rethink it. I've set aside $200,000 to cover his education and get him established as a physician. He doesn't know how much. I simply told him if he was cautious, it would be sufficient."

"I'd say so."

"You're the administrator after my death. He's not to know how much is there. That way he won't be wasteful."

Her presumption that he was there to do her bidding suddenly irritated him. Martin irritated him. "And if I refuse to act as administrator?"

"You wouldn't," she said.

He remembered a time when she would have cajoled, but they were apparently past that.

"Is there a problem?" she asked.

"It's your money, Rose, and there's plenty of it."

"Then what's eating at you, Captain?" She leaned forward, "Is there anything I can do?"

"No."

Her voice had softened now, and she put a hand out to touch his arm. "Are you ill?"

"No, Rose." He covered her hand with his. "I'm fine. Busy

with the building, that's all." He wasn't about to tell her he was dealing with a son he'd never counted on. Not until he had a handle on it.

✢

When Dooley called, J.J. was checking the weather channel. A storm system had been centered over south Texas for the past week, with high wind alerts and intermittent thunderstorms. The coast guard had spotted some water spouts in Galveston Bay and was issuing standard warnings.

"This is Dooley," he said, almost breathless. "Just got in. Got your message."

"Did you hit bad weather?"

"Sure did. It was pretty exciting. So when can we talk?" Dooley's voice was so open and inviting, it embarrassed J.J., reminded him of early dating days, calling a girl on the phone, hearing her soft approval leaking through the receiver.

"Dinner tomorrow? I'll pick you up about six."

"That's great," Dooley said.

J.J. tried to imagine the boy doing a victory dance. You don't search for someone for years, he thought, and finally catch up with them without having some price you want them to pay.

✢

They went to Mario's for dinner. It served good food, slightly off the tourist path. It also had high-backed booths that would work for a private conversation, and the waiters didn't hover. J.J. had brought Rose here often. She liked the opera music and the chilled lemon liqueur they brought gratis after the meal.

"Pavarotti," Dooley said, sliding into his seat, nodding toward the speakers.

"You like opera?"

"I don't know opera. But this guy's great. Sometimes he hits notes that make my eyes sting."

J.J. nodded, wondering where they were headed.

"I make you uncomfortable, don't I?" Dooley asked.

"Let me put it this way," J.J. said. "I had no idea you existed, and now, not only have you appeared, but you tracked me down and know things about me I've worked damn hard to get past."

Dooley smiled. "I've wanted to know my father all my life. Then I learned you'd been in prison and I thought maybe I should give it up."

"But you kept looking," J.J. added.

"Well, Mother always talked nice about you. And I read the newspaper articles from back when it happened, and they painted you as a regular guy who'd made a mistake."

"A serious mistake," J.J. said.

"I talked with a couple of people you'd screwed. They still acted mad, but I could tell they carried it around like a trophy. One man told me you got his beer stein collection worth more than $5,000. But he had it insured for $8,500. So, he collected his insurance, took a trip to Vienna on the money, and came back with a good start on a new collection. And there was a woman who lost her grandmother's silver who called you 'a riverboat rascal.'"

"That made you proud?"

"There are worse things. Something about the way she said it sounded . . ." His explanation began to drain off.

"What do you want, Dooley?"

"To know you."

He was unwavering. "I'm not a very chummy guy," J.J. said.

"You like the ocean, don't you? Why don't we go fishing? How about Thursday? I can be at your place at seven."

"You're going to ride out on your bike?"

"Sure."

"Make it eight."

J.J. lit his pipe, and Dooley excused himself and headed for the bathroom. Relieved to be alone, he called for the check and busied himself verifying the bill and figuring the tip. Dooley definitely made him uncomfortable. This wasn't how people he knew handled themselves. Everything out there on the surface. And now a buddy fishing trip? Jesus!

He moved toward the front desk to pay. Dooley was standing in the foyer talking to Jesse Martin. He waved him over and started an introduction.

"I know Captain Broussard," Jesse said, looking like someone who'd taken a bite of fish and found a bone.

"Doc was in my mammal rescue class last June," Dooley said. "How do you guys know each other?"

"We have a mutual friend," J.J. said, and Jesse nodded.

"This guy has good stories about medical stuff," Dooley told J.J. "I almost went pre-med, was a biology major, but I have too much salt water in my veins." He turned back to Jesse then. "Hey, maybe you'd like to come fishing with us on Thursday."

"I have a lot to do before classes start."

"Oh, come on," Dooley urged.

"Yeah, why don't you join us," J.J. said, hoping to sound sincere. What he wanted was a buffer, someone to fill the spaces between him and Dooley for those six hours. And he might as well get to know Jesse better if they were going to be locked together in this thing with Rose.

"I'm glad he's coming with us," Dooley commented when Jesse was gone. "He needs to stop thinking about being suspended."

"Suspended?" J.J. asked.

"He's pretty sure he'll get back in."

J.J. wondered how much Rose knew about this.

⁜

Dooley and Jesse arrived at the cabin at eight on Thursday morning. J.J. heard them pull in. They had met before seven to bike out together. They were talking about having the road to themselves, about the tail wind, and the awesome sunrise. Their energy was palpable. J.J., who was on his second cup of coffee, was surprised to find them on time. Kids, he thought. Hard bellies. So full of themselves! Don't have arthritis, calluses, knees that go out. Still think anything's possible. Lucky for them, he reminded himself, and stepped out on the deck.

"Hey, J.J.," Dooley called up.

"Hey," he answered.

Elena had come up as they were leaving and Dooley asked if she wanted to come. She had shook her head, embarrassed, and said she'd come to work and looked over at J.J. who had agreed with her. Then Dooley took J.J. aside and said he and Jesse would pitch in and help with the cleaning if that was important. He said four was a better number than three, especially because Elena had told him she liked being on the water but didn't get out as often as she liked, and she seemed like someone who'd be good company and why didn't they give her a day to remember.

They traveled out of the bay, out of sight of land, in search of deep water, big fish, adventure. They'd been going more than an hour when Dooley asked J.J. if he'd checked the gas gauge.

"There's two tanks,"

"We're getting close to two-thirds on the first tank."

"Yeah?"

"So, allowing an extra third to get back in, we ought to drop anchor pretty quick."

J.J. took his eyes off the horizon to study the advice-giver.

"Sorry," Dooley shrugged, "it's habit. You know, 'the ocean is my classroom.'"

"I knew I'd heard that somewhere," J.J. said. He knew the school motto. He also knew the rule: Save an extra third of your gas in case you have to come in under rough conditions, or something else unexpected comes up. But J.J. didn't worry about it unless the weather was threatening. Today was perfect if he'd ever seen it—a day to be on the water. If he wanted to give these people a pleasant time, this was promising. Elena sat between Dooley and Jesse, quiet, interested, mysterious. Anyone seeing the four leaving the dock would have thought for sure she was with one of the young men. J.J. took silent pleasure in the fact that her connection was with him.

It was Elena's idea to go offshore. "I would like to see the *Atlántico*, not just the *Golfo de México*," she said as they headed out.

"I can't take you to the Atlantic," J.J. laughed, "but I can take you out far enough to pretend."

"Dramamine, anyone?" Jesse said, pulling a plastic sheet of pills from his pocket and waving it around. "Special price today."

Twenty-two miles offshore, the sea was as calm as a summer pond. They tied up to an oil rig and dropped lines. Nothing happened for almost an hour, then a flurry of bites, and it got quiet again. Dooley stripped to his swim shorts, put on goggles, and explored the rig. Jesse watched from above, humming the theme from *Jaws*.

"Amazing things down there," Dooley told Elena, when he was up, toweling off. "You ought to come see."

She shook her head and wrinkled her nose.

"It's an incredible ecosystem, from the tiniest sea life to some of the largest. What goes on under a rig is the best show in town. Come on," he held his hand out. "The oil's just on the surface. You'll be through it before you know it."

Elena smiled. "I don't swim that good."

"Maybe we can do it with a snorkel some time."

She nodded.

"Jesse?" Dooley asked.

"I think I'll wait for the snorkel moment, too."

Dooley stepped to the side of the boat, shook his head hard to whip the water off his hair. He spread his towel and sat, cross-

legged, on the bench. "You guys don't know what you're missing."

They broke out cold drinks and sandwiches. Jesse began to
entertain Elena with charades of various creatures taking or
avoiding the bait. She guessed in Spanish. Dooley translated.
She giggled. J.J. watched their game in silence, thinking she
seemed more friendly, less serious, than the young woman he
knew. He'd never seen her with her peers, never seen her with
young men. It irritated him.

⁂

Jesse was the first to notice the change. "Wow," he said.
"Feel that breeze. It's like—from the north."

Elena turned her face to the sky. "A gift from God," she
said.

"It is from the north," Dooley said, looking at J.J., who
looked at the sky and said nothing.

A couple of minutes later, J.J. got up and checked the
weather radio. He tried to be casual. When Dooley heard him
start the motor, he untied the moorings. Jesse and Elena, still
playing, hardly seemed to notice.

"You all might want to secure your stuff," Dooley told
them.

He moved around the boat, picking up loose items; he
pulled out life vests and a tarp, then put on the shirt and tennis
shoes he had shed earlier in the day.

"What's going on?" Jesse asked.

Dooley pointed to where gray clouds had gathered. The
cool wind continued, still welcome, still unthreatening. J.J. had
the boat humming now and began accelerating. "It's a squall
and it looks like its coming our way. They come in real fast, and
we're more than an hour out. It's liable to be a rough ride, with
the wind kicking up swells. You're gonna get wet. You don't
melt do you, Elena?"

She smiled as if she wasn't sure what the question meant,

while Jesse helped her into her life jacket, and they hunkered in a rounded corner of the boat to brace themselves for the ride. "If this was Six Flags, we'd call it the KIDNEY CRUSHER," Jesse shouted over the motor, waving one arm like a cowboy on a mechanical bull.

After thirty minutes it began to rain, easy first and then picking up speed. Pretty soon it was pelting them, cold and stinging against their skin. Jesse and Elena sat on a tarp with the end pulled over their heads, eyes alert, peering out from their cave. J.J. stood at the wheel with Dooley behind him.

"Can't see a thing," J.J. shouted. He cut back the motor and wiped a forearm across his eyes.

"Try these," Dooley handed him the swim goggles. J.J. took them but didn't put them on.

"I'm thinking we ought to anchor up long and wait for it to pass," he called.

"Couldn't be more than twenty minutes out." Dooley was insistent.

"Doesn't help if I can't see. I'm not sure where the hell we are."

"What about your GPS?"

"Don't have one."

When Dooley said nothing, J.J. could hear the question ringing in his ears. He didn't have one because he seldom went offshore, and you don't need one in the bay. He wasn't doing fishing charters any more. He was a sailor before all this new-fangled equipment came around. He liked things simple. He didn't have a computer either, or a cell phone, or an automatic ON for his weather radio. If he had, it would have beeped him when the squall developed. But they were okay—just wet and cold—and this thing should be over before long. Could spend the night out here if we had to. He looked back to see Elena huddling against Jesse. Shouldn't have let her come, he thought.

Dooley was fumbling in his backpack. He pulled out a wind-breaker, put it over his head, and squatted low, then fumbled some more. "I've got a hand-held, with the Freeport jetties plotted," he shouted from underneath his tent. "If I can keep this thing dry I can help you get in."

J.J. shook the water from his hair, put on the swim goggles, opened up the motor, and let Dooley guide him into the bay. If the boy had been one bit smart ass, if he had criticized or wanted to take the wheel or even raised his voice, J.J. would have reminded him whose boat it was, and whose grand idea this outing had been. But he didn't. Dooley read his equipment and let J.J. drive the boat.

When they reached the dock, the boy turned and extended his hand. "Thank you, sir," he said.

J.J. wondered if he was thanking him for the trip, or for taking advice without balking. Neither deserved a thank you. It had been an adrenaline rush for him. The first in a long time.

By four P.M., they sat enjoying warm drinks at the Seaside Inn, drying out, waiting for the clouds to lift. It looked like the sun might come out again before the day was over. J.J. and Dooley sat quietly, relaxing in a similar rhythm, letting the shared accomplishment settle in between them.

"That was impressive," Jesse said. "Couldn't believe how fast it came on," his eyes still glowed with excitement. "We could have been in trouble if you all didn't know what you were doing."

Elena looked over and nodded. "We thought it was very wonderful, like a movie."

"So you weren't frightened?" J.J. asked.

"Jesse protected me," she smiled.

Back at the house, when they were alone, J.J. found himself irritated by her continued good humor. She moved around the kitchen, humming to herself.

"I like your son, Dooley," she said.

"Seems like you like his friend, too."

"Jesse?"

"Don't be coy, Elena. What went on out there?"

"What is coy?"

"Never mind." He picked up the newspaper and went out on the deck.

Elena followed a few minutes later, bringing him a cold beer.

"You are *celoso?*" she said.

"I don't know what that means."

"You do not like seeing me with him?"

"I saw what was going on. You were practically sitting on his lap, your heads so close together I couldn't tell where one started and the other stopped. I just want to know, did he hit on you?"

"He did not hit me."

J.J. had never known her to play games with him before, but he could swear she was enjoying watching him act like a jackass. Something about Jesse Martin stuck in his craw, and the fact that the two of them had been huddled together, giggling, while he and Dooley were trying to save their asses hadn't set well.

"He makes me laugh," Elena said. "He is a nice man, and funny, and he did not touch me improper, if that is what *hit on* means."

"Maybe you wanted him to." He knew when he said it he had gone too far.

"Maybe," she said, and turned to go inside, then stopped at the door. "Maybe I will go home this evening. I do not feel welcome here."

He stood up and took her hand. "Elena," he said, pulling her to him, "you're soft, you're beautiful, you smell like a woman. I know what he was thinking."

"I am not responsible for what another is thinking," she said.

✥

Later that night J.J. lay awake thinking. Territorial. That's what he'd felt, watching her with the boys earlier—each of them vying for her attention. Surprised they didn't get into a diving contest. He should have known better, should have said no when the idea came up. He was too old for this, J.J. thought, feeling her move against him.

Outside, it had begun to rain softly. From the window, he could see the light on Woody's deck spreading its yellow glow in a soft haze, inviting flying creatures to be trapped against its incandescence. His neighbor would be out with a gig tonight in rubber boots up to his hips, wading the marshes, looking for tomorrow's supper. It was a solitary diversion, a facet of J.J.'s life he seemed to have misplaced.

PART II

The Good Death

"It seems to me most strange
that men should fear;
knowing that death, a necessary end,
will come when it will come."

William Shakespeare
Julius Caesar,
Act 2, Scene 2

20

A year had passed since the summer Jesse worked for Rose, and now that he was looking back, that period stood in his memory as an idyllic time. It wasn't long after being reinstated in school before he found himself drowning in course work and clerkships—Surgery, Neurology, Radiology, Dermatology, a four-week acting internship, twenty weeks of research electives, plus preparation for two different examinations required for graduation. There was hardly time for sleep. Still, he managed to share a dinner or lunch with Rose at least once a week. She wanted regular reports on his hospital life and never failed to ask about his finances. She insisted on writing a monthly check for expenses, more than he actually needed. After a while it didn't seem awkward to take her checks, but he tried to be diligent about the weekly meal. It wouldn't do for her to feel slighted.

"Did I ever tell you about my grandmother?" Rose asked Jesse one day, not allowing him a chance to answer. "After my grandfather died, she traveled around, visiting all her children. There were five, and she'd stay with each family for a period of six weeks to three months, depending on how smoothly the visits were going, or how much she might be needed. She always spent a long time at our house, because she got along well with my parents, and since I was an only child, having her there kept me entertained. She slept in my bed when she was with us, and always on the first night of her stay she'd say, 'Now, Rose, you know I'm an old lady and sometimes old ladies die in their sleep, so if you wake up and can't rouse me, just call your mother. Don't be afraid. It's a blessing to die in your sleep.'"

"And did she?"

"Die in my bed? She did. I remember my parents were afraid it would traumatize me, and the minister even came and talked about how nice it was in Heaven where she went, and that I shouldn't worry. I was only ten, but it struck me then that if dying wasn't a bad thing, people shouldn't get so worked up about it. My grandmother prepared me perfectly."

He had nodded, wondering why she was telling him this.

"I'm telling you this because I want you to know I'm not afraid of dying, but I do fear losing my mind and some of my other major functions before I do. It's apparently something you think about as well. I recognize your little memory tests."

"I'm committed to keeping you as healthy as possible."

"And you've done pretty well, though I might as well warn you, I'm planning to smoke a cigar at the grand opening party. But here's what I want to tell you." She fumbled in her end table and brought out an envelope. "My attorney has drawn up a new power of attorney for health care, in which I've stated my wishes and named you as my agent. Any problems with pulling the plug on me, knowing my wishes?"

"No."

"Then be advised." She refolded the papers, put them back in their container, and handed it to him. "Addled as you may think I am, I haven't forgotten that I asked you for a final pill, nor has the fact that you've ignored my request gone unnoticed. I'm hoping this added responsibility will get you on the ball in that respect."

He fumbled for an explanation, but she continued.

"I found the information I wanted. Self-deliverance, it's called. My sources said to shop for a doctor, communicate your wishes to him, and get his reaction. Young doctors, they said, are more open to new ideas and better versed in medical ethics than their elders, but none of them are likely to jump up and assure you that they'll be there when you need them. It's still against the law. I'm counting on you, Jesse—oh, not to do the deed, I know it has to be self-administered.

"I could use cyanide," she continued, getting breathless now, "but they say there are mixed reactions to that. Some die instantly, and some convulse for significant periods of time. I don't want anything that would have to be cleaned up after. Freezing is a nice alternative, but not likely in Galveston, unless I could get myself locked up in the old ice house. And there's always the plastic bag over the head. The book says you can secure it with a rubber band or a ribbon. I'd opt for the ribbon. Probably yellow."

"This isn't funny, Rose."

"Just want you to know I've done my homework. Spent a lot of time thinking about this. There are more physicians than you probably imagine, Mr. Innocent, who discreetly prescribe for terminal patients. And they're seldom prosecuted. If I approach you in good faith and tell you I'm having trouble sleeping, you can give me a prescription for some heavy duty barbiturates. I fill it a couple of times, and voilà, my escape is in place, a lethal dose locked in my safe. I'm planning to put a sign on it that says, 'Eat Me,' so that if Alzheimer's hits, and I can't remember anything, these will look like candy."

Jesse, at a loss for words, gave Rose a wry smile to acknowledge her little joke, and told her she'd just have to trust him.

"I trust you'll do what you think best, young man," she said in a voice unnaturally sharp, "but this is my life and it's winding down and there are ways I don't want to go out. Let there be no doubt in your mind that I expect your help."

Jesse nodded and turned to tuck the papers she'd given him

into his backpack. Rose, graciously, let the subject drop.

❖

Their visits were not casual. She was always carefully dressed, with makeup and jewelry, and Pearl served their meals on china, with real silverware and crystal. He had come to be comfortable at the table, being served, making conversation, using a napkin. Sometimes, exhausted from whatever had come down in the past twenty-four hours, Jesse ached to cancel. But he didn't.

Rose liked to tell him about the fiction she was reading or a show she'd seen on television. He brought her stories from the hospital. She loved gossip.

"Dr. Jefferson stopped me in the hall the other day."

"Jefferson?"

"You know, the one you visited on my behalf."

She shook her head, indicating she wished she didn't have to remember.

"He asked about you."

"Still wants a sizeable donation, I imagine. I'm relieved they never sent a grant proposal. Could have embarrassed me with that. But I should probably give them something." She hesitated, obviously in thought. "I have a little lot in east Houston that faces on the freeway," she said. "I rent it for billboard space, which makes enough to pay the taxes, but a realtor called me a while back. Said she thought she could get me $45,000 for it. I could give them that and they can keep it or sell it or do whatever they do with such things, and save me the trouble."

Jesse nodded. Forty-five-thousand dollars was a year's salary for a doctor starting out in public health. Rose saw it as a bone you'd throw a dog—something to get rid of. How much money does it take before you start thinking like that, he wondered. Would he get that out of touch someday? He could already see himself changing. Didn't look for specials on pizza coupons anymore. He bought butter instead of whatever margarine was on sale. He'd started taking vitamins, and they weren't cheap.

And he'd just bought a ninety dollar pair of tennis shoes. Like a child showing off, he'd put them on to visit Rose.

Their meeting that day had started with him taking her blood pressure, checking her pulse, listening at the carotid artery, checking her hands for temperature, skin tone, telltale signs. She was impatient with his ministrations.

"This is no way to visit," she complained.

"You could always see your own doctor."

"I much prefer seeing you," she smiled and looked down, allowing him to palpate her neck. "It's about time you got new shoes," she commented dryly. "Now, tell me what else is going on with you." She patted the chair beside her, and he dutifully went through whatever of interest he'd tucked away for her pleasure. Last week he'd filled her in on the secrets of prescription language: *hora somni,* at bedtime; *per os,* by mouth; *ut dict,* as directed; *ad effect,* until effective.

"It's simple Latin," she had observed. "They use it to keep us confused, completely forgetting that some of us took Latin in high school back in the dark ages. Same with the illegible handwriting. It adds to the mystique. You're not that kind of doctor, are you?"

"Of course not, Rose. I tell my patients everything I know, and I admit there are still some things I don't know, and then we argue about their plan of treatment."

"Don't get smart."

She liked it when he teased her, and he had come to appreciate the fact that she was opinionated and manipulative. She might be difficult, but she was seldom boring. He noticed she had recently started calling him "Doctor."

Jesse had applied for a residency in Family Medicine with UTMB, in spite of Rose's intensive lobby for a prestigious specialization. She had an image of the kind of professional she wanted him to be, even though those were the doctors she refused to see.

"I've been thinking about how many people suffer from

allergies these days." Rose interrupted his thoughts as he checked her pulse one afternoon, "Just imagine your office filled with rich old ladies with runny noses and watery eyes. Nothing too messy. It's just a matter of prescribing the right pill."

Jesse adjusted the stethoscope and listened more carefully, wondering if he'd picked up something unusual.

"Wasn't an allergist what you wanted me to be last week?" he asked, more to check her memory than to make conversation.

"Last week I suggested orthopedics, and you rejected that," she answered.

"And the week before that?"

"A proctologist. Are you testing me?" she drew back and looked at him sharply.

⊹

She had asked one day. "Do you have a girlfriend, Jesse?"

"Not really," he said, caught off guard.

"What about the girl whose party you attended last Christmas?"

"That was two Christmases ago, Rose."

She shrugged. "Time flies when you've been sick. Well, what about her anyway?"

"We stay in touch."

Rose raised an eyebrow.

"No, Rose, that's not what I meant. We're friends. There's no touching there."

"Well, what's wrong with her? Doesn't she know a good man when she sees one? She doesn't have to go all the way, but healthy young men require a sexual outlet. Everyone knows that. Do you go to gentlemen's clubs, massage parlors, avail yourself of women of the street?"

"That's none of your business."

"I know. I heard on *Oprah* that a large percentage of young people are having unprotected sex because, for some reason, they think they're invulnerable to STDs. And I know you're on top of this, but there was a young medical student on the show who was careless one time with a woman he picked up in a bar and contracted genital warts." Rose made an appropriate face of disgust. "You're young and strong and maybe you think you're invulnerable, but did you know that some very famous people died of syphilis?"

"I *did* know that," Jesse told her, "and I *can* and *do* take care of myself. Is there anything else?"

"If you can ask me about the movement of my bowels, I believe I have a corresponding right to invade your privacy," she said, pretending an insult. "We never talked about sex in my day," she told him. "Not with our parents, not even with our husbands. Most of my experiences were what you'd call silent and furtive. My goodness, when I read *Lady Chatterly's Lover* I realized I had missed something. Almost went out and hired myself a gardener, but I wasn't so much needy as curious. Of course, so was she. Lady Chatterly. Curious. Now I turn on the television day and night, and they're talking about sex as casually as you'd recite *Mother Goose*."

✢

"I'm pooped," Susanna slid into the booth at the hospital coffee shop, where Jesse was waiting for her. She was taking a prep course so she could transfer to Intensive Care. "It takes similar skills, but I'll have fewer patients," she told him. "Eventually I'd like to get qualified as a nurse/practitioner so I can act more independently. I get so tired of taking bullshit from doctors." She stirred sugar into her coffee. "So what's new with you?"

"Thought you'd never ask," Jesse, ignoring her blast at doctors, pushed a newspaper article her way. "Have you read about this?"

"The pirate's house? Yeah. Looks like they're really doing a job on it."

"I think we should go to the grand opening."

Susanna gave an exaggerated sigh. "More doctor bullshit."

"Nope," Jesse smiled. "This is Rose's project, and she expects me to bring a date."

"Your landlady? The one we saw in the emergency room? Maison Rouge is her deal?" Susanna was piecing it together, looking incredulous. "Why didn't you tell me?"

"The last time I mentioned her you acted like I was trying to impress you."

"Well, now you've succeeded."

"So, I can give her your name, to send an invitation?"

She nodded.

"This is a real date," he said seriously, verifying.

She sipped her coffee slowly, then looked across with a dimpled smile. "Dr. Martini, I'm well aware of that."

⁜

Jesse had a minimum of free time but still tried to meet Dooley for a beer now and then. It kept him grounded to talk about something other than medicine, plus the guy was a safe and comfortable sounding board.

"So, this lady my dad's working with is the same one who's helping you through school?" Dooley asked after Jesse had mentioned something about Rose.

"Yeah. She's my benefactor. Benefactress?"

"That's a mouthful."

"And even more awkward to explain. First I rented a room from her, and then I started helping her out, and now I guess she's taken me to raise. She's paying for me to finish school and wants me to choose a specialty."

Dooley whistled appreciatively. "Heck of a deal." Then he leaned across the table. "What's she like?"

Jesse hesitated, trying to sum Rose up in a few words. "Very smart, overbearing, nosy, funny, and incredibly loyal if she takes a liking to you."

"Dad invited me to the big opening, said something like it was time for me to meet her, but I'm not into fancy parties."

"Me neither, but I have a date and a tux."

"That lets me out."

"You don't have to wear a tux."

"That's what he said."

"How's your dad these days?"

"Different."

"Good or bad?"

"It strikes me as one of those mid-life crisis things. He was a fisherman and almost a hermit a couple of years ago, and now he's all wrapped up in this business."

"What about Elena?"

"He never took her seriously enough, seems to me, but I think she's going to bring it to a head."

"Does she think he'll marry her?"

"I doubt it. She just needs a way to get her kids here, and I think she kept hoping he'd step up to the plate. About this woman—Rose—I gather she's rich."

"Very."

"And my dad advises her?"

"That's what she says."

"And he spends a lot of time with her?"

"Not lately. In fact, she's been complaining that he's too busy to come around."

Dooley slid his beer bottle in circles on the table. "I'm just trying to figure out their relationship."

Jesse chuckled. "I've been working on that one for a long time."

✛

When Jesse left Dooley that night, he had the sense of something having gone unsaid. Dooley had been looking for information. Maybe he wondered if his father was indebted to Rose—or trying to take advantage of her, both of which had occurred to Jesse from time to time. Life with Rose was complicated. He was pretty sure the captain questioned his motives. And maybe Dooley would too if he'd told it straight: "Rose likes me a lot. She pays me to keep her happy, and it may involve eating dinner one day, talking about my sex life the next, and writing her a prescription for sleeping pills in the future. So far, I've done everything she's wanted."

What was he going to do about Rose? She was pushing for at least two more years of specialization and then a traditional city practice. It was the kind of thing that had looked appealing at the beginning, but now had lost its call. The thought of jumping from the discipline of school to the discipline of a practice had a negative appeal these days. He might as well step up on Rose's treadmill and never think about hitting the surf again.

There were things he'd been looking into, but they were things he couldn't do if he had to support himself immediately. Doctors without Borders was a chance to travel and function at that emergency-room level he liked. He'd heard talk about clinics in downtown Manhattan, and San Francisco, where you work like hell during the day but, at night, you're living in the Big Apple or the City by the Bay. That sounded like something he could handle. A family practice residency would prepare him for that kind of medicine without ruling out more exciting stuff down the road. He wanted to be a doctor, not a zombie. There were even bands and sports teams that had doctors on staff. You could travel with them and stand around backstage and share the groupies. Pretty far out stuff, but thoughts like that could get the juices flowing when his energies were totally depleted. He knew what Rose would say to any of those ideas, and he wasn't about to rock the boat by mentioning them. She had made a couple of minor changes to her will in the past year, maybe just to keep him on his toes. He'd make a decision after she was gone. Hated to think of it that way, but she wasn't going to be around forever.

✣

A couple of weeks before the party, Jesse uncovered his new Perry Ellis tux and tried it on. He checked his reflection in the mirror, then turned around and craned his neck to get a view from behind. It looked sharp, a far cry from the cheap tuxes he'd rented for weddings and proms. Rose had insisted they go shopping and had made him try on a bunch of styles until she made a final selection based on criteria he felt sure she was exaggerating. But it was her $600.

"Most men don't know the least thing about shopping," she told him, "and, judging from your clothes, you're no exception. If I let you shop alone, you'd probably buy the first one you tried on."

The first one that fit, he had thought, not sure there was anything wrong with that.

"A professional man always needs a tuxedo," she had told him, making him turn around in each one, so she could assess it from the back. "There'll be more opportunities to wear this than you can imagine."

"I'll probably put on weight before that time comes."

"You're not the type," she had said while she straightened his tie. "Now, you're going to need some good black shoes. Nate always said the shoes make the man."

He fished in the closet for his new shoes and went back to the mirror again to get the total effect. He straightened his tie and practiced some James Bond moves, talking under his breath. *This is your life, Jesse Martin. You're a doctor, now, going to a grand opening, not a kid going to a prom. Stay in control, Man. Always in control.*

21

Rose pressed hard on the channel button of her television remote. She knew it wouldn't respond more quickly to force, but, disgusted with *Oprah's* program, she used it like a gun.

"Terrorists," she spat out the word. "Blowing up buildings. Don't these people have anything better to do?" She was impatient with the subject. She refused to give them the time of day—people who killed indiscriminately, who flouted the most basic of human values, whose philosophy, if it could be called that, set back the civilized world by thousands of years. Leave them to the military, she thought. However, a war on terrorists sounded a little ambitious. None of the wars she could remember had accomplished anything they promised.

Galveston wasn't a likely spot for terrorists, though it had seen a bloody battle between Lafitte and the Karankawas in the early 1800s, been fired on by the Union Navy during the Civil War, and German U-Boats had been spotted off the coast during World War II; but the island's greatest threats had always been from Mother Nature, and from human greed, or enterprise, however one wished to characterize it. There were regular reports of sand being washed away and ground sinking from the harvest of oil and gas. Salt water marshes were disappearing because of building and development. Water supplies and quality were threatened. And the island was long overdue for a serious hurricane. One of these was more likely to do her harm than terrorists, Rose decided.

✛

A full year had passed since her summer of recovery, since Jesse had whisked her around town and supervised her life. He'd done his job for her and returned to his studies. He was older and less playful when she saw him now, and, though she realized that might be necessary to his development, she didn't like it. "Why don't you go fly a kite," she told him when he looked especially worn. He sometimes responded with expressions of concern about people across the world in need of basic food and medical help, talked about special medical missions, something about a Harvard doctor who was doing amazing things in Haiti.

"I give to the Red Cross," she told him. "Lots of people give to various well-established agencies. If you must be a hero, be one at home. You can't go risking your life. I won't allow it." She made a mental note not to say that again. She didn't want to sound like she was telling him what to do. Jesse was a free agent whom she'd continue to reward as long as he made good decisions.

✛

On the afternoon movie channel, a band across the bottom of the screen announced tornado alerts for the bay area. Rose sipped her scotch. It was too early in the season for so much activity. Every week or ten days another eastern hemisphere storm was born, watched, weighed, and measured. Rose was doubly perturbed this year. The weather was messing up her schedule.

She had them addressed and ready—engraved invitations to the finest party of the season—set for the weekend of Labor Day, masks optional. Because of these damn storms she didn't want to send them out and then have the party go bust because a hurricane showed up. She wanted to monitor it down to the last minute. That's what she'd decided, and she didn't want to discuss it. Seventeen. Her magic number. Seventeen days between the mailing of the invitations and the party. Seldom could a hurricane be predicted seventeen days in advance, but Rose had been specific with this, as she had with many of the details of the party.

She had invited Galveston society—the Moodys, Kempners, Gaidos, BOI families she had met back in Nate's day, professional people from architecture, law and medicine, historians, journalists, and preservationists from across the state, politicians, past and present, up to and including the governor and his lady. She had sent thirty invitations to the developer from whom she'd bought the land, with a note of thanks and a request that he distribute them as he saw fit. She was hoping to snag some classy Mafia connections, if such a thing still existed, which she knew it did. Through Jesse, she had hired eight medical students at outrageous fees and rented tuxedos for them so they could greet and mix with the guests. A little bright new blood gets things moving, Rose knew, and she impressed on Jesse the kind of young person she was looking to hire, but said he couldn't be one of them. She wanted him there that night, visiting with her, with a date. When he had told her he didn't date, she had told him it wasn't up for discussion.

She had handed J.J. ten invitations, and he had handed them back to her, saying there was no one he wanted to invite.

"I know you have friends, neighbors, maybe just someone you'd like to impress with an invitation."

"No, thanks," he had slid them back across the polished end table.

"Surely."

"Thanks, Rose, but my neighbors aren't into the social scene."

"Nonsense, Captain," she had said, her voice getting sharp. "This isn't just an opening, it's the best damn party anyone's going to see around here for years. I expect you to bring guests, and I've set aside four places at the head table for your party. You mustn't let me down," she had announced, pushing the invitations once again into his court.

Months earlier the captain had suggested that she hire Blair, the woman she'd liked from their initial meeting at the Tremont House, to help with the planning. Together they had worked out the guest list, the menu, the entertainment, and publicity.

"I'm thinking we'll send out invitations with no other announcement. Make it elite, so those who are invited will know they were hand chosen," Rose had told her.

"I think," Blair offered hesitantly, "it might be even more appealing if you let everyone know it's happening, but hold attendance to invitation only. Put an announcement outside Maison Rouge, run an ad in the paper, get it spotlighted on local television, invite some media people from Houston. Let everyone in the area know what's happening. Then an invitation will become a prize."

Rose had agreed that was an even better idea. "I wish we could offer an added incentive," she frowned. "A chance to see the place will draw the curious, but, God, I'd hate a spotty showing. I used to run in the social circles, but I've been out too long to expect attendance just because my name's on the invitation. They're likely to say, 'Rose Parrish? I thought she was dead.'"

"How about a charity auction," Blair ventured.

"Of what?"

"Something unusual your guests might like to see."

Rose nodded, thinking. She had such a thing—sitting in her bedroom safe—a gold doubloon mounted in gold, set with diamonds and emeralds, hanging from a braided gold chain. It had been Nate's gift on their twentieth anniversary. She had been forty-one; he was sixty-two. It was the year she almost left him. The gift was an appeasement, a promise, a bribe—she didn't know. It had never pleased her, had seemed ugly, too outspoken in its quest to be unique, alien to Nate's ordinarily excellent taste. It was designed especially for her, but she'd always felt it wasn't intended to complement her as much as to tag her. She had smiled and accepted it, had even worn it occasionally. Those had not been good times, when their appetites and energies ran at cross purposes. She decided he was tedious and uninteresting. He complained she was flighty and willful. They quarreled in the mornings and didn't speak at night. She threw things. He ignored her. She went on shopping sprees. He closed the checking account. She took a job at an art gallery in Houston, where she flirted with the owner's son and made lunch dates with prospective clients. She couldn't remember how it all ended, how they got back together. Maybe it was Paris. That was probably it. She remembered that he was charming and debonair. The French respected older men. Well, so did she. Hadn't she married him? My God, she had almost forgotten about that time. When you have forty good ones, a couple of bad years are easy to overlook.

Blair was talking now about food and entertainment, gypsy fortune tellers, wandering magicians, exotic delicacies. "You want it voluptuous and exciting. We'll put bands in various locations with music for every taste—blues, salsa, reggae."

"I don't want to be garish," Rose interrupted. "Less is more."

"Not at a party, Rose. Here, the only question is, how much is enough?"

"I want my guests to be surprised and pleased, but I'll be damned if I want anyone thinking I'm out just to impress them. I don't even want Maison Rouge to be the star of the show. I want to stir up a passion for this strip of land we call the island. There is a shared history. I didn't choose Maison Rouge because

I wanted it to be a moneymaker. I want to free people back to their roots—give them a taste of a different time, a place where rules can be broken. I want to give them something to be excited about."

"You're seriously committed to this, aren't you?" Blair had removed her glasses and was studying Rose with a look of admiration.

"I'm thinking of it as my swan song, dear. It better be good."

✣

Invitations went out on August 15. Rose had one mailed to herself so she would know if the mail was prompt. She also wanted the experience of receiving the announcement in the mail, opening it, letting its festive sense wash over her. They had been mailed to arrive on a Friday or a Saturday. She didn't want anyone coming home out of sorts, opening their mail, and tossing the invitation aside because they didn't have time to think about it. She had created a happening a couple of times before in her life, but nothing matched this. And she realized she was possibly too far out of touch with the real world to know what would capture the imagination, but that's what she hired Blair for, and that's why she spent all that time talking with the printers and the caterers and the interior decorating team. Many of the decorations would be permanent fixtures—the splintered canoe, the N. C. Wyeth oils of pirates, the candelabra.

"What do you think, Pearl?" she asked, unrolling the scrolled invitation, lettered in calligraphy.

"Mighty fancy writing. Can hardly read it."

"It's intended to look ornate."

"I suppose."

"Oh, come on, Pearl, can't you get excited about this. Just a little?" Rose hated that she couldn't get anything from the woman. "I'm expecting you to come, you know."

"Oh my, no." She suddenly appeared flustered.

"And your husband and son. You will be my guests. You'll need a costume, of course."

"I don't wear costumes."

"Then just wear dress-up clothes. Something you'd wear to church."

"I don't think the Lord would like it."

"The Lord has nothing to do with this, Pearl. It's a party. You like music. You like good food. Put on your Sunday best, and I'll send a car for you. You work like a Trojan, you give to everyone, and never question whether it's in your best interests."

"It's not for me to decide," Pearl answered proudly.

"Well, the world is full of people who do things without questioning them. You certainly don't want to be one of those."

"I don't question," Pearl told her pointedly. "The Book doesn't say anything about questions that I know of; it's about faith. It also says: *By your actions shall you be known*." She turned and left the room.

Now what did that mean, Rose thought. Surely she isn't accusing me of not acting. She's seen me put this whole thing together.

✜

The grand opening was overdue. If the building had been finished earlier, they'd have missed hurricane season altogether, but there was one delay after another. And then, just when they got the roof on, a small twister swooped down and blew it off. That's when Rose had called Ellsworth King.

"El, I thought we'd done everything possible to make this building impervious to the weather."

"Well, Rose," he drawled. "It isn't finished yet."

"What's to keep this from happening again?"

"Storm shutters. If the wind can't get inside, you take a lot of pressure off your roof."

"Did we arrange for the best?"

"Your man did. He chose that Bahama style, like I recommended. They're not motorized, though. You'll need some hands to secure them when you need to, but I figure, with the kind of place you're going for, that won't be a problem."

She hung up, pleased. There was so much to think about, and she had been sick back when a lot of decisions were being made. Not that she didn't trust the captain, but he had never done this before, and sometimes she wondered if he had his whole mind on his business. Jesse had found out some things for her last year—that he had built a new house, and there was someone staying in his old one, someone Jesse met on the beach, and he told her that the cleaning woman often stayed for dinner.

"She cooks dinner for them?"

"No. The captain cooks for the three of them."

"How old is this woman?"

"Late twenties."

"Pretty?"

"Very."

"And you say the boy is a friend of yours?"

"Yeah. A really nice guy I met on the beach."

"And he knows the captain? That's quite a coincidence."

"Yeah."

"Oh, for goodness sake, Jesse, just tell me the story. Don't make me pry it out of you."

"Well, the captain's his father."

"His father?" Rose leaned forward, eyes sharp as points, demanding more.

"He's been looking for him for a long time and he found him here, and the captain didn't know he had a son because he broke up with Dooley's mother before he knew she was pregnant."

"He has a son named Dooley? Like Tom Dooley?" Her voice was sarcastic now.

"Dooley Thomas, actually."

"Hmmm," Rose said, thinking. "So, this boy and the girl are spending a lot of time with the captain? Sounds like a scam. Are they a couple? Working as a team?"

Jesse smiled at the idea. "No way."

"Why do you say that?"

"I don't want to speculate."

"Very admirable, but it's just between us."

"Well, Elena belongs to the captain."

"No! Belongs?"

"No, Rose" Jesse took a breath and rephrased. "Goes with. She and the captain are friendly."

"Lovers?"

"I guess you could call it that."

Rose was consumed with curiosity, but Jesse said he didn't

woman hanging on to her health and her mind, with occasional blips, trying to manage with some kind of style. Sometimes she looked at her reflection from across the room and could still see the Rose who had set more than one man's heart aflame. She remembered soldiers begging for kisses before heading for war, an artist who pleaded to do her portrait, a pilot who showed up regularly to take her for joy rides, and that colleague of Nate's who sent flowers every week for a year. She thought he'd never give up. It was possible no one could still see in her the woman who had attracted men in that way, but vanity dies hard.

That's why what she wore to the party needed to be perfect. She might not be up to a foxtrot, but she'd be sporting an Italian silk dress the color of port wine, with a matching feather boa. She had seen the gown in the Neiman's catalog and had a seamstress copy it, with a few changes intended to flatter her sagging, but not completely out of shape, figure. In her hair she would wear a tiara—a bit much, but this was a costume affair. Diamond earrings and necklace. The doubloon necklace would be displayed on her dressmaker's dummy, which would be draped in the same cloth as her own dress. It was scheduled to stand in a central place, with its letter of authentication and $5,000 value, so that interested parties could inspect it at their leisure before the bidding began.

As August 31 drew closer, Rose tried to walk on the treadmill for a few minutes each day and downed large quantities of vitamin C. Blair called daily with a count of bookings at the Tremont and the Galvez hotels, where she had negotiated a special guest rate for out-of-towners. One week out, fifty-six rooms had been reserved. If that many were coming from a distance, she had to believe those living on the island would make every effort to attend. Rose was ecstatic.

On Thursday afternoon, August 29, the U. S. Weather Bureau issued a tropical storm watch for Galveston and vicinity. Rose, unperturbed, called Blair and arranged for a canopy to be set up at the entrance to the building so the doorman could help guests from their cars into a protected area.

On Friday, the rain and winds began, and Rose, her stomach queasy, drank tea and watched local weather reports. At one point she called Pearl into the parlor.

"I understand you have a reputation among your church people as a prayer warrior."

"Yes'm." Pearl bit her lip and looked at the floor.

"I'm wondering if you could say some words for better weather?"

Pearl looked up. "I only pray for people."

"But it works?"

"It does."

"Then, it wouldn't hurt to ask for good weather for tomorrow. Would it?"

"I only pray for people. I go to battle with the evil spirits in them. I fight when they're not able."

"Storms have been considered evil spirits," Rose told her. "I bet you can do this if you try."

"I pray for people," she said.

Stubborn woman, Rose thought.

When Pearl retreated, saying nothing more, Rose felt she had at least made an effort. If the weather cleared, she'd be sure to give the woman full credit, whether it was due or not. She broke a rule and poured herself a scotch before five P.M., hoping the captain would stop by. She knew he was in town supervising last minute activities. Blair and her team were managing the party, but the captain was coordinating with the new general manager who'd come from a swanky club in Houston, bearing credentials, but a minimum of experience.

"He's young," the captain had warned her.

"Children are running the world these days," Rose complained. "I'm glad you'll be there to keep an eye on him."

"He insists on a computerized order/billing system that I've never heard of."

"Why don't we do it the old fashioned way—with waiters who remember your order. And if you come in often, they remember what you drink."

"I don't think he'll go for that," the captain said.

"I'll talk to him," Rose said. She had sat down with the young man and told him about how it used to be. Told him what it was she was trying to recreate. Told him this was a historic project, as well as an expensive one, and, while she respected his expertise, she thought there might be some things she could show him about old style elegance. He agreed to forego the computerized system and to hire only waiters with good memories.

Rose had been involved in a lot of decisions these past months. When she awakened in the morning, she had a list of things to do. Many could be accomplished from her telephone, but sometimes she hired a taxi and kept the driver with her until her business was complete. She didn't like to walk far, but had found she could avoid that by calling in advance and being expected. It was wonderful the treatment people offered a rich old woman looking to spend large quantities of money.

✥

It rained and blew all Friday night, the thirtieth, but Saturday morning dawned clear. Rose made her way to the window and smiled to see blue sky. There were still clouds on the horizon, and the wind was whipping the trees, but Rose was relieved. The captain had called to say he'd send a driver for her at six. Guests wouldn't be arriving until seven, but she didn't want to be rushed.

When Lisette, the hairdresser, came at two, she reported that it had started to rain again.

Rose went to the window to see a sky the color of gunmetal.

"Damn," Rose stamped her foot. "This is going to ruin things."

"*Au contraire,*" Lisette looked up from where she was setting up for a manicure. "This will discourage only those with no spirit of adventure, and who needs them?" She snapped her fingers and tossed her head.

"Maybe you're right. Who needs them?" Rose tried for the same effect as she settled into her chair.

Lisette gave her a facial, then washed and dried her hair, pushing it into rich waves, softening it around the face with a curling iron. At four-thirty she helped Rose into her dress and fastened her necklace.

"Elegant," the girl said, stepping back to admire.

Rose sat at her dressing table, back to the mirror. "Now do the face. Just don't make me look 'painted.'"

Lisette applied toner, concealer, base, blush, eyebrow pencil, eyeliner, shadow, mascara, lipstick, and powder with a practiced hand. She then handed Rose a mirror and watched as she studied herself from first one angle, then another.

"What is it you don't like?" Lisette took her silence for displeasure.

"My dear," Rose told her, "You've done a good job. I'm just trying to assimilate your handiwork." She turned her head and looked again, quickly, into the mirror, trying to catch herself by surprise. "I seem to have lost perspective. Maybe I should leave off the tiara. Wouldn't want to overwhelm," she laughed a throaty laugh.

Lisette hugged her. "I have to get dressed now. See you in a few hours." She stopped at the doorway and looked back. "You look like a queen."

"I feel rather queenly." Rose could feel her heart beating irregularly. Excitement! It didn't hurt. She leaned back in her recliner, delighted she had managed to make it to this point.

It was five-thirty, a few minutes to rest before the limo came. It was almost dark now. When the weatherman on television advised viewers in the area to stay inside, because it appeared they were in for a rough night, she snapped him off. When was he ever right? She would walk into Maison Rouge on her own steam, assisted by her driver, and using Nate's old gold-headed cane Pearl had located in the storage closet. It was her plan to greet people at the door for the first hour. She had practiced resting her left hand on the cane as she extended her right hand. And there would be a chair behind her when she needed to sit down. Didn't want her ankles to swell. She could still greet from a sitting position. But that chair should be a wooden one with arms, and it would be nice if the upholstery were white or gold, to set off the dress.

22

John Broussard stood in the foyer of Maison Rouge and greeted guests whose energy seemed to be feeding off the storm's supercharged atmosphere. The crowd was buzzing with stories of traffic signals malfunctioning, a billboard blown over, high water on Fifty-second Street. Judging from the large numbers who made it, only the over-cautious would cancel their plans on a hurricane threat. People walked around congratulating one another for being of hardy stock, knowing when you could—and should—brave a storm.

"This is worth a little inconvenience," J.J. heard one elegantly dressed woman say. "Isn't the place marvelous? Doesn't it make you feel decadent?"

Because of the weather, they had scrubbed the plan for Rose to greet people near the front door, so Blair had seated her prominently in the lobby and was making certain guests had a moment to exchange greetings with their hostess. There was also a team of attractive young women in sleek black dresses welcoming people, putting on name tags, and directing guests to food and entertainment centers. Jesse's cadre of students had been assigned to certain areas and instructed to act like perfect hosts—which, in case they weren't sure what that meant, Rose had specified: See to the guests' needs and entertain them at the same time, and never let it enter their minds there's something you'd rather be doing. "In fact, gentlemen," she had finished her little speech, "I hope there isn't. Welcome to Maison Rouge."

⁘

"I'd like you to meet the governor," Blair whispered in J.J.'s ear.

He turned slowly, marking the sound of those words, and followed her across the room. Heads turned as he passed, and he stopped to shake a few hands. Some of these people had already approached him with business possibilities. More would come. He'd bet on it, if he was a betting man. He'd gotten his wish with this project—bought himself some respectability and kept the door shut on his private life. Blair, standing now with the governor, the governor's well-endowed wife, and the editor of *Texas Monthly*, smiled broadly, and motioned for him to join them.

243

⁘

When he moved into his new house, J.J. hadn't put the old horseshoe back up over the door. He tried it for sentiment's sake, but it looked out of place. He'd decided then that the foundation of Maison Rouge was a good place to plant his luck and had set it in fresh cement in the northeast corner. He didn't realize at the time he was burying a piece of himself.

When he'd been supervising construction on the building, there'd been no time to follow sports. He'd been too busy with the club opening even to track this storm—and she was no small one. His bookie had stopped him at the barber shop to ask what was wrong because he hadn't been by. J.J. had lost interest. His prison therapist had told him it could disappear someday—like a backwards puberty—a change, arriving unbidden, on some schedule of its own. Simon had said, "If you don't nurture it, you'll likely turn around someday and find your call to gamble has gone." It probably was a good thing, but the realization didn't set well with J.J. He didn't want to get too careful to take a risk. And he had already lost the sense of traveling light.

⁙

Guests exploded into the lobby, breathless, and J.J. knew the club was off to a memorable start. These people will talk about opening the Maison Rouge with a storm roaring outside until the day they die, he thought. Maybe it's the horseshoe. He checked his watch and made a circle through the kitchen to see how things were going.

At seven-forty-five, the canopy set up to protect guests from the weather blew over, after which, doormen with umbrellas escorted ladies from their cars, while most men scrambled in behind them. J.J. asked a doorman with a radio tuned to the weather channel to keep him advised. At eight-thirty, a severe weather watch was issued, marshalling local emergency forces and requesting that people take cover. At eight-forty-five guests were still arriving.

"This place weather-proof?" someone with a name tag bearing the title honorable, asked J.J.

"According to the architects, our ballroom is the place to be in the event of a storm," J.J. assured him.

"You hear that, Mother?" his honor turned to his lady. "This is the place to be. Now let's go find us a martini."

J.J. took a quick walk through the downstairs rooms, looking for Ellsworth King, and found him surrounded by a group that included a few who were taking notes.

"We considered location within the building, structural reinforcement, elevations, you name it, when we planned this room," he spoke with obvious pride. "We've all heard the story about folks dancing all night at the Hotel Galvez during the 1915 storm. Well, Rose Parrish wanted a room like that, so we gave it to her."

J.J. excused himself and made his way through the group to speak to the architect. "The newspaper wants a picture of you and Rose in front of the mural."

"I'd be delighted. She still holding court up there?"

J.J. nodded and smiled. As they started up the stairs, he was paged to come to the front lobby.

"Some latecomers here asking for you," the security man said.

Rose had been openly disappointed at his refusal to bring guests, so he'd reconsidered and asked both Dooley and Elena. Elena said she wouldn't be comfortable at such an event. Who would she talk to? What would she wear? Dooley had said he wasn't keen on parties, but he'd bring Elena if she'd agree to it. J.J. was often caught by surprise at the rapport between those two. Now, here they were, dripping wet, in the foyer, apologizing.

"Her street was flooding, and they were telling everyone to stay in, but I got through with the truck." He mopped his head and neck with a damp towel one of the doormen had offered.

"I was afraid, but he said. . ."

"I said," Dooley broke in, "that we needed to get here. I read about the ballroom being storm-proof."

J.J. made his own apologies for not being able to stop and talk right then. He pointed in the direction of food and drink and said he'd find them later. Meanwhile, he and his new manager scurried through the crowd, arranging for the likelihood that many guests would be staying the night. There was enough food, but forty blanketed cots in the upstairs storage closet wouldn't begin to accommodate 250 guests. A sleeping room was designated, and cots were set up. Easy chairs and sofas were readily available, and some, intent on planning ahead, were already staking claims. Alcohol was flowing freely. The musicians, seeing they might be called on to play all night, had petitioned for time and a half.

"Pay whatever you have to," Blair advised him. "And keep it upbeat."

In the grand ballroom, J.J. located Rose sitting at a round table with El King and a handsome older woman. Jesse Martin was at the table with a pretty blonde, and there was another couple J.J. recognized as a city councilman and his wife, both local attorneys.

"Captain," Rose extended her hand when he approached the table. "Do you know all these people?"

"Some of them," he shook hands with Jesse, El, and the councilman.

"Well this," she motioned to the blonde beside Jesse, "is Susanna, a nurse who once upon a time stole my heart. And this," she motioned to the councilman's wife, "is another bright young woman making her way in a man's world. The young people have been chewing on the problem of malpractice claims, while we silver-hairs have been summoning up the past. Please join us, Captain, and meet my friend Daisy."

He pulled up an empty chair and sat where he could keep an eye on the ballroom.

"Daisy was a Kempner, but we won't hold it against her. She's also a storehouse of island history, and she's been telling me the most fascinating story of Lafitte's dark-haired mistress, who was said to be a ravishing beauty and a shameless flirt." She raised her hand to summon a waiter passing by.

"Benedictine and brandy," she said.

"Yes, ma'am, Mrs. Parrish."

"Anyone else?" Rose asked, smiling smugly at J.J. because the waiter knew her name. "Anyway, this mistress was much younger than Lafitte and caused quite a furor in camp. So, as his virility waned, he allowed her to take lovers, with one stipulation. When not in his bed, she was required to sleep in a hammock, while rattlesnakes roamed the floor of her boudoir. Those who would approach her were required to take their pleasure in the hammock, which discouraged all but the most ardent."

J.J. turned to Rose's friend. "Truth or fiction?"

The woman shrugged playfully and smiled back.

He looked at his watch and excused himself. "It's almost time for the auction."

Rose clapped her hands. "I've bet Daisy and El we'll get $8,000 or more. They don't want to bid, but if it goes that high, they've agreed to throw in another thousand apiece."

As the waiter appeared with Rose's drink, the band struck up a medley from *Phantom of the Opera,* and a man in a partial mask danced through the room with a handful of black and white balloons.

It was almost midnight before J.J. went in search of Dooley and Elena and found them sitting quietly at a table in the cigar bar.

"I expected you two to be in the ballroom," J. J .said.

"It's crowded in there. We decided it was safe enough in here."

"If you don't think, you wouldn't know it was a storm out-side," Elena said. "I can't hear the wind, but I know it's there." She seemed nervous, tapping her fingers against the table top.

J.J. caught tension in the air, but it was interrupted by the sight of Jesse Martin ushering Rose into the cigar bar.

"Jesse," Dooley stood and motioned them over. "And this must be the lady I've heard so much about," he held out a hand to Rose. "I feel like I know you already."

"I don't know what they've been telling you," Rose purred, "but it's not all true."

Elena put out her hand. "I'm Elena."

"Well, aren't you lovely," Rose said.

As the others started to sit, Elena excused herself and headed for the ladies room, followed by the captain who said he needed to check with the manager. He caught up with her in the hall and took her by the arm.

"Relax. You look worried."

"I am worried," she said. "I need—Dooley and I need to talk with you."

He frowned. "Tonight?"

"Soon."

"If you say so." He checked his watch. "You going back in there?"

She nodded.

"I'll be back later—when things quiet down—if things quiet down."

Her face relaxed slightly as she smiled a thank you, and he noted how stunning she looked. Her blouse, shimmering like mercury, was bare across the back. Nothing to wear? Must have borrowed something from her roommate.

⁂

Thirty minutes later, when J.J. returned to the cigar bar, he found Rose dominating the table, using a lighted cigar to emphasize her words. It trailed small curlicues of pungent smoke.

"Captain, I believe I've found the most interesting table in the house. Not only are these young people handsome, they're smart. We have a doctor, a nurse, an oceanographer, and, did you know Elena was studying to be an engineer before motherhood took her out of school?"

J.J. looked in Elena's direction and raised his eyebrows, as if impressed. It was news to him.

"And I'm finding out things about you I've never known."

"Such as?"

"That you have a regular poker game at your house. If I'd known, I might have asked to come. I love a poker game."

"Another B & B, Mrs. Parrish?" the waiter who had obviously been assigned to Rose stopped by the table. "This is the last call."

"By all means, Scott. And bring us a deck of playing cards and some chips. All right," Rose turned to address the table. "Who's up for a game? I'll stake each of you to a hundred dollars in chips."

Elena shook her head, but the others grinned and pulled

their chairs closer. The captain begged off, saying he needed to keep tabs on things. Rose wanted five players.

"Could you hunt up the gentleman who put in the high bid on my necklace? The antique dealer. Tell him I'm going to give him a chance to get some of his money back."

⚜

As the mahogany grandfather clock struck three, waiters were circulating through the rooms with coffee and chocolate. Most of the older guests dozed on cots or easy chairs; a lively group had claimed tables in the ballroom, where at least thirty couples were line dancing to "Boot Scoot Boogie;" the poker game in the cigar bar had attracted some onlookers. An hour later, a weather advisory announced that the worst was over but recommended that people not get out on the streets until daylight. While some debated making a run for it, the majority elected to stay and "see what they're serving for breakfast."

249

It was almost dawn when J.J. retreated to his office, shut the door, and put his feet up on the desk. The party had been going for twelve hours. He leaned back and was rubbing his forehead along the brow line when someone knocked.

"Yeah?"

Dooley stuck his head in the door.

"How'd the poker game go?"

"I came out with fifty dollars." He patted his pocket and smiled. "Jesse took Rose home. She kept up like a trooper until about an hour ago. Then, all of a sudden called it quits. We're going to clear out, too."

"Think you can make it?"

"It'll be daylight by the time I get to Thirteen Mile Road. It should be open by then." He smiled and ran a hand through his hair. "I'm glad you asked us. It was some kind of deal." He started to close the door, then stuck his head back in. "I need to talk to you sometime about Elena."

"What about Elena?"

"Nothing that can't wait a day or two."

J.J. nodded, too tired for curiosity.

⁘

At seven the next morning J. J headed home, exhausted, needing to see what the storm had left in its wake. The sun had come out, the flooding had receded, and most of the damage appeared to have been done by wind. Signs, construction material, small boats, and assorted trash were strewn across the landscape. A few cars sat deserted by the roadside.

A white flag whipped in the breeze outside Kelly's, Mrs. Kelly's signal that she was in and had information for west beach owners. J.J. stopped.

"Top of the mornin'," Mrs. Kelly called, with unnatural cheerfulness. Woody, sitting at a table by the window, raised a hand.

"Thought I recognized your pickup on the road back there," J.J. said. "Trouble?"

"Headed in about eight last night, when the storm looked like she wasn't goin' to let up. Got a surge in that low piece of beach and I stalled. Beach patrol picked me up. But I could'a spent the night in the pickup if I had to."

"Where did you spend the night?"

Woody jerked his head in the direction of Mrs. Kelly.

"And where did you spend the night, Captain?" Mrs. Kelly, unembarrassed, studied J.J.'s wilted tuxedo.

"It's a long story," he said and turned back to his friend, "Sounds like you were a little slow in clearing out, Woody."

"Maybe so," Woody mumbled. "Used to count on talkin' it over with you."

"I remember those phone calls."

"I called Dooley, but he wasn't there neither."

"How'd your cabin fare?" J.J. asked.

"It's okay," Mrs. Kelly volunteered. "We checked it out first thing this morning. San Luis Pass is still closed. Tides're four feet above normal. I lost my sign and some shingles, but came out okay again. I respect Mother Nature, you see, and she never gives me a hard time."

J.J. excused himself from the conversation and headed home. He was too tired to think clearly, but not so tired that Mrs. Kelly's banter didn't irritate him. Like she'd expect a bull not to charge her if she was a vegetarian. And she had put out that flag, not because she had information, but because she wanted to show off Woody, who'd apparently appeared at her door in town last night. J.J. realized he didn't understand women, but why would anyone want to brag about Woody?

He drove by to check on the old cabin, which looked mangy, with shingles missing in numerous places. A window was broken where something had sailed into it. Dooley was removing glass from the frame and waved as if to say he had things under control, but J.J. stopped anyway.

"Need a hand?"

"Just going to tape this up until I can replace it."

J.J. took a pair of gloves and got out of the truck. "It goes easier with two."

They picked glass in relative silence and then began taping garbage bags over the open space. The bags flapped and were hard to hold in place.

"Not sure this will stay if the wind picks up," Dooley said.

"Hold on and I'll get my staple gun," J.J. told him.

"I can help." Elena suddenly appeared from around the corner. Her hair fell around her face and shoulders, rumpled and abundant, and she had on a UTMB T-shirt that hit her at mid-thigh.

"Where'd you come from?" J.J. did a double take.

"I was asleep in there," she motioned, "but I heard voices."

J.J. looked at Dooley. Dooley shrugged. "Her place had some water in it, and I said she could sleep here."

J.J. felt a flush of irritation. That same thing as before. Only then it was Elena and Jesse. Now Dooley?

"It's nothing," she looked at him and shook her head.

J.J. stopped to look from one to the other and decided he needed to ask. "So what was it you wanted to talk to me about?"

"I have asked Dooley to marry, and he says he will," Elena announced in a voice one might use to dedicate a bridge.

"We've been talking about it for a while," Dooley added, when J.J.'s silence got uncomfortable. "Wanted to run it by you, but you've been hard to catch."

"I hear yesterday that the immigration people talk of stopping work visas like mine," Elena added. "When I go to México next time, I may have problems getting back."

"So if we get married, she can bring her boys over."

J.J. looked at Dooley, then at Elena. He folded his arms across his chest, caught his lip between his teeth, and waited before he spoke. "You were going to run it by me? To get my blessing?"

"Captain," Elena put her hand on his arm. "It's for the citizenship."

He didn't look at her, just lifted her hand from his arm and wrapped it around Dooley's in a motion of handing her off. "I thought you were smarter than this," he said to the boy.

"Smarter than to marry with me?" Elena, indignant, raised her voice. "And what's wrong with me? You have never complained before."

"Smarter than to take on a family that isn't your own," J.J. said to Dooley. The fact that he had to look up a couple of inches to his son didn't help.

"I'm not promising to raise Elena's twins. I just want to help her get them here. Thought you might let me buy the old cabin for them to live in."

"I'm the one who said it first," Elena broke in, "and he agreed. And there's nothing *sexual*." She said the word in

Spanish, and it sounded more suggestive. "But if we marry and that is what he wants. . ."

"I don't want to know," J.J. said, waving his hand at them to stop as he walked toward the truck.

Dooley followed and caught the driver's door as J.J. was starting to shut it. He leaned down and spoke slowly. "I'm willing to do that for her. It's no big deal to me."

"Marriage?"

"Just legal words. As long as the three of us agree, and we're comfortable with it, you all can still have your thing."

"Our thing?"

"Your relationship," Dooley half-mumbled the word.

"That bothers you? Is this what it's about?"

"Bothers me that you don't take her needs any more into consideration when she's so loyal to you. But it's none of my business. I know that." He rested against the open door and rubbed his palms together. "I know this feels awkward, J.J., but it doesn't have to be."

J.J. started the truck and let the motor idle. He'd never seen Dooley nervous, never seen him so serious. He was so well-intentioned, and incredibly naïve, much like his mother had been. It was hard to sustain anger at him.

"What's she going to do?" J.J. asked.

"She's going to look for work at a hardware store, or maybe Radio Shack—some place where she can learn and move up. She's sharp. She has the equivalent of two years of college."

"I know," J.J. said. But he actually hadn't known about the college. When had she had time to go to college? He put the truck in gear.

"You mad?" Dooley asked.

"Nope," J.J. answered. He was rubbed sore that they had gone behind his back and had chosen to spring this on him when he was too tired to think straight. But he had asked for it. As for being mad, long-term, split-the-sheets mad? No. At thirty, he was masterminding a robbery ring. People do crazy things—especially when they're young.

As he shut the door and rolled down the window, Elena walked up. She leaned in toward him. "You be proud of your son," she said. "He has a big heart. I won't bring him trouble. Not you either."

It was impossible to look at her without desire. Even now he wanted to smooth her hair, trace the line of her lips with his hand. "That's not the problem," he said.

She raised her hands and threw back her head. *"Dios,"* she whispered, as if she needed help but knew she wasn't going to get it. "What is the problem?"

"Our relationship. *You* married to *my* son. *Your* children."

"You are ashamed?"

"Maybe. Or jealous."

She smiled softly.

"It's a lousy idea, Elena." He started backing out.

"I give it my best shot," she shouted after him. "Maybe you will get used to it."

J.J. drove on, relieved that Woody had been back at Kelly's and not next door to catch that scene. He found that his new house had survived the storm well. Beyond a bunch of trash and mud, he couldn't see any wind or water damage. On the dock, a snake was sunning itself. He poured himself a glass of water, took two aspirin, and fell across the bed.

⁜

The telephone awakened him harshly. It was hot in his bedroom. The circuit breakers must have gone off during the storm, and the air conditioning wasn't on. Drops of sweat were forming on his forehead.

"This is Jesse." J.J. could hear other noises in the background, the rattle of metal, a jumble of voices. He sounded shaky. "I'm at the hospital, Captain. With Rose."

"What happened?"

"She lost consciousness. I, *uh*, I called 911, couldn't find a pulse, tried to give her CPR. God, I've never done it on a live person. It was," he hesitated, "not easy. But we got her here pretty quick."

"And?"

"She had a stroke. She's been given medication that should minimize the damage. The next twelve hours are crucial, but she's able to breathe on her own, and that's a good sign."

J.J. wiped his forehead and took a deep breath. "She's going to be mad as hell when she wakes up," he said.

"I know," Jesse sighed.

In the background, J.J. heard someone being paged on a loudspeaker, heard the sound echoing off the white hospital corridors, saw an image of Rose, pale and limp, lying semi-conscious, monitors attached, being attended by people who hadn't the slightest idea that only a few hours earlier this body had been so full of life, dealing five-card stud and drinking the finest liqueur.

23

Rose's eyes flicked open, then fluttered shut. Open. Shut. The lids were heavy and slow to respond. Maybe they needed oiling. She set out in search of oil, but became lost in a dark hall. There were other voices, just around the corner. She struggled on until her hands reached out in the dark and felt the smooth, white coolness. Ironed sheets, from out of her childhood. She was lying horizontal. But this wasn't her bed. She opened her eyes again. A face looked back at her. A pretty face, smiling. She wanted to get to a sitting position, but something didn't work. The pretty face leaned close.

"Don't try to get up," it said in her ear. "You might pull out your tubes."

A question formed in her mind. "Waaa," she said.

"What's that, dear?" the pretty face leaned down to her.

"Waaa." Her lips didn't work.

The girl picked up one of her hands and caressed it like someone would pet a small bird. "You had a stroke," she said. She put pillows behind Rose's head and lifted a glass to her mouth. "Can you take a sip of water?"

She was thirsty. The liquid fell from her mouth and down her front.

"That's good," the girl said and wiped the spill away.

From behind the girl, the others came into focus. She couldn't think of their names, but she knew them. A man and a boy. They stared down at her with heavy faces. A stroke. Not good. Her eyes fluttered shut.

She opened her eyes.

"Can you eat something for me?" Pretty Face was extending a spoon toward her.

Rose shook her head.

Pretty Face laid down the spoon. "No?" she said, smiling. She stood up and moved the food tray aside. "Something to drink?"

Rose moved her head up and down and tried to raise her hand toward the water pitcher.

The nurse poured a glass of water, supported Rose's head with her arm, and held the glass to her mouth. A little spilled. Susanna, the name on the nurse's chest, put a straw in the glass and held it to Rose's lips. She fumbled, but was able to capture it and hold it between her lips. A trickle of water reached her mouth.

"Excellent, Rose," the girl's dimples twinkled in her cheeks.

How does she know my name, Rose thought. The images fell in on one another—*this girl, and that boy I saw before. Jesse. They work at the hospital. There's going to be a party. The captain was here a while ago, with Jesse. Why am I here? She said a stroke. A stroke of luck. Not luck. Why can't I get this clear? I had a stroke. People die with strokes. Am I dead? You may wish you were. Who said that? Rose? I'm Rose. I'm lost in a tunnel. Someone, help.*

⁙

"Can you raise two fingers, dear?" Pretty offered her a drink from a straw as she talked. "Good," she said when Rose complied. "Now, I'm going to ask you some questions, and if the answer is yes, I want you to raise one finger and if the answer is no, I want you to raise two fingers. Okay?"

Rose raised a finger.

"You're coming along," the pretty nurse told her. She asked some more questions, then excused herself to return with an official looking man in a white jacket. *What do they call them?* Rose thought. *Doctors that stay at the hospital all the time, like they live there, like residence—no, that's a house—like, resident. Resident.*

After some silly questions and some simple tests, the resident, apparently pleased with her progress, ordered that she be taken off the catheter to see how things were working 'down there.' He also called for physical therapy the next day. "It's our program here," he explained to Rose, who nodded, trying to understand what was going on. "We have an outstanding record in stroke recovery. You may be walking out of here next week."

✢

"We're taking the catheter out now, dear. This may sting a bit. Did you feel that? No? Well, sometimes it's dead down there for a while. You ring, now, when you feel the need, and someone will bring you a bedpan."

Rose understood what the nurse was saying, but she didn't like the sound of it. She followed a bumpy path backwards. *I was at the party and now I'm here. I had a stroke, at home, I think, and they got me here, somehow, and I can move a little better than I could yesterday or the day before and I may be recovering, but I have to pass some tests. Damn degrading! I knew it would come to this. Well, stop whimpering, old girl, and get on with it.*

Within another twenty-four hours, Rose could lift crackers to her mouth and get them soft enough to swallow. She could take a few steps with a walker, though her left leg worked better than her right, but the thoughts came jaggedly, and the words wouldn't come at all. She was angry. She tried to do as she was asked. She had failed the bedpan test and was wearing diapers. People cheered when she took six steps. Reduced to infancy.

Jesse stopped in to congratulate her on her progress. She stared at him with ice in her eyes, trying to say what she was unable to articulate.

"We're going to get you out of here, Rose," he promised. "Hang in."

She sat, or lay, in her bed and brooded. Most meals she refused. Sometimes she pushed at the strange hands that tried to feed her, spilled the food on the bed, a mess to be cleaned. She knocked things off the table in clumsiness, sometimes in exasperation. The hospital chaplain came to pray with her. She wouldn't look at him. He prayed anyway, a beatific smile on his blank face, asking God to have mercy on her soul. "If there is a God and there is a soul," she tried to say, but he misunderstood her mumblings and took them for appreciation. "You're welcome, dear," he said.

She wanted no consolation. She wanted to express her misery, to spew it across every face that smiled down at her and asked her to roll over and say "Ah." *Like to see* you *when the tables are reversed,* she thought. *You think you'll never be like this. Just sure somehow* you *can avoid it, so you coo to me, and I'm supposed to like it.* She practiced speaking when no one was around but, embarrassed by the slurred results, she communicated increasingly by hand signals and words painstakingly written on a tablet someone had made available.

After ten days, Rose was moved to the recovery wing of the hospital. Her day was filled with appointments—physical therapy, occupational therapy, speech therapy, a daily bath, three meals, visits from doctors, nurses, social workers, the nutritionist, the chaplain, and assorted others. The activity left her exhausted and irritable, but nights, when she was alone, were worse. Television had become long and complicated. She found it hard to follow the plots of movies and preferred her daytime shows, but in the daytime someone was constantly carting her off to therapy, where she refused to comply, except with the simplest of tasks. One day Jesse came in with a VCR and a video tape. He set the time to record between noon and five P.M. and told her she could see her shows that evening.

Sometime after dinner, Pretty Face appeared in her room with a sandwich and a glass of tea and settled herself in the visitor's chair. "We just changed shifts," she explained. "I told Jesse I'd stop in and run back your tape."

Rose nodded.

"He thinks about you a lot," she went on. "You remember your party? I hope so. If you don't now, it should come back. We were going to check out the ballroom when he got back from taking you home, maybe dance," she dimpled. "But he never showed up, and I didn't know what to think. Finally he called, all out of breath, and asked if I could meet him here." She unwrapped her sandwich and took a bite. "Ummm. You want to hear this?"

Rose nodded.

"He paced up and down in that corridor outside ICU for hours. I think he blamed himself somehow. When I first met Jesse, I thought he was a smart-off, the kind of guy that never takes anything or anyone too serious, always looking to make a joke, further himself, maybe at my expense."

Rose shook her head.

"I realize," the girl smiled. "He's not like that at all. He's complicated."

She slipped off her shoes and talked as she finished her sandwich. "I had a hard day, Rose. How about you? It's ridiculous, isn't it, the way they take you all over the place. Won't let you get a minute's rest? But they say it speeds recovery. You're coming along, Rose. I know it seems slow, but before you know it, six months will have passed, and you'll probably be able to do just about everything by yourself. I see a lot of people in your situation, and you're doing very well," she smiled and punched the remote to begin the taped *Oprah* show. "Mind if I watch with you? I like this woman."

Rose didn't mind. When the girl was her nurse, she was reserved and businesslike, but when she came in after hours to talk, she was natural and didn't make Rose do anything she didn't want to do. Susanna took to stopping by after work. She talked about patients a lot worse off than Rose. Sometimes she read to Rose from the newspaper. Sometimes they watched television together, and Susanna gave her commentary. "Uh-oh, she's getting fat again. That woman has freed us all from apologizing about weight. Still, it's got to be a drag to yoyo up and down so." The girl had opinions. She also was stuck on Jesse. Rose could tell when they were in the room together. The way she tilted her head to listen to him. The way she managed to stop in the room whenever he visited.

❖

One Saturday morning the captain brought a young Mexican woman, whose dark eyes shone like the seeds she used to fill her pockets with when she was a girl. She couldn't remember what those were called, or where that was, just like she couldn't remember this girl, although the captain acted like she should know her. Elena, he called her. She assumed he'd hired her, like a babysitter, and found the idea irritating.

"They say weekends are hell in a hospital," the captain said, "and I have to be at Maison Rouge. The club is doing better than we imagined, Rose." He leaned down and squeezed her hand. "You'll be out of here soon, and I'll take you to see it."

She pulled back her hand, let the papers in her lap slide to the floor, and looked away. The captain turned to go, ignoring her bad humor, while the strange woman pushed the wheelchair out of the way and stooped to pick up the papers.

"He cares much," she told Rose, "but doesn't know how to say it."

Then she moved the chair around and sat down in the visitor's chair opposite Rose. "Do you play checkers?"

The girl pulled a checkerboard from the tote bag she carried and set it up between them. Rose couldn't work her hands to complete a move, but she could indicate the checker she wanted to move, and to what position. They played until she was tired. Elena helped her into bed. Rose awoke with a cramp. Elena massaged her leg, pulling the toes forward, relaxing the cramp. She spoke softly under her breath as she worked.

Rose had picked up some Spanish over the years. There was a Spanish speaking nurse she had when Nate was alive and on his last legs. With hours together at his bedside, they had passed the time trying to talk about ordinary things, making the best of an otherwise tedious situation. Nellie, that had been her name. Strange name for a Hispanic, Rose thought, but she had been a bright woman, and a good cook. Rose shifted in the bed. This girl has good hands, she thought. There, she just about has that cramp rubbed out.

Rose had drifted off when the girl turned her over, pulled the covers over her legs and whispered, "I'll see you *mañana.*"

❖

The patient offered no response. Someone had written that on her chart. She had read it from her wheelchair. Every morning someone helped her dress, put her in a wheelchair, and there she waited, a cog in the wheels of medicine. She had managed to inspect her chart. *Left hemisphere stroke. Mild hemiplegia. Aphasia. Impaired cognition. Depression.*

She had stopped trying to talk. She didn't care to improve. *To hell with them.* She tried to think it out at night, lying in the dark after the evening shift had taken her to the bathroom and given her all those damn pills. She wanted to pretend to take them, the pills, and collect them until she had enough. But she couldn't remember how many were enough, and some of them might be making her better. She was confused. No one was going to help her. She had to get home. There she could think this through. Do some research. Something needed to be done. And 'twere well it were done quickly. Where did that come from? She strained to remember.

Hospital activity slowed on the weekend. No therapy. No visits from miscellaneous personnel. Fewer visits from medical personnel. It should have pleased her; instead it made her restless. The previous weekend she'd been too sick to notice, but this was her second full week, her third weekend, and she sensed a rhythm. There was that flurry of activity at the morning change of shifts, followed by room cleaning and baths, then quiet until lunchtime, then shift change again at two, a meal at five, shift change, *ad infinitum*. Without therapy classes, she had time to think, time to be angry. "Count your blessings," the preacher on the television beamed at her. *Go to hell*, she thought, and managed to change the channel. She got cartoons. She pressed again. The preacher again. Damn. She pressed again. A tour of the hospital came on the screen. *Spare me*, Rose thought.

She had thrown the remote control on the floor and was wishing she hadn't when Elena slipped into the room. She had said she'd be back, but Rose wasn't counting on it. Yesterday, she hadn't much cared.

"Good morning," the girl said.

Rose nodded.

"Checkers today?"

Rose nodded.

When lunch came, Elena offered to feed her. Rose declined, choosing instead to pick at her food. Lifting a spoon, trying to get it to her mouth, chewing, swallowing—these were awkward movements now, and eating was work. Did it used to be pleasure? After her tray had been removed, Elena slipped downstairs and brought back a large chocolate milkshake with a straw. Its creamy coolness felt like moonlight in Rose's mouth. She worked on it all afternoon, so that at dinnertime she had no appetite and pushed her tray off to the girl. When the orderly came, she complimented Rose on cleaning her plate. Elena smiled at Rose over the orderly's head, then reached in her tote bag and pulled out a plastic container. "Massage today," she announced.

Rose shook her head. The girl approached the bed, sat on the edge, and poured some of the bottle's contents into her hands, then rubbed them together before picking up Rose's hand.

"I know," the girl said, stroking Rose's hand with her own. Her touch was firm, working the joints of the fingers, rubbing at the fleshy pad below the thumbs, pressing in the center of the palms. "You don't want to be touched," she said, "because you're mad at this body. Because it won't do what you want. But I am telling you it's okay. I ask you, *por favor,* to let go." The sureness of the girl's touch accepted Rose's anger and coaxed it away. She closed her eyes against a sudden sting of tears, the first since she'd found herself in this Godforsaken place.

The girl continued to massage, her hands sliding up Rose's arms in a long, seamless move that recognized her flesh as something alive. Rose relaxed as the girl positioned pillows for comfort, rolled her to her side, and began to rub across her shoulders, up the neck, down the spine, out across the buttocks. She had a problem there, with the girl's hands on her backside, feeling her own helplessness, remembering the humiliation of baths and diaper changes, but she willed it away. No place here for pride.

The soothing hands continued down her legs, to work on the calves, where the cramp had come yesterday and had lingered, with a hinted promise, throughout the day. When she reached Rose's feet, the girl stopped to refresh the oil. Rose lay quietly, hoping it wasn't over.

As she worked, Elena spoke softly, as if to herself. Her voice, low and rhythmic, had the quality of someone reading poetry. Remote. Requiring no response. Rose didn't catch all the words, but let them splash across her.

"I used to do this for my *abuela*. My grandmother. She liked it very much, too. When I massage, I talk to her, but she could only listen and couldn't give me her thoughts. I wished for her thoughts. She had many stories of the old days. *Cuentos de la patria—México—*our beautiful land, and always *los conflictos*.

"But here, also, are conflicts. *A la frontera*. When I cross the border, I may not be able to return.

She had her hands beneath Rose's shoulders now, palms at the shoulder blades, pulling gently upwards, thumbs pressing softly at the base of the neck. *"Es bueno,* this feeling of skin on skin. No? Too bad it gets a woman in trouble. It brought me an *esposo, muy guapo, muy estúpido*. And two *niños*. How you say? Twins. The captain says you have no *niños* and I say, *pobrecita*. He tells me you are rich. *En México,* to be rich allows one to live in a nice house, to pay her bills, with some left over, to have a new car, pretty clothes, and the children, to get an education.

"My boys—*tan precioso*. I want that they grow up well and maybe there is a way. Dooley says he will marry with me. The captain *no le gusta*, but what can he do? Dooley and I are not *amantes*. Should I marry with him? You are almost asleep, I think. It's good you don't hear this. You have your own *proble-mas*. He tells me you were a wise woman. *Una sabia*. Maybe you still are."

Elena laid the cover lightly over Rose and washed her hands at the sink. Rose, silent and relaxed, could hear the water running, hear the girl reach for a paper towel, hear the towel dropped in the trash. She wanted to roll over and look at her again. Maybe try to talk. But it was hard to turn by herself. With

265

the mental image of a turtle flailing on its back, she rejected action for a remnant of dignity. She needed to think about what she had heard. What did she say about the captain and someone who would marry her?

✢

After two days with Elena, Rose was irritated to find that Monday had come, and hospital routine was back to normal. The social worker appeared, with a clipboard in hand, to discuss her release and future arrangements.

"Two more weeks," the woman told her. "That will make a full month of rehab. That's the standard. You're doing well, they tell me, except for the speech. Your therapist thinks you're reluctant to talk. Could that be so, dear?"

Rose glared at her.

"We need to have a plan for when you're dismissed. Will you go home?"

Rose nodded.

"I need to speak to someone responsible for your care. Otherwise, I can recommend some excellent nursing facilities where you can be helped."

Rose shook her head vehemently and reached for her writing pad.

Dr. Martin, she wrote.

✢

Pearl had come every Monday, Wednesday, and Friday to report on Thomas the cat and to bring Rose's mail, which was now accumulating in a box on her hospital room window sill, beside the flowers the captain sent every week. Pearl entered the room cautiously, sensitive to her employer's ill temper. Rose motioned for her to sit. *Home in 10 das,* she wrote. Something looked wrong, but Pearl could figure it out.

Pearl's face brightened, as if she thought that was good news.

Rose waved her hand and frowned. There would be no celebrations.

"With you down here," Pearl said, "I haven't had enough to do. I planted bulbs for spring."

Rose shook her head as if the other were demented. *Send handchiefs,* she wrote.

Pearl reached for a Kleenex box, her eyebrows raised in question.

Real, Rose wrote and underlined the word.

The next day she took her pad and pencil to occupational therapy and indicated she wanted to practice writing. She also practiced in the mornings before breakfast. She needed to be able to communicate, and this talking wasn't coming along. Her tongue felt like a thick slab of bacon, and, though she knew the words, they hung trapped in her head, as reluctant to emerge as her cat from under the bed. The therapist had her looking into a mirror, trying to form vowel and consonant sounds, doing exercises with her lips. It was not a pretty sight, not to mention the drooling that occurred from time to time, even when she wasn't trying to speak.

❖

On the third Saturday of what she had come to think of as her incarceration, a tall young man came to her room. Rose was dressed and seated in her chair by the window, trying to do a crossword puzzle, cursing the spaces in her brain, aware that every day she was thinking a little better than the day before.

"Hi," he said, standing at the doorway. He stood almost at attention, removed his cap, and held it in one hand. In the other hand was a black tote bag.

Rose waved him forward, thinking him a messenger of some sort.

"Elena couldn't come today," he said, "and I told her I'd like to come. If you don't feel like seeing me, I'll go."

He was familiar. She motioned for him to sit.

"I'm Dooley," he extended his hand, and she laid hers in it. His hand was large and warm and very alive. Was this the one Elena spoke of? Had they met?

She wiped at her mouth with a lace-edged linen handkerchief and tried to smile.

"I'm not too good at crosswords," he nodded toward her newspaper, "but I admire people who do them. My father likes to do them."

She looked at him, hoping he could read the question in her eyes.

"My father?" he got it. "That would be Captain Broussard. You and I met at the opening of Maison Rouge, but that was the night you had your stroke, and Jesse told me part of that might have been erased. I sure am sorry it happened, but you're looking good." Rose's instinct was to like this person, though her nature questioned that anyone with brains could attain maturity and want to go visiting infirm old ladies in the hospital. He must want something. Maybe he was simple minded, she thought. Maybe they sent him to her because they'd be a good match—the half-wit and the half-wit.

She pointed to a crossword clue—"a nautical term"—then showed him the five spaces provided, where she had an "m" in the final position.

"That should be *abeam*," he said. "That's like the crossways of a ship as opposed to the length of it. Right angles to the keel is the proper definition."

She looked up to see if he was laughing at her.

"I can help with nautical stuff. I'm a marine biologist."

Seems like she did remember something like that. And didn't they play poker? She dabbed at her mouth and reached for her yellow pad.

Poker, she wrote.

"You want to play poker?"

She shook her head impatiently.

"Did we play poker? At the party?"

She nodded.

"We sure did," he smiled. "I won fifty dollars from you. Well, I went away with $150, actually, since you staked us all in the first place and you wouldn't let me pay you back. I donated the money to the dolphin rescue program I work with. Thought you might like that. It was a fine party, by the way. My dad tells me you did most of the planning."

She nodded, wishing she could remember more of it. When she lay awake at night, she tried to remember, and little pieces kept coming back. Like now. She could remember the poker table now and smoking a cigar and Jesse, frowning.

What's your story? she wrote. She was proud of that question. She had thought it up this morning when waiting for the nurse to help her out of bed. A way to get other people to talk, so she wouldn't be required to. The only thing she hated more these days than trying to talk was being alone.

"My story is about looking for my father for the last few years. Now I've found him, and *I'm* glad, but I'm not so sure *he* is. Other than that, I love the water. I get my masters in marine resources management next May, and whatever I do after that is almost sure to involve the ocean.

The girl? she wrote.

He shrugged and looked confused.

Elena, she wrote.

"We're friends," he said, and offered nothing else, though she waited.

Your mother? Rose wrote.

He thought before he spoke. "My mother has a roving nature. You might call her a gypsy, but she says she's managed to organize her life so she can do only what she wants to do, and that's something most people don't ever achieve. She's in Florida right now. That's where she likes to spend the winter."

When she didn't write any more questions, he asked, "You want to play checkers, or gin rummy?"

She chose checkers because she didn't think she could manage holding the cards for gin, but she appreciated that he'd given her the option. It wasn't just his eyes and soft manner, or the fact that he didn't treat her like she was disgusting that pleased Rose. She liked his choice of words. A roving nature. She could follow that.

The stroke had wiped out trails in her brain. Sometimes when she came across a word or an idea, she could dig around a bit and uncover a path, and it would become clear and useable again. Sometimes she dug and dug, and nothing came clear, like when she read the headlines or watched the news. People who called themselves pro-life were voting in favor of the death penalty. The president was saying we might have to go to war so the world could have peace. Only a month ago, she must have understood.

She looked up at Dooley. Was that his name? *Your name?* she wrote.

He reached questioningly for her pencil. *Dooley,* he wrote.

She nodded and tried to smile.

24

Jesse used to imagine how it would be, receiving his M.D.
In that picture, he'd be surrounded by family and friends, and
there would be serious recognition, and a celebration. In reality,
the moment passed, and all he could think of was how over-
loaded he was at work. And that he was worried about Rose.
She was mad and depressed. Still proud. Severely limited. Her
disabilities were possibly more physical than mental, which
made for a bad scenario. She tried to pin him with her eyes every
time he came in her room, and so far he'd avoided a confrontation, but one was sure to come.

Jesse had gotten the residency in Family Medicine he'd
applied for. His assignment was underway, working with indi-
gents in the county, and it was interesting medicine, even
though the patients shot themselves down, literally and figura-
tively. The work felt important, and the people he saw were less
demanding and more unpredictable than those who paid for
their health care. Rose would surely disapprove—if and when
she found out—but now he thought she might be happy that he
was staying close. He'd paid his dues to her over the last year,

and would continue to, except for this escape pill she's looking for, not that such existed. He wasn't going to put his future on the line. How could she want that? She hadn't invested in him to see him throw it away, he reasoned.

⁜

He had a new family now. There were seven of them—six first year residents and a senior resident—people who could understand how crazy his life was, because it mirrored their own. They shared cases and humor and pieces of their personal lives, along with pizza and doughnuts and coffee. There were two nice girls with good minds and sisterly attitudes that made them easy to work with. One of them was married, as were two of the guys. They had all chosen this Family Medicine route because they weren't quite ready for the hotshot specialties.

"So, Jesse, how's it going with Susanna?" someone asked one morning just as he had filled his mouth with heavily sugared coffee.

He swallowed. "Might be going better if we had a little time. I see her at the hospital most days, but that's not exactly the ultimate in romantic settings."

"Still looking after your godmother?"

That was how he had described Rose to the team. It was a convenient tag, and close to the truth.

"She gets out next week, and I've got nurse Victorias lined up to take care of her at home."

"The monarch of the fourth floor?" one of the girls asked with a giggle. "Now that lady's a piece of work."

"So is my godmother," Jesse said, considering the power struggles he'd observed between the two of them when Rose was in with pneumonia. He considered himself lucky she had agreed to come. Nurse Victorias had retired from the hospital and was doing only private nursing now, but she didn't take just any job, and had made it clear she was doing this because she thought he was a nice boy and she had high respect for Pearl.

The topic of the daily noon lecture series at the hospital was patient suffering and medical ethics. Jesse made it a point to attend, along with some of his team mates. Later, they argued among themselves about euthanasia.

"If modern medicine can extend life past any decent quality, a patient has the right to ask for a dignified death."

"And doctors have the right to refuse," Jesse said. "I will give no deadly medicine to anyone if asked, nor suggest any such advice," he quoted the Hippocratic oath.

"I don't think we can hide behind that any more. Tell me what's worse—providing an independent means of checking out, or doing some of those things we've all seen or heard about, like failing to refill an oxygen tank, or dragging your feet on the way to a code red, or disconnecting the food supply so the patient starves to death?"

273

"This dialogue's only going to increase as the population ages. They've had a form of voluntary euthanasia in the Netherlands since '84. If you lived there, you might be used to the idea, not think it was any worse than a therapeutic abortion."

"I couldn't get used to helping someone die. It's not my idea of being a doctor."

"Get real. We watch people die all the time. I could find you a situation just about every day, where, if you're honest, you'd agree the kindest thing is to put that person out. . ."

"Not for us to decide," someone broke in.

"I agree," one of the girls said.

"If we don't decide, who does?" the other girl said. "I say it isn't immoral for a doctor to assist in the rational suicide of a terminally ill person," she drew the words out so they sounded legal. "And I'm not the only one that feels that way. A lot of doctors share that position, and some are brave enough to say so publicly."

"Brave is right. They've probably got their careers behind them," Jesse said, "because I'm not risking what I've worked for. It's trouble with a capital T."

"Not if you do it right. The discreet ones are never charged or convicted."

"For sure, if you're going to do it, you know your patient, you get a second opinion, and you sure as hell don't administer it yourself."

"It could still backfire."

"Yeah. Well, sometimes you might have to go out on a limb to help someone. I see people who are just waiting to die. They've outlived all their friends. Can't do for themselves. When they start starving themselves, they need an easier out. I'm not sure I can say no to that."

"It's a question of conscience," Jesse insisted.

"What if it was your mother?"

Or your godmother, Jesse thought. He had made his decision, but the question continued to dog him and having some of his medical family taking the other side didn't make it any easier.

✛

Jesse was on call for the newborn nursery every fourth night. He usually checked with the OB floor before he left the hospital to see if anything was cooking, but this Friday night it looked quiet. He turned on the cell phone his dad had given him for graduation, checked the battery, and stuck it in his shirt pocket, feeling self-conscious and showy as a kid on a skateboard. He and Susanna were going on a date. He'd bumped into her about three in the afternoon drinking tea in Rose's room.

"Just finished my shift," she explained, "and brought Rose some tea. She's mastered the cup."

Jesse had nodded enthusiastically, not looking at Rose, who was sure to be wearing a sarcastic look. When he did look her way, she was busy making a list of things she wanted him to bring from the house. She had gotten good at this, giving him lists of things to do almost every day. When he said it might be a day or so before he could get to it, she'd frown. Sometimes she'd ask Pearl for the same thing, so that when he went out of his way to do her bidding, he often discovered it had already been taken care of. He couldn't tell if her manipulation was planned, or instinctive.

"She's keeping your attention," Susanna declared when they were outside the room. "Like a child."

"Except she's not a child. She knows what she's doing. At least as far as I can tell. I just don't know if I should let her get away with it."

Susanna shrugged. "She doesn't have much else to do."

When he frowned, unsatisfied with her answer, she took his arm and focused her eyes on him. Maybe she even batted them. "What if I said I'll go with you, and we'll get her stuff and then maybe you'll buy me dinner, since you're a salaried doctor now." Her dimples crinkled when she said 'doctor.'

He picked her up a few hours later, driving Rose's Mercedes. That made Susanna smile, too. He had noticed how proudly she declared she wasn't hooked on material goods—she was a nurse after all—but it showed anyway, her taste for nice things. She was going to like seeing the inside of Rose's house too, Jesse thought, not the least ashamed of his intention to impress her.

He slipped his key in the front door, opened it into the foyer, and flipped on the light. Under Pearl's daily care, the wooden floor was polished to a rich, dark shine, as was the reception table. A hint of lemon oil hung in the air.

"Nice," Susanna nodded, looking down the picture-lined hall and into the sitting room at the right.

"You want a tour?"

"Sure."

He took her hand. "Come with me, my little chickadee."

She shook her hand away and laughed.

"She doesn't have any family?" she asked, following him through the downstairs, stopping to admire the copper pots in the kitchen, a breakfront that displayed china and crystal in the dining room, a curving vase of silk flowers on a pedestal at the bottom of the stairs.

He shook his head and started up.

She followed. "So who's getting all this stuff?"

"I don't know." He went into Rose's room.

She stopped at the door, looked around, and nodded. "This room looks like her. So, maybe you?"

"Maybe me what?"

"Maybe you're getting her stuff?"

He shook his head. "She's set some money aside for me. Not sure how much."

"When do you find out?"

He shrugged and looked at her, eyes wide as if to say your guess is as good as mine. No one had gotten this close to his Rose story.

"Wow. She does have you on a string. Do you owe her anything?"

"Not exactly."

Susanna was nice enough not to ask any more questions. Or maybe she was just distracted, admiring Rose's antique dressing table with the three-way mirror and the petit point chair cushion. She sat down, looking beautiful in three directions, and gathered emery boards and cuticle clippers from Rose's list. Jesse kept thinking about where they might go for dinner and not run into anyone from school. He wanted her to himself. Maybe tonight, he thought. She glanced up, caught him staring at her, and winked. Just then his phone rang.

"Dr. Martin? Got a four-pound preemie here," someone named Della told him. "Need you here to give your blessing on standard procedures." He thought he could detect the sarcasm that experienced nurses often laid on new doctors. Well, she'd have to get over it. He was the one with the M.D., and it had interrupted his life again. He took Susanna home and headed for the hospital.

⁂

Jesse's father called looking to borrow money, marking a new level in their relationship. Jerry had lost his job and gotten a DWI, his dad reported, and there was a good-sized fine and lawyer's fees to cover, and it had been a hard month. He was still with Serline, who was working in telephone sales, and they were hoping to buy a house in Baytown or Alvin, so they could be closer to him because she believed in families sticking together. Thanksgiving was coming up, and she sure hoped he'd be able to come eat with them. His dad wanted him to know that Serline was quite a cook, always trying new recipes and concentrating on nutrition, low-fat and low sugar and all that. She made some killer vegetarian enchiladas and a chocolate cake approved by Weight Watchers, and whenever she served it, she talked about how she thought his doctor son would approve.

"So, Jesse, you think you could lend me $500? I can probably pay you back over the next couple of months."

"How many times are you going to help him, Dad?"

"I've told him already, this is the last."

Jesse grimaced over the phone as he agreed to send money.

"Something else I wanted to ask," his dad's voice lowered and took on a different tone.

"What's that?"

"Can you get that Viagra?"

"I could probably get some samples."

"Does it work?"

"For some people."

"It's not for me. It's for your Uncle Ed."

"I understand." Jesse said. "Got to be sure to follow the instructions."

"I'll tell him," his dad said.

⁘

He asked his team if anyone else was getting uncomfortable requests.

"Sleeping pills? Tranquilizers? The purple pill? You name it, they want it. Your friends. Your family. The guy next door. You've got to draw the line."

"Sometimes they don't ask for medicine, they just want free advice. I went to a party the other night where this good-looking girl cornered me for an hour with a list of her symptoms."

"What was wrong with her?"

"She mentioned Chronic Fatigue, Epstein Barr, TMJ, PMS, and Carpal Tunnel Syndrome."

"Did you get a date with her?"

"After the first thirty minutes, I lost interest."

⁘

278 He had a call from Bobby Calhoun, looking for antibiotics for his boss.

"He's picked up a social disease, you know what I mean, and doesn't want to go to his own doctor for it. It's embarrassing, a man in his position, and I thought you could give us something that'll clear it up."

There were antibiotics at the clinic. He could dispense some without much trouble, but he should at least talk to the patient first. He didn't even know this man, and if he did this favor, wouldn't there be others? He'd have to examine him, he told Bobby, who said he'd get back to him.

"How'd you know to call me?" Jesse asked.

"I asked J.J. if you hadn't graduated by now, and he said you had. I guess congratulations are in order. Me, I graduated from Penn State in '65," he chuckled.

"That's no small accomplishment," Jesse said, doubtful.

"Sometimes I say Penn State; sometimes, the state pen. Don't know which gets more attention." Calhoun laughed again.

Jesse was silent. He didn't have time to encourage jokers, but something had caught his attention. The first time he'd met Calhoun the guy said something about spending time with J.J. back in the '60s. Jesse hung up, swiveled his desk chair around and located a web site that claimed, *Our criminal background check will provide a prison history on anyone who has been in prison.*

❖

J.J. Broussard called to meet with Jesse to talk about Rose. The captain had been friendlier since the night of the party, or maybe it was because Jesse, with Rose's POA for healthcare, shared the power now. Last summer on the boat, Jesse thought they'd broken through, thought the captain would start treating him like a person and not an intruder. Then, the next time he saw him, he was cool again. Icy. He sure was a moody one. All Jesse knew was that since Rose's stroke, he'd definitely changed attitude again, which was good if they had to work together.

"I'm not at the hospital much because I'm busy as hell with Maison Rouge. I owe it to Rose to keep the club going," he told Jesse. "And," he ran his hand across his face and looked uncomfortable, "the truth is, I can't stand to see her like that."

"She's getting better," Jesse tried to sound official. "They're sending her home at the end of next week."

"To do what?"

"To continue improving, let's hope. I've lined up a nurse I know to come in during the day, and I'd like to find someone to be there during the night, in case she needs help. Pearl will do it, but I don't think Rose wants Pearl up close and personal."

"I don't think she wants anyone up close and personal." J.J. rubbed his forehead and leaned toward Jesse. "Frankly, I'm glad she made this your responsibility and not mine. I have to force myself to set foot in that hospital room, to look at that woman I've known for years, see her looking like hell, not able to talk, being spoon fed."

"She's graduated from that since you saw her."

"Is she talking?"

"No."

"What a nasty kiss of fate. She loves to run the show. Can you get a read on what she's thinking?"

Jesse slipped into his medical voice. "Stroke patients are hard to read. Some have inflated opinions of their abilities; others have to be coaxed. With any stroke you expect some memory gaps, a shortened retention span, difficulty in conceptualizing. How much, it's hard to know without some pretty extensive testing, and she's not cooperating."

"Did she ever talk with you about a . . ." The captain hesitated, ". . . a check-out pill?"

Jesse nodded, not smiling. "Never called it that, but I know what you mean."

"She used to ask me to get her something," the captain said. "Something that would kill a big fish, she used to say, should be good enough. She wouldn't use it until she needed it, she told me, but if she waited to get it until she needed it, she wouldn't have it when she wanted it. I didn't give it much thought back then, but it makes sense, now that her life isn't worth a damn and she has to go on with it. I hope she isn't clear enough to realize what's going on, but I bet she is. The last time I saw her, she was mad as hell."

"She's still mad," Jesse told him, "but she's better—much better than I think you're imagining. It was a good idea to send Elena and Dooley."

"Dooley went to see Rose?"

"Last weekend. They played checkers, and he read poetry to her."

J.J. shook his head. "She can play checkers?"

"Pretty well."

"Why can't she talk?"

Jesse shrugged. "Like you said. A nasty kiss of fate."

J.J. motioned for the waiter and reached in his pocket to pay the bill. "Do this for me, will you, Jesse?"

"What?" He felt suddenly on guard.

"If she asks, see that she gets something."

"She's not terminal. In fact, she's getting better all the time."

"She ever going to be like she was?"

"Probably not."

"Then help her out."

"It's against the code."

"Screw the code. You've got the keys to the kingdom with that M.D. after your name, and we both know she helped you, and she's set aside a handsome sum for your future. Now you figure something to help her out of this with some grace because she deserves it. You owe her." J.J.'s face was getting red, though he kept his voice low.

Jesse felt off the chart too. What he was asking was unreasonable. "You could just hand her a loaded gun."

"I don't want her dead. I want her to have some decent choices, one of which is to check out when she's ready."

"We don't even know if she's capable of that decision."

"You damn well need to find that out. And talk to her. Give her some reassurance."

Jesse rubbed his temples with one hand and tried to think clearly. Where the hell did J.J. Broussard get the idea he could tell him what to do?

"You may have chosen to live outside the law, but I won't be bullied into something that could ruin me."

"What the hell does that mean?"

"I know you've served time for burglary and theft."

"And?"

"It's food for thought, considering you have almost complete control of Rose's financial affairs."

"You threatening me?"

"No. I'm weighing my responsibility to Rose."

"Why don't you tell her, you little prick," J.J. grabbed his hat and turned to go. "See what she says."

⁜

By the time Jesse stopped in to see Rose three days before her scheduled release, he'd decided he could reassure her without promising anything specific. He thought he could escape a confrontation, especially if she wasn't talking. "Typical male solution," he could imagine his female teammates complaining. He'd convince Rose that when she wanted help, he could provide it. He'd take a chance she'd never get to the asking point, because if it came to that, he'd have to back out. If that was a betrayal, it would still be easier to live with than a mercy killing on his record. As for the captain's shady history, he wasn't about to lay that on her.

He sat on the window ledge and faced Rose in her chair. Her hair had been washed and combed into place and her cheeks were brushed with pink. She wore a wine colored dressing gown and held a handkerchief in her lap. The muscles of her right hand had relaxed a little, leaving her a wider range of motion and a more natural appearance.

"Can we talk?" he asked.

She shook her head and gave him what appeared to be a quick smile.

"Well, I'll talk then, and you can interrupt me any time you like."

She nodded and reached for her pad and pencil.

"You're recovering very nicely, Rose. When you go home, you'll have help there around the clock for a month or six weeks, and I'll get with your doctor to reevaluate at the end of that time. I'll check on you every day, just like old times."

Bedside manner, she wrote.

He grinned and continued. "I haven't forgotten our earlier conversations, and I know your feelings about controlling your own destiny. I assure you, if and when the time comes that your quality of life has become very poor, there are options we'll explore together. But you're doing well, and I expect you to improve in the next month as much as you have in the past one. Let's make a date for Maison Rouge for Christmas. How's that?" He stopped and smiled as she wrote on the tablet and turned it for him to read.

Bulsiht, it said.

25

In prison, John Broussard had come across a volume of Shakespeare's complete works. It was a surprisingly compact book, with tissue-thin paper and small print. It was a textbook, he assumed, highlighted in pink and yellow, a donation from some matron who had weeded her bookshelves. In desperation, he had decided to try it and had found it tedious. Then he came across an annotation in the margin of *Hamlet*. *Fatal flaw: a quirk of character that brings one's downfall.* He went on to read the play, many times, and to ponder the idea of a fatal flaw.

J.J. recognized his willingness to take the easy way out. He saw it now in the fact that he was squeamish about visiting Rose. He didn't like visiting hospitals, seldom attended funerals, and avoided people who mourned, whether it was over a lost boyfriend or a drowned child.

He had watched one of the poker gang on west beach dying of colon cancer. Old Charlie had refused to give up. He dragged himself to the cabin on Mondays, sometimes after a day of treatments, weak and colorless, unable to eat or drink, fumbling his cards, making bad bets, nothing working but his courage,

which everyone admitted was screwed in place. It was awful for
J.J. to watch, and he found himself wishing the guy wouldn't
show up, but he did, up until two weeks before it was all over.
J.J. never got comfortable with it. People can get beyond reason when they're on their last legs, he knew that much, which
left him to wonder what Rose had in store. He thought he knew
what she was thinking and had tried to put the pressure on
Martin, but the guy didn't seem to be buying.

When he'd walked into that hospital room and seen her
barely able to wiggle a finger, he wished Martin hadn't been so
efficient with his CPR. There are things worse than dying. He
and Rose had said that more than once. They'd said a lot of
things, like how he'd help her go out easy—take her out in the
boat and let her slip over the side. Those scotch-fortified conversations were a joke now that the time was here. Her mind
wasn't gone, or so Martin had convinced him. She would be
expecting something of him, another reason he was in an avoid-
ance mode. He hadn't actually seen her since the day he took
Elena in to sit with her.

Soft, his father had called J.J., when he opted for business
instead of pre-med. "Doctors have to make hard decisions every
day, but you're too soft to do what's necessary. Always want
things to be comfortable, an easy ride." He could hear his
father's words. "When push comes to shove, you can't face up
to the hard task." It didn't bother J.J. The pre-med hadn't been
his idea, and once he hit physical chemistry, he knew it would
never make.

Later, when he'd bitten the bullet and done hard time, his
father hadn't been impressed, had wanted him to cut a deal, get
out of it somehow. And maybe he could have—by worming on
his connections. "If you have information of significant value,
we might be able to reduce your sentence," the feds had told
him. "Maybe get you probation." He had thought about what
he knew—insider trading in his stock firm, a ring of fences

across the southeast, drug and gambling machinery in Baton Rouge and New Orleans, the cover-up on the girl that died at the KA house.

"Nothing," he had said, with a smile.

"What's so funny?" the officer had asked.

"Guess I've led a sheltered life," J.J. said.

"Well, that part's over," the officer had said.

He had done what seemed the right thing for probably the first time in his life. Had taken his medicine and kept his mouth shut. Hard time, they called it, but it hadn't been that hard. He had polished his golf game, gone swimming every day, eaten decently, and no one had tried to rape him. He had proved he could handle whatever came, but that didn't change the fact that J.J. still chose to avoid uncomfortable situations. And this thing with Rose was the worst. The two of them had a history. God, he didn't like seeing her slide down the drain in a slosh of body fluids and bitterness. Beyond the loss, he felt a creepy sense of time bearing down on him, slow and heavy as a tank. She was, he found himself remembering, a woman he had been attracted to.

He remembered the night they had watched *Out of Africa* on her new VCR. She fancied Redford's character and insisted on making comparisons.

"Blonde, handsome, a loner, a rogue. Your story, here, Captain."

He had looked over at her, legs tucked neatly beneath her, a balloon glass of red wine in one hand, twiddling a strand of hair with the other, eyes moist in the subdued light of the television. She was inviting him, as she so often did.

"Think you could do that?" he had asked, turning the conversation toward her. "Live alone in Africa?"

"I could do anything I set my mind to," she had told him, with a flash.

He had nodded. Including getting me into bed, he'd thought. But neither of us really wants that.

"You'll have to leave now while we prepare her for bed," the nurse had told him when he went to see Rose the day after the party. Rose's blank eyes met his briefly, and looked away. Did he only imagine anger in that look, and mortification, and some kind of accusation? She never wanted to be caught by surprise. She never wanted him to see her at less than her best. He quit going to the hospital, and though they said she was improving, he still found himself wishing she hadn't made it through that first night. The rest of this wasn't going to be pleasant. He called the florist and ordered more flowers.

✥

Elena, who still came on Thursdays to clean, had offered to spend time with Rose in exchange for what she called her extra pay. She didn't want to stay the night with him until she decided about the marriage, she had told J.J., speaking with the calm of someone discussing what to have for dinner.

He wondered when that decision might come. It had sure seemed pressing the night of the party. What factors was she weighing? And if she decided not to marry Dooley, would she come back to J.J.'s bed, and how would that be? He respected the way she hadn't belabored him with icy looks or sighs. Could he believe that she and Dooley hadn't slept together? Did it matter? She was friendly toward him, and self-contained, and she talked about her time at Rose's house.

"Such a big house," she told him, "and so many pretty things. She wants to give things to me. Like these," she reached up and touched a dangling earring of silver and onyx. "It's okay, you think, that I take them?"

"She wouldn't offer if she didn't want you to have them."

"She likes me to read to her in Spanish. Poems. Children's poems. She likes the rhyme. How much, you think, she understands the Spanish?"

"I don't know," J.J. said.

"You don't know?"

"It never came up. What else do you do with her?"

"I do her hair, paint her nails, join in the exercises," she lifted alternate arms and legs in an awkward motion. "She writes questions, and I tell her about myself."

"Is she angry?"

"Not at all," she answered quickly. "She's very sweet. And she's getting better every day."

"So I understand," J.J. said.

"She wants to see you," Elena told him.

⁜

Maison Rouge was a roaring success. A feature article about the stormy all-nighter opening ran in the *Houston Chronicle* and was picked up by newspapers for Sunday human interest stories as far away as Santa Fe. Even with tourist season over and travel numbers down, the club rode a wave of curiosity and approval which kept J.J. busy eight to ten hours a day and didn't leave much time to dwell on people problems. Rose, Dooley, and Elena had taken a back seat to his duties as general manager. Before long, he planned to get Rose's personal financial records in order, in anticipation of tax time. He might not be at the house holding her hand, but he was taking care of her business, and that was their original deal.

The club was closed the early part of the week, and poker night had continued, but the climate of the game had changed. One of the men had moved to a retirement community in the past year, and another had died. More than that, J.J.'s new house with its shiny, white surfaces didn't invite cigar smoke and red sauce like the old cabin had. J.J. had become an outsider, no longer in on fishing trips or neighborhood gossip, and the strained feelings were strong as garlic. But everyone still showed up. Some were willing to see if time would take care of it; some, like Woody, pretended everything was the same.

Dooley made an appearance early on a wet Monday night in November. "Peace offering," he said, while he dug in a paper sack and laid three rings of venison sausage on the counter.

"That'll do," J.J. said.

J.J. and Dooley had talked only once since the party, and, with a minimum of words, had covered the subject.

"You insulted Elena," Dooley had told him.

"The two of you insulted me."

"We didn't set out to insult you. We were working on Elena's problem, one you aren't inclined to get involved with," Dooley had told him.

"I think you're way out of step," J.J. had said. What he didn't say was that he felt an obligation to give him a warning. Women are unpredictable. If Dooley didn't realize what he might be getting into, someone needed to tell him, and it might as well be his father. Wasn't fathering what he was after?

"Possibly," Dooley had said quietly.

⁜

Dooley lifted the dutch oven lid and breathed in the aroma as J.J. opened a package of chips and poured hot cheese dip into a heavy brown bowl. The men would be coming soon, and some wouldn't have eaten all day, anticipating chili night.

289

"I graduate in May, and I've been offered a research position here. Thought I might stick around. You have a problem with that?"

"Nope."

"Can I buy your cabin?"

"Not if you plan to house Elena in it."

"No, sir. I won't do that." He fumbled with the strings on the sausage, removing the tags. "You know, I'm really sorry about how this has worked out."

J.J. put up his hand. "Let's don't get into it."

"Rose Parrish has been home from the hospital for a couple of weeks now. She's wondering why you haven't been to see her."

"She tell you that?"

"I guess I'm wondering, I mean with the flowers you send and all."

"Rose understands."

Dooley reached in the paper bag and pulled out a book. "She sent you this. Sorry if it smells like smoked meat," he added. "Didn't think about that when I put it in there. It's cowboy poetry. I guess that kind of fits the smell."

J.J. took the gift from Dooley, wanting to ask about Rose, somehow irritated that the boy knew more about what she was doing than he did, amused by her choice of book.

"She started writing her own poetry the day she came home. Limericks. Every time I go, she's got new ones for me."

"For you?"

"For whoever. Whomever, I think it is. She's a stickler for grammar too. Corrects me with a look." He imitated a Rose gesture that J.J. recognized. "Jesse said you weren't too comfortable with her disabilities. I've gotten used to things like that."

"Things like what?"

"Like not talking, motor dysfunction, fear-generated inactivity. We get it with the beached sea mammals."

"She'd love to hear that," J.J. said.

"She's getting better, you know."

"That so?"

"You skeptical?"

"I am, Dooley. Why do I feel like someone put you up to this visit?"

"Probably because they did. We've run out of excuses for why you haven't come."

"We?"

"Jesse, Elena, and I. She's after all of us about it."

"So the book isn't from her?"

"Picked it up where I got the venison," he took off his cap and smoothed his hair. "Thought it was worth a try."

"You're not much of a liar, Dooley."

"I know."

Woody came through the door about then, happy to see Dooley, calling out to him from across the room. "Y'all through chartin' them crustaceans?"

"Hell, Woody, we'll never get through. Ocean life keeps changing just like everything else."

"So why do you do it?"

"I'm not real sure. I think Congress appropriated some funds for it a long time ago and they forgot to cut 'em off."

"You shittin' me?"

"Yeah."

"I was 'bout to get mad and stop payin' my taxes."

"Spoken like a patriot, Woody."

⁜

J.J. felt pride whenever he saw the boy, fully realizing he had no claim. He wanted to shake this marriage notion out of his head, but they had pretty well put that subject off limits. Was J.J. jealous? No more of her, than of him. Elena was a woman he liked being with, but there had been others. Dooley was flesh and blood, and this was new territory, sketchily charted. He had that same open spirit, lack of anger, and determination that J.J. remembered in the boy's mother. He wondered what Brenda would think about Dooley and Elena. Wondered if he should give her a call.

⁜

Late on a Saturday night in mid-December, J.J. was poring over paperwork in his upstairs office when he got a call from the club manager. Some guests in the cigar bar were asking for him. He stopped to wash his hands and check himself in the mirror. If they want to see the head honcho, he thought, adjusting his tie, I'm it. Wednesday through Friday nights he wore a suit. Sunday nights, it was a sport coat and white shirt, no tie, but on Saturday nights it was a tux.

He liked this job. If anyone had told him a couple of years ago he'd be running a premier club and mixing with the public after twelve years of hiding out, he'd have dismissed it as so much hot air, something he had no interest in. It was good to be surprised, great to find something new that keeps you on the edge when you think you've exhausted your lifetime of chits. He liked getting calls from the mayor, and developers, and reporters; liked having customers asking for him.

He might not like it forever, might get tired of the grind, the paperwork, the routine. He was only too aware that even the best things get old, but for now, he was on a roll. According to the most recent will, on Rose's death the building was to revert to the historical society. J.J. had already planned his pitch to run it. Without a mortgage, all he had to do was cover overhead. He could offer them a profit that'd be hard to pass up. His main concern was how the historical society would justify getting support from a nightclub, but that was something for the tax lawyers to ponder.

He made his way down the stairs and through the lobby, past twelve-foot murals of pirate ships and stores of loot. He straightened his tie once more and grinned, remembering Rose's insistence on the specifics of that particular scene, then headed around the corner to the glass-enclosed cigar bar, where about ten people appeared to be involved in some kind of fracas. A woman was standing on one of the tables, and two men were on chairs, removing icicle-shaped ornaments from the crystal chandelier. J.J. called security and waited. Someone from inside the room was waving him in.

Bobby Calhoun and another man hustled around the corner like keystone cops.

"What are you doing here?" J.J. asked Bobby.

"Visiting with Sam when he took your call. Figured maybe you could use some help," Calhoun said. His eyes darted toward the room as he spoke, and he all but strained at the leash. "What the hell do they think they're doing?"

"Let's check it out," J.J. said, happy to have such eager

backup. He opened the door and stepped in, followed by two experienced security men who were hungry for action.

"J.J." A man's voice called to him, but he didn't look in that direction because his view was frozen on the woman standing on the table, now emptying a glass of wine. She looked him boldly in the eye, then threw the empty glass against the brick fireplace with a flourish while the others clapped.

"Saralee?" J.J. asked.

"Yes?" she answered, climbing down from the table, looking now a little embarrassed, but still in control. She adjusted her blouse at the waistband of her skirt in a familiar tidying motion.

He looked around the room and recognized most of the faces. Saralee, obviously a little drunk, proceeded to act as spokesperson.

"We read about you in the newspaper and thought we'd just come and see. 'Wonder what old J.J. is up to,' everyone says from time to time, so when we read about your club, we just climbed into the SUV and popped over. A pirate's den. That's good, J.J. Actually, it's done in very good taste. Do these people know what a pirate you really are?"

"Now, Saralee, we agreed. That's over and done with," one of the men stepped in and extended his hand. "Long time, no see, J.J. You're looking good. Better than some of us." He patted his paunch that was tightly secured by a red vest. "Yeah, we read about you and were curious. Bunch of us drove over this morning, had some dinner, took in the harbor parade with the Christmas lights, then came over for a looksee and a nightcap. No more hard feelings. You did your time. We got our claims settled. You remember Jane and Harvey, Paul, Sammy. . ." He went through introductions, most of which were unnecessary. Two of the men had remarried. One of the ex-wives was there with a new husband, as was Saralee, who seemed to have traded her innocence for something more brittle.

"No hard feelings?"

The man nodded. "Absolutely."

"Then, what's up with the chandelier and the wine glasses?"

"That was my idea," Saralee popped up. "I've always wanted to do it. Don't you remember? Always wanted to go somewhere and crash my glass against the wall like they do in the movies. So when I got here, I thought, here's my chance. J.J. owes me something."

He looked behind him at his backup men, then turned to face the others. "I'm going to have to ask for the chandelier pieces back, but I'd be happy to bring you gentlemen some brandy and champagne for the ladies," he motioned to a waiter. "And we won't clean the hearth up yet. Someone else may have an urge."

"Haven't lost your sporting sense, J.J.," one of the men said.

J.J. saw that the group was seated and served, then left Sam stationed outside the bar door, just in case the party got rowdy again.

"Good Lord, man," Bobby said, following him up the stairs, "These are the people you've been worried about? I thought they were going to break into "For He's a Jolly Good Fellow.""

"Nothing succeeds like success," J.J. mumbled, thinking he sounded like Rose.

⁜

On the morning after his surprise visitors, J.J. received another unexpected call from a Will Parker, who identified himself as Rose's attorney. J.J. remembered the name.

"Mrs. Parrish asked me to set up a meeting at her house tomorrow afternoon," he said, "and asks that you be present."

"Regarding?"

"She wants to change her will."

"Again? Isn't this the fourth time?"

"Depends on how you count."

J.J. thought he detected some mild exasperation, maybe just amusement, in the lawyer's voice.

"You think she's stable enough to make a change?" He hoped that didn't sound threatened. It was a valid question.

"I'd stake my license on it, Mr. Broussard. She has it all down in black and white."

26

From the moment she got home, Rose felt thwarted and bedeviled by her nurse.

"Ms. Parrish, you're actin' like a child," Victorias told her when she refused to get dressed, or take a bath, or eat. "You can do better than this, honey. I thought you wanted to come home."

Rose nodded. She had wanted to get home, but now that she was here, she could see how bad off she was.

"Why can't you just work with me? Relax. Enjoy what comes your way. Forget about bein' angry and let your body heal."

Rose turned her head away until the nurse left the room, knowing the woman spoke the truth. She was angry because she awoke disoriented every morning and stayed that way most of the day. She poked around in files, tried to read things, made notes, then couldn't decipher them later. She couldn't relax. There was a feeling of things calling to be done, and time was not her friend. Victorias and Pearl were catching the worst of her frustration, which wasn't fair, she knew, but she had to stick it somewhere. If she could get a little relief from this fuzzy head, she could be more gracious. Didn't want to go out ranting and raving like her mother-in-law. All she could remember about the woman was her meanness.

Pearl was driving her crazy—standing at her doorway, or at the foot of her bed, praying silently or aloud, whatever she thought she could get away with. Usually Rose waved her away, angrily. Finally, she wrote her a message—corrected many times before it was delivered. She wanted to be sure the woman understood, and just in case this prayer warrior thing worked, she wanted to be very clear. *Pray for a peaceful death,* she wrote.

"I can't do that, Miss Rose," Pearl said, after studying the message Rose had left on her food tray.

Rose raised her eyebrows as if to ask why not.

"Can't pray for someone to die."

Rose stared her down.

"Well, yes, you're going to die someday, but the Lord doesn't want us to think about that. That's His business."

Peaceful, Rose tapped her finger on the word.

"Okay. I see. A peaceful death. We're not telling him when or how, just asking that it be easy."

Rose nodded.

"I can do that."

Rose clasped one hand in the other in a victory sign.

"I'll do what I can," Pearl told her, still measuring her commitment.

Rose nodded, trying to look appreciative. She had been hard on Pearl over the years, but the woman deserved it. She was impossibly stubborn.

❖

When Jesse stopped by a couple of evenings later, she was ready for him.

Drugs, she wrote on her pad.

His face blanched.

Too many. She wrote.

"You're taking too many drugs?" he asked for clarification.

She nodded, and motioned to the array of containers on the sideboard.

He studied them, noting what each was for. "I can't second-guess your doctor, Rose, but I'll check with him. It's possible some of these are unnecessary."

"Hope he'll listen to you better than he did to me," Victorias chimed in. "I told him this mornin' she was overmedicated. But doctors don't like nurses telling them their business, do they Dr. Jesse?" She gave a smile, as if to say he shouldn't take her criticism personally.

"Officers should listen to the people on the front lines, is what they teach us."

"Well, we don't all practice what we preach."

Rose clicked her pencil against her pad impatiently and saw Victorias exchange a look with Jesse that said, *she don't like being left out of this conversation.*

"I was afraid she wanted more," he said to Victorias under his breath as he picked up the telephone.

Rose had heard him. Just because she didn't speak didn't mean she couldn't hear. But she wasn't clear why he had said that. Why to Victorias and not her? Why had he lowered his voice? Why were they keeping things from her. Why would she want more drugs?

She listened as Jesse called her doctor's office, then watched as he put down the phone and picked up a footstool. He walked over and deposited the stool in front of her. Then he leaned down, lifted her feet up gently and crossed them at the ankles, just like he'd done that first day he came to her house. She remembered it like it was yesterday, even though she couldn't remember the name of those orange vegetables rabbits eat that Pearl insisted on cooking.

Jesse straightened up and smiled at her, looking relieved. "To want to cut back on your drugs is a real statement of hope, Rose. I knew you were a fighter."

After her meds were changed, and Rose could think clearer, she figured it out. Jesse was afraid she was going to confront him again. Well, she hadn't given up on the idea, but it was clear her *lily-liver'd boy* wasn't going to be any help. She'd have to rely on herself, and how could she do that if she couldn't think? It was a conundrum, wherever that word came from.

⁂

Her days were filled with ditty work, almost as bad as in the hospital. There was the business of getting nourishment into her old body and getting it out. Then there was personal hygiene, for which she didn't give a damn any more, but her nurse seemed to think it was terribly important. Victorias wanted her to bathe every day, had an arrangement of a chair and railings in the bathtub, and a moveable shower head. She was expected to soap and rinse every part, while the other supervised. *Bubble, bubble, toil and trouble,* she thought. It was unnecessary and degrading, not to mention that it reduced her to shivering gooseflesh. She would never get used to it. What did she do to get dirty anyway? She could live the rest of her life with a warm washcloth once a day and never be the worse for it. But try to tell that to Victorias. There were exercises, too, a routine she was taken through twice a day.

Damn doctors. She never wanted to hear the word *procedure* again. Every time someone used that word, it meant being wheeled off somewhere for tests that were often tedious, and sometimes painful. Then there was *prognosis.* She had looked that one up in the dictionary for clarification. It was very close to *prognostication,* but sounded fancy and knowing when uttered by someone in a white coat. She had the feeling they had set her on the conveyor belt of the old and the sick, and there was no way off. The doctors don't give a damn about me, ROSE. All they see is this shell to be poked and prodded. Keep me drugged up so I won't give trouble. Even Jesse was showing signs of disaffection, talking about her instead of to her, and she was half mad at him. But he was young, she told herself, and worried about his career, and he was trying. She could make allowances.

If she was upset with Jesse, she should be furious at the captain. But she knew what was bothering him, why he wouldn't come around. He can't tolerate incapacity. And I certainly fall in that category, she thought. One minute I can recite the Koran and the next, I've forgotten how to tell time.

Mornings were the worst. Of course, mornings had never been her favorite, but now it seemed to take forever before she was allowed to settle in with the newspaper and a cup of tea. Once again they had taken away her coffee. And her food was bland and mushy because she was still having some problems swallowing larger pieces. The list of irritations went on. But, as the day progressed, things got better. By the time *Oprah* came on at four she was usually settled in her favorite chair, able to let go of many of the day's frustrations.

She didn't have her conversations with Nate any more. He had been gone too long. It was the captain whose absent counsel she sought, and when she fashioned their conversations she addressed him as John J. Well, of course, she didn't actually address him, but the name seemed to fit, as if he were no longer the captain in her mind, but a trusted companion. She couldn't understand how things had become so complicated in his private life, but life gets messy sometimes. She could remember that much. And when she imagined consulting with him, she appreciated his answers and felt she could trust his judgment. It was his voice that told her to lay off the drugs if she wanted to think clearer. The same voice suggested she get out the will and try to make some sense of it. He was the one looking after things. She wished he would come around in person.

❖

Elena came in the evenings and stayed the night. Sometimes she read to her; sometimes they sat quietly, and she rubbed her hands or brushed her hair. Rose offered her the use of her old sewing machine in the upstairs bedroom, which delighted her. There was material there also, and thread and zippers and a load of things she should have cleared out years ago. Many nights the girl sewed upstairs and left Rose to work, unhampered, on her computer. If she needed help, all she had to do was call, since Pearl had rigged up a monitor to connect their rooms, like something you'd use with a newborn to be sure it was still breathing.

Elena didn't talk much, but when encouraged, her conversation was fresh and sprinkled with ideas and revelations that kept Rose wanting to hear more. Apparently, she had a wild hare about going to mechanics school, though Rose thought that didn't seem fitting for a young woman from a poor country. The women Rose had seen in México were mostly barefoot and pregnant, subject to men and the church, but that was forty years ago, so things had probably changed. Still, she had to wonder who would hire a mechanic down there, especially a female. Elena said she could take her truck apart piece by piece, said lots of people in the town where she lived drove old cars, said she could make good money fixing cars, said she thought she could get a job in the garage at the Sears store, that she had a friend there who would put in a good word for her. There hadn't been any Sears stores when Rose visited México. For all she knew, these days there were shopping malls and those ubiquitous restaurants with the yellow arches.

There was the day she tried to ask Elena about the captain, and the girl had told her he was busy and she didn't see him so much. *Upset?* Rose had written and the girl had shrugged her shoulders. Either she didn't understand the question, or she didn't know the answer. She wanted to know about the girl and the captain. Had they been lovers? Had he used her? Had she used him, or hoped to? Would they get back together? She thought not. Whatever John J. had found with her, it wasn't likely to continue, considering the difference in their ages, and how determined she was to do something with her own life.

Sometimes Dooley came with Elena. Rose sometimes had a hard time remembering the boy's name. Kept wanting to call him Huck. They didn't seem to be lovers, he and Elena. That's what both of them claimed, and she thought she could still tell the difference. But friendship wasn't a bad place to start.

Dooley talked straight to her, like Rose wished everyone would. He told her he hoped someday he and the captain would have the parent thing behind them and just be friends. Once, when Elena wasn't around, she wrote him a question about the captain and Elena, but Dooley said she'd have to ask one of them. He told her Elena liked to read, but mostly in Spanish, that he had given her a book in English by a San Antonio woman who wrote about Hispanic women trying to cross over, that she had liked it, seen the truth of it. Rose wished she had energy enough to read. So many losses.

Rose asked about Dooley's work, and he told her more than she could ever understand about mollusks and cephalopods, but she was pleased by his enthusiasm. Couldn't remember when she had felt that kind of pleasure in anything. Now that she thought of it, she had been excited about Maison Rouge. Had it only been three months ago?

Rose had problems trusting her own judgment. She used to value her intuition, used to like flying by the seat of her pants, but her confidence was shot. When she was wrong back then, no one questioned it. Now, everyone thought they were smarter than she. Even Pearl. What they didn't understand was how much things had changed since the stroke. Money had lost its importance. Very Christlike, she thought, though it would make the Republicans nervous. Appearances had gone to hell, too, but her vanity hung on like beggar's lice. She studied her face in the hand mirror when she was alone, trying to learn to straighten out her lower lip and raise the eyebrow of the droopy eye.

When the sun came up, she was surprised that she still wanted to wash her face, comb her hair, and look at a newspaper. She found herself wondering when the next killer hurricane would hit. Would the Muslims keep blowing things up? The stock market hit 10,000 again? She wanted to see what would happen with Elena and Dooley. One more soap opera unfinished. Something else to tend to. *Oprah* talked about that yesterday—or was it today? Something about curiosity being healthy.

✛

One day, Dooley brought her an assortment of small paper bags.

"It's tea," he told her. "My mother sent it for you."

She raised her brows in question. "I told her about you when she called the other day, and she said these were good for stroke patients. They're supposed to," he hesitated and reached in his pocket for a piece of paper. "She made me write it down because she said it's important."

Rose leaned forward and nodded.

"Release barriers to movement, clarify thinking, and promote spiritual dreams," he read dutifully. "Use in combinations, as desired."

Do you? Rose wrote, and made a sipping motion.

He shook his head. "Not often. But Mom puts great store in her teas."

Rose motioned that she wanted to keep his list and he laid it with the tea.

"She also said if you have any thoughts about reincarnation, the tea can help you find a past or future life." Dooley said.

How? Rose wrote.

"Through your dreams," Dooley said.

✛

Rose thought about her own mother a lot these days. Wished she could thank her for letting her be left-handed. Back when she was growing up, kids were supposed to be right-handed, but her mother saw that it came naturally to her and wouldn't let anyone change her. She'd have a hell of a time writing with her right hand, which wasn't good for much now except resting in her lap, or steadying the paper. Maybe she should start trying to talk, but the writing was working out. People kept stopping in—everyone except John J., and perhaps he'd come more often when he saw she could still make decisions.

As the weeks passed, she found she was able to do more, physically and mentally. This didn't cheer her so much as impel her to action. Her keepers—Victorias and Pearl and Jesse—were visibly pleased and impressed. She had learned to keep them happy by being compliant and as pleasant as possible. Perhaps it was the tea. She had begun drinking it in the mornings and then had included it in her evening regimen as well. Pearl brought a pot of scalding water and she mixed it herself, some from each of four bags.

> *Eye of newt and toe of frog,*
> *Wool of bat and tongue of dog.*

The words sang themselves in her mind. It was a satisfying ritual, and amusing, though she'd prefer pouring single malt scotch across crystal clear ice cubes, or ringing a margarita glass with fresh lime and salt.

Her dreams had become quite interesting. One night, she was assisting Mother Teresa; the next, she worked for Big Tit Marie. She was a dolphin, following Dooley's boat; another time, a cat, wandering the automotive bays of a Mexican Sears & Roebuck. Once, she was a child, alone on the prairie, the wind ruffling her hair as she walked into a sunset made red by dust.

She asked Dooley what he thought about an afterlife.

"I'm not sure where I stand, Rose. Life's a big mystery, and I feel like my job is to come to peace with it. I try to keep my eyes and ears open and give things the respect they deserve."

Oh, she approved of this boy! She made a note to write his mother and thank her for the teas and to tell her what a fine son she had raised.

✢

Victorias told Rose, while drying her off vigorously after one of those chilling baths, that she was finally learning humility, and it was high time. Rose scoffed silently. The only thing she'd learned was another way to stay in the game. Not talking set people off guard. She liked the changed dynamics, liked the power, enjoyed being the only one who knew her full capacities. Not that there was anyone to best. These people seemed to care about her. At least they stuck around to take care of her, and she knew how much of a pain that was. She needed to reward them, *to throw away the dearest thing she ow'd, as 'twere a careless trifle.* Now who was that talking? Voices still popped into her head, unbidden. What was this telling her? Turn sweet and selfless? That seemed a pitiful bid for attention at this late stage.

Nothing in his life became him like the leaving it, another piece of words came back. She did want that—to go out well— and would work on it until she could stomach it no more. Stopping eating was probably the easiest. She didn't have much appetite these days anyway, though a scotch sounded nice. It would probably run through like a dose of salts.

She found an old diary in her bedside table and reread it, then wished she hadn't. It was one she had kept during those years when Nate was slipping downhill, just as she was doing now. She was reminded of the times she had dressed him in robe and slippers, helped him into his easy chair, lit his pipe, and handed it to him, before visitors stopped by. She liked to believe he was following the conversation, though he never spoke.

> *Dismissed Nate's nurse. She was bright and cheerful, silly as hell, and without judgment. Nate is losing all con - trol of his urine and much of the time exposing himself. She giggles at him—and I'm sure repeats his antics to neighbors. Will use the aide one day a week for exercises, but, with Pearl's help, will do the rest myself. Physically*

demanding, but he responds best to me. Must protect his
privacy.

✠

It came to her regularly, the knowledge that at any minute she could take a turn for the worse, or have another stroke, God forbid. In rebellion, she refused her sleeping pills so she could work at the computer late into the night. She studied her assets, reacquainted herself with her business, wrote bad poems and bitchy letters to the hospital and the AMA. It was tedious typing, but her fingers worked about as fast as her brain.

> *There was an old sinner who said,*
> *'I'll repent before I am dead.'*
> *But her memory was shot,*
> *All her sins she forgot,*
> *So now she is hell-bent instead.*

> *Dear Sirs:*
> *I am writing to protest your position on euthanasia.*

✠

On the appointed day of her meeting with Will Parker and John J., Rose dressed herself, only requiring help to comb her hair. The hands still couldn't find their way to the back of her head. Satisfied with her appearance, she arranged herself in her chair, handkerchief in hand, her papers and pen on the side table, along with a glass of water.

Will Parker arrived a few minutes early, briefcase in hand. He greeted Rose warmly, then fumbled in the case for his papers. Her papers, to be more exact. They had been in communication by fax for the past two weeks. He explained that, given her inability to speak, her faxed communications would establish clarity of mind at the time of the will changes.

"How do you think Mr. Broussard will feel about these changes," he asked her.

They'll grow on him, she wrote.

John J. arrived on time. Pearl showed him into the sitting room, where he looked surprised to see Rose dressed, sitting erect. He took her hand and leaned down to kiss the air beside her cheek.

Cosmopolitan, Rose thought, wondering if that was a word or if she had made it up.

"You look wonderful," he said. Still holding one of her hands, he stood back, appraising. "Stylishly thin."

She nodded, knowing gaunt was the word, and gave the smile she'd been practicing.

"Mrs. Parrish has four items for our attention today," Will Parker began. "I've already incorporated these into her will, and we'll sign the document here with you as a witness, but she's requested that the changes be made clear to you, as you are so closely involved in her personal affairs."

J.J. nodded.

"First, in the matter of the living trust, she asked me to change the beneficiary of the tax-sheltered trust back to the Galveston County Library Association, where it was some versions back." The attorney looked over at Rose. "In Mrs. Parrish's words," he read, "'literacy never goes out of style. All else is fluff.'"

J.J. nodded. "Those are her exact words?"

The lawyer assured him they were. Rose nodded and dabbed at her mouth.

"As a side issue," Parker went on, "she wants Maison Rouge taken out of the trust and is deeding you a life estate in this property. In her words, 'he seems to have found a home there.' The property will pass to the historical society at your death, or earlier, should you choose."

"There is an increase to $250,000 in trust for Jesse Martin for further education and establishment in the practice of medicine over the next five years. She's taken you off as trustee and has designated her bank. She also requests that you two try and resolve your differences."

"She's making a personal bequest to Elena Lara, in the amount of $100,000."

"What in the world for?" John J. was on his feet.

Parker scanned his notes. "'Symmetry,'" he read. "'I'm old and rich. She's young and poor. I also believe she can do what she says, so I'm making a small, foreign investment.'" The lawyer looked up at Rose again and nodded slightly. She had told him Captain Broussard would have questions about that one.

"Finally, there's a directive here to you, Mr. Broussard, as administrator, to allow Pearl and Nurse Victorias to select any personal items from the house you don't wish to keep."

As the lawyer packed up, John J. walked across the room and stared out the window. Rose rang her bell, and Pearl appeared.

"A drink, Captain?"

He nodded, looking slightly confused. "You don't do drinks, Pearl."

"I do what she needs," she said, looking at Rose. "Pray for her, too."

Rose lifted her hand ever so slightly and shook one finger back and forth at Pearl, as if to say, that's enough.

"You want one, too?" Pearl asked.

Rose nodded. She had to be on her last legs to get the woman under control.

After Will Parker left, J.J. stayed on. Pearl brought their drinks. Rose's, served with a straw, looked like water, with a breath of scotch, but she didn't challenge it. At least it smelled right.

"You've made a great recovery," he told her.

She shook her head and scribbled, *not 1st choice.*

"I know, Rose," he avoided looking at her. "I want you to see Maison Rouge," he stumbled on, filling the silent spaces. "It's quite a place." Then he told her about the opening party, about the visitors from Baton Rouge, about the wedding at

Thanksgiving, the Christmas parties scheduled, the events already booked for 2003.

Thanks, she wrote.

"For what?"

She studied his face. What did she want to thank him for? Years of conversation, and companionship.

He leaned down to kiss her cheek. "I brought you something," he whispered, tucking a vial into her good left hand.

She held it up to study its contents. It held a handful of small pills.

"Black beauties. They'll put you right to sleep, like we always talked about."

She raised an eyebrow in question.

"My neighbor. Woody. Tells me he can get anything, so I put him to the test. Also put a couple to the test on a stray dog. He just went to sleep, sweet and clean."

Rose scribbled on her pad. *"Maybe not just now."*

"For God's sake, Rose. You don't have to use them. I wanted you to have them because you'd asked, and Martin isn't going to do it. He's too afraid to take a stand."

"You two still at war?" she wrote.

"Not really," he said.

⁜

When Elena came that night, Rose asked her to locate a favorite book and a large brown envelope, and then to leave her alone. She had a letter to write, and it would take a while.

Dear Dooley,

I'm used to receiving information on religion from people intent on rescuing me from a hot eternity, but am NOT in the habit of passing it on. This is a first for me, and surely a last, but I wanted to leave you something of my treasures and you don't seem to have much use for material things. Perhaps this book will enlighten your path.

After a lifetime of knowing what I DO NOT believe, I would love to know what I DO believe, but will certainly dance in the four winds not having it worked out. I do like the idea of God being all around, within, and responsible for establishing the laws of the universe, but not responsible for every miserable thing that happens in this world. As for reincarnation, I like to think I was convicted in the Salem trials, but shall return again as a future warrior in the good fight.

I charge you with taking care of your father when I'm no longer around to worry about him. He is a valuable person, more so for his muddied past.

She read it over, not quite satisfied. It needed work, but Rose was tired.

PART III:

The Sweet Hereafter

27

Rose was dreaming of a tornado, thin and ropelike. It appeared on the far horizon and moved quite slowly toward her. All her life she'd dreamed of tornados, swirling torrents of black that wanted to suck her up, from which there was no escape. In those dreams, she couldn't find the car keys, couldn't get the door open, was frozen on the spot, trapped in a vulnerable position beside a huge window, or outside, pinned against a flat, red barn watching as the monster approached, its gaping mouth revealing screaming children and topsy-turvy trees.

In this particular dream there was plenty of time to get away. She got her purse, went to the garage, started up Colette, and opened the sun roof. Then she drove through town and across the causeway, where she stopped and looked back to see the rope hovering at a respectful distance, as if to say it could wait. She stopped by the florist and bought an armful of tulips, then to the cemetery to pretty up her mother's grave. Back home, she put the car away and went to her bedroom. She opened her windows and lay and watched as the rope slipped through the window. It stood, circling and whirring beside her bed. She felt no fear, only curiosity, as she turned back the covers and invited it in.

✤

*Rose Parrish died in her sleep on New Year's Day in
the year of our Lord, 2002. She was discovered by her nurse,
Victorias Brown, and housekeeper, Pearl Lowman, both of
whom were taken by surprise at being unable to rouse her.*

*"She seemed in good spirits when she went to bed,"
Nurse Brown remarked.*

*"I never expected her to go so soon," Mrs. Lowman
added. "But she had an easy, peaceful look on her face."*

✤

On the morning of June 1, 2002, J.J. Broussard chose his
clothes with special care. If anyone could reach from beyond the
grave, it would be Rose, and she'd undoubtedly want him looking spiffy. He chose white pants, new deck shoes, a blue denim
shirt. *Matches your eyes,* he could hear her say.

How many times was her voice going to ring in his ears? She
was dogging him. At work, at home, arranging her memorial, he
could hear her. Funny. Irreverent. Caring.

It was an interesting piece of irony, he thought, how hard
she'd worked to stay aloof, to dress up her goodness in a scarf
of sarcasm, and build a barrier of pride around herself so no one
would suspect the softness of her heart. Rose was always careful
with her money until she decided to give it away. But, if he'd
known enough to notice, he might have suspected her generosity in the way she listened to him, and thought about what she
heard, and then focused her light on it.

Now, when only memory remained, J.J. was able to fully
appreciate her—the depth of character, the sharpness of wit, the
contradictions that defined her charm. To be in her circle, she
had to approve of you first. And since she made it clear she did-
n't suffer fools, one had to be honored. He thought about her
self-proclaimed simple beginnings, how she'd changed over the
years he'd known her, and how she'd faced the end with grit.
He didn't like to dwell on the end. Better to remember the
good days—Rose, with raised glass, toasting: *Fight, fight,*

against the dying of the light. She took liberties with the poet's words, she told him, because she had always been fond of a rhyme.

Rose's light hadn't died. No one who was enjoying the benefits of her generosity these days stopped hearing her voice. He'd heard as much from each of them. It was as if she were still hanging around, sitting on their shoulders, whispering in their ears. Maybe the memorial would quiet her down. Rose had indicated in her papers who was to be invited, and, of course, she wanted it at Hall's Lake. To be dropped off with Nate. J.J. hoped the gulls would lay off.

Their relationship had been a good story to the end. She had trusted him. That was the heart of it—that, and an attraction that resisted definition. She approved of him, just as she found him, and wasn't afraid to show it. In fact, she laid it on him with everything she had. Maybe he should have taken her to bed. *Out of pity? Captain, shame on you.* He heard Rose's voice, indignant now. She continued to stand by, making comments, reminding him of himself.

Would she be upset if he sold the house? He knew he wanted to live on the water and would never be comfortable in town. It'd be a shame for it to sit empty. There were memories tied up in that place. His and Rose's, and Nate's and Pearl's and Jesse's. And that was just for the last fifty years. Would it be better for it to sit empty, or come alive again, with dinner parties and late nights in the library and cocktails on the porch?

Maybe J.J. would take his proceeds and see what else life had to offer. He'd keep hold of Maison Rouge, of course, but Rose wouldn't want him to continue as a bean counter. Thinking about her made it easy to fabricate a comfortable rationale. She had always been able to justify her actions, even when she changed her mind. Especially when she changed her mind. Good on you, old girl, he thought. He arranged his cap in the mirror, wishing, sentimental as it might sound, that he could extend his arm and take her to the gathering.

315

"Dr. Jesse isn't going to be in the clinic today because he has to attend a service." That's what Jesse asked the clinic receptionist to say. Everyone in those parts knew that meant someone had died, and it would keep his people from thinking he'd deserted them. The patients he saw, "the indigent and underserved population of Galveston County," were incredibly tough in some respects, impossibly fragile in others. It made him, Jesse, feel more normal. Especially normal. Ready to give something back, including compassion for people who made dumb mistakes.

He was riding a crest. Getting his M.D., freedom from debt, and connecting with Susanna had all fallen in place. He didn't know if he'd feel so gratified by serving the needy if he had to count on getting paid for his services. But that was the freedom Rose had given him. Rose and J.J. Broussard. He regretted having misjudged the captain, but that's what silence and secrecy get you, he thought. He planned to never have anything to hide. It was a head trip for Jesse—looking back at his beginnings, knowing where he was now, wondering where he might end up in ten or twenty years.

He had made no firm decisions about his future, but was looking into specialties. He and Susanna wanted to stay in Galveston for now, and he felt sure Rose would approve. He had looked forward to this day—a chance to pay his last respects—a time to stop his constantly pulsing life and think, reverently, about what she had done for him.

She'd balk at that reverence. Well, maybe it was just serious appreciation. But, she was some kind of woman. Captured him, like a butterfly, that first day he walked in, looking for a cool apartment. When she decided to pounce, I was history. She picked herself a boy, and I was what she got.

As Dr. Martin, Jesse had to watch how he dressed with his patients. If he wore the prescribed white shirt and tie, he'd scare them away. Same with golf shirts. T-shirts were the thing.

Under the white coat. And old tennis shoes. That softened them up a little. Today, he pulled out the ninety-dollar ones he bought a few years back—the ones Rose had commented on. That's what got him into thinking about what to wear. *How would she like to see me?* he asked himself. The minute the question was laid out, the answer appeared. *White coat.* Of course, Jesse thought. Come as a doctor.

Rose had taught him so much, just by being herself. Taught him some things about sex, too. Flirted with him. Embarrassed him. Asked him touchy questions. He needed to know that in his business—all the things sex is for people. All the fears and denial it generates. People need to acknowledge it, he thought. He thought too much. He knew he was on a ride. Sex was really good for him right now.

What did he remember best about Rose? The time, right out of the blue, when she said he had pretty teeth. He had worked for those teeth. No one ever said they were pretty. She gave him a fresh look at himself. She expected him to be his best self, and he wanted to make her proud.

✛

J.J. had rented a luxury deck boat for the occasion and took it to the marina at Bay Harbor to pick up the attendees. Pearl and Victorias came together, both dressed for a service. Victorias wore a feathered creation she had selected from a Neiman Marcus box on the top shelf of Rose's bedroom closet. It was an impressive hat—not what she might have bought for herself, but this was for the lady. That had been her thinking.

Pearl wore a hat also, and white gloves, and the dress she had worn to Rose's party. It was blue, like the gulf, and Rose had complimented her on it. Pearl had become more assertive in the six months since Rose had died. She had invested her money, with the advice of Captain Broussard, and she had a new job, a government job that would see her into old age.

Rose had told her once that getting older was no fun, but you must learn to pretend. Pearl had said she didn't like pretending and had thought to herself she wanted real things, like an annuity. Those always sounded good. Well, she had an annuity now, and a husband that didn't displease her, and a son that wouldn't win any prizes, but he was hers. She was happy and she blessed Rose Parrish.

✢

Elena liked ritual. It was her place of feeling. It was her escape. She had waited for this time. This time for Rose. She loved the woman. *That is the truth,* she thought, knowing there were those who would question her loving a *gringa*. Why do such things have to be uncomfortable?

When Elena had learned from the lawyer Parker that Rose had left her a world of money, she was amazed. She had liked the woman from the first. Great spirit, she had. A sense of humor. A kind ear. *Buen carácter.* She thought about her almost every day. She would never forget what she gave her. A chance to work, to be recognized, a chance to give her boys a chance.

Elena was taking her course in mechanics and doing well. She was back with her sons in México. It was *mamá* who convinced her. Her mother, present at her babies' birth, had taken the umbilical cord and planted it in the back yard. *Loca,* Elena had thought at the time, crazy woman, trying to insure that her grandchildren stay near where they were born. Now, she had begun to think the boys were meant to stay in *México*. She had enough money to do it all—to be with her family, to complete the circle. But she had stretched the circle. She, Elena, was different. So would her boys be different. So would the times. And to the service she would wear a white blouse, the kind the native women wear, trimmed with lace and embroidered with a large red rose. *Acuérdese de las mujeres,* she thought. Remember the women. Elena would carry the memory of Rose as far as it could go. She was her hero.

✢

Dooley stood in front of the mirror, shaving. He didn't have much of a beard, and what he had was blond, so he didn't shave every day. But today was Rose's service. He'd never been to a memorial service before, but guessed it was time to learn about such things.

He had liked Rose a lot and wished he'd known her better. She had a generous dose of honesty about her, which had made him inclined to listen to what she told him, even when he didn't always understand it. The important thing was she'd known his father for a long time. Trusted him, too, in spite of his past.

Dooley would look out for his father, like she'd asked. They'd finally gotten past that sticky place with Elena. He'd been stupid to agree to her plan, but she had been lit up with her dream, and hard to resist. He and J.J. were planning to sail to Florida in a couple of months and they'd visit his mother when they were there. It would be interesting to see those two together. Dooley felt glad to be invited to this event, proud to be part of this family, strange as it was. Rose had left him with a lot of thoughts, unfinished conversations, and a book he'd value for its ideas as well as its source.

✛

Susanna had asked to attend. She and Rose had made a connection that began and ended with Jesse. And since she was involved in most everything that was happening in his life these days, she figured Rose wouldn't mind her coming to say good-bye.

Susanna had been ready to give up on men a few years back, and then Jesse had shown up, persistent as a puppy, and he'd won her over. It wasn't easy, juggling a profession with the needs of a man for sex and attention and some kind of pampering, but Jesse seemed happy, and she woke up happy these days, and that was something to hold on to. Her friends said it was just her clock ticking. It was more than that. She had moved in with him, and they'd been taking care of Rose's house for the past six months for Captain Broussard. She loved that place.

Susanna dug in the closet and pulled out a belt made from rattlesnake skin that she'd bought at a second-hand store when she first came to Galveston. She thought it made a statement about being adventurous, something she figured Rose had been, in her day. Help is as near as your call button, she had tried to tell Rose. Susanna's help came with dimples. And she would wear an outfit to Rose's funeral that would meet with *Oprah's* approval. That much she promised.

⁂

It was a flawless day. June on the island. Blue sky, smattered with puffy clouds, warm sun, a fresh breeze. The boat had been on the bay for more than an hour. They had moved through the intercoastal canal, then east toward Alligator Slough and Chocolate Bay. The passengers visited quietly among themselves or stood at the railing, watching the fishermen and wake boarders and kids on jet skis, strangers for whom recreation was their mission that day.

Entering Hall's Lake, J.J. drove along the shoreline. "In wet years you can take a small boat through those bayous," he gestured to the north, "all the way to the outskirts of Houston." His passengers nodded. It was a pleasant ride, more isolated now. Aged trees, graceful water birds, here and there a glimpse of an elegant home. Peaceful, everyone agreed.

Elena had brought doves. *"Palomas,"* she announced, her eyes on J.J. like a caress, as she carried the cage aboard. After the ashes were scattered, she released them. There were seven, one for each person present. Instead of taking off, as anticipated, they chose to hang around the boat. Dooley recaptured the birds and tossed them, with a flourish, into the breeze, but they wouldn't go. Some stayed close on the deck, as if to show loyalty. Others stayed high, resting atop the cabin, at a distance measurable for their freedom. The birds studied the passengers. The passengers watched the birds. No one could think what to do.

"That's spooky," Susanna whispered to Jesse.

Victorias gave a chuckle of recognition. "Stubborn, I'd say."

"Maybe she's sticking around for a drink," Dooley drawled softly, drawing a scattering of laughter.

J.J. opened the champagne and filled plastic glasses all around. Even Pearl took some, remarking, in reasoning reminiscent of the deceased, that if Jesus could turn water into wine, she could partake on very special occasions. As they lifted their glasses in a final toast to Rose, another boat of travelers passed close enough to recognize a celebration. They called out and leaned over the side, waving greetings. The doves took off at that moment, first two, then the others, and Rose's party followed their flight across the summer sky until they disappeared from sight, lost behind a biplane's banner that fluttered in the breeze, inviting all within view to happy hour at Jim's on the Boardwalk.

Galveston Rose

text set in 11/15 Galliard
title set in Centaur and Boulevard
book design and colored pencil illustration by
Barbara M. Whitehead